Moe's Books 8/7/17

THE BEAR WHO BROKE THE WORLD

JUSTIN McFARR

To Urmi,
Lovely to have you at my reading.
Hope you enjoy the novel!
Best,
[illegible]

WSP

WHEELER STREET PRESS
Los Angeles

Cover photographs © by Justin McFarr
Book Design by Jakob Vala

ISBN 978-09976131-4-8 (trade)
ISBN 978-09976131-5-5 (e-book)

Library of Congress Control Number: 2016952415

Published by Wheeler Street Press
www.wheelerstreetpress.com

10 9 8 7 6 5 4 3 2 1

First Edition
Printed in the U.S.A.

For

Lynn, who inspires me at every turn,

and

Mom, who always believed

Chapter 1

My first memory from the summer of 1976 should have been the sound of a school bell ringing like freedom or the sun on my face as I jumped onto my dirt bike. Instead, my earliest recollection from that June was of a Thursday night spent in a neighborhood pub.

Ken, my mother's boyfriend back then, got home from work early and had movies on his mind. Home was the house on Emerson Street in Berkeley that he shared with me; my younger brother Demian; and our mom Rose. I was ten. Demian was six. It was the day before the last day of school. A night of cartoons and an old slapstick comedy sounded like the perfect way for us, as a family, to usher in summer.

A few short blocks from our house was The Starry Plough, situated near the invisible border between Oakland and Berkeley. Demian and I had been worked into a frenzy by Ken's promise of us chowing down on hot dogs as big as our heads while watching things we'd only seen on our little black-and-white TV—if we'd seen them at all. "That's really big, Steve," my brother kept saying on the walk over, measuring his face from all different angles while he tried to imagine the size of those monstrous English bangers. "We need to get there and get those."

The two of us were determined to beat the local crowd that would soon converge on the corner tavern. I wanted desperately to secure a choice spot on one of the long, weathered benches stationed in the alcove where the pull-down movie screen promised hours of entertainment. The way Ken had painted the experience, I didn't want to risk missing any of it.

We rushed past the bar stools that came to my chin, wooden stork-like things planted below the long bar. The smell of cigarette smoke already lay acrid in the pub. The unvarnished, deep-russet tables and rickety wooden chairs made the place appear rundown and seedy, but the setting sun's glow, leaking through the stained-glass window behind the bar, filled the room with an unexpected brightness.

When my father was still around, before he packed a bag and headed three thousand miles away from the life he had apparently grown bored of, he brought me to the Plough once. At the bar, he arranged my plump body on the stool beside him and ordered up a pint. The owner, Virgil, yanked on what looked like a Ping-Pong paddle, and dark, foamy beer shot out into a mug so glacially frosted I was convinced it would shatter. Dad drank his Guinness, which created a bubbly moustache over his upper lip that I wanted to stick my hands into and pop. He ran his long, yellowed fingernails over the bar's surface, unraveling a story about the relic, shipped over from a coastal tavern in Ireland just before the entire town was nearly washed away by an angry sea. Why it was angry Dad never said, but he pressed his nose against the bar and encouraged me to do the same. He told me I was smelling the sea of our homeland, even though both Dad and I had been born in the United States, and that every nick and stain I saw on this scuffed top were like small engravings from its long history. I breathed in the bitter smell of beer and cigarette ash, but no ocean. He ordered me a Roy Rogers and then scribbled a few lines of a poem onto a napkin.

I was caught up in thoughts of my dad and had slowed my pace. Demian shot past me to the head of the bench. It stood closest to the back wall of the pub, where the coiled white plastic screen rested until seven o'clock, when it was unfurled and the movies began. He sat down with a squeal. "Beat ya!" His feet dangled above the floor, an untied gray shoelace kissing the hardwood. "You snooze, you lose," he said, parroting a phrase he'd heard before. It prompted me to sit on top of him.

"I what?" I asked, joking.

"Stop, get off," he squealed, laughing as he tried to shove my huge body off his tiny frame. With my eleventh birthday less than two months away, I was a small bear of a boy. My bangs, which hung down and covered my eyes, looked like a mass of tar. I was meaty, with something that resembled muscle lurking under the skin to give my shoulders width and my arms heft. But no amount of clothing could conceal the bakery rolls of fat that had gathered from my chin to my knees.

Gramma, my mom's mom, made frequent attempts to reassure me about my weight. "You're simply going through a growth phase, Stephen, and once it's over, you'll be—what do they say?—lean and mean."

I wanted to believe her, but it was difficult for me to get past the fact that I looked and felt like a blubber-butt. A hideous beast. On the flip side, Demian was skinny, and everyone he ever met thought he was cute, adorable, and vivacious; no one ever used those words to describe me. It was impossible to tell we were related, a fact needlessly pointed out to us at house parties, on the street, at school functions, and wherever we had to introduce ourselves as brothers. I thought the confused looks and sideways stares of disbelief would eventually cease to bother me. But they never did.

Demian was the right size for his age, but so skinny that with his shirt off I could count the ribs. His skin shone white and transparent as an icicle, his long, sunburst-colored hair loaded with curls that corkscrewed down past his shoulders. His cheeks bloomed with color and his chest sunk inward, like a piece of paper folded in half. He was sometimes mistaken for a girl, which, whenever she happened to be in earshot of the remark, seemed to please Mom for reasons I learned later that summer. To friends who came to the house, she revealed that his kindergarten teacher, Mrs. Frost, thought he was the spitting image of St. Raphael, the archangel. After the hundredth time I heard Mom say this, I looked up the saint in a book about the Vatican from the school library. I could see the resemblance, but I thought Demian looked more like St. Michael in a painting I'd seen on a field trip to the Oakland Museum. The image—one that never quite left my mind—was of the angel, whose face, despite the sword raised high against the devil himself, revealed nothing like malice or even divine anger. The description was something like, "God's winged soldier Michael, standing majestically in battle mode, vanquishing Satan."

The devil and the angel—that's what I thought maybe we looked like to all those people who stared when they saw us together.

I pinched Demian's knee through his dirt-caked blue jeans as I slid off him and parked myself on the bench. Only a few people occupied the other end of the bench, near the bar, but I knew it would fill up soon.

"Hot dogs, hot dogs," Demian chanted, lightly banging on the table as if he had a knife and fork in each hand, "big as your head, big as your head." It made me hungry.

Mom and Ken took their time getting to us, his arm around her and an unlit cigarette in his slightly crooked mouth. When they reached the table, Ken poked his head between our ears. His cigarette almost jabbed me in the eye. "You boys got us a good seat," he said, his nicotine-stained moustache curling out a little at each end of his lips. He smelled like the embers of a dying fire. "Way to go."

Ken led Mom around the end of the bench and made a big show of helping her settle in across from us. He liked being chivalrous, as he called it, opening doors for people and pulling out their chairs in restaurants. Mom seemed to like it; once he was seated and had tossed the cigarette on the table next to an ashtray and an open book of matches, she rewarded him with a long kiss.

"Are we going to eat now?" I touched my stomach, its groaning cries for food smothered by the Rolling Stones song blaring through the pub. "I'm really hungry."

"What else is new?" I thought I heard Ken say. Mom drew her lips together in what looked like a *shush* sound.

"What are you going to order?" she asked Demian and me.

"Those banger things," I said.

"As big as your head / Your head, your head." Demian turned the words into a little song.

Mom removed her tan suede jacket, the one with all the thick fringe at the bottom, and draped it over her legs. She said, "I'm keen for the fish n' chips tonight. And a glass of wine."

"Yes, m'love." Ken lit his cigarette and scooted off the bench. To us, he said, "Pepsis, right?" We nodded and Mom said the name of a wine I'd never heard of. It sounded French. Or maybe Italian.

With Ken at the bar, Mom turned her attention to us. "Excited about the movies?" We both nodded. Demian's feet exploded into kicks of energy under the table. "You know, I used to watch movies like this, with the little projector and a sheet for a screen, with your grandparents when I was a girl."

"You mean with Gramma and Grampa?" Demian leaned his body against the edge of the bench, eyes big and focused on Mom. My stomach still grumbled, and I was impatient for Ken to order our food and bring our drinks.

His hands were full when he got back, and he spilled some of my soda. "Three dollars for a glass of wine?" he said to Mom. "Your mom has expensive tastes, boys."

She did? I looked down at the Adidas-like, no-name-brand shoes I had been wearing since the beginning of the school year. Now they were too small, and the soles were in tatters. Demian's boundless energy had put holes in his cords, and Mom had patched them up with mismatched thread. I didn't understand what Ken meant.

"Geez, babe," Ken said as he watched Mom sip from her wine glass, "you could get a half a lid for that."

"I would rather use *this*," she held it to his nose, "to relax instead of the skanky pot you buy, anytime."

He glanced around the pub, like he was looking for someone. "Yeah, I'm working on that."

The food came and Demian stared at his sausage, pooching his lower lip into a pout. "It's not *that* big," he mumbled.

I was starving, so I pierced mine with a fork and cut into it, steam escaping from the middle.

By the time I finished everything on my plate, the pub owner's son Conor had introduced himself and the movies were set to begin. Demian had only eaten a small fraction of his dinner. "You finished?" I asked.

He nodded his head, then looked up at me. This was our normal routine. He ate like a bird, and I didn't, so I got his leftovers. Something else I heard, more than once from other kids, was, "Jack Sprat could eat no fat / His *brother* could eat no lean." It was so funny I forgot to laugh.

Around eight thirty, the Marx Brothers movie, *Horse Feathers*, ended. Conor came back to the front of the screen, made a quick announcement about a fifteen-minute break until the next film, and then rushed to help his father behind the bar. Groucho's off-key songs and Chico's mangled English still played in my head, making me giddy.

"You guys want more soda?" Ken asked. Of course we did. "Another glass of wine, babe? I may have to knock over a bank to pay for it, but anything for you."

Demian giggled and stared up at Ken, my brother in puppy-dog mode, hopeful for a soft pat on the head. Ken gave him a wink, then sauntered off, his body swaying to the beat of a Van Morrison song from the overhead speakers. I craved another Pepsi, so I kept a close eye on his progress. Ken stopped when he saw our next-door neighbor, Kirby Johnson, standing halfway between our table and the bar. He leaned his face into Kirby's ear and whispered something.

Their conversation lasted a long time, until Ken patted our neighbor on the arm and finally edged up to the bar. Kirby, whose tie-dye shirt and bright red headband stood out among the muted browns of the pub, glanced in my direction before turning away. A slight shiver coursed through me.

Ken was ordering his drinks when a kid, younger than me by a couple of years, passed by our table.

"Hey, Omen," he said to Demian, making it sound like a threat. I only caught a quick glimpse of him—stringy hair, ripped white tee, what looked like a permanent scowl tattooed on his face—before he vanished to the other side of the pub.

Demian sat with his head down, the silly mood in him abruptly shifted into something somber.

"Who was that?" I asked.

"I don't know," Demian said in a way that didn't make me believe him.

I was about to push it, force his lie into a truth, when the music stopped and the lights dimmed. A Laurel and Hardy short crackled and popped on the screen. I nudged Demian in the back, reminding him that we'd seen it before, on TV. Once the bumbling piano movers started bickering with each other like an old married couple, my little brother chortled and everything else faded away.

Ken stood at the table, a shot of whiskey in one hand and a red wine in the other. He set the full glass in front of my mother, whose attention lay on her hands. The brick-red emery board she used to file her nails looked like an oversize Band-Aid.

"Another glass of your Chateau Latour," Ken said. "Only the best for my lady of expensive tastes." I didn't see my Pepsi, only their drinks. When she sipped her wine, Ken licked his lips over and over again, as if his mouth was on fire. It was weird, and I didn't think I'd seen him do it before. When I asked about my Pepsi, he cussed, said he'd forgot. He tossed a dollar on the table and told me that while I was at it, I might as well get a water back for his drink. I hurried to the bar before the next movie started.

A Tex Avery cartoon strained into focus just as I returned to my seat. By the time it was over, I had finished my Pepsi and was ready to head for home.

The projector got packed away, the screen was rolled up, and the music was back. My mother sipped her wine while Ken double-fisted his drinks: a highball of whiskey cupped in one hand and the tumbler of water I'd fetched for him in the other.

"So what'd you boys think?" He lifted the whiskey to his lips. It was the same russet color as the benches, creating an illusion of Ken drinking liquid wood.

"I liked the harp guy," Demian said, still giddy but his energy fading. It was almost nine o'clock.

"You mean Harpo, sweetie. His name is Harpo," my mother corrected him. She placed both hands—small, with unpainted fingernails—on her head and reined in her long braid. Her cinnamon-brown hair slowly rose from her waist until she had wrapped the tightly wound braid into a giant bun at the nape of her neck.

As she wove and twisted her hair, Demian whispered incessantly, like he had just been given a mantra, "Harpo, Harpo … yeah, Harpo."

Ken looked nervous, constantly glancing at my mother and fidgeting on the bench while doing that lip-licking thing again. He tapped out a Camel from his nearly empty pack, lit it, then wedged it between his lips. The smell of smoke wafted through the pub and into my nose. I winced, then looked away from the table. I caught sight of a kid from my school leaving the pub, his mother steering him gently outside. Most of the other parents with kids were already gone, the place left feeling quiet, vacant, and too grown-up. I wanted to be back home in my room. I wanted to be like the other kids.

"Why were you home so early? What's going on with the job?" Mom asked Ken.

"No reason. It's fine, babe." He took a big sip of his drink, and some of it dribbled onto his chest. The shirt buttons were undone to just above his belly button. He ran two fingers through his dark chest hair, then licked them.

Ken looked to Mom for a reaction, his fingers outstretched to her, but her face got dark, like she was worried about something. He wiped his hand on his jeans and began to fidget again.

"So, Stevie," Ken said, his attention shifted to me, "I hear you got a girlfriend." He poked Mom, "You hear about this?"

I didn't know what he was talking about. What girlfriend? Seneca? But I hadn't mentioned her to anyone. Had I?

"I read about her in that book, your diary thing. You left it out there for the world to see."

He had read my journal? Why would he do that?

I gave him a dirty look—feeling violated without exactly understanding what that sensation was—and he held up his hands, palms out like I was a cop or something. "Hey, I just wanted to see if there was anything in there about me. There wasn't." He sounded disappointed.

"Why would there be?" Mom asked, then went back to her wine. Her voice was low, but it sounded like she was slurring her words.

"So this girl, is she a fox?" he asked me. "What's she like?" Ken turned to my mother, who half listened while she mouthed the words to an Allman Brothers song. "What are ten-year-old girls like these days? Huh, babe?"

She either didn't hear him or was too lost in the wine and the music to answer.

"She's not my girlfriend," I said, staring down at the table. Wanting to not talk about this. Wanting to go home.

He sucked down a lungful of cigarette smoke and squinted. "She's not? But all that stuff in there—"

"There's a girl at school I … like," I confessed. "But she's not my girlfriend." I could see Seneca vividly, her wide blue eyes and shoulder-length hair the exact color of Johnson & Johnson's baby shampoo. "Not yet," I muttered softly, to myself.

"Well, if you like this girl, Stevie, you better get your butt in gear. Right? Tomorrow's last chance, ain't it, to score her number or 'fess up your love?" Ken began singing over the music in the pub, a song about school being over and summer being here and something something forever.

He laughed, and my mother's lips stopped moving. She looked up, shook her head in that disapproving way I knew all too well, then kissed him. While they locked themselves into an embrace, I turned to Demian. His eyes were red and his head bobbed slightly in a semicircle.

I checked my Casio watch. The oversize hands were stacked on top of each other over the nine; it was a quarter to ten. Clearly, Mom and Ken, snuggled up on the opposite side of the bench, had no intention of leaving any time soon.

Then I noticed it. A change in the air, the moment before my mother raised her voice.

"You asshole," she screamed at Ken, slurring her s's. She backed away from his embrace and bore through his face with her eyes.

Ken leaned forward, an attempt to curl back into her embrace. "It wasn't even a real job," he whined.

"It was the only job you had. And it was better than what you have now. Nothing."

I felt Demian scoot closer to me, wide awake now.

"Just calm down, Rose. It was a shit job, squandering my talents. I'll get another one, that'll recognize what I'm capable of."

"Bullshit you will. And don't tell me to calm down. I hate that!" Mom's voice had gotten to the level where it challenged the volume of the music. One of the few remaining families—a tweedy professor type with his wife and daughter—stared at us as they gathered their jackets. I imagined them getting into their expensive car, something shiny and free of dents, with the father driving them toward the hills near the Claremont Hotel, where Ken had told me most of the tenured professors lived. The houses in that part of Berkeley, close to the UC campus, were large, majestic, and filled with a special kind of splendor that was a mystery to me. Watching the three of them, tenderly holding one another's hands as they left the pub, made me feel poor and unclean.

A half an hour later, the argument still hadn't ended, but Ken had gotten Mom to lower her voice. He had also gone back to the bar for more drinks. There were refilled glasses of soda in front of Demian and me, but we weren't thirsty. Another thirty minutes and they were both really drunk. Ken dragged her to the small dance area, where they hugged each other through another Allman Brothers song.

Demian and I alternated between laying our heads on the table and kicking the underside of it. We played games using the tiny pools of spilled beer, half-empty glasses, and cigarette butts around us. With the tip of my finger, I drew the words *I want to go home* onto the scratched wood of the table over and over again.

By the time Mom and Ken stumbled back to us, all the other families had gone back to their homes. The pub was now dense with smoke. More people, different people, younger and louder, had replaced the earlier crowd. The music switched from Mom and Ken's kind of music to something newer, hard and rocking and dissonant, for these big groups of people with Cal jerseys and short hair, their laughter flooding the entire pub. Time inched by, and Demian got so tired he slipped off the bench and fell backward. I barely caught him before he hit the floor.

"Mom, can we go now?"

She didn't seem to hear me. She and Ken were in lovey-dovey mode, all the fighting from before forgiven or forgotten. I raised my voice until I thought I was yelling. "Mom?! D's falling asleep."

"Just a little while more, sweetie. He can crash on the floor if he's tired. Take my jacket." She handed me her suede coat with the fringe at the bottom. I kept my hands in my lap.

"We've both got school tomorrow," I said, competing with the pub's powerful sound system. "Last day, remember?"

She just nodded and dropped her jacket onto the table. A strip of the fringe landed in a small puddle of beer.

Ken leaned over to me, his eyes glazed, the words forming sloppily on his lips. "So, Stevie, why don'tcha walk him home, 'kay? Your mom and I wanna finish our drinks, keep our mellow going, you know?"

I stared at him, not sure I'd heard him right. I had walked home alone after dark before, but never this late at night and never with Demian. Did Ken actually want us to leave by ourselves?

Ken met my stare, then jerked his thumb toward the front door. I looked to Mom, whose gaze was on a fixed point elsewhere. I swallowed, searched for something to say that would convince them to leave with us. When I leaned over the table to get Mom's attention, Ken stood up. He was unsteady, a strand of his long hair over one eye, the other eye with streaks of red in the part that was normally white. "Go on home."

I felt like a small dog cowed by a much bigger dog. I nudged Demian awake and together we shuffled across the floor. I pushed open the heavy oak door. The smoke, body heat, ceaseless chatter and clinking of glasses followed us into the street. The brisk night air shocked me. Goose bumps crawled along my arms, a ratty T-shirt my only protection from the cold blowing in from the Bay.

The corner was empty of people, cars whishing past intermittently along Shattuck's two lanes. My brother and I drifted up Prince toward Wheeler, Demian's eyes puffy from fatigue and cigarette smoke. His voice was raspy and spent.

"They're not coming too?" he asked, like he'd woken up just then, no idea that we were alone on the dark street.

"Nope. They'll be home later." I touched the top of his head, gently, and when he craned his neck with a tired smile on his face, I felt a sliver of better.

"I liked the harp guy. Harpo … Harpo."

"Yeah, he's funny," I said.

We walked in silence, past houses with their porch lights off, overgrown trees that draped above the sidewalk and seemed like they could hurt us if they wanted. So many flowers, leaning into us from each wild garden we passed, nipping at our ankles in the dark. All the green leaves became black. Our own footsteps sounded like someone else, close behind us.

As we disappeared under more trees, the wind from across the Bay swept in hard and batted Demian's nylon jacket around his tiny waist. At the corner, I took his hand in mine.

"Left, right, then left again."

"I know, I know."

"Every time, though, okay?"

"I'm not a baby, you don't have to hold my hand."

"I know, it's just … It's dark and …" My voice trailed off as we crossed the street.

"Okay," he said, and let me hold his hand until we reached the sidewalk.

We passed more paneled wood houses, suffocated by darkness, as we hurried toward our own little stucco home. We were nearly to our street before we saw anyone, the neighborhood quiet except for the bark … bark bark … bark … of a dog up the street. Humphrey, a terrier mix, appeared at the corner, tugging on a long leash held by Mrs. Hunter. She lumbered up the street in her light blue housedress and furry slippers.

"What you boys doing out so late?" A heavy woman in her sixties, she spoke like every syllable was its own sentence.

"Coming back from the movies," Demian said. When he leaned down to pet Humphrey, the dog's tail gave a few shakes of approval.

"The movies? Where your parents at?"

"They're right behind us, Mrs. Hunter," I quickly said, before Demian could open his mouth. "They wanted to see the credits."

I grabbed Demian's arm and pulled him away from the dog. We left Mrs. Hunter and neared our house.

"The credits?" she muttered, behind us now. "Letting them boys walk out alone in the middle of the damned night. I swear, these poor kids parenting they own damn selves."

A few houses down the block I noticed the hot red cherry of a lit cigarette. On the porch of the house next to ours, Kirby Johnson, who lived there with his parents, sat concealed by an overgrown shrub. He was in his early twenties, and I thought I'd once heard Ken mention that Kirby had graduated a few years behind him at Cal. Our neighbor had only ever said a few words to me in the three years we'd lived next to him, but whenever I saw him, including earlier that night at The Starry Plough, he gave me the creeps.

"Nosey old bitch," he said as we passed his house, a deep voice cutting through the night. "She needs to mind her own business."

I stole a glance at his obscured face, the light from the cigarette momentarily illuminating his thick, yellow curls. I couldn't see it at that moment, but I knew, hiding underneath all that hair and slightly raised off his brow, was a thin, jagged, three-inch long scar. Flowing red like lava, it ran down from his hairline to just above the bridge of his nose, in angry relief against that pale white canvas. He made me think of the boogeyman, a silly, made-up, monster-in-the-closet I was supposed to have outgrown when I was Demian's age. But I couldn't shake it, the feeling that my neighbor was someone, something, to fear.

Chapter 2

THE NEXT MORNING, A FRIDAY, DEMIAN was dressed for school before I had even opened my eyes. He sat cross-legged on his bed in our cramped room, silently mouthing the words he read from one of my Fantastic Four comic books. The worn wooden headboards of our twin beds grazed the bottom ledge of a crusty white window frame, where Demian's action figures were positioned like a battalion of soldiers. The room was already drowning in light, no curtains on the windows to keep the sun from bursting inside. His plastic Spider-Man, which used to be mine, was backlit in yellow from its perch at the top of his bed. Powered by the light of the sun, it looked ready to spring down upon his bedspread, where Pinocchio and Bambi lay unaware that the web-slinger was on the hunt.

I lay under my own bedspread, faded and torn in places. Library books and my personal collection of oversize Tintin paperbacks—filled with the adventures of a Belgian boy and his dog Snowy—lay scattered at the foot of the bed. A half-empty glass of Pepsi and a ravaged box of Chips Ahoy cookies commanded the majority of space on the dresser that separated our two beds.

On Demian's side of the room, posters thumb-tacked against the cotton-candy-colored walls struggled for space. A Benji movie poster nuzzled up against an Incredible Hulk banner, which loomed above a March of Dimes walkathon announcement. The blast of colors and shapes and material—from glossy to newspaper print to the black velvet from a flea-market-bought mini-painting of the Fonz—stood in contrast to the walls on my side of the room, bare but for a small calendar of the Alaskan wilderness.

Sprawled along the floor, miles from the bamboo hamper in front of the closet, were our unwashed clothes. From under the bed poked more T-shirts and holey socks, in addition to half-broken toys and comic books that had been neglected and abandoned. I had deliberately left the dirty clothes on the floor for days now; Demian would never pick them up and I had a bet going with myself as to how long it would take before Mom said something about it. She hardly came into our room now, not even to tuck Demian in like she used to, and the filth in here reminded me that she had begun to treat us the same way we treated our old toys.

I struggled into a sitting position, my undershirt soaked with night sweat. I remembered my dreams. They had been filled with Seneca Reed, the girl from my fifth-grade class who wasn't my girlfriend.

Not yet.

That same phrase had run through my anxious brain all night, prodding me to fulfill the promise I'd made to myself months ago. It was the last day of school, my last chance to tell her what was on my mind—that I liked her more than just as a friend—before summer came and some other kid made her his girlfriend. Other fifth graders had hooked up throughout the year, and some of them were even having sex already. I wasn't sure I was ready for that, but I knew I wanted to kiss her and put my arm around her and be part of a couple with her. The girl advice that Ken, all whiskey-happy at the pub, had thrust at me was something I hadn't asked for. But he was right. I had to find my nerve and make a move, risky as it might be, or lose my chance with her forever.

I was pretty sure that Seneca didn't see me the same way I saw her, but I had heard the saying *nothing ventured, nothing gained*, so I felt emboldened to take some kind of action. It was time to venture and gain myself a girlfriend. I had even started a list, in my journal—the one I now hid under my mattress, away from Ken and whoever else felt entitled to read my private thoughts—of things I wanted to accomplish over the summer. It was by no means complete, barely a list even, but making Seneca my girlfriend before summer's end was at the top of it. That it was written down, and not just an idea in my head, seemed to give the goal power. Urgency.

I made an effort to, at least temporarily, clear my head of Seneca and the hazards of the day ahead. I kicked my covers off and hopped onto the cold, hardwood floor. Demian finished the comic and reached down between our beds into my long box of *MAD Magazines* and Marvel heroes, replacing the FF with an Amazing Spider-Man.

"What time is it?" I asked.

His nose in the comic book, Demian sung out, "Half past a monkey's ass and quarter to his balls."

"Who taught you that?" I asked.

"Nobody. Just heard it," he said.

"Well, what time is it, really?"

Gramma and Grampa had given us matching Casio watches for Christmas. I always removed mine before bed, and couldn't always find it in the morning, but Demian never took his off. His wrist was so small that the strap nearly doubled over the plastic face. He lifted it to his face, then mouthed the seconds as they ticked by until he squeaked, "Six forty-seven." He dove right back into the comic.

"Did you have breakfast yet?" He never remembered to eat.

Demian shook his head, eyes never straying from Spidey.

"Why not? Are we out of cereal already?"

"Don't wanna wake Mom and Ken. They're still sleeping," he said.

"You sure they're home?" I asked, and instantly regretted it.

"What do you mean?" He looked at me for the first time.

"Nothing." I moved toward the bathroom and a shower. "Just go get breakfast and don't worry. You're not gonna wake them up. Trust me."

By 7:20, Demian was on the back of my second-hand dirt bike, his skinny bottom perched on the hard, uncushioned seat while I pedaled standing up. With his elementary school the destination, we climbed our street to Wheeler, hung a left, and then cruised over to Ashby, where the traffic was already heavy in both directions.

"I am stuck on Band-Aid brand / 'Cause Band-Aid's stuck on me." Demian sang his latest, favorite commercial. "I am stuck on Band-Aid / 'Cause Band-Aid's stuck on me!" he repeated, louder this time. Past favorites for him involved the Oscar Mayer Wiener and McDonald's two-all-beef-patties recipe.

I tuned him out and allowed my gaze to climb upward into the Berkeley Hills, where houses stood like castles, magical places filled with wonder and opulence. The part of the city that wasn't part of the city, that place where rich people did rich things and lived incredibly special lives. I shifted my eyes and looked for an opening in the traffic. We blazed across the intersection, crossing the two lanes of momentarily open space, and sailed through to the other end of Wheeler.

I maneuvered between the concrete pylons, there to prevent cars from entering the short block, and Demian slapped at an overgrown weed sprouting from the top of the octagon-shaped barrier. We rode by the hulking apartment complex where my friends Telly and Irod lived. I had spent a lot of time there after school and before dark. The back area of the apartments was hidden from the street, and that was where the neighborhood kids congregated, in a huge open area filled with climbable trees and leaf-strewn, perpetually damp ground. It was where alliances were formed and battle lines drawn. Where our imaginations were unfettered and wild energy overflowed from every one of us. I'd eventually have to share that place with Demian, now that he was getting older and more interested in my friends and my world, but at that moment I was happy to keep its secrets to myself.

My feet pumped harder on the pedals as we rounded the turn onto Russell and ascended toward Le Conte Elementary School, where I'd spent four of the greatest years of my life and where Demian was finishing kindergarten. It was the place I'd learned not only how to read but how to enjoy books and to trust my own imagination. It was where I'd eaten free breakfasts in the cafeteria, before I knew that being poor was something to be ashamed of. It was where my hard work had resulted in praise, surrounded by a family of teachers and schoolmates five days a week. It was where I still came sometimes, by myself on the weekends, when Mom and Ken's friends took over our house with their wine and their weed and I needed to be alone.

Sweat dripped into my eyes as the bike rolled past the auditorium. I felt Demian's nose brush against my back, then his ear press against my spine. It felt like he was burying his face into me, and I couldn't understand why until I saw the kid standing all alone on the sidewalk. He had his arms folded across his chest, wearing the same ripped T-shirt I had seen on him the night before at the pub. The scowl he had flashed at Demian was still smeared over his face.

A few feet past him, I skidded to a stop at the gate leading into the kindergarten play area. Beyond the fence and the smattering of playground equipment were the two rear doors of Mrs. Frost's and Mrs. Birchman's adjoining classrooms. Demian was early for class; I was running late for mine. He hopped off the bike, mumbled a thanks, and then ran through the gate to join his friends at the monkey bars.

I watched him dart off before I turned to stare at the kid who had spooked my brother. I pedaled to where he lurked in front of the closed auditorium doors, stopped the bike, and rested my arms on the handlebars. When his eyes met mine, he said, "What the hell you staring at?" He was fearless.

"What's your name?" I cracked my knuckles in front of his face, the joints popping loud enough for both of us to hear them over the excited screams and yells of the arriving school kids.

"None of your business." He had dirt ground into his eyebrows, and hard snot filled both nostrils. I didn't answer him, but steered my bike's under-inflated tire closer to his small, grimy body. "Get outta here. You don't go to this school."

"My brother does, and I want you to leave him alone. You got it?"

He just stood there, arms still folded, staring dumbly up at me.

"Hey! You hearing me or are you deaf?" I grabbed at my ear, made a twirling motion with two fingers.

"I seen you before. You're the Omen's brother."

That was the second time he'd called Demian that. The horror movie about the devil's offspring wasn't even out yet, but every kid I knew had seen the commercial on TV, with that crazy nanny screaming my brother's name. Demian made me get up and change the channel every time it came on.

"I'm *Demian's* brother, you little turd, and if he tells me you messed with him, I'm gonna kick your ass."

His lips were cracked and his fingernails were caked with filth. I tried to feel sorry for him, but from his silence and the way he looked at me, I could tell that he had been bullying my brother. I was pissed that it took me so long to figure out, that it was the last day of school before I got the chance to do something about it. I wasn't sure why Demian had kept this a secret from me, and I wondered if there were more kids at the school like this one.

I raised my fist, threw a fake punch at his face, and watched him flinch. "You got it?"

"I won't do nothing to him," he finally mumbled, his defiance waning. "What do I care for him for?"

"Good. Remember it." I backpedaled a few feet and then rode past him, close enough to notice the raised goose bumps on his bare, hairless arm. His face was slack. His eyes avoided mine.

I glanced over my shoulder when I reached the corner. He had moved onto the sidewalk and stood facing me, hands by his sides and a trembling lower lip poised to speak.

"Fat-ass!" he screamed at me. Both hands went up and he double-flipped me the bird. He turned and retreated to the safety of the school's main grounds.

I raised my fat ass from the seat of my bike, caught my brother staring at me through the playground fence, and furiously pedaled off to my last day of school.

I RUSHED UPHILL TO MY SCHOOL, Emerson, nervous, shaky, and a sweaty mess. My hair was wet and tangled, and my shirt back was soaked through. All I needed now was a big pee stain on the front of my jeans to make the morning complete.

I locked my bike to the rack in the entranceway, my damp fingers making the combination lock moist and slick. My plan for the day, the only thing I had set out to accomplish, involved a certain fifth-grade classmate. The last thing I wanted was to stink when I asked Seneca Reed for her phone number.

There was probably no way she would give it to me, even if I wasn't sweaty and huge and gross. I'd never even had a girlfriend before, but when Seneca transferred two months earlier with her long hair and blue eyes, dimpled chin and intoxicating smile, I imagined her as my first. I cozied up to her, found out what subjects she liked, what kinds of things she enjoyed, and swiftly became a chum.

"Chump is more like it," Trevor Kruemann told me when I confided in him a few weeks after her arrival. "She's not going to go for you. Barry Varta's gonna swoop all over her and you're gonna look like a dick."

"She already told me she doesn't like Barry. I just have to play this right and she could be my girlfriend by the end of summer."

"You're ... what's that word my brother used the other day? Delusional, yeah, that's it. You're delusional, thinking you've got any chance with her besides just being her 'good friend.'" Trevor laughed then, his crooked upper teeth and pug nose inciting my rage. I wanted to punch his stupid face in, but I didn't. He was one of my best friends.

Jogging down the school hallway, I ducked into the boys' bathroom before I could bump into anyone I knew. The white-tiled smell-a-torium was empty, the echo of my tennis shoes keeping me company as I sidled up to one of the sinks and wasted time waiting for hot water that would never come. I doused my face and hair in the ice-cold flow from the spigot before slapping my underarms with handfuls of water. I dried everything off in the hot blast of the wall dryer, grabbed some toilet paper, and dabbed up all the remaining droplets. I wasn't sure if I was any cleaner, or smelled any better, but I felt fresher.

Before I reached Mrs. Kennedy's classroom, Trevor and a kid I couldn't stand, Ryan Miller, cornered me in the hall.

"Hey, Daedalus, looking sharp, brother," Ryan said, using the name my father had given me, the one I no longer answered to. "What's up with the wet-dog look?" He laughed an odd, sniveling laugh that I tried my best to ignore.

"What are you going to do this summer?" Trevor asked me, turning his back on Ryan and changing the subject.

"I don't know," I said. "Maybe—"

"Lose some weight?" Ryan said it like he was reciting a punch line from a sitcom.

Trevor came to my defense. "Ryan, why do you have to be such an asshole?"

"What? What'd I say? Daedalus, what'd I say?"

Instead of engaging in a battle of words with him that I wasn't sure I could win—his dad was a lawyer and Ryan knew how to talk people into a corner—I just nodded at Trevor and moved toward class. I could hear them fall in line behind me, Ryan whispering something about how he had to be honest with me, especially since nobody else was. My heart sped up, and I wanted to punch him right in the face, but I was too scared about getting in trouble if I did.

As I entered the classroom I felt low, but when Seneca looked up at me, her face full with that sweet, engulfing, ear-to-ear grin of hers, my mood shifted upward dramatically. This was my first real crush, someone that I had dreams about, a girl who could serve as my salvation and fill all those empty holes littered inside me. I convinced myself that if she became my girlfriend over the summer, I would come back to this school in the fall with pride in my step, a sense of purpose to my life, and joy etched on my face.

I took my seat and dropped my backpack to the floor. Mrs. Kennedy, a hunched-over woman whose gray eyebrows always stretched to her temples when a thought stymied her, promised a half day of minimal work and plenty of good times. The only assignment was to finish our class yearbooks: colored construction paper as front and back covers, with book reports, tests, art projects, and photos from the entire year stuffed inside. It was a "keepsake," Mrs. Kennedy said, of our fifth-grade "experience." Some of us would give them to our parents; the rest of us would probably throw them in the garbage on the way home from school.

I was pretty sure Seneca would give hers to her father, considering the way she spoke about him and how he seemed interested in what she did at school. She didn't seem embarrassed that he was so involved in her school life, which made me embarrassed that my mother was so completely uninvolved in mine.

I watched her walk to her desk from the back table, where she had used the three-hole punch. Her eyes landed on mine and I felt heat at the back of my neck. She sat down and I looked at the clock. I had less than three hours before class, and the school year, would be over.

My hands were so damp I scrubbed them against my pant legs. I had to find a reason, a good excuse, to get close to her. Her desk was two whole aisles over from mine. But it was near the pencil sharpener. I grabbed my yellow No. 2 and felt the sword-sharp tip of it. I shoved it against the underside of my desk until I heard a small crack and felt the lead break.

After sharpening my pencil, I walked slowly down her aisle. The undersides of my arms began to tingle, and I wondered if this meant I was about to have a heart attack. The thought tried to plant itself in my head, but I resisted it. I was going to talk to Seneca, and I was going to get her phone number if it was the last thing I did on this earth. This was serious business, and the imagined threat of hospitalization and surgery on my suddenly faulty heart was not about to stop me.

"Hi," I said, sounding stupid in my own ears. "I, uh, I … Ooh, what's that?" I pointed to a drawing that Seneca was placing inside her yearbook.

She looked up at me standing over her, then back down at a watercolor of what was obviously the front of our school.

"It's the school," she said, looking down at it. I stared at the part in her shoulder-length brown hair. I imagined tracing the line with my index finger. Her head angled upward and she asked, "Didn't you do one too? I thought we all had the same assignment."

"Yeah, sure, it's just … mine didn't turn out as well as yours there. I can't draw for shit … I mean, I'm not … I'm not good with it." The tingling in my upper arms had returned.

"I guess I'm not, either, if you didn't know what it was." She laughed a nervous laugh, her cheeks crinkling up and that tiny mole on the side of her nose expanding ever so slightly.

"No, I'm just stupid. That looks just like it. It does." The soles of my feet throbbed, and I fought the urge to rub them right there in front of her. "So … your book is looking pretty good. Better than mine, definitely."

"I don't have much, though," she said, thumbing through it. "I really wish I had started here earlier. But I guess I have enough, so it's okay."

"Yeah," I said, wanting to say so much more. "Well, I should get back to my desk. See ya."

"Okay. See you, then."

I went back to my desk, slapped my yearbook together as quickly as I could, and waited quietly until it was time to go home.

Mrs. Kennedy collected our textbooks, gave us a heartfelt farewell, wished us a great summer, and let us all go as the final bell rang like it was the start of a horse race at Bay Meadows. I hung back and waited self-consciously for Seneca to leave the classroom before me and then trailed her. Waiting for my last chance.

She was talking to Hailie Jones, who I sort of had a crush on back in third grade, but she never saw me in that way, despite the two-dollar valentine I'd spent most of my allowance money on that year, which had resulted in a bored, "Thanks, Stevie."

I overheard a snippet of their conversation, something about them maybe going to Great America in July, if they could both convince their parents to let them. There was no way I had enough nerve left to ask Seneca for her number in front of Hailie. My final opportunity to connect with Seneca was rapidly disappearing, but I tried not to panic. I crossed my fingers inside my pocket and hung back.

Hailie ran off, and Seneca turned around to face me. "Steve, hi. You know, we never talked about the summer." She smelled good, like she had strawberry ChapStick on her lips.

"We didn't?"

"No," she said, a mock scolding tone in her voice. "Here." She handed me a folded piece of paper. I swear she blushed.

I caught the handoff just as she turned around and was swallowed up by a mass of cheering, yelling, excited kids rampaging through the halls on their way to summer vacation.

I stood by the lockers, not sure what had just happened. I opened the piece of stationery to discover a pretty flower pattern surrounding seven numbers, her phone number in full bloom. Above this was her name in cursive letters, the script flowing and swirling in perfection. From the slight wear on the paper, I deduced, in detective-like fashion, that she had been holding onto this for longer than I would have imagined.

The doors at the end of the hall sprung open, and a giant burst of sunlight flooded in. The light and heat enveloped me; energy rushed through my body. I muffled a yawp of joy, but nothing was able to contain what I felt inside.

Chapter 3

On my last day of fifth grade, with Seneca Reed's phone number neatly folded in my jeans pocket, I rode my bike away from school in a satisfying daze. Normally I picked Demian up from school whenever he didn't have plans to walk home with Rafe, his buddy from kindergarten who lived down the block from us. Today was a Rafe day so, at barely two in the afternoon, I neared home alone. I suddenly got a clear vision of Ken, newly fired, butt planted on the couch at home, getting high and watching TV snow, or sleeping off last night's hangover. The notion of being stuck inside with the guy who had sent Demian and me out alone in the middle of the night made my stomach hurt. And Mom, at her job down at the phone company, wouldn't walk through the front door until at least six. That left four hours. I had a sudden impulse to ride to the UC campus.

I headed toward Telegraph.

At the corner of Ashby and Fulton, anticipating the taste of a Top Dog bratwurst with relish and mustard slathered inside a massive poppy-seed bun, I spotted Demian and Rafe. The desire to tell my brother about the confrontation I'd had with his bully, and for him to fess up about keeping secrets from me, became a fresh need and my hunger faded for the moment. I got impatient waiting for the light to change. When I saw a hole in the traffic, I swiftly pedaled across two lanes toward them.

"Demian," I said, almost ramming into them. They both jumped. "What's up?"

"Nothing," he answered. He was focused on the sidewalk, his feet alternating between long strides and stuttered steps, in order to avoid stepping on any of the cracks. He had no intention of breaking our mother's back.

"Hey, Rafe," I nodded at him. A goofy smile was his response. With his moptop haircut, a plaid shirt over yellow, striped slacks, and scuffed-up, oversize Buster Brown shoes, my brother's friend seemed primed to enroll in clown school. "I thought you got out early today. You two just heading home now?"

There was a sly exchange of looks between Demian and Rafe, but they continued walking without answering me. I alternately sped past them and slowed my pace, furiously working the pedals to keep myself balanced and avoid toppling sideways.

Rafe caught my tightrope act out of the corner of his eye. He blurted, "Mrs. Frost wanted Demian to have something. A gift."

"Aww, Rafe, I was gonna tell him." Demian stopped for a moment, then started again, his little legs driving him forward in a zigzag pattern.

"What'd she give you, D?" I pointed at his ratty backpack, which Mom had found in a free box the year before.

Demian snapped the fingers of his left hand, a habit picked up from Ken; this was Ken's nonchalant yet hostile way of dismissing an idea, a person, or a subject he wasn't interested in talking about. "Nothing too great," Demian said. "Just a book."

"Really? What kind of book?" I asked, genuinely interested. I had an oddly Pavlovian response whenever books were mentioned. At least, that's what Mom had thought out loud more than once.

"I'll show you later. If you really want to see it." Demian's right heel barely missed planting itself on a slim crack.

"But the book, you know the book from Mrs. Frost? We're not just coming home late 'cause of that," Rafe said, his eyes lit up with excitement.

We turned the corner at Wheeler and passed our landlord's house, but it didn't look like Mr. Takadakos was home. He had lost his wife to diabetes on New Year's Day, and I had overheard Mrs. Hunter from across the street gossiping about him to another neighbor. She said that he liked to take long drives where he would talk to his dead wife, pretending she was sitting next to him.

I asked Rafe, "'Cause why, then?"

Demian shoved his hands in his pockets, as his feet stepped on crack after crack.

"Eric Zydenski beat up Chris Ogilvy after school." Rafe pounded a fist into an open palm, the sound like a wet towel slapping a large rock.

"Who's Eric?"

I looked at Demian, but Rafe answered. "You don't know who Eric is? Man, he's been hassling Demian all year. Messing with him on the swings and—"

Demian swatted Rafe with an open hand and said, "Shh."

"Okay," I said, "who's the other kid, then?"

"Chris? He's a total dork. From Mrs. Birchman's class. Nobody likes him; they all think he's maybe retarded. Eric just did what everybody wanted to do anyways. So, you know, it was cool-city." Rafe swiped a few stalks of sour grass as we passed a small patch near the end of the block. He ripped the yellow flower off and tossed it into the street, then bit into the green body, sucking in juice and stem through his teeth.

"How bad did he kick his ass?" I was relieved it hadn't been Demian.

"Kinda bad. There was definitely blood." Rafe gave Demian a playful shove. "His nose, huh?"

"How old is Eric?"

"Second grade," Rafe said. "But kind of big for how old he is."

"He sounds like a shit-bag. Does he beat up a lot of kids at school?" I pedaled beside Demian. "Does he beat you up, Demian?"

My brother's voice was so low, the only thing I could make out was, "... doesn't ..."

"What'd you say, Dem?" I asked.

"He doesn't mess with me that much."

"He shouldn't mess with you at all." I imagined Eric's dirty hands all over my brother and nearly steered the bike off the sidewalk.

As we passed Kirby's house, I couldn't help feeling relief that he wasn't sitting on his porch like he had been the other night.

"You wanna come in, Rafe?" Demian said when we were in front of our house. "I think we got some Pop-Tarts. The Co-op kind, but still good."

"I gotta get home. I'll come by later, 'kay? Maybe after dinner. We gotta talk about that thing." He waved at me and ran three houses down to his place. His mother did seamstress work for a cleaners on Shattuck Avenue and took care of Rafe's two-year-old sister, so she was home most of the time. She doted on Demian whenever he visited their place, but I always got the sense she didn't think much of me.

"You guys have a *thing*, huh? Ooooh." I reached out over my handlebars, trying to muss Demian's hair, but he ducked away from my grasp.

"Shut up. It's not like that. You're stupid."

"You're stupid," I said, then swatted at his head. He ducked out of the way just in time. He danced a little victory jig. I got off my bike and Demian sat on our first step. He didn't make any moves to go inside.

"You think they're here?" he asked. "Now?"

"Mom was supposed to work, I think, and Ken … his car's here. But, I don't know."

"I don't want to go in yet," Demian said.

I sat beside him on the step. "You wanna go somewhere else? Get some candy at the liquor store? I've got some money." I had abandoned the idea of cruising along Telegraph, not wanting to leave Demian alone, but I was still antsy.

"Nah. Just wanna sit," he said. "Uh-huh."

So we sat there, at just past two in the afternoon in the first hours of our summer vacation. My excitement about the phone number had deflated with the talk of Eric. But the quiet moment allowed an opportunity to pat my front pocket where the number lay (even though I had it memorized minutes after she placed it in my hand) and envision a summer of possibility that I hoped might change everything for me.

"You'll love it at Levitz!" Demian yelled the furniture store's slogan, which made it sound more like a command than what it was, just a stupid commercial jingle.

I crinkled my forehead at him. He tried to do the same, but he couldn't quite pull it off. We stared back into the empty street.

"You wanna hear something?" Demian turned to me, his knees knocking together in that way they did when he had something exciting to share.

"I don't know … *do* I?"

"Everybody at school's been talking about it. I mean, for, like, weeks. This old man, he shows his ding-a-ling to kids at the park."

"You told me that was a rumor some kid started a long time ago." I picked at a tiny scab on my elbow.

Demian jumped up from the steps, then stood in front of me so that he had my full attention. "Unh-uh. Jenny Gribendi—she's in third grade and everybody says she's not a liar—she and this other girl saw him doing it. You know, showing them his, you know, showing his thing."

"Flashing them?" I asked. My brother nodded his head. "At Willard Park? *When*?"

"I don't know. Tuesday, I think. Yeah, Tuesday."

"You don't think Jenny's trying to maybe get people to think she's cool or something, give her a rep there?" A beat-up Mustang sped down our street, Jethro Tull pounding through the car's bass-heavy speakers. The friction of tires on asphalt mixed with the music in such a way that I swore I could smell the guitar and hear the burnt rubber.

"Well … that's what me and Rafe are gonna do. The thing."

My mind had wandered, and I had lost the thread of Demian's story. "The thing?"

"We're gonna find the guy, the old guy, and take a picture of him doing it. Rafe is gonna borrow his mom's camera and we're gonna picture … *take* a picture. After then we're gonna take it to the police. Like Encyclopedia Brown, you know, from those books you read me. His dad's the police."

"That's not such a good idea, Demian. What if you find him and he decides to, I don't know, hurt you guys?"

This gave him a moment of pause. "Rafe and me were talking and maybe, maybe, maybe … if we go like real detective-like, so he doesn't know we're there until, well, we, you know, take the picture." He thought on it, absent-mindedly rubbing a small fist against the crotch of his jeans. "Then we run."

"Well, sounds like you two really have it all thought out." I decided I was tired of standing outside my own house. I didn't want to listen to Demian anymore; I just wanted to be inside with my own thoughts of Seneca.

Demian followed me through the gate, watched silently as I steered the bike to a spot next to the rusted metal garbage cans. When I turned around, he stood slack-jawed in front of the back door.

"Don't you have your key?" I asked, wondering why he stood there like he'd lost the use of his arms.

"Yeah. I just wanted you to ... I don't know, go in first."

"I'm sure if they're not home, they've gone off to work. I didn't see Mom's car parked anywhere out there, so, you know. Don't worry about it—they came home last night." I wanted to reach out and give him a pat, or hold his vulnerable hand like I had the night before, but I didn't. Instead, I stood there, feeling self-conscious and powerless.

"I didn't think that. I just ..." he trailed off. Then he looked at me with impatience as I fiddled with my three keys. I finally opened the back door and we walked into an empty house.

We split up without planning it, Demian taking the back of the house and me scoping out the front. Nobody was in the dining room, the living room, our room, or theirs. I took a seat on the purple paisley couch by the front window and waited for Demian.

"They're not here?" he asked, panicky. He still wasn't convinced they had come home the night before.

"Nope. Like I said, they're probably at work. You see this?" I held up an ashtray with four or five cigarette butts in it, the smell of smoke still pungent around them. "Ken smoked 'em today. And look," I pointed to the chair across from the couch. "Mom's jacket. They probably woke up right after we left."

"Okay," he said, then wandered into the kitchen. I heard the fridge door open.

I picked up a Furry Freak Brothers comic sticking out the side of the couch and yelled to my brother, "Bring me some Pepsi. And Wheat Thins." I fingered through the black-and-white strips inside, crudely drawn panels that focused on Fat Freddy's cat, who did nothing but get stoned and then crap all over the place. Bored with it before Demian came back with my food, I tossed it at a pile next to our fireplace, on top of *High Times* magazines and issues of the *Berkeley Barb*.

I stared up at the potted plants dying on the mantle, the hanging fern growing like a weed near the window, and wondered the point of having living things that weren't cared for. Looking at the mess of books exploding outside of Ken's makeshift cinderblock bookcase, I thought about the downtown library and how many books they owned that I couldn't wait to borrow.

Demian juggled two glasses of soda and a yellow box, nearly spilling it all before he reached the couch. I helped him, then broke open the box of square crackers and grabbed a handful. As he raised the glass of Pepsi to his lips, I said, "Turn on the TV, it's almost time for Beaver." He put down the glass, let out a fake-agitated sigh, walked over to the set, and switched it on.

What my dad had always called 'the idiot box' was barely warmed up, the sound for a Charmin toilet paper commercial beating the picture by a few seconds, when the front door opened and Ken strolled in.

"So, I called him a philistine and explained that I had more brilliance in my johnson than he had in all his fucking degrees, and I'd be buying and selling *his* pencil dick soon enough," he said to someone behind him. Ken saw us occupying the couch and gave me a quizzical look. "Hey, aren't you boys supposed to be in school still?"

I caught Demian's eye and gave my head a slight nod toward the TV. He dutifully turned it off and grabbed his glass of untouched Pepsi. Ken didn't say a word, only sat down in the spot I'd just left, but Kirby waved a creepy hello at us. "Hey, little men, how's by you?"

I gave him a non-committal half-smile, then led Demian toward our room.

"Why's *he* here?" my brother asked once we were safely behind our bedroom door.

This was the first time I had ever seen Kirby inside our house. It was unsettling.

"Maybe they're friends. I don't know." I shrugged, then threw my pillow up against the headboard. I didn't want to think about Kirby, or Ken, or even Eric, my brother's bully. I just wanted to hold Seneca's phone number in my hand and focus on our upcoming summer together.

Music suddenly crawled under our door from the other room, an album of Ken's that sounded like Frank Zappa or Captain Beefheart—discordant and unpleasant. Used to music playing in the house at all hours of the day and night, I had learned how to tune most of it out, especially if I was engrossed in a good book. I placed my drink and the box of crackers on the dresser that stood between Demian's bed and mine, before dropping to the floor and shoving my hand under my bed. As my fingers brushed a few paperback spines, I stared at the Wacky Pack stickers plastered on the sides of the dresser drawers. I chuckled for the hundredth time at the screaming woman and baby on a detergent box, covered in icicles and snow. Mom used the brand the sticker parodied, so I thought it was a riot to see a skewed version of reality right there in my room. I reminded myself to buy another pack, once I got my next allowance.

My fingers finally settled on a thin volume, a book of short stories by Jack London that I had started a few days before. Usually I only got a little more than halfway through one of them before falling asleep under the covers with my flashlight still on. But sometimes I'd completely finish a story and spend all night dreaming adventures in the Yukon among the native people and wild animals.

I always read two or three books at a time, currently deep into both S.E. Hinton's *Rumble Fish*, which was much too real and depressing for the beginning of my summer vacation, and *Stranger in a Strange Land*, a sci-fi book that the school librarian, Mr. Ventner, had recommended. The plan had been to finish it before school ended, in order to tell him what I thought of his favorite book, but I never go that far into it. Once I stumbled upon London, which opened up avenues of escape that not many other books I'd read offered me, I was hooked. I had found my new favorite author.

Back on my bed, I turned the London book to midway through "Nam-Bak, the Unveracious" and reached for my Pepsi. As I brought it down from the dresser top, the glass knocked against a half-open drawer and spilled soda all over my shirt and the book. I yelled a multisyllabic obscenity I'd heard from one of Ken's colorful friends and stifled the urge to smash the glass against the wall.

Now a sticky mess, I changed my shirt and waved my wet book in the air to dry. Demian was too busy with his Lincoln Logs to do more than glance up at me once. I headed toward the kitchen for paper towels and a Pepsi refill. Ken and our neighbor Kirby sat in the living room, passing a joint back and forth and talking while the record player spun loud chaos. They didn't bother to acknowledge me. I made it to the kitchen without a word exchanged between us.

"Philosophy is the core, man, of human evolution." Ken battled the music for vocal supremacy, and I could hear him clearly from the next room. "Fuck the body. It's the mind, how it conceptualizes ideas—that's what we're all about. That's why pot is so amazing, I mean, it doesn't mess with the body and it actually opens portals in your mind that aren't accessible without it. All these pathways awaken in there and allow you access to all kinds of amazing ideas. Take the concept of ..." Ken had another toke of the joint and kept on rambling.

As I refilled my Pepsi, I thought about how Ken reminded me so much of my dad, the way they both talked about things that seemed so big and important and totally beyond my comprehension.

Thomas O'Neill was twenty-two when he met my mother on the UC Berkeley campus, finishing his senior year while she did secretarial temp work for the administration in Sproul Hall. My father used to brag about how the first time he saw her, a Monday after his political science class, he knew she'd marry him and bear his children. That first day, though, he didn't say a word to her. He came back the next day, even though he had no classes, and struck up a conversation with her. By the third day she had accepted an invitation to lunch at LaVal's in Northside and less than six months later they were married and I was on the way.

They lived with my mother's parents while figuring out how to pay for a place of their own. My father landed a job delivering auto parts throughout the East Bay for a Turkish boss who paid him under the table and occasionally gave him hash from "back home" instead of actual money. By the time I arrived, they were living in a tiny apartment near the campus, and making enough money between them to feed us all, and still afford their "little bit of grass" now and again.

It was 1965 and my father's hair rivaled my mother's hip-length tresses. They had jumped on the hippie bandwagon and even considered joining a commune until smarter heads (hers) prevailed and they decided to raise me outside the village.

I was christened Daedalus Stephen O'Neill, my father's homage to his Irish birthright and James Joyce's supposed literary stand-in from *Portrait of an Artist as a Young Man* and *Ulysses*. Not until I was nearly eight years old, and dad had been out of our lives for over a year, did I finally convince everyone that I wouldn't answer to that weird name, and Steve or Stevie was how I demanded to be addressed. Stephen became an acceptable alternate, but my given name was strictly *verboten*. In addition to its implication that I was a *dead* kid, I also realized something even worse: *Daedalus* sounded like *dad-less*. Look at me, I'm a boy without a dad! That was not how I wanted to be seen by the world.

Until I turned eight, however, I was known as Daedalus, my parents' friends endlessly impressed with how clever and literary they were for christening me that tragic name. My father had a group of friends from school who stuck around Berkeley after graduation, some who pursued regular jobs like my dad, while others enrolled in master's studies and Ph.D. programs in order to stay in school as long as the student loans and grants continued to come through. These were his overeducated, politically aware, highly opinionated cohorts who eventually helped convince him—once Demian was a toddler and Thomas O'Neill's life was being consumed by two kids and a dead-end job, with the '70s fast approaching—to abandon us and move to New York in pursuit of his poetry ambitions. He claimed North Beach in San Francisco had been used up by Ginsburg and Kerouac, and even though Ferlinghetti and his City Lights were still beacons for emerging poets, my father thought the Big Apple would better appreciate his unique brand of verse.

So, a few short years after persuading my mother to name her second son for yet *another* literary character—this time, from Herman Hesse's underground novel—he packed a U.S. Army duffel bag with a few belongings (ironically, he had dodged the draft and his duty to country, but used the military's supplies to flee his family), borrowed some money from his relatives in Omaha and headed out of our lives, never to return. My mother was devastated, alone to raise a barely-two-year-old and a six-year-old. She leaned on my grandmother quite a bit, who never resented it and actually took amazingly good care of us whenever she drove from Fremont to our little place in Berkeley to make dinner and console my mother.

My mother found a better, full-time job, put Demian in cheap daycare in Oakland, and let me fend for myself at Le Conte Elementary. She met Ken while shopping at the Co-op, her purse stuffed with the multi-colored food stamps we received once a month. Within a few weeks he was sharing breakfast with us every morning, and within six months they had found the rental house on Emerson and had officially shacked up together. It was a good omen, Ken had said, finding a place on a street named for Ralph Waldo, a free thinker and genius mind. My father's ideals, regurgitated out of the mouth of this fake dad, an interloper whom my mother had chosen as a substitute for what she had lost.

I was eight by that time, and Demian was four. I went by Steve only, never by Daedalus. As far as I was concerned, I wasn't my father's son anymore. I was my own person, finally allowed an ordinary name for an ordinary boy. Let my little brother keep his odd name, I thought with a bitterness that would only intensify as I grew older, let him carry on the tradition of Thomas O'Neill's literary slavitude until he figured out for himself what kind of man his father was.

Listening to Ken drone on to Kirby, I stood in the kitchen and pondered the kinds of conversations I actually remembered from when my dad was around, the ones he had with his hippie, highly educated peers. While they all went entirely over my head, they had the same flavor to them, the same important-sounding tenor, that the conversations Ken and my mom had with their friends. Especially when they were getting high. I was sure I was the one missing something, left out of the conversation as well as its meaning because I lacked the maturity, the intelligence, the knowledge of things past, present, future and unknown. I was only ten years old, and they were all college-educated, some of them with multiple degrees. They were the geniuses. I was the idiot.

I went back to my bedroom, joined my little brother, and checked on my Jack London book. It was ruined.

Chapter 4

SATURDAY MORNING ARRIVED, WEIRD AND WONDERFUL. My first day of summer vacation, and I could do anything, I could do *everything*. Most of all I wanted to travel up to the avenue, Telegraph, and spend the allowance I'd been saving from the last three weeks: on Spidey and X-Men comics, hot dogs, and maybe a 45 or two. The sun had already found its way inside my room, so I hurried to dress before sweat could gather in the folds of my neck and the base of my back.

I heard voices from the kitchen. "Mom got donuts," Demian said when I joined him, Ken and Mom. He had a face full of chocolate, the last edge of an old-fashioned clutched in his sticky hand. Smoke hovered in the air around Ken, who leaned against the refrigerator and puffed on a cigarette. He looked like he had just woken up, naked everywhere but below the belly and above the knee, a pair of wrinkled khaki shorts hanging loose on his hips. Mom drank her coffee at the table, halfway through a French twist, looking as if she'd been up for hours.

"I saved you a jelly," she opened the top of a big pink box with at least half a dozen donuts inside. "Still your favorite?"

I nodded, reached for the big, round ball of dough, and was surprised to find it warm. Before I had finished swallowing the last bit of strawberry filling, my hand was back in the box, plucking out a chocolate bar. Demian savored his final bite, in no rush.

"Do either of you have any plans today?" Mom asked, while behind her Ken rubbed his eyes and plowed into a new pack of cigarettes. I watched the red strip of plastic twirl off the top of the box and flutter to the kitchen floor. Ken's dirty big toe prodded it under the fridge. He beat the bottom of the box with his palm until a single cigarette broke from the pack.

When he stuck his tongue out to the tip of it, I turned away and said to Mom, "It's our first day of summer vacation." It wasn't exactly an answer, but my way of letting her know that today was the beginning of something special. That it meant a little more than the days that had come before, and the days that would come after. I wanted it to mean something to her, as well.

"There's a small festival happening at People's Park," she said. "Live music, artisans, lots of food, maybe even a juggler. Ken and I thought it could be fun. What do you think?" Mom tried to close the white donut box, but one of the sides refused to fold in.

"Sure, Mom, I guess." I popped another sticky chunk of dough into my mouth as she rifled through our junk drawer. Scotch tape in hand, she pushed down the top of the box and sealed it shut.

"There," she said, before sliding it on top of the refrigerator. "These should keep for a day or two."

"Not if Stevie can reach it," Ken said, hopping onto the kitchen sink butt first.

Mom said, "Be nice," while he smoked and began picking at his feet. She turned to me. "Get dressed. We'll leave after Ken finds the gold between his toes—"

"Hey!" he said.

"—and gets himself a shower. Right?"

Back in my room, I heard voices outside. The window was closed, but it sounded like adults talking. It sounded as if someone was crying. My hearing had always been what the testers at school called "above average," and as much as I wanted to be able to hear a pin drop a mile away like I was Superman, I didn't seem gifted with anything heroic or extrasensory. I just heard higher tones clearer than the majority of people out there and could sometimes make out words other people next to me could not.

At the window, I saw Mrs. Hunter next door, talking to Kirby's dad. I ducked down and pushed the wooden frame a few inches upward.

"—didn't do nothing." Mrs. Hunter kneaded her fists deep into her eyes, her hands looking wet. "Just a gentle little soul, my only companion since Mr. Hunter passed."

Mr. Johnson, in a sweater and slacks, towered over her. Larger all around than him, she wore a thin dress that covered everything but her billowed folds of arm fat. The way her body jiggled when she moved, that was so familiar to me. Mrs. Hunter was bigger than me, but I knew that jiggle: how it looked, how it felt, how embarrassed I was when I caught other people staring at it. Kirby's father placed a hand on her shoulder and said, "I'm sorry about your dog, Elma. I truly am. But my son wouldn't do this. Couldn't do this. You must know that."

"I know he did." She stepped back until his hand dropped from her body. "In my heart, I know that boy poisoned my dog. I'ma call the police. I'ma get justice here."

Mr. Johnson nodded. "I understand how upset you are. Let me get Kirby. He'll assuage all of your concerns."

"I don't need that," she protested, but he had already gone into the house. I tried to see past her, up the street to her house, but it was blocked by trees and parked cars. Was Humphrey really dead? Did Kirby kill her dog? Why? I had never had a dog before, but I liked petting them and the sloppy feel of their tongues on my hands and face.

Watching Mrs. Hunter stand there on the porch alone, the sobs causing her entire body to quake underneath her faded, over-washed housedress, I felt her pain. Watching her made me want to cry, too. Even though Humphrey hadn't been mine, I understood her grief, and I shared it.

Kirby appeared on the porch, one hand rubbing sleep out of his eyes. "My old man says—"

"You killed my dog. Kilt him!" she raged, her voice deep now and hard for me to hear.

"What are you talking about? I didn't do anything to anybody." Kirby moved away from her, back toward his house.

"I know you did it. God, He sees everything you do." She pointed a shaky finger toward his face. "Everything."

"You got a little bit of the crazy in you, lady. You hear me?"

"You poisoned my baby." Mrs. Hunter's voice trembled so badly now I thought her whole body might topple over. I had read a story in a magazine once about a man who had gotten so angry that his face had filled up with blood and he died right where he stood. I didn't know if it was really true, but I figured if it was in the magazine it had to be.

"Prove it then," he said. He jutted his neck at her, his unwashed curls flinging downward near her face. "Go ahead," were the last words I heard him speak before she backed away from him and stumbled up the street. Now she was bawling.

Kirby stood for a moment watching her go. Then he turned and looked directly at me, my face peering out behind the partly open window. He stared at me, with a look I couldn't quite make out. I ducked right away, but it was too late. He had seen me.

My thoughts went wild, out of my control, and I got all paranoid. Would he poison *me* now? Demian? Why was I so stupid, listening at the window where I knew all along I never should have been? I quickly got dressed, all the while imagining poor Humphrey lying in Mrs. Hunter's back yard, dead because of Kirby.

KEN LIKED MEXICAN FOOD THE WAY I loved hot dogs, so we ate lunch at Mario's before heading across the street to People's Park. We were at one of the window tables, with a view of Telegraph Avenue's long stretch. The vendors had taken over the sidewalks, selling hand-woven clothes, jewelry, buttons, pipes, toys, books, and rugs that added color and vibrancy to my view from the other side of the glass. I ate my wet burrito slowly, still feeling the lump of dough in the center of my stomach from breakfast. A girl passed close to the window, and for a minor moment I believed it was Seneca. A hot flush rose from the back of my head to my face, and my eyes blurred for a second. She pushed a strand of hair behind an ear as she disappeared down the street, and I knew it hadn't been her. I felt both relieved and disappointed—glad that she hadn't seen me with food in my face but wishing she was here with me now. Seneca was on my mind all the time, and I thought there was something wrong with me. She spoke to me in my head, and I answered her. We had conversations, held hands, and it was fantastic even though I felt guilty for carrying her around inside me like that without permission.

We had all stepped outside the restaurant when Ken yelled, "Juan! Qué pasa?"

A guy about Ken's age, dark sunglasses covering his eyes, approached us from up the street. He saw Ken and his face burst into a broad smile.

"Kenny, hey," Juan said. He wrapped his skinny arms around Ken, then took off his glasses. "Was just thinking about you, man. They were shooting a documentary up at the campus just now. You still into film and all that?"

"See 'em whenever I can. I seriously need to check out that Bergman film before it slips away. Supposed to be really powerful, and Sven Nykvist, man, that Swede knows how to light and set up his shots, you know? Every frame a goddamn masterpiece, waiting to be hung in a gallery somewhere." I waited for Ken to introduce us, wanting to be included in the moment.

"You should teach, man," Juan said. "You know a lot." He opened his mouth wide again, in a grin that made him look like a little kid. Demian stood beside me, also attracted to the relaxed, infectious joy coming off of Ken's friend. "Hey, who you got there with you?" Juan said, catching our stares.

"Oh, yeah. This is my old lady, Rose. Those are her kids."

Juan offered his hand to Mom, then to us. I could feel his smile in that handshake, could sense something good all over him. I wished that Mom had met him before she'd met Ken. I fixated on that idea as he shook Demian's hand with that same kindness and warmth.

"So why don't you ever come by the house?" Ken asked. "I know I extended a few invitations through Raisa and that crowd. You need to hang out with us."

"I would love to, really. I got a kid now, don't know if you heard. Gotta stay at the homestead more."

I stared at Juan's face and knew he was thinking of that kid of his, probably a little girl. My fantasy unraveled, and Juan disappeared from our couch, where he had had his arm wrapped around Mom, with me and Demian tangled up at his feet.

"Why?" Ken asked.

Juan laughed, stuttered. "Um … why? Because that's my family, man. More important than anything else. No offense, but my number one priority is always gonna be to them. No matter what."

Ken had a blank look on his face, like he didn't understand. I understood. I wished for Mom to insert herself into the conversation, say something like, "That's really nice, Juan. You're a great person. What a great dad, huh, Ken?" but she wasn't even paying attention, her gaze up toward the park.

"Well, hey, you're out here alone now. Got time for a coffee or something? We can hit the Med right there, catch up some." Ken moved closer to Juan, like he had forgotten we were even there.

Juan turned his attention to me and Demian again, and then he lowered his voice. "I don't want to interrupt your own family thing here, Kenny. We should find another time."

"Nonsense." He turned to Mom. "I'll meet you up there later, okay?" He kissed her, drawing his lips away from her just as she puckered her own lips. She quickly covered her mouth with a hand.

"Nice meeting you all," Juan said, before Ken led him down the avenue, toward the coffee house.

We stood there and watched them cross against the light. They narrowly escaped a car as it sped through the intersection.

"Why's Ken in a hurry? Doesn't he want to be with us?" Demian said the one thing I was pretty sure both Mom and I were thinking. But I knew the *us* was just me and my brother. He loved Mom but not us. We weren't his family. We were his old lady's kids and that was that. I thought about how lucky Juan's kid was. I hoped the kid knew how lucky it was, too.

Mom rolled her head and bent her legs to the beat of the four musicians up on the park's bandstand. Demian and I danced with her, surrounded by grooving, moving bodies underneath a cloudless, pale blue ceiling of sky. The sun spread its heat over the top of my head, and even though I felt moist and hot under my clothes, it didn't matter. This was what my first day of summer was supposed to look like.

When we were headed toward People's Park, I was trying to decide whether I was mad at Ken or happy that he wasn't part of our group. Mom had seemed put out, but as we stepped onto the grass and Demian took her hand in his tiny grip, her mood shifted. She pulled me into their union, the three of us strolling toward the throng of Berzerkeley locals who had brought festivity to an area that sometimes felt dank and kind of scuzzy. Homeless people were usually scattered around the park, alone near the benches talking to themselves or congregated around curious college students who argued about something Ronald Reagan had done years ago, or what Jerry Brown had done just yesterday. I rarely ventured into the park alone, having witnessed too many people going to the bathroom in plain view of the busy sidewalk or jutting needles into their bodies while high school kids, a few feet away, swung on branches and threw rocks at each other's heads for fun.

But today the park was overrun with families, and the sense of safety and violent-free fun prevailed. Demian's fascination with a lady midget who wore multi-colored scarves around her wrinkled neck and spoke in a strange accent lasted until it was his turn to sit in her chair to get his face painted. He turned shy and wouldn't budge, so I went first. Once she had finished painting an impressively close rendition of the ship Ghost from London's *The Sea-Wolf* across my forehead and down to my chin, and Mom had gamely gotten a few butterflies sketched upon her cheeks, Demian finally took a seat and told her he wanted to be a Blue Meanie. Shortly after that, Mom pulled us into the circle of dancing figures. The music was light and seemed to float into the air, confined to the park by that endless ceiling of bright sky above us, and Mom shook and swayed her body with a joy that seemed directed at Demian and me. She belonged to us, and we to her, just like it used to be.

WHEN MY FATHER LEFT US, I was six. Old enough to feel the loss. Demian was only two, but he had been saying "Dada" long enough that when it became a question instead of a statement, I believe he understood something important had disappeared from his life. I went to first grade and pretended nothing had changed, even though every time Mrs. Kellis read us a story about a mommy and daddy who loved their children more than anything else in the world, my stomach ached and I balled my hands into fists until my fingernails scraped blood from the palms. I watched my mother withdraw into herself. She asked more and more of me with regard to the caretaking of Demian until I smeared a diaper full of shit all over his face and left him screaming in the kitchen sink. I locked myself in the bedroom with a pillow clamped over my ears.

My mother eventually shifted gears and became more involved, clinging to us with the same level of focus she had used in her withdrawal from us. Everything suddenly became about *us*, and even though she replaced her part-time job with a full-time one, put Demian into daycare from nine till night, and turned me into a latchkey kid who became expert at doing my homework and setting the table before five o'clock, I sometimes felt overwhelmed by her attention and smothered by her love. Without my father around—the man I heard her tell friends was "the love of my life, and I'll never love anyone … *no* one, the way I loved him"—did she feel she had to thrust all that unused, pent-up emotion on Demian and me? Did we become the recipients of all her absorption and affection because he was no longer there to receive it? Were we the default receptacles of our mother's rudderless yearning? We had come from him, so we were *of* him. Was there any groundswell of emotion that belonged to Demian and me that was separate from her love for him? Something that we could call our own?

Those are questions I never would have thought of at six, but I know I have always carried around that doubt about how much my mother truly cared for me and for Demian. I've obsessed over it, tried to quantify it somehow, qualify her love as true or untrue, until I thought I would lose my mind. Or my heart. My father abandoned us only once, and there was an ultimately pleasant finality to the act. He had stripped us of his love and attention a single time, never to reappear and pluck it away again. My mother, on the other hand, had proven that she could dismantle my world again and again. She could relinquish her responsibility, her love for me, on numerous occasions, without warning and without seeming remorse. Then she would reappear, present me with her love as if it were a gift on a receiving tray, and without waiting for a response, go on loving me until it was time to transform back into the familiar role of Indian-giver and again snatch her love away as if it were just some stupid toy.

But at six years old, with my father gone and my brother unable to share my grief, I depended on my mother's all-encompassing love and the way she devoted herself so fully to her sons. So I took it, greedily, not aware that it could ever go away, that things would ever change between the three of us. And it was wonderful. I was loved, and doted on, and paid attention to, and cared for, as was my brother. Maybe I knew it wouldn't last forever, but I wanted it to go on longer than it did. It lasted almost two years, just the three of us with all that love.

And then she met Ken, and all that love shifted to him.

Chapter 5

It was a rare Sunday night, with everyone in bed before ten. No loud music or TV sounds from the living room to keep Demian awake or me from diving headfirst into the world of Jack London's danger-filled adventures. The house was peaceful, quiet. The only things I heard as I sat in bed with *The Call of the Wild*, covers over my head and a flashlight nestled in the crook of my neck, were Demian's snuffled snores and the crackling turn of the pages in my worn paperback.

Revisiting the canine world that London's Buck inhabited reminded me of a dog that I was sure never would have survived the Klondike. Humphrey, Mrs. Hunter's domesticated pet, appeared in my mind with his mouth hanging open and his eyes staring directly into nothingness. I had never actually seen a dead animal, but everything I read about them—and there were so many: *Old Yeller, Sounder, The Red Pony, Where the Red Fern Grows*—served to fuel my own visual picture of poor Humphrey in his *rigor mortis* state. I wondered what kind of poison it had been that killed him; Mrs. Hunter hadn't been clear about that when she confronted Kirby, but I figured it had to be something made for roaches or ants or rats or something. Possibly small pellets put into his dog food or a liquid poison poured into his water bowl.

The thoughts began to blend and blur until the flashlight's beam faded and my eyes closed.

I couldn't have been asleep for long before a scraping, metallic sound pierced my semiconscious state. It was the dull grind of a garbage can being dragged across concrete. I flicked the flashlight off and peeked out from under my sheet. The room was completely dark. The only brightness emerged by way of moon shine, from over two hundred thousand miles up in the sky, gleaming through my window. Outside, Kirby ambled down his driveway toward the sidewalk. Monday was trash day, but the garbagemen were notorious for coming late in the day, which meant most of the neighbors didn't bother hauling their big cans to the curb until the sun had already risen. So the fact that Kirby, who always seemed to be at home during the day, was taking his trash out at night struck me as suspicious.

He stopped with the can just shy of the street, rested the metal bottom on a strip of newly cut grass, and secured the lid. Kirby leaned on the cover with both hands, like he was trying to seal it up tight, while he glanced around. The lamppost up the block threw a small streak of light in Kirby's direction, which reflected off the lid's handle and landed under his chin. The noisy trek to the street didn't seem to have aroused anyone but me. I fell away from the window before his head could swivel toward it.

Kirby's footsteps padded up the driveway and into his back yard before I latched onto a thought that would keep me up and alert for another two hours. I needed to see inside that garbage can, because that's where the poison that killed Humphrey was hidden.

Once I had officially deputized myself, as a member of the Concerned Citizens Brigade of Berkeley California of the United States of America (or CCBBCUSA, an acronym that looked a little like my friend Trevor's last report card), it was time to lead the investigative team of one outside and into the street. Convinced that I was serving the greater good of not only my city but the country itself, the butterfly-like sensations in my belly that had bothered me for the past hour—unpleasant and a little nausea inducing—finally subsided. I was ready to uncover the truth, despite the dangers inherent in the mission.

When you're ten, the worst ideas in the world can somehow seem like the greatest ideas ever imagined. That's why my friends and I jumped off roofs and swung bats at wasps' nests and shoved our penises into thin-necked soda bottles. Not because any of those decisions were particularly smart, but because we could.

I am convinced that in every boy, between the ages of eight and thirteen, is a secret little death wish. Not a suicidal desire, nothing as depressing and morbid as that, but instead a kind of dare issued to the universe. I dare you to let me die if I fall backward off this tree and onto the hard, unforgiving ground below. I double-dare you to let that speeding bullet of a Trans Am run me over if I dart into traffic to retrieve a rubber ball I bought at Pay 'n Save with my very own one-dollar bill. Wrapped up in that juvenile death wish is, of course, the sense of invincibility, the belief that kids will live forever. The normal amount of fear that accompanies every potentially dangerous or foolhardy act is overwhelmed by this greater sense of immortality and the belief that no harm will ever come to them.

I believe it was this idiotic combination that reinforced my decision to venture out into the midnight air, cloaked in black pants and a black T-shirt, in search of damning evidence against my suspected dog killer of a neighbor. There is no other logical or rational way I can explain the choice I made that night, which led to similar and increasingly more perilous choices in the months that followed.

I slipped out the kitchen door and moved around in the dark toward the Johnsons' garbage can. I used the lamppost a few houses up from me to show the way, the moonlight above obscured by the cover of late-night clouds blown in by a Bay breeze. No one was out on my block, and no cars traveled up or down the street. I was alone to indulge my detective fantasy. If my younger brother and his not-too-bright neighborhood buddy could plan to photograph a pervert flasher, then I could surely nab myself a dog murderer.

At the front of Kirby's house, I took note of all the closed and darkened windows. With the trash can only a few feet away, my gaze took in our house, the Johnson driveway, the smooth sidewalk, the pock-marked street, the quivering trees, and my own dirt-scuffed tennis shoes. I waited in the silence until finally allowing myself permission to step forward. My fingers roamed around the circular metal garbage lid, tugging slightly upward in an effort to test the tightness of the air lock. When my hands met, I dug my fingers in farther under the top and felt it separate from the can.

After more than a minute of careful, quiet lifting, the cover came loose with a scraping sound. The smell of raw onions mixed with fried meat wafted up to me and I believed for a moment that I had unleashed the poison into the neighborhood, up into the atmosphere, and my work here (under the auspices of the CCBBCUSA, of course) would tragically be responsible for the death of our entire race.

The thought passed, and I peered down into the mouth of the can. I recognized the black bags as Glad brand, the expensive ones that were always advertised on TV. At home we used the white, no-brand kind that had an inevitable tendency to rip and tear whenever it was my turn to empty the garbage. I covetously touched the pliable rubber, my fingers tracing the smooth thickness of the top bag.

The *chug-chug* of what sounded like a mini-train echoed downward to me and I watched two projectiles of light swerve around the corner at Wheeler and straighten out onto Emerson. Instinctively, I leapt away from my spot by the garbage and found protection from the thickness of a nearby tree. My nose pressed against the rough bark as I waited for the sputtering of the car to continue down the street and away from me. When it did, I surveyed the whole of the neighborhood again.

It was placid, peaceful. I returned to the mission.

When my eyes adjusted to the light flow from the lamp-post, I resumed my task of investigating the contents of Kirby's garbage can. I unraveled the bright-white twist-tie and peered inside the opening. A few empty food cans and bunched-up paper towels were visible, but unless I was willing to dig my hand deep into the bag or dump the trash out onto the ground, there was no way I would find what I was looking for. The night air crept under my clothes and chilled my skin. I yawned, and almost covered my mouth with a hand until I remembered where that hand had been.

I stared into the guts of this metallic vessel of garbage and knew I was beat. Even if I managed to pick through the first bag of somebody else's smelly refuse, there were still three more bags underneath that one. And if Kirby was smart, like I thought he probably was since he had gone to college, then the likelihood of him stashing the poison he had used on Humphrey at the very bottom of the garbage can was incredibly high.

I retied the twist-tie, resealed the garbage lid, and was then reassigned by my Citizens Brigade to get back in bed and report this mission as a failure. The mission had been birthed out of such hope, and the disappointment over its uncompleted status was crushing.

THE NEXT MORNING, I WAS RESTLESS, the mystery of whether or not Kirby was responsible for poisoning Mrs. Hunter's dog frustratingly unsolved, and Telegraph once again beckoned. I realized I needed to explore the avenue on my own, without the family, and without worrying about Demian. Leaving him alone made me feel guilty, so when I offered my bike to him and he happily accepted with his own plan to swing by Rafe's house, I was relieved.

There was a soothing breeze at around 9:00 a.m. when I hung a left at the Co-op, my eyes drawn to the Campanile. Sather Tower summoned me, like a hypnotist, from its spot in the middle of campus. I purposely avoided the view of the hills above, still shrouded in a light mist. That secret, inviting world above reminded me that I was a lesser person than the revered souls whose homes shared the same atmosphere as the sky. I was their inferior in every way. I didn't necessarily consider myself poor—I ate three meals a day, sometimes more, went shopping with Mom and Demian a few times a year at Mervyn's or Hink's, and even got a two-dollar-a-week allowance for doing my share of the chores around the house—but I knew that I didn't belong around rich people, didn't deserve the cool toys or the popular clothes that the privileged kids got without even asking for them.

"Spare change?" was the first thing I heard as I crossed Haste and approached the display window of Shakespeare & Co. Books on the corner. The guy was familiar, a fixture on the avenue, and seeing him made me feel both better about myself and guilty for wanting more than I had. A scraggly white guy, his hair was matted, his clothes unwashed for probably years, a long sheepdog beard to match the wild gray hair on his head. His hand was out, caked in dirt and grime and germs that I was sure would mutate into cancer cells or bubonic plague and attack my insides if I touched even a finger of him. There was all of that, and he smelled.

He muttered it again: "Spare change?" All I had on me were ones from my allowance, with nothing to spare. I looked away, muttered a meek, "I'm sorry," then picked up my step and lasered in on a banner halfway up the street that declared, *Comics & Comix*. This was the first stop on my quest for the perfect first day of summer. I rushed into the store, which felt enormous, endless, and without equal anywhere else in the world. The new comics were stacked atop an extra-long table in the middle of the store: all the DC and Marvel titles that I consumed like air. Once in a while I would sneak a peek at the independent comics, the ones flaunting long-haired hippie girls, with their crazily oversize breasts and scissor-sharp legs. They were fun to thumb through, and I'm sure I could have bought a copy from Harvey or Pietro at the counter, but I knew that four or five regular comics was the sacrificial price for just one of the irregulars.

I scooped up three different Spider-Man titles, a new Avengers, and some other comics with covers designed to make my head explode. Those ultra-bright colors, the glossy covers, all the action up front that promised even more extreme action within—I was a sucker for anything with a superhero inside. I wandered the store, picking up this one and putting down that one, until I found myself back at the front counter.

"Haven't seen you in a while. What you been doing?" Harvey, a skinny Cal student who was waging an unheroic war against pimples and a slight stutter, leafed through my selections.

"Saving up," I said. "Friday was my last day of school. Thought I'd start the summer out right."

"You bet. I've read most of these already. You're gonna love the new issue of Spidey Team-Up. The dialogue is kind of for shit, but the battle scenes are pretty epic. The writer was definitely channeling some Milton and Pound. I mean, the literary antecedents to the specific mythology this book cites are unmistakable."

I smiled up at him, nodding like I knew what he was talking about, before laying down a third of my allowance and walking out with my loot.

Outside, I was nearly run over by Demian and my own bike.

Rafe skidded to a stop just behind Demian. "Hey, Steve-ereeno!"

"Don't do that," I told him. I was too old for stupid nicknames, and I'd warned him before.

"He didn't mean nothing," Demian said, coming to his friend's defense.

Then I heard them. Faintly, at first, until the sounds crept closer, became more lucid, yet never wavered from their monotonous repetition. "Hare Krishna, Krishna Krishna,

Hare Hare, Hare Rama ..." The words were delivered in a sing-songy rhythm, male voices mixing together to deliver a chant that was both simple and kind of creepy.

They had a temple on Stuart Street, just below Telegraph, and every day a procession of finger-bell-snapping, flowy-robe-wearing, sandaled freaks would fill the air with their holy mantra. We stood on the sidewalk right outside Rasputin Records, Rafe and Demian squeezed against the wall, as the nearly bald men danced and skipped past us; the only hair they had was at the top of their heads, tiny patches that spread down their backs in long, skinny braids. Two kids, both younger than Demian, brought up the rear of the group, their hair shaved the same way as the older Krishnas. I felt sorry for the kids, but Demian seemed to be fascinated by them.

"They're pretty cool," he said, mimicking their finger movements and trying out the chant.

"Cool?" I said. They looked and sounded pretty stupid, and I was annoyed by their jangling parade down the avenue. They weren't cool; they were lame, deluded into thinking they were happy because of their weird religion.

"Well," Demian stopped clapping his fingers together as I stared at him, and Rafe mounted his bike, "not cool, maybe." Demian got on his bike but took a last look at the backs of the group and said, "They're ... interesting."

"See ya," Rafe said, and Demian waved to me as they rode to the corner and disappeared around it. I transferred my bag of comics from one sweaty hand to the other and decided what to have for lunch.

THE SOUNDS OF KIDS SCREAMING AND splashing in water attracted me to the pool at Willard Park. I still had a few dollars left on me, after skipping the new singles at Leopold's Records, and gave serious thought to spending some time in the giant pool. I stood at the bottom of the stone steps leading up to the entrance, the smell of chlorine tickling my nose. Excited kids of every age loitered around the front door, wearing their street clothes but holding onto their two-piece suits, Mark Spitz-like Speedos, and water shorts in anticipation of swimming and diving their day away.

It came to me then that I didn't have a suit. Not that I hadn't brought one along but that I didn't even own a swimsuit. I thought about what I looked like whenever I accidentally caught myself in a mirror wearing only my white underpants, sickened by the idea of my body in a pair of swim trunks. Maybe no one else really cared how fat I was, like my grandmother was always trying to convince me, but I knew, and I cared. And if I was ever going to get a girl like Seneca to want to touch or even kiss me, I had to look more like Peter Parker than the Blob.

Even though I was in jeans and my crappy shoes, I convinced myself that a jog would do me good. I shoved the comics deep down into my back pocket and started uphill toward Hillegass Street and the park Berkeley locals called Ho Chi Minh Park, after the Vietnamese leader responsible for the deaths of a slew of American soldiers. I knew about the conflict from listening to first my dad and his friends, then Ken and his old college buddies. None of them had been in the war, and a few of them told elaborate stories about what they'd done to "beat the draft," but they all seemed to have plenty of opinions about who was right and who was wrong in the whole thing. I tried to understand why the Viet Cong, who I thought was the enemy, came across in their eyes as the heroes, and our government and the U.S. soldiers were "cowards and killers." It all seemed to make sense to them, and even though I thought I was pretty smart for my age, I couldn't get it to make any sense for myself. It was only lately that I had begun to understand a word from one of my book assignments for school: *hypocrisy*. I didn't understand exactly what it meant, in the same way I didn't fully get *irony* and *orgasm*, but the more the adults around me talked about the state of the world, the more the word seemed to define their conversations.

Halfway through my jog up Derby Street, I realized my stupid mistake. I had only finished my lunch fifteen minutes earlier, the incline was steeper than I initially had judged, and the most exercise I had seen lately was a semi-vigorous game of tetherball during recess the week before. My legs suddenly wobbled like Jell-O, sweat gathered in a puddle on my forehead, and my throat began to burn like I had a fire smoldering in there. I brought the jog to a slow walk and was about to sit down at the tennis courts to rest. Then I saw Demian, a hundred yards away.

My brother kneeled behind a small bush, staring out at the middle of the park. Beside him crouched his buddy Rafe, a Polaroid instant camera gripped between his palms. They were obviously on the lookout for the rumored flasher, but clueless how out in the open they really were. They looked like two midgets casing a joint before the stickup. With their bikes up on kickstands, there was the anticipation of a big getaway.

Rafe saw me approach their spot before Demian did, and he immediately snapped my picture. The flash blew, and a couple snoozing on their blanket a few feet away jerked awake and looked in our direction.

"Demian, we got the old perv!" Rafe said, shaking the picture for its required thirty seconds, the smell of sour chemicals wafting toward me as I joined them.

"You want me to beat your ass, Rafe?" I grabbed the picture from his still flapping hand and shoved it into my front pocket. "You guys are a couple of 'tards, you know? Sherlock Dumbass and Mr. Without-a-Clue here."

"We're trying good," Rafe said.

"Well, try a little *gooder.* I saw you from a mile away." I physically moved Demian closer to the bush, positioned him at an angle that helped to obscure him from view. Rafe watched us, and then repositioned himself around some leaves at the same time he dug his body downward into the dirt.

"There, that's better," I said, finding a space that could accommodate me as well. I knew that I'd stick out however I crouched or shoved my body into the bushes, like Fat Albert playing hide-n-seek, but I tried my best.

"Hey, over there," Rafe stage whispered, getting into his role as private detective on stakeout. He pointed to a tree about fifty yards away, slipped the plastic binoculars from around his neck and handed them to me.

Our next-door neighbor, Kirby, had nestled himself into the crook of a tall oak tree, with a multicolored blanket laid out at his sandaled feet. I took the protection of the bush and the intimacy of the binocular vision to size him up the same way Frank and Joe Hardy did in their books. I'd read a few of them to Demian, and my silly desire to have adventures like them or Encyclopedia Brown had most likely been the catalyst for my brother and Rafe's escapade here at the park. I stared at Kirby's hand-woven cap, which barely covered all of his dirty yellow curls, and slowly registered all the details of his face and body. His skin was pasty, the color of bleach or sour milk; his face was clean shaven and unremarkable except for that angry red scar on his forehead. His eyes just below it looked blue or green, and when they stared straight at me, I quickly ducked and pushed the binoculars to the ground.

"What'd you see?" Rafe whispered, excited.

I shook my head, then peeked through the bush to see Kirby a distance away, his focus not on me or the bush. He had looked *toward* me, but there was no way he had actually seen me. I continued my close-up examination of him, trying to figure out what it was about him that scared me so much, made me fear that he could hurt me or my brother in the same way that he had killed Mrs. Hunter's dog. The nervousness I felt around him suddenly seemed so irrational, now that I saw him in loose, dust-brown clothing and worn out sandals that lacked any rational degree of menace. He was simply a guy, hanging out in the park, who had maybe … maybe … poisoned a dog. But there was no proof that he'd done anything, just like he told Mrs. Hunter. And I'd learned enough from my readings that you needed proof to convict someone of a crime, no matter how much you thought they were capable of pulling it off.

I handed the binoculars back to Rafe.

"Nothing to see here. Move it along," I said in a brusque, cop-like voice.

Rafe squirmed and said, "But that's the guy. My mom, she told my dad, when she didn't think I could hear because I was watching TV, but really I could hear her 'cause I can watch TV and listen to what somebody's saying at the same time, and she said that that guy killed a little dog that didn't do anything but bark, which was sometimes annoy-a-ly but not something to hurt somebody about."

"He lives next door," Demian said, trying to get the binoculars from Rafe, who held firm. "Next door to us. Doesn't he, Steve?"

"The cops were there, about the dog—that's what I heard Mom say—but they went away and he stayed there. Hey, have you sawed that sign they have by the door? It says, *The Johnsons*? That means 'dicks.'" Rafe laughed, and Demian joined in.

"It's their last name, you dork," I said.

"I know that." He glared at me with his six-year-old brows furrowing. "It still means dicks."

Demian piped in, "He's not doing nothing, he's reading a book. Can you see it, Rafe?"

"Looks like a big paperback. Paperback writer," he sung, whispering the lyrics to the Beatles song. "Two naked people on the cover," he giggled, "kinda like those statues I seen with leaves in front of their things. It's, like, '*History of Sex-u-all-tee*' or something." He placed his fingers on his lips, as if he were deep in thought, and then said offhandedly, "Don't know it."

"Hey, look," Demian said a little too loud, and the couple lounging a few feet away looked up again. He lowered his voice. "There's a guy, over there. Going up to him."

We all watched a long-haired white guy in flared blue jeans—what Ken called elephant bells—and an Indian shawl wrapped around his bare chest saunter up to Kirby. The guy leaned down, and I couldn't see what was going on. A few seconds later he sauntered off.

"What happened?" Demian asked Rafe, who peered through the binoculars. "Did the guy flash our neighbor?"

"Nah. He gave him some money. Mister dick-man gave him a plastic bag," Rafe said.

"Drug deal," I blurted. Then I did the Detective Baretta voice, gruff and smoky. "I'm thinking pot. The baggie is probably just like the ones Ken brings home sometimes."

Rafe looked shocked, and a little in awe. "Ken smokes pot?"

"Yeah, don't your parents?" I mimed smoking a joint.

"No. We're Jewish, we don't do stuff like that." He said it with such innocence and beefed-up pride I wanted to laugh in his face.

"Yeah, okay," I said, letting it go. I figured that if he was already six years old and still naïve about drugs and what his parents were up to when he wasn't looking, I wasn't about to rob him of that sweet innocence.

Demian had moved closer to Rafe, sharing the binoculars and joined at the head like a pair of Siamese twins. I looked up in the sky and felt peaceful. And a little bored.

"All right," I raised my voice a little, "I'm gonna leave you Encyclopedia Brownies to it. Just try not to get into any trouble, or piss anybody off, got it?"

Rafe waved me away with a hand. Demian didn't move but said, "See ya."

I crouched backward out of their hiding place, turned forward near the tennis courts, then headed back down the way I came. I pulled the Polaroid from my pocket. The exposure had gotten smudged when I rammed it in my jeans, but the image was still very clear. I didn't look like a perv, as Rafe had said, but like a kid who ate his weight in Twinkies and McDonald's french fries.

I tossed the picture at a garbage can, made sure the comics were still secure in my back pocket, and slowly jogged down the street toward home. I didn't have much reason to think about Kirby again after that, until the day Demian told me everything that had happened, and then I couldn't *stop* thinking about him.

Chapter 6

DINNER TIME. AS MUCH AS I liked to eat, our nighttime meal was so unpredictable I tended to approach it with hesitation, if not a sense of impending disappointment. Ken always preferred we go to a restaurant or eat take-out—both choices favorable to the alternatives: leftovers, something home-cooked but usually flavorless, or a meal consisting wholly of breakfast snack foods, like cereal or cinnamon toast with butter. Mom had gotten home a little early and was in the kitchen cooking away. She asked me to make a salad, but the lettuce was wilted and the only other vegetable in the crisper was a small basket full of molding cherry-red tomatoes, discolored slime poking through the tiny square holes. Mom threw some frozen peas into a pot on the stove, and by six thirty everyone was seated at the kitchen table with warm food in front of us.

"The meat was going to go bad unless I did something with it, so ..." Mom spread her arms out across the table and toward our plates.

"... So here it is. And it looks *lovely*." Ken took her hands in his, doing a Julia Child impression, with a little extra screech at the end.

Demian giggled, and I bit into my Hamburger Helper-helped burger. The Wonder Bread was soggy under my fingers, and there was a chalky taste to the meat. I added more ketchup to it and forced down another bite.

I had gone with Mom to the Co-op a week before, when she had bought most of this meal. We had traveled up and down the aisles of the supermarket—which was close to our house and they took food stamps—picking up the staples: Challenge butter, kefir milk, regular milk that came from Berkeley Farms ("*Farms in Berkeley?*" was printed on every carton), cereal, TV dinners, Pepsi bottles, and whatever produce was fresh.

After palming a few tomatoes and replacing them with a sour look on her face, Mom moved the cart toward a new aisle. "Mom, how about some of the fruit?" I asked.

I held up a bunch of grapes. She glanced at the price per pound and shook her head. "Too expensive." I looked at the special cheeses she had stacked in our cart, along with two big bottles of wine and a box covered in lace, the label written in French. "Besides, we're supposed to be supporting Chavez and the farm growers with a boycott on grapes."

I dropped the thick vine back into its bin.

"Do they serve grapes at school?!" She looked at me like I had done something wrong. I shrugged. "Grab me a bag," she said.

Mom scooped up a few red apples and dropped them into a clear plastic bag. She broke off two bananas from a bunch of five and tossed those into our cart, next to the apples. "There we go," she said. "Fruit."

At the checkout area, we only had one person in front of us, a lady with gray hair and two canes hanging from the handles of her shopping cart. She struggled to place a few cans of cat food and a box of powdered milk on the black rubber conveyer. I slapped the flat red divider, which looked like a giant Twizzler, onto the moving surface behind her food and unloaded the cart as Mom ran a finger over her handwritten shopping list.

When the old lady was gone, and the checkout woman—always smiling and pleasant, she had checked and bagged our groceries before—was ringing up our stuff, Mom asked for a carton of cigarettes. Camel, Ken's brand. "My old man loves his smokes," Mom said to her, then counted out a handful of colored food stamps from her purse once everything was totaled.

"We don't accept those for alcohol or cigarettes. I'm sorry," the checker woman said.

Mom stood there with her hand out, the government dollars looking like Monopoly money, not at all like real currency. "Yeah, right. I forgot." She just stared at the woman, like she was waiting for her to change her mind. "How much without those things?" Mom finally asked, her lips moving but her teeth glued shut inside her mouth.

The woman gave her a new total, and as Mom dropped a few of the food stamp bills into her purse and handed the rest over, she said, "I'll pay cash for the rest."

"Of course," the woman took the bills, her face still kind and her mouth still smiling. "That'll be eight twenty-seven all together."

Mom handed her a real ten-dollar bill, and the woman opened the cash register, a bell ringing loudly as drawers filled with all denominations of change and paper money, even a few fifties, shot outward as if exploded from a cannon. She tucked Mom's ten in with what looked like the twenties, then handed her back two fives, a one-dollar bill, and a jingle of change.

I looked at Mom, to see if she was seeing what I was seeing, but her expression stayed constant. It wasn't until we were out of the store that I said something about it.

"She made a mistake. It's not my mistake. It's hers," she said.

"But isn't that stealing?" I said, my voice low in case anyone around us could hear.

She steered the cart toward our car in the parking lot. "Nonsense. It's not stealing. Not when they have so much more money than we do." She stopped the cart, put her hands on my shoulders. I could feel her fingernails digging in through my T-shirt. "Which they do. Just because it says it's a 'co-op' that doesn't mean they're not still screwing people left and right. Did you see those tomatoes in there?"

She let go of me, and when we reached the car, I loaded the thick paper bags full of our groceries into the back seat. "I deserve it," I heard her say as I started to wheel the cart to the entrance. Walking back toward the car, I wondered what I would have done if someone had made a mistake and given me the wrong change. Would I have given it back? I wasn't sure, but I thought I probably would have. It didn't seem right not to.

AT THE DINNER TABLE, MOM SPOONED a crowd of peas into her mouth, then gave a small, satisfied *mmm*. I wondered if she was thinking about the free money she'd taken from the Co-op.

"What'd you boys do all day?" she asked, and it sounded more like an accusation than a question.

"Nothing," I said, and Demian said the same.

"Come on," she said, "tell me one thing you did today."

We were both silent, which Ken took as an opening. "I read the new Pat Conroy book today. Fantastic."

"The entire thing?" Mom held her hamburger just below her mouth. Her eyes were fixed on Ken.

"Hey, Archie loaned it to me. I wouldn't buy a hardcover, you know that."

"I wish I had all day to read books." Mom finally took a bite from her burger.

"I'll read you some of it in bed tonight, you'll love it. Real masculine writing, South Carolina backdrop, with a whole pre-civil rights sub-plot. The South, man, those are some fucked-up, backwards assholes." Ken clenched his jaw, and I thought I heard teeth grinding against teeth.

Mom wiped her hands on our paper towel napkins, then swung her ponytail of hair around and onto her chest. She played with the ends of it, her attention focused on each strand.

"Carter's a Southerner, but he's gotta have more sense than *Geraldine*. Ford's a serious idiot, another Yalie pud-wacker. Jesus, this country, we know how to elect our leaders, don't we?" Ken licked his fingers until the yellow stains were visible. He fished into his back pocket and shook out a cigarette.

I suddenly wished we had a dog. I'd seen all those movies where kids fed their dinner to the dog who sat at attention under the table, waiting for scraps. The peas in my mouth were undercooked and hard as pebbles, but I was sure that if I had a dog he'd eat them for me. I thought about what Mrs. Dillon, the older lady from across the street, had told me a few hours before about Mrs. Hunter's dog, that it died by eating poisoned raw meat that had been thrown over the front yard fence. The neighborhood was kind of freaked out over it, and after the cops came to Kirby's door and didn't haul him away to jail, everyone seemed more afraid. The few other dogs that lived around us were now kept in the house all the time, and even the cats I used to see licking themselves in the sun had disappeared behind front windows, peering out at me with insistent but silent meows. If there were no more animals to poison, was there a chance that person would think about poisoning kids instead? I looked at my half-finished burger and lost my appetite.

"What's on tap for tonight?" Ken asked. "You wanna trek on up to College Ave. and do some window shopping? It's a beautiful goddamn night for it." He blew out a cloud of smoke, and I watched some of it hover just above my burger.

Just when I thought both of them had forgotten that Demian and I were there at the table with them, Mom said, "Stevie, are you and Demian interested in doing that?" I said uh-huh, and my brother nodded his head. He had removed the burger from the bread, scraped off all the crap from the meat and was squashing his peas down with the fork handle.

"They can come, sure," Ken said. He stuck the cigarette in his mouth and picked up his half-empty plate. I watched him shovel most of the food Mom had cooked into the trash can and then rinse the plate before leaving it in the sink. He stubbed his cigarette out on a tin ashtray above the faucet. "That was good, hon. Hearty. Juicy, too." He rubbed himself down there, over his jeans, and poked a finger into his mouth.

Mom flung her hair back and opened her arms to Ken. He sank into her, his moustache brushing against her chin before his lips met hers. Demian stopped mashing his peas. I could feel the bits of burger I'd eaten sitting in my stomach like lumpy blobs of tar.

They stopped kissing and Mom got up from the table, led Ken by the hand out of the kitchen. "Stevie, we'll be right back. Clean up for me, okay?"

She was out into the hall and heading toward their bedroom before I had a chance to respond.

"I'm gonna watch TV," Demian said. His chair scraped behind him and his feet hit the floor at a run. I cleared the table, ran Palmolive over the dishes, and washed them as thoroughly as I could. The scent of Ken's still-smoldering cigarette filled my nose the entire time.

IT WAS TUESDAY AFTERNOON, LATE INTO a day I'd spent mostly sleeping and making lists in my journal: TV shows I watched, all the streets in Berkeley I could remember, names of kids I'd gone to elementary school with. If I had had any talent as an artist, I would have doodled. I didn't, so instead I wrote lists.

I thumbed through the fake-leather book I'd bought with my allowance at the beginning of fifth grade from Papyrus, a small stationery store on College Avenue. I had aspirations of filling it with details of my school days, but after only a few nights of writing in it before bed, I had let the habit go. Summer, however, was a time for fresh starts, for re-purposing the old with things that mattered for my future.

The other list I had begun, with *Make Seneca my girlfriend* as the top priority for the three short months that led up to sixth grade, looked anemic compared to my dopey, extended lists about random movie actors and books that started with '*S*.' I stared at the mostly blank page and considered what to write: goals that I could, and should, accomplish by summer's end. I wrote a title, all in caps, that read, *THINGS THAT I MUST DO THIS SUMMER*, followed by about fifteen exclamation marks. I made a dash in front of the Seneca goal, then multiple dashes down the left-side of the page to fill with more goals.

"Lose weight—lots of it!" came right away and I wrote it down. Nothing else leapt out at me. I peered out my bedroom window, the sun still burning bright in the sky, and awaited inspiration. Kirby and Mrs. Hunter's dog, and the night I dug through his garbage can, sprung to mind. I hesitated, then wrote, *Find Humphrey's killer.* I stared at the page. I briefly considered adding the goal of helping Demian and Rafe with their supposed flasher before I realized that was a stupid goal.

I fumbled the pencil across the page until it slid off and onto the floor. My eyes scanned the list, which seemed like a lot and at the same time not, until I focused on the first entry. I had procrastinated long enough. The day had been filled with a mixture of boredom and anxiousness. It was now four days since she had given me her number—time to call Seneca and ask her out. On a date? I had no idea how to do that, at what part in the conversation I needed to ask that, and where exactly our date would take place.

I shouldn't have worried about it because it never came up.

"Steve, you called!" Seneca was on the other end of the phone, and butterflies swirled around in my stomach with the worst/best feeling I'd ever had. "I didn't have your number. I wasn't sure if I wrote my number down wrong, or you lost it or something."

"No," I said in my living room, empty except for me and the lingering smell of Mom and Ken's weed. "I would never have ... I mean, I wouldn't lose it."

"I was hoping we could, you know, do something, now that we have all this time with no school, but my dad, well ...

we're going back to Seattle this week." The sadness in her voice was no match for the crumpling I felt in my heart. How idiotic I was, believing a girl as amazing and pretty as Seneca could actually become my girlfriend. I wanted to hit myself in the head or slam the bottom of the phone, the hard metal part, on my hand as punishment for being so goddamn stupid. Stupid, stupid, stupid.

"You're, you're," I could barely get it out, "you're going back to Seattle for good?"

A pause. A pause wasn't anything good.

"No, we're not moving back there. My dad, he's got some stuff to finish up there, and my mom's still there, I guess I need to see her. Anyway, I'm leaving on Thursday and we're not coming back to Berkeley until after the Fourth of July. I really wanted to see you before I left, but—"

"I could come over right now," I said, anxious to be with her.

"Yeah, that would be ..." She paused, but I know I heard the enthusiasm in her voice before it all changed. "That's probably not a good idea. My dad's kind of flipping out about the trip, and he's really strict so me having a boyfriend—I mean, a boy, a boy over here could get me in trouble. You too. So, I'll just see you when I'm back, okay?" We talked a little more after that, but my brain was buzzing, overcome with disappointment and a touch of anger, so I don't remember much of it.

My mood turned sour, then sad. Seneca would be gone for almost a month, and I thought about all the other boys she might meet, up there in Seattle where maybe she'd forget all about me. Now the chances of us actually going out on a date and becoming boyfriend-girlfriend seemed so remote that I felt stupid and defeated.

I remembered a conversation between Mom and her friend Pam, soon after Dad had left us. "He'll be back before New Year's," Pam assured my mother. "No one spends a winter in New York if they know what it's like in California. He'll be back."

"If I *take* him back," Mom said, with that self-righteous anger of hers.

Pam caressed Mom's chin and said, "You will."

"Maybe," my mother said, but she was never given the chance to make a choice about him coming back into our lives. Because he never did.

The scent of weed, sharp like something gone bad in the fridge, caught my attention and I spied the roach right away: sitting all alone in a tin ashtray on the edge of the sofa arm. On a bookcase just above it, a little silver clip served as a bookmark inside a paperback by Camus. The idea of removing it, and using the tiny metal tool to smoke Ken's unfinished joint, leapt into my brain as a way to escape the unpleasant crush of my thoughts. I had smoked before, mostly whenever they threw parties at the house, or when we went out to other parties that Ken's Cal buddies threw. But I'd never done it on my own, without music playing and everybody around me already drunk or stoned. I thought about how it had felt, inhaling it down my throat, burning everything inside my mouth, and decided against it.

My next thought was food, something that made my mouth water instead of burn. There was the leftover pizza in the refrigerator—pepperoni, sausage, and Canadian bacon from Chicago Lou's—and Rocky Road ice cream in the freezer. There was also a new bag of Oreos waiting, unopened, in the cupboard.

And then I felt inspiration finger-flick me in the forehead. Instead of wallowing in food and self-pity, I could approach this month-long catastrophe as an opportunity. I could get my fat ass in shape and by the time Seneca got back maybe look less like a pig and more like somebody she might seriously consider kissing. I had already done some running the day before, when I was at Willard Park, so it was possible I could handle a little more training.

I remembered that Manny's dad had a weight set in his garage, and two minutes later I was out the door and headed to my friend's house.

MANUELITO HESPERIAN, A KID I HAD known since kindergarten, lived a block over, on Essex Street. I took the long way, warming up my muscles so that'd I'd be ready for the bench presses and barbell curls that I'd seen weightlifters do on TV. It was a little after four o'clock, so I figured I had about two hours before Mom was home from her job at the phone company, Ken was settled in front of the hi-fi set in the living room, and Demian was back from his day. He had gone to Fairyland in Oakland with his buddy Twahn and his mom, who was pretty cool and always super eager to take her son and his friends anywhere they wanted to go. She didn't have a lot of money—I think Demian had said Twahn's dad was a bank teller or something—but she managed to take her son on day trips more often than they could probably afford.

I headed down to Shattuck Avenue, hung a left at the corner where the barber shop was and peeked inside the window. A burly black man, wearing a muscle tee, sat in a swivel chair reading an *Ebony* magazine while the barber put curlers in his hair. I wondered if being black felt any different than being white, or if it all pretty much felt the same. There was a commercial I'd seen a few times on TV, showing a kid younger than me at his school, and spending time with his parents. He had a full afro and was missing a couple of teeth. At the end of the commercial, he said, "I'm proud to be an African-American." He seemed to know who he was, what he was, and liked himself for it. I liked that kid, too, and I was curious if he'd like me if we met somewhere, even though I wasn't particularly proud of myself and figured I was just a plain American.

I passed the liquor store at the corner where Ken got his cigarettes and booze, and where all of us kids bought our candy and sodas. It was also where you could sneak a peek at the newest *Playboy*, if you were slick about it and didn't let the guy behind the register see you.

The house next to the store was Manny's. I climbed up the tall lime-green stairs to his front door and knocked. His mother came to the door in a macramé dress I thought she had probably made herself, and minutes later Manny and I were back down on the street, the garage door open and our muscles pumping. From Flint's, just down the street, I could smell the meat cooking and their sweet barbeque sauce. I thought of pork ribs slathered in the little shop's homemade sauce, and I nearly abandoned the workout before it even began. But then the wind shifted, the smells disappeared, and my cravings slowly passed.

Neither one of us were very familiar with the weights, but Manny's father worked out from time to time, and he had watched his dad put on and take off the weight plates, tighten the metal clamps, and do multiple reps and sets. His father wasn't a big man, but he was in good shape everywhere, except for his beer gut, which pooched out like a bowling ball.

Manny and I took it slow, because we hadn't really used the equipment before, and also because we didn't want to break anything. He thought his dad would be fine with us using it, although Manny hadn't specifically asked for permission. But we would be careful and everything would be fine.

Until it wasn't.

I had just finished a set of chest presses on the flimsily padded bench when it was Manny's turn, and he wanted more weight on the barbell. We secured it to the two bar holders—like miniature goal posts, the way they looked on the field at Memorial Stadium the one time I'd watched a Bears football game for free way up on Cheater's Hill—and loosened our respective clamps. Manny had shown me how you had to keep the bar balanced, so whenever weight came on or off the bar, both guys had to remove the same weight at the same time.

I don't remember what happened exactly because it was so fast. It was probably a mixture of me being a little fatigued from pressing half my weight into the air and Manny being a little too enthusiastic to start his own sets, but whatever it was, it ended with my side tilting upward and his side wrenching down, like a see-saw. The result was that a fifteen-pound weight smashed into the concrete floor of the garage and the hard blue plastic of the plate cracked.

It looked as if someone had taken a big bowie knife and sliced the plastic open. The gash was long, but not deep. Manny put his finger inside it, many times, and made me do the same. The tip of my index finger jammed against the block of cold concrete that the plastic was molded around. The weight was still intact, but the rip was hard to ignore. Manny stared at it with a weird intensity, as if he could will the weight to magically repair itself. But it didn't. Both of us had lost our motivation to continue working out, so we stacked the weights—with the slightly damaged one on the very bottom—and closed up the garage.

"He won't even notice it," I assured him, my arms tight and warm. I felt powerful, the temporary rush from the workout filling me with energy. I suggested a run, so we ran around the block, punching our fists in the air and kicking our feet in karate-like motions.

We got back to his house around five, and his mother greeted us at the door, wearing an apron over her dress now.

Her body smelled like spices from faraway lands. Manny's father would be home soon, the food cooking in the oven for their dinner at six. She offered us a snack. I was hungry after all that exercise, but I had to avoid extra meals if I was ever going to lose all that weight before Seneca got back from Seattle. I told her no, thanks, but she insisted in a way that made me think I would offend her or hurt her feelings if I didn't eat her food. I sat down at the living room table next to Manny and across from his little sister Juanita, and we feasted on tortillas and sweet corn cakes.

I sat enjoying the snack when his father walked through the door. The table jumped slightly when he entered the house, and it took me a few seconds to realize that Manny had bumped the table with his leg. I looked over, and he seemed nervous, his mind most likely fixated on the ripped weight plate.

Manny's dad gave his wife a kiss, then one to Juanita. He walked over to Manny and me, gave his son a playful swat, and said a quick hi to me.

"What did you boys do today?" he said in his fractured English. He had moved to the Bay Area from Mexico when he was a teenager, and his Spanish bled into everything he said in English.

"Nothing." Manny looked into his plate, then said almost inaudibly, "We lifted some weights for a while."

"You building *musculo, hijo*? Getting big and strong like your papa, eh? *Bueno*." He smiled, patted his son on the back, proud.

Manny's dad walked away, undressing as he moved toward the back of the house, where their bedrooms were. Once his dad was gone, Manny exhaled a breath that seemed to have been held a long time, believing the worst had passed.

Then his dad came back in, sat in his big recliner and switched the TV from a kiddie show Juanita had been watching to an A's away game. "Did you put everything back the way you found it, Manuelito?"

"Yes, Papa."

The inning ended, and Manny's dad got up. "I need to go out to the garage for a minute. Dinner almost ready, Maria?"

She nodded, then got up from her chair and went to stand by the stove in the kitchen.

He walked out, and we all sat in silence. The game resumed on the TV, and we all tried to lose ourselves in Reggie Jackson up at the plate against the Expos' starting pitcher, Don Carrithers. I had never been a big sports fan, but at that moment, it was the most important thing ever. I focused on how Jackson held his bat, his stance, the way the helmet fit his head, everything but what Mr. Hesperian was doing down in the garage.

When Manny's dad came back up the stairs and into the house, his manner had changed completely. "Why do you lie to me?" he asked from the front door. I could tell Manny was afraid, the way he refused to look up at his father. "Everything is *not* the way you found it. Is it?"

"What's wrong, Eduardo?" Manny's mother asked, hesitant and cowering.

"Your son, he destroyed my weights. The entire set is ruined now. Come, Manny, in the back room." He stripped his leather belt from around his waist and walked calmly down the hall and into the darkness.

Manny's eyes looked crazy and got so big in his head I would have laughed if it wasn't so serious. Then his face relaxed, like he had become resigned to his punishment. He took small, laborious steps into the back room. Shortly after, I heard Manny screaming. Crying. Taking the kind of abuse I had never faced in my entire life. The few times when Mom actually put her feet down about Demian's and my bad behavior, we were never physically punished. And my dad had never raised his hand to me. In fact, I don't ever really remember him even raising his voice to me. He usually just left the room or the house whenever conflict or disappointment threatened to replace his calm and peace-loving attitude.

The beating lasted for what seemed like forever, or maybe ten to fifteen lashings. I sat there at the table with his mother and sister Juanita, all of us staring downward, pretending we didn't hear Manny's screams or the horrible crack the belt made every time it struck him. When Manny came out, he was wiping his wet, tear-flooded face on his shirt sleeve. I watched his father follow behind and felt like I was going to pee myself. Was I next? Was he planning to beat me with his belt too, since I was partly responsible for breaking his weight plate?

But he passed both of us at the table—I was still sitting and Manny stood, trying not to let anything come in contact with his backside—and resumed his spot in front of the TV. The Astros were now up to bat, and the game looked like a close one. Not that I cared much for baseball, but my heart was banging so hard in my chest that I wanted my brain focusing on anything but the beating Manny had taken, and not on how afraid I was that his dad might suddenly start beating the shit out of me, too.

"You better go, Steve," Manny whispered to me. "We're gonna eat in a little bit."

I didn't know what to say, so I didn't say anything. I nodded to him. I saw his mother and sister, still silent, as the sound of the baseball game eclipsed everything else.

I got the hell out of there.

Chapter 7

WITNESSING THE BEATING MANNY RECEIVED AT the end of his father's belt really spooked me. It also made me reconsider my own family, which in comparison seemed like *The Partridge Family*. The worst thing I had ever seen Mom do was when she slapped Demian on the butt in line at the Pay 'n Save when he was about three. My brother had not been able to contain himself, touching everything he saw, down every aisle of the store, until my mother finally lost it and hauled off on him. She immediately apologized, lifting his bawling, skinny little body up and into her arms. He looked more shocked than hurt when she hit him, and within a few minutes his tears stopped and all was forgiven.

Guilt was never something my mother embraced for long, and whenever a mistake was made or a slight was delivered, she took a blameless stance. At least, that's what it looked like from my perspective, as inexperienced and unadult as I was then. I didn't know if she had learned that approach from my grandparents, or if it was something defensive, born out of a sense of self-protection.

Of course, when I called my grandmother the morning after the weight debacle at Manny's, I wasn't consciously thinking about corporal punishment, or the denial of responsibility in the face of accusation or conscience. I was only thinking that I hadn't spoken with her in over a week and that I missed her.

"Steve, oh my goodness," Gramma said after I told her it was me on the phone, "it's so wonderful to hear your voice."

"Yours too, Gramma," I said. The house was empty, and I had her all to myself.

"Everything okay at home?" she asked, and I wondered why worry crept around the edges of her voice. "How's Demian?"

I nodded my head vigorously, as if she were right in front of me. "We're good. School's all done, so we're playing a lot."

"What kinds of things are you playing?" she asked. I gave her a quick rundown of our summer so far, leaving out Mrs. Hunter's dead dog and Manny's ass-whooping.

"When do we get to see you and Grampa?" It had been months since we'd had dinner at their house. Sometime after Christmas, our visits to Fremont had become less frequent, until we finally stopped going over on Sunday nights altogether.

"Soon, I hope," she said, not blaming Mom at all, even though I was pretty sure it had been her decision to keep us away from them. "Perhaps I could make a special trip out during the week, since you're both out of school now."

"Without Mom," I said, my voice quiet like we were sharing a secret.

"Without your mother, yes. Would that be okay with you? Just the three of us?" I could tell she wanted me to say yes, so I did. "We could have a lovely little day. Lunch, of course, then maybe some clothes shopping. Do you have swimming trunks for the pool?"

I thought about standing in front of Willard Pool, unable to go inside even if I had wanted to because I didn't own a suit, and was embarrassed. "Yeah, I got everything I need." Then I felt like I had to defend Mom, that she was under attack. "Mom buys us everything. We go shopping all the time."

"That's good. Then we'll do something else. Maybe I'll take you to the park. Or ice cream."

I was hit with a sudden urge to watch TV and not be forced to think or feel anything anymore. "I gotta go. Thanks for talking to me, Gramma."

"Uh … okay, then. I love you, Stephen."

"I love you too," I said, ready to hang up the phone.

"Give my love to Demian," she said, right before I said bye and pushed the plastic nubs on the phone cradle down.

As the sound of the TV came to life, and the picture appeared out of the darkness, I leapt onto the worn couch and waited for Gomer Pyle to make me laugh.

DEMIAN AND I LAUGHED LIKE SILLY people in the small bathroom of Snoopy's Ice Cream Parlor on University Avenue. He had come home from his spy adventures in Willard Park just as another episode about my favorite marine had begun. There had been no sign of the flasher, which I was relieved to hear, but Demian had found a five-dollar bill hidden under some bushes.

"Do I have to put up a sign, like on *The Brady Bunch*?" he had asked, cradling the bill like it was a baby.

I eyed the money, thoughts of ways to spend it orbiting around in my brain. "So some old man can say it's his and then give you, like, twenty-five cents? Unh-uh. It's yours, Demian, fair and square."

"Mine," he said softly as he ran one thumb methodically over each corner, like he was trying to get the number five to rub off and tattoo itself onto his finger.

I had been craving ice cream ever since Gramma had mentioned it on the phone earlier, so I floated the idea over to Demian. He was torn between saving the cash and spending it right away, so I nudged him toward getting rid of it before its rightful owner could reclaim it. That's how we ended up in the bathroom of the ice cream store, alone with the water faucets and hand dryers.

I had already washed and dried my hands when Demian came out of a stall with his pants down around his ankles. "What are you doing?" I said, catching sight of his little penis poking out from under his yellow T-shirt.

"I got dookie on my fingers," he shuffled toward me at the sink, his hands outstretched.

"Eww!" I pointed at the open door of the stall, "Did you wipe them on some toilet paper?"

"No more." He reached the ceramic bowl and used a knuckle to turn on the spigot. Water streamed out, splashing up and out of the sink and onto his shirt. "Oh, man!" He broke into a silly grin, laughing as he plunged his hands into the full force of the faucet.

"Soap! Don't forget to use soap," I said, wondering if he remembered to flush.

He cleaned himself, then whacked the big metal thing, which looked like a doorknob, on the hand dryer. Demian's hands flew downward as the air hit them. His mouth opened, and a squeal filled the room. It echoed around the walls and tiled floors just as he broke out laughing.

"You're an idiot," I said, trying not to laugh myself.

"*You're* a goober," he yelled, then shoved his head under the warm air. Strands of his thin blond hair whirled around as if they were the tentacles of some underwater creature.

We traded insults until the door opened and a teenager in the Snoopy's uniform stepped inside. He glanced at us for a moment, then headed right into Demian's stall.

My brother pulled up his pants before he pushed me toward the door, and when I opened it, he whispered, "I didn't flush."

I laughed down at him, and he joined in with his hiccup-like giggles.

"If it's yellow, let it mellow," I whispered back.

"But if it's brown, you better flush it down!" He screamed up at me.

We ran out of the bathroom, laughing all the way to the front counter.

Once we'd ordered a big banana split with all the fixings, I grabbed a table. The huge fans, big white metal things that were bolted to the ceiling and spun crazily around and around and around, kept me cool as we waited for our number to be called. I handed the ticket to Demian

"Number thirteen," he said, smoothing the scrap of pink paper on the tabletop. "Why do people say it's unlucky?"

"Do they?" I said, teasing him a bit. I wanted to know what he knew. I was always amazed by some of the things he said, the information he had learned somewhere. When he asked me questions about things, it was because he was testing my knowledge against his own. When he spoke about a subject with full authority, it was because he didn't know shit about it.

"It's supposed to be stuper ... What's the word, it's ... uh ... you smash a mirror and black cats and stuff?"

I folded my arms, looked away and into the half-full restaurant.

"Come on!" he shouted in that little voice of his. "What's the word?"

"Superstitious," I said, still not facing him.

At the front counter where the more than thirty-one flavors were kept under a long glass dome, I saw something that almost made my heart stop.

"Yeah, stuperstitious, that's the one," Demian said, but I barely heard him.

"Number thirteen. Number thirteen," came a woman's voice from a small loudspeaker at the counter.

A few feet away from this woman, who held up our enormous banana split, was Seneca. Her dad, tall with skinny arms and bony shoulder blades that pointed out from his white T-shirt, stood next to her, peering down at the open containers of ice cream on display.

"Yay, us!" Demian squeaked as he handed me the ticket. "You get it."

He peeked back at the woman with our order. She squinted out into the dining hall. "But I might drop it."

"No you won't. Don't be a fag."

"I'm not a fag," he said, with all the defiance he could muster. "What's a fag?"

I glanced over again, saw Seneca's long, beautiful hair hiding her equally gorgeous face, and grabbed the number from Demian. "I'll do it."

A half walk-run erupted in my legs and I went with it, hoping I could move in fast enough to avoid Seneca noticing me. I wanted nothing more than to see her face, talk with her, and of course kiss her. But her dad was with her, and I was afraid that even if I said a simple hi to Seneca, he would be able to see right into my brain and know exactly how I felt about his little girl.

At the counter, I placed the paper scrap down. "Number thirteen," I said, trying to keep my voice from carrying over to Seneca, who stood no more than ten feet away.

The woman flashed a tight, all-lip smile before extending her arms to me so that I could remove my banana split from her impatient grasp. I muttered a thank you and hurried back to where Demian sat licking the back of his hand.

"Demian." I put the wide glass dish down and sat in the plastic chair across from him. He drew his tongue back into his mouth. "Do you taste good?"

He grabbed one of the long, skinny spoons and dug into a cloud of whipped cream. He shoved the bite into his mouth, white puffs sticking to the outside of his lips. "Not as good as this," he said with his mouth full.

It looked so good and I was so hungry that I grabbed the other spoon and dug into the middle of the dish. I lifted out equal parts chocolate ice cream, banana, caramel sauce, and whipped cream. My mouth opened long before the spoon reached it. A little slurping noise came out of the side of my mouth, and Demian laughed.

"Shut up, hand licker," I said, and indulged in another spoonful.

He did it again, and a thin line of whipped cream trailed from his tongue onto his knuckle. "Mrs. Dillon, her cat does this." He licked and licked. "It keeps doing it. Even on her thingie."

"You're gross," I said, another bite in my mouth.

I turned my gaze away from his cat impression and got a cold jolt through my chest: Seneca and her father were seated only two tables away. Her eyes were trained on me, her dad's attention elsewhere. I could feel the wet, sticky globs of ice cream on the sides of my mouth, could imagine what my face looked like all bloated with banana split on both the inside and outside.

She looked at the back of her father's head, which was turned away from her, then flashed me a big smile and gave me a low, side wave. Her face shifted away from my sight as her dad asked her a question I couldn't hear.

The metal napkin container was empty. I stared at it, frantic, until my vision went blurry. The damp lumps around my mouth crawled down to my chin, but all I could do was let them continue their slide. I turned my entire body away from Seneca, so the only thing she could see if she looked in my direction was my back, and open-palmed the wet, sticky mess until it was gone. I wiped my hand on my denim knee and looked back into the half-eaten bowl of melting mush.

She had smiled, sure, and even waved at me, but I knew without any doubt that she was just being nice. Polite. Because I was a disgusting slob, a whale beached at the ice cream parlor, unable to eat without getting food all over myself. I was glad she was leaving for Seattle the next day. This way, she would have a good excuse never to see me again. Never to call me, or me call her. Nobody in their right mind chooses to go out with a whale. Why would they?

I told Demian to hurry up and finish, and I would meet him outside. I looked down at the ice cream stain on my pants, a stain I knew wouldn't come out no matter how much water I splashed on it in the bathroom, and wanted to punch myself in the head. I rushed out of the restaurant, afraid to see a look of disgust or pity or shame on Seneca's face. I wanted to remember her the way she looked when I thought there was a chance she could be my girlfriend. I wished I could be someone who deserved her.

We were out to dinner the following week, as a family, at a Cuban restaurant apparently both authentic and affordable, according to Ken, who pronounced it "Coo-bin." On Shattuck, just below the campus, in a brightly colored, tiny place with about seven tables, all of them full, we sat at our table by the window and waited for our food. Ken told us how he used to eat here all the time when he was a student at Cal, but wasn't sure why exactly he hadn't been back until tonight. They served us our drinks but didn't offer any bread while we waited, and I made a stupid joke about how I guessed that people in Cuba didn't have bread.

"That's not funny," Ken said, his ruddy face stern and serious. "I know you're just being glib, trying on a little shade of American superiority, but it's not gonna fly, okay? Not in here. Not tonight."

He took a sip from his glass of white wine and made a show of cracking his knuckles. I was onto his whole tough guy, tough love act with me, the subtle threats of "putting me straight" about some of the things I did or said. I knew it was only an act, empty posturing that would never amount to anything, as long as my mother had her say in things. And her say was law, at least when it came to me and Demian. The two of us were her kids, her boys, and even though he was living with us like a father, he really never acted like one. Or deserved to be treated like one.

His word meant nothing.

I thought about how Manny's father's word meant *everything*, how he beat the shit out of his son in front of his mother, sister, and me, and none of us said a single word about it, during or after. Ken wasn't a violent man, and never seemed to me like someone who would want to hurt me or my brother, but my mother refused to allow him any disciplinary power over us, which meant I could ignore pretty much anything he told us under the guise of a commanding father. It failed to cross my mind how he might feel about their arrangement, whether it was at all emasculating or painful to live with two kids who never thought of him as anything other than their mother's boyfriend. Because I didn't particularly like or respect him, I rarely spent much energy on his inner life. I thought of him as a houseguest who wasn't planning on leaving anytime soon. He was here to stay, but he would never come close to being a father for either one of us.

"Sorry, Ken," I said, really not meaning it but trying not to start a thing. I just wanted to eat. I had starved myself all day, imagining someday looking more like a dolphin than a whale.

His manner softened, and he smiled too broadly at my mother, proud of his college-educated victory over a ten-year-old. "It's cool, Stevie, it's cool. Summer vacation and the living is easy, right? I can dig it, you know. It's just that folks in Cuba, under Mr. Castro and his communist regime, they get enough disrespect in their own country without privileged capitalists like us making judgments on how they live their lives. You understand?"

I nodded, still not sure how my crack about the waiter not bringing us any bread had turned into such a big deal. Mom spent her energy on drinking her glass of wine, rather than commenting on our discussion in any way.

The dinner finally came. Demian and I sat quietly shoving shredded pork and beef into our mouths while Ken and Mom talked about what a prick Ford was and how if only Carter came into office, the state of the union might just have a fighting chance at turning a corner for the better. They were passionate about their position, totally in sync and agreement on all the political nuances and practical possibilities. I tried to order flan for dessert, but they only had rice pudding, so I ate that, and then we left.

It was still early, not even nine o'clock on a Tuesday night, and because we were within walking distance of the UC Theatre on University Avenue, that became our destination. The marquee lit up the middle of the block with its bright-white bulbs, and Ken led the four of us to the box office. They always showed a double bill, with a different pair of movies playing every night of the year, so you could conceivably come to the theater three hundred sixty-five days in a row and see seven hundred thirty movies without catching the same one twice. The marquee advertised Marlon Brando in *Last Tango in Paris* and Jack Nicholson's *One Flew Over the Cuckoo's Nest.* Ken pulled out his wallet at the island's window.

"Two adults and two kids," he said, slapping down a twenty-dollar bill on the metal ticket generator.

Inside the circular tower, a guy with a wispy beard and a small staircase of earrings rising above his lobe pointed to the showtimes on a board above his head. "*Cuckoo's Nest* doesn't start for about another hour."

"I don't care," Ken said, the money still poised between the two of them. "We'll sit through the end of the first movie, then see the second one. No problem."

I wandered over to the posters on my right. I acted as if I wasn't listening, but my intention was to catch every word of what was unfolding at the box office. Mom, on the sidewalk a few feet behind Ken, tried to engage Demian in a game of rhyming words, but I could see her attention was pulled toward the scene too.

The guy's hands gripped either side of the ticket machine, refusing to touch the money. "Look, I've seen the Bertolucci film, and quite frankly it's a little … graphic for your kids. Besides, it's rated X, so I can't really sell you tickets for it."

"So you sell us tickets for *Cuckoo*. Who gives a shit? You're not gonna lose your job." Ken smiled at the guy, pushed the money toward him.

"That's kinda not the point," the guy inside the box said.

"Then what *is* the point?"

"Listen, why don't you bring 'em back in an hour, when the Forman movie runs."

Ken had gotten worked up over my little comment in the Cuban restaurant, but I could tell those three glasses of wine with dinner hadn't managed to mellow him out. He lowered his voice, but every word still managed to reach me from ten feet away. "You go to Cal, right? What are you, a film major?"

I couldn't hear the ticket guy's response.

Ken went on in that same loud whisper, "Well, I was a fine arts major, and you and me, we could bullshit through the night about the *graphic* content of film and its suitability for our oh-so-impressionable youth and maybe even discover fresh insights about Brando's method genius and the auteur fucking theory, but frankly I just want to buy my tickets and get the fuck into the theater. Is that okay with you?"

I strained to pick up the response to this, but all I heard was silence, then the repetitive click-clack of tickets fed through the machine.

"Thank you," Ken said loudly to the box office. He walked toward the open double doors and we all followed. Even though we'd already had a full meal, and I'd even had dessert, Ken got popcorn, sodas and two boxes of Jujubes at the candy counter.

Inside the theater, everything was blindingly dark. The only illumination came from the huge screen down at the bottom of the aisle, and it only lit up the first dozen or so rows. I fumbled down the aisle behind Mom, aware that Ken was leading her and I was leading Demian.

Mom turned into a row, and I plopped into the seat next to her, spilling some of the popcorn Ken had given me to hold. It took us a while to settle down, as we passed drinks and candy around, but as my eyes adjusted to the darkness, I could see we were surrounded by empty seats. The backs of heads were visible six or seven rows up, with most of the people seated in the middle or near the front of the theater.

There were only two people on screen, both just talking in what looked like an almost empty apartment building, and we'd missed over half of the movie, so I sat munching popcorn and tried not to be bored. Twenty minutes later, I wasn't bored anymore.

The two people on screen were naked, the man old but powerful somehow, and the woman fleshy and wonderful to stare at in the dark theater. He was on top of her, grunting and pushing himself at her. I felt myself get excited and covered my lap with my hands. I strained to see Mom and Ken, difficult to make out their faces in the quick flashes of light that shined off the movie screen. I could see their heads pressed together, Ken's hand in Mom's lap. Then I turned to Demian, next to me, and he wasn't looking at the movie screen. His eyes seemed to be staring into the wooden-backed chair in front of him. They darted up once, then quickly down again. When I looked at the screen again, the sounds of sex loud and animal-like filling the entire theater, the man's body lay slumped over the woman. My excitement was still there, in my lap, but I didn't know how to feel about Demian. He seemed so lost, so small there next to me.

I WOKE UP IN WHAT I thought was the middle of the night, and I had to pee. Probably all the soda from dinner and the movies. We'd stayed awake for the end of *Last Tango*, but both Demian and I fell asleep for most of the other one. I woke up in time to see the big Indian smother Nicholson's shock-therapied vegetable in his bed, then smash the sink through the wall and run away. It was a pretty cool ending, I thought, but on the walk home, Ken kept telling us the movie wasn't nearly as brilliant as the Ken Kesey book it was based on, which he was going to make sure both of us read once we were old enough.

I didn't want to turn any lights on, for fear of waking Demian, who slept soundly in the bed next to me. There was a half-full moon in the sky, so I grabbed my watch and moved to the window, where enough light came through that I could see it wasn't even 1:00 a.m., less than an hour since we had all gotten back from the theater. I got out of bed and did my best to be quiet as I stepped into the hall.

Before I reached the bathroom, I heard noises that I had definitely heard before. Usually they were muffled, but I heard them clearly now, full-throated and coming from the open door of Mom and Ken's bedroom. I really had to pee, and the only way to the bathroom was by passing their room, so I was stuck. I waited. When the pee started dribbling into my underwear, I knew I had to get to the bathroom or I was going to piss myself.

I planned to sneak by without me seeing them or them seeing me. The hall had hardwood floors without any rug to muffle my footsteps, so I had to do it just right. I made it to the middle of the hall, directly across from their room, a muted red light escaping from their nightstand, when I heard my mother say something that made me stop.

"Ooh, fuck me, you dirty cocksucker. Fuck me."

I didn't want to look—it was the last thing I wanted—but when I heard that I couldn't help it. She had said *fuck* before—not very often, and usually when she'd hurt herself banging into something—but the other cuss word was new from her, at least to my ears.

I turned to see Mom fully naked, pressed against their big dresser by the wall, with Ken mounting her from behind. The sweat on his back shone a sickly orange from the tiny light bulb by their bed. He was fully concentrated on what he was doing, his eyes closed and his body thrusting violently into her.

I mentally prodded my body to move forward, to get the hell into the bathroom, empty my bladder, and stay on the tile floor in there until it was safe to venture back to bed. Stuck in place, my eyes fastened on their excited nakedness. I was freaked out, not sure what the hell to do, when Mom abruptly turned her head toward the door and saw me standing there. Her eyelids were half-closed, but it seemed like she could definitely see me. And see me seeing her.

She continued moving with the motion of Ken behind her, moaning and pushing herself backward into him. And staring at me. We held each other's eyes for what felt like five minutes, but it was probably no more than thirty or forty seconds, before her head turned away and she gazed at the top of the dresser.

I no longer had any urge to pee. It must have crawled up inside me. I wanted to crawl up inside myself and die, scared and unsure of exactly what I felt. I hurried back into my room, got under my covers, and shut my eyes, with the intention of blocking out what I'd just seen, what I'd heard.

But I couldn't escape the vivid memory of her eyes, staring at me as Ken shoved himself at her again and again. I had heard stories of kids mistakenly walking in on their folks having sex, where everyone ended up embarrassed and awkward afterward. But this was something else. This felt really wrong, off-the-rails bad in a way that I didn't understand, or necessarily want to understand. It felt fucked up. I felt fucked up. And angry. Angry at them for doing it, and horrified that I had stood there and watched it happen.

Crazy, surreal images that seemed to build on each other filled my head for over an hour until, exhausted, I finally fell asleep. When I woke a few hours later, the sun was up and my bed was wet with urine. I longed to cry, but instead I gathered up my sheets and pressed them into our wicker-basket hamper, stuffed between Demian's and my clothes, hoping to hide them from sight and smell.

I was wide awake, and it was barely 6:00 a.m.

Chapter 8

NOTHING SEEMED DIFFERENT FOR MOM WHEN she saw me that morning. She and Ken were both hung over, but she still went to work and didn't say a word about the night before. I knew I hadn't imagined it, but maybe she was so drunk or stoned or tired she didn't remember us staring at each other while she and Ken had sex with their bedroom door wide open. I was weirded out by what had happened, but I knew I could never say anything to her about it. Especially if it had never happened for her. I was determined to get past it, to forget every bit of it, if that meant I could still look at her at the dinner table without seeing her the way I did that night: her face not my mom's face, her words not my mom's words.

It was the middle of June. Seneca was still in Seattle with her dad, and I was in bed at eleven in the morning reading *Tunnel in the Sky* under the covers and grieving the loss of my Jack London book. Not that I wasn't enjoying Heinlein's story of Rod and Grant, young colonists visiting strange planets—I was just starting to get a real taste for the sci-fi stuff—but I was bummed out that my London short story collection had been so doused in Pepsi that it was literal ly unreadable. I'd even gone up to Moe's the week before in hopes of finding another copy, but it was a lost cause. I missed the outdoorsy adventures detailed in the London stories, imagining myself in those situations, out in the tundra or the wilderness or at sea. Space was fantastic, but I honestly felt that Alaska—even though it was literally as far off for me at that moment as the outer reaches of the universe were—was a place I could actually inhabit, a world where I would fit in, and maybe even thrive.

My stomach told me I was hungry, even though I'd eaten Corn Flakes with Demian less than two hours earlier. I knew food right then would be a disaster on scale with *The Poseidon Adventure*, especially since everyone was out of the house, and I could see myself eating mouthful after mouthful of crap in front of the TV for the rest of the day. Even though exercise seemed to curb my relentless appetite, I had no compelling reason to work out.

Demian had urged me to go back up to Willard Park for more private-eye adventures with Rafe and the possible flasher, but I didn't feel like hanging out with six-year-olds all day. I dug under my mattress where my journal had lain undisturbed for over a week and flipped it open. When I got to the page with all of my summer goals, the one about Seneca being my girlfriend made me feel like the list itself was pointless. The one about losing weight, that was something within my power to complete. Or at least attempt. I hadn't really pursued getting justice for Mrs. Hunter's dog, Humphrey, and now there was shame attached to that goal. And some fear.

I found a stubby yellow pencil with barely a nub of lead in it, dragged my fingers down to a dash that had nothing but empty space next to it, and wrote *Have adventures* in sweeping cursive letters.

It was fine to read about space and the icy wilderness, but ultimately it was all make-believe. I loved imagining myself in those stories, but I had done nothing to try to make any of it a reality. Sure, going out in a rocket or riding a dogsled were impractical, given that I was only ten years old and lacked the kinds of funds I would need for those extraordinary adventures. But I could work with what I had.

I stared at the open journal until my eyes blurred and I felt there had been a true melding of the words on the page with the motivational area of my brain. Seneca's voice leapt into my mind, loudly and clearly saying, "*Me*." I closed the book and stashed it back under my bed.

That one word served as a trigger, and I knew I had to do something, right at that moment, or else I would never accomplish my goal of becoming "lean and mean" for Seneca's return. I rolled out of bed, grabbed a quick shower, and by noon I was on my bike heading over to Manny's. I had no idea if he'd be there, or up for anything that involved exercise—especially after the whole weight plate debacle—but I gave it a shot.

He was bored, looking for something to do. Since I'd been lamenting the loss of my London book and had put into writing the goal of going on real adventures rather than only imaged ones, I suggested biking out to Oakland and over to Jack London Square. Neither one of us had been there on our own, but our families had driven us there at one point or another, so we knew vaguely where it was. I figured if we just rode down Telegraph far enough, we'd run into it. It was logic like that I planned to use if I ever made it to Alaska and found myself without a map or unsure of a clear path to a specific destination.

We farted around at his house for a while, until we grabbed our bikes and pedaled down Shattuck. When it merged with Telegraph, we moved to the sidewalk and away from car traffic. I kept my eyes on the concrete below, but my attention was also drawn to all of the activity around me. Across the street, I spied a do-it-yourself car wash; more than one laundromat, with the spinning clothes visible through those small, circular windows; a hippie guy with a backpack strapped to his shoulders and a collie at the end of a leash in front of him; as well as billboards raised high in the sky with advertisements for Schlitz Malt Liquor, Squirt soda, and hair products made just for black people.

We hit a stretch where three kids, about our age but wearing rattier clothes than us and talking at each other all at once, blocked our path. I slowed, expecting a collision as they barreled toward me, no space between their side-by-side formation. I stared at them, my legs tense and ready to brake, desperate to meet their eyes. Not one looked up as my tires rolled over the cracks in the sidewalk on my head-on approach into them. I wanted to yell, "Hey," get their attention before we collided. My mouth opened and before anything came out, two of the boys slipped behind the third to form a straight line that I glided around. The sound of Manny's bell *bing-binged* and I swiveled my head back. His face was covered in a full-cheek smile, laughing as he jerked his big thumb at the kids. They walked side-by-side again, still talking at each other like birds crowded together on a telephone wire.

Manny's handlebars inched up next to mine.

I said, "Street?"

He turned his head to the curb, gazed past the parked VW bug with its passenger door dented in, and scanned the flow of seemingly endless moving cars. "Nah," he said out of the side of his mouth, his feet no longer pedaling. I cruised in front of him to retake the lead and heard the faint click of his chain as the pedals rotated forward.

As we rode, I peeked into doors of stores I had never seen before, never knew existed: a darkened bar, with all the light sucked from it but the pounding groove of Curtis Mayfield's "Pusherman"—a song I'd heard when this kid Kiley Dent and I were friends and he used to play his dad's *Superfly* album non-stop—filling the sidewalk; a huge place with a Day-Glo *Pawnbroker* sign over the door, everything from musical instruments to mounds of jewelry flooding the windows; a gun shop, where a mean-looking security guard in a faded blue uniform stared out from behind thick, solid bars; and a bunch of restaurants that poured out spicy smells and sweet smells and smells that made my nose itch and smells that pierced my eyes and turned the world blurry for a second.

I tried not to let all the unfamiliar sights—the big churches next to the nail salons next to the motels next to the huge empty lots filled with weeds grown wild—keep me from moving forward, deeper into territory that was not very far from home but which felt like another world. I thought of London and all the adventures he had purposefully entered, not just in his imagination but in his real life, too. True, most of the areas he ventured into were barren, and bereft of people and houses with bars on the windows and metal gates lining the sidewalk, but that was the place for his time, his personal journey. Oakland was my Alaska, my uncharted urban expanse. I would mentally record the unusual things I saw in this enclave and then faithfully regurgitate them into my journal back at my Berkeley homebase. I owed it to London, I owed it to myself, and maybe I even owed it to the world.

A burger place, with an area for car hop service, appeared before me and stirred my hunger pangs. I fought the urge to stop, to refuel with a big, juicy hamburger, and averted my eyes. I had intentionally skipped lunch in hopes of shedding more pounds, and when I caught a whiff of French fries, I literally salivated.

I swallowed my tangy spit and pedaled faster, toward a freeway underpass. Above me, partially obscured by a suspended wall of cement, half cars and half trucks whipped past; a hum of movement declared itself as the exact sound that The Flash made as he zoomed from point A to point Z in seconds flat. When we entered the darkened cavern beneath the overpass, the sounds took on a more thunderous, condensed, auditory vibration that was deafening at times. Halfway through, a bus chugged beside us, and when it passed, my bike swayed toward the parked cars, shoved by the exhaust and a strong wind generated in its wake. I steadied myself, took a quick glance backward at Manny's own unstable handlebars. I raised my butt off the seat and threw all my weight into increasing the motion of my feet.

Half a block past the mouth of the underpass, Manny pulled up alongside me, and I veered to the curb and stopped.

"Where we at now?" he asked.

We looked around. A freeway overpass was behind us, a creepy-looking mortuary right next to a liquor store across from us, and just miles and miles of cars, street, sidewalk, and billboards, a spot of smog in front of us.

"I'm pretty sure this is the way, but … I'm thinking we should have been there by now." I was the captain of a ship that had possibly veered off course, adrift in a sea that spread out like forever in all directions. Not a trace of land or our destination anywhere.

"Should we go back, then?"

"I don't know. Do you wanna?" I checked my watch to see that it was early still. A little after two o'clock.

"And do what?" he asked, *bing-bing*ing his bell like he was bored.

I stared over my shoulder at the overpass and said, "Only time I ever went to Jack London was my mom driving the freeway. Maybe if we just follow it, we'll get there quicker."

He nodded, and my confidence surged. I took the wheel of the ship and steered it toward 34th Street. I hung a right and kept the freeway, one block over, in my sights.

We rode up onto an overpass, where traffic ran in both directions, the steady flood of vehicles big and small filling the air with that particular hum again. I could make out downtown, off in the near-distance. I pointed at it, then told Manny we could keep going, find a big street, and ride it all the way to downtown and then to the waterfront. We left the drone of freeway noise behind us on a search for an alternate route.

At Grove Street, we veered off to our left, and it was like we both knew where we were now. This was another familiar street, like Shattuck and Telegraph, and even though it was a main thoroughfare, it was like we'd left a big city and arrived in a small town. Right away I noticed things here that I hadn't noticed up on Telegraph.

The sounds from the freeway had followed us, a constant, high-pitched thrum, like yellowjackets crowding around their hive, which mingled with intermittent explosions of noise. A pickup truck, its bed filled with rusty cargo, wires, and dirty mattresses streaming over the sides, rumbled past us from the opposite direction, backfiring as it slogged down the street. Loud, disembodied voices, more urgent than angry, volleyed back and forth as we ventured further. I hoped we were close. I needed us to be almost there.

The air emptied of noise suddenly, and I looked behind me, worried that there was nothing there, a giant void that was quickly moving to consume Manny and me. But the terrain was unchanged, house after house surrounded by bars: bars on the windows, bars on the doors, bars surrounding the yellowed and scarred earth that passed for front yards. I craned my neck back to the road ahead and noticed that Manny had started pedaling faster. I wondered if he shared in my sense of fear and approaching danger.

Then the thumping started.

It was faint, like a small boy beating on a toy drum, until it got louder, more expressive. Tiny explosion followed tiny explosion as the sound of guitar strings mingled with the measured booms. I was afraid to look behind me, and there was soreness in my legs as my front tire closed in on Manny's rear one.

"Don't stop, man, don't stop," Manny muttered to himself, his agitated voice careening over his shoulder toward me.

A song formed out of the guttural rhythm, with words that I couldn't quite make out. The soft pads of skin on my fingers were covered in sweat. I heard my breath through the thunder claps behind me, and it reminded me of the wolf trying to blow down the pig's brick house. And then I recognized it, the lyrics struggling to break free from the bass that surrounded it; it was something I'd heard before on the radio, and the familiarity of the song, out here in this alien world, filled me with calm.

Then I ran directly into a huge pile of garbage strewn in the gutter. All along the street, I had managed to avoid the discarded bags of chips, empty cartons of cigarettes, and assorted bottles and cans, but this heap of trash seemed to appear out of nowhere. My front tire hit it dead-on center, a squishy thud barely audible above the approaching monsoon of sound behind me. I flopped sideways, half in the gutter and half on the sidewalk. Manny must have gotten around it, which is what I would have done if my mind had been on the road instead of that song, because he was already half a block ahead of me when I untangled myself from the bike.

I sat on the curb, head down with my hand cupping a scraped and slightly bleeding elbow, as the source of the music rolled slowly by me. A shiny, long car that looked brand-new glided past as if it were running on the beat of the music instead of gas. The driver wore sunglasses and was slumped down in his seat. I stared at him, waiting for his head to turn, for him to acknowledge me there in the garbage—with a laugh or a mean word—but he acted as if there was nothing around him but his music and the road.

Manny, almost at the end of the block by now, turned and stared gape-mouthed at the car. Then he saw me. At the same moment, I saw the older boys across the street.

The car passed, and Manny pedaled back to me, his head shifting quickly between me and the four guys staring at us from a front porch. As Manny closed the distance between us, one of the porch dwellers hopped down the two brick stairs and unlatched a metal gate. Two of his buddies followed him onto the sidewalk.

"Hey!" the guy in the lead shouted.

The rhythmic fusillade drifted down the block and turned at the corner.

Manny leapt his bike onto the curb behind me. "Get up, Steve," he said to my back.

"What you doing with my bike?" The guy across the street was just a blur now, my mind empty. I knew I needed to move, to be scared, but it was as if I'd left my body there on the curb and I was floating around above it all.

Manny kicked me, said, "Let's go," just as the three guys walked off the sidewalk and straight toward me.

I sprang to life then, on my feet. I ignored the pain in my elbow and grabbed up the bike by the handlebars and led it onto the curb. Away from them. Next to Manny.

"Take off," he said, and then he was sailing down the sidewalk, not waiting for me. I hobbled onto the seat, my toes unsteady beneath me as I struggled to match my feet to the pedals.

More than halfway across the street now, the lead guy came into focus; his bare, wiry black chest expanded as he spread his arms like wings and raced toward me. "That's my bike," he growled. One of the guys behind him laughed into a fist as the other one clapped his hands like it was the end of a show.

I pushed my whole upper body at the handlebars, willing myself to move faster. My feet pedaled furiously, my legs full of new energy. Purpose.

Manny took a quick look over his shoulder, where I was gaining on him. "Shit!" he yelled, and his legs pumped so rapidly they were a blur. I chanced a look behind me, stunned to see all three of the guys already on the sidewalk, only a few feet from me.

All thought left me again, but this time my body took over, and I sped up to Manny. Then I was past him.

"Shit," he said again, and I looked back to see them still chasing us. We came to a corner, and I impulsively turned off Grove and onto whatever street it was. My entire body swayed one way, then the other, my feet pressed so firmly onto the pedals it was like they had fused.

At the next street, I turned again, not thinking about anything but getting far away from danger. I was like a wild animal, tracked by hunters. They were Jack London now. I was the prey.

After two more turns, I heard a loud skid in back of me. I stopped pedaling and swiveled my head around. Manny had stopped, and he was coughing. I looked past him and couldn't see anyone else around. I cautiously wheeled the bike into a wide arc and drifted back toward him. I slowed my bike, but didn't allow it to stop. In case they were still after us, I wanted to be ready.

"Where'd they go?" I asked, suddenly looking at all the houses around us, expecting them to pop out from behind one at any moment.

Manny coughed a few more times and then started to pedal in a tight circle. "I think they gave up. I don't know."

"We keep going then, right?"

"Not back that way!" He gestured wildly, his head vibrating in a series of violent shakes. "Goddamn *mayates*," he mumbled.

"Let's just ... keep going this way. Okay?" I rode up beside him and pointed away from the direction we'd come.

I pedaled slowly until he was right next to me. My heart pounded all through my chest. I gasped, coughed, and sucked in a big breath of air.

He said he was thirsty, and I said I was too. We rode for a while, and every time we saw anyone standing on their porch, or playing in the street, we sped up and didn't look back.

The sweat that had warmed me before now chilled my skin. Biking through the neighborhoods that seemed identical to me, with all the peeled paint on the houses and the battered bars on the windows and the garbage in the street and black face after black face with no faces that looked like mine or Manny's, my body shivered and I gave up all hope of ever reaching Jack London Square.

I thought if we just kept riding, we'd find a big street that we knew, something that ran through Berkeley. Something that would lead us back home. But we seemed to get farther and farther away from home. I couldn't seem to keep the goose bumps from forming on my arms and legs, over and over again.

"We gotta get home, Steve. My dad, he's gonna kill me, man."

I looked at my watch. It was after four o'clock. Manny's father would be home in little more than an hour, and there was no way we'd be back in time.

"I know," I said, but I didn't know anything. "I know."

We kept riding, then heard a siren from a block or two over.

"Cops," Manny said, and he rode in the direction of the sounds.

I raced to catch up. "Where you going?"

"The cops, they know how to get us home. Right?" Manny pedaled, his head cocked toward the sound of the moving police car.

"We don't need them," I said, everything my mom and Ken and all their friends had said about the "pigs," the "fuzz," the "fascist fucks" flooding into my head. I slowed my bike, more afraid of the police now than even the three guys who had chased after us. More afraid of asking them for help than being lost.

"Come on," he yelled, but I slowed down even more. Manny hesitated as I ceased pedaling and the siren cycled down to a stop.

"Where'd they go?" he said, thinking aloud. I pulled my bike to the curb. Manny looked at me. "What are you doing? We need to find them."

I had heard all kinds of stories at the parties Mom and Ken had thrown, at the parties we had gone to, about "police brutality" and "the totalitarian regime of the SFPD, BPD, and all the other fucking PDs all over this unjust country." That was Ken's voice I heard now, and even though I had begun to not entirely believe in it, his was the only authority I had access to.

"Trust the people to do right by you," Ken had said, on the tail end of a rant about civil liberties and fascism. "Help isn't on the way, because it's up to us to protect each other."

I pedaled again, with a purpose. Trust the people.

Manny followed me, his teeth chattering. The air was crisp now, but I knew it wasn't only the cold that was responsible for that sound. It was his father.

I told him that we just needed to find someone and ask them where we were and how we could get home. "And have them steal our bikes? Then we'll be really fucked, Steve." His shouting was interspersed with a squeak that emphasized his nervousness.

I didn't have the energy for an argument, so I let him lead us toward what we hoped would be a way home.

On we rode, veering left at this corner, right at that one. I didn't recognize a thing, but since I had gotten Manny into this, I figured I owed it to him to let him get us out of it. When we rode down a block where some kids about our age were smacking a Whiffle ball around, I wanted to stop and ask them how to get back onto Grove. But as I decreased my speed, Manny pedaled harder, arcing away from the kids with his head locked straight ahead. I pumped my legs into fast motion, not about to let him disappear. But I glanced over at the two boys and one girl. She waved at me, friendly, and I gave a nod back.

The shadows were getting longer, and my arms lay covered in little bumps of cold. A wind whipped under and over me, a tiny whistle accompanying its migration. I thought I heard crying ahead of me, from Manny, but his head was down, and I couldn't be sure. A few blocks more and I was like a mouse in one of those mazes where they run around until they finally get to the exit and the waiting cheese. But were stuck in the middle of the labyrinth, no reward in sight.

He slowed to almost a crawl, and I wheeled up beside him. His face looked wet, but I wasn't sure if it was from tears or sweat. He looked back at me, but neither one of us said anything. He folded his arms over his handlebars and stared off into nothing as his feet propelled him forward.

An old man, black and craggy-looking, stood on the sidewalk in front of what I figured was his house. He held a faded green hose and dribbled water over half-dead plants in the front yard.

"Hey, boys, whatcha doing round here?" he yelled out to us. It didn't sound mean, even though his voice was raised. He reminded me of Mrs. Hunter, the way he looked right at me and seemed interested in what my answer would be.

Just as I was about to turn around and ask him for a way out of there and back to Berkeley, Manny came to life.

"Shut up! You old nigger!" The words spewed out of my friend's mouth, and my feet stopped pedaling.

Manny spit onto the street, his legs became lightning, and he dashed away. My own body stopped completely, and I looked over at the man on the sidewalk. His face had changed. No longer the curious, open face that had spoken to us just a moment before, it now looked completely different. Damaged. His face was crumpled inward, as if it had been hit with a battering ram.

He caught me staring at him. "Don't you call me nigger now, boy." His voice cracked, but his eyes remained steady on me.

I swallowed hard and didn't believe I had enough saliva to speak when I said, "I didn't." He waited. "Sir."

"Don't you do that," he said. I didn't blink. Finally, he stared back down at the water dripping onto the ground.

I turned away and rode off as fast as my exhausted self could manage. I didn't want to look at him anymore. Something in my chest hurt. My heart hurt.

It felt late, very late, by the time we finally found Grove Street again and headed toward what we both believed was home. I was afraid to look at my watch. When stores began popping up on our trek back, I yelled at Manny to stop. I led him to a small liquor store that had a phone booth outside it.

"What?!" he yelled at me, panicked. "You thirsty? We ain't got time for this. My dad, he's gonna kick my ass. No lie!"

"I'm gonna call home. Maybe somebody's there. Ken or maybe even Mom." I hopped off my bike and peeked inside the wide door filled with posters of black girls in bikinis holding big bottles filled with brown liquid. The clock inside read 6:50.

My throat clenched, and I hurried over to the empty phone booth outside the liquor store. I was afraid to tell Manny what time it was, afraid for him when he finally walked inside his house where his father was probably waiting with that belt in his hand.

I fished a dime out of my pocket and dialed my number. It rang. And rang. I knew that Mom had to be home, had probably been home for a while now. I started to worry about what kind of trouble I would be in, especially if they had to come way out here to pick Manny and me up. And our bikes, which Ken would probably have to shove in the trunk or tie up on the roof of his car.

After what seemed like forever but was probably only three or four minutes, I hung up.

Manny, still on his bike, tiptoed over to me. "What?"

"No answer," I said dumbly. "But I'll try again." I retrieved the dime from behind the little silver door at the bottom of the phone and shoved it back into the top slot.

As it rang and rang, Manny's body moved so much it looked like he was wrestling with himself. After two minutes he pleaded, "Let's just go. I gotta get home, man. Now."

I counted five more rings, then forced the phone from my ear. I hung it up, so tired and hungry and scared that all I wanted to do was curl up in front of the store. Instead, I got back on my bike, and we rode. We rode and rode until finally we reached our neighborhood. The sun was descending into the west, and the sky would soon be a hundred shades of dark. At Manny's house, we said goodbye to each other with our eyes. Nothing good was going to happen for either one of us, so we saved our words for another day. A day in the future when something good would be possible again.

MOM, DEMIAN, AND KEN WALKED THROUGH the front door at 10:14, and I stayed where I was on the couch. Scowling. The TV was on, but I wasn't watching it. It was just white noise to me.

"Hey, buddy, you missed dinner," Ken said as he slipped off his corduroy jacket and went to the bathroom without waiting for my response.

"Did you have fun? We figured you were out with your friends, had dinner at one of their houses." Mom managed a half smile, then went into her bedroom.

Demian stood by the door, shoulders slumped, jacket still on. It looked like he was going to cry. "I told them, Steve."

I was pissed at this point but didn't know if Demian should share the blame for the feelings of worthlessness and abandonment that Mom and Ken had provoked in me. They hadn't even bothered to leave a note. I stared at a far spot on our grayish wall and waited for him to tell me the rest.

His tears trickled out, and I involuntarily jerked upward to go to him. But I caught myself and stayed seated. "I told them to wait for you, but Ken said he was hungry." He tried hard to keep his voice from getting loud enough to reach Mom and Ken. Then his words got quicker, running together in a jumble. "I didn't want to go, I wanted to wait for you, but they made me."

At that, I got up and went to him. I took off his jacket, led him over to the sofa and sat him down. I pressed my lips to his ear, "It's okay, Dem. Don't cry, okay? You don't need to cry."

I heard the toilet flush, and Ken appeared from the hall and sat across from us. Demian had wiped his tears away, but there was still a streak of moisture on his cheeks. It made his bleach-white cheeks darken into what looked like Red Delicious apples. Ken didn't seem to notice.

"Archie and some of my buddies are coming by in a little bit, so don't get too involved with the boob tube. They're bringing over the new Rainbow album, we're all gonna listen to that. You guys are welcome to stay, but no TV."

"I think I'll just go to my room," I said, staring at him with a sick, dead feeling in my stomach. I hadn't eaten anything since breakfast. "I'm really full from dinner."

"S'alright. Suit yourself." Ken stretched his leg out until his big toe brushed up against the little silver nub at the front of the TV and turned it off. I headed for my bedroom, not surprised when Demian followed me. When I shut the door behind him, Mom was still in their room doing God knows what, and Ken had put on an album and kept screwing around with the volume, making it really loud, then quiet, then loud again.

My stomach ached from hunger, but I was afraid that if I ate anything I would throw up. And I refused to go out there again. With them.

Demian and I sat quietly and read comic books until Ken's friends showed up, the music went on to full decibels, and my concentration went out the window. I'm not sure when Demian fell asleep, but I sat and stared at the walls until well past midnight, when the music stopped and the party slowly broke up. I crawled into bed and tried not to think about anything, especially not how hungry I was.

Chapter 9

ONLY A FEW DAYS HAD PASSED since my disastrous bike ride to Oakland and back, but in that time I felt like a seismic shift had occurred within me. When my mother, Ken, and Demian had waltzed into our house past ten o'clock, bellies full and without a hint of concern for where I'd been or when I'd gotten back, a new sadness and loneliness had consumed me. I had never gone in much for religion, firmly placing all faith in my mother, never wavering in the belief that she would take care of me. Midway through that summer, I found myself a practicing atheist, no longer under the conviction that my mother's love for me still existed. I sort of drifted after that, with no sense of who I really was or what I really cared about. I ate a ton of junk food and did nothing but watch TV.

That Saturday afternoon, I was in the throes of what I would only later realize was depression: at the time, I was just "in a funk." Life had little meaning, but there was still a strong urge in me to reverse the feelings, to turn myself around and get some positivity flowing through my veins. I abandoned the black-and-white movies on TV for my room, where I dived into my journal. I rolled my neck, heard a loud snap, then another, smaller, crack, and took a deep breath. Mentally pumping myself up, I turned to the page where all my summer goals lay. Not one of them had been completed yet; Seneca was still in Seattle, my body hadn't broken a good sweat in days, Humphrey's killer was still out there, and the lone adventure had resulted in a beating for Manny and a major depressive episode for me. Utter failure all around.

It was my fault, I knew this. I needed to start working out again, start an investigation into any other possible dog poisonings in Berkeley, and embark on another unfamiliar journey. I also needed to add more stuff to the list. Easier things to accomplish, and one big one. Something bigger than them all. In my state of mind, straining to think only made me hungry. I fought the urge and started to write.

Play an instrument, *Go to sleep before 10*, and *Don't watch as much TV* were erased as quickly as they were written, but a few goals survived the brainstorming session. I knew I could *Run a mile every other day* and *Beat 3 Friends in arm wrestling*, so those goals stayed. I played with the wording of my favorite, the one I had no idea how to complete but the one I thought had the most potential to be life-changing. Or life-defining. It was: *Do One Heroic Thing*. I had no idea what that "thing" would or should be, but I knew it had to be a selfless act, something amazing that I did for anyone but me.

I thought maybe it could be rescuing a cat from a really tall tree or stepping in if I saw some small kid getting beat up by a bigger one. I wasn't sure what it was, and I didn't necessarily think planning it in advance would qualify as "heroic" exactly, but I knew this was a goal worth throwing out there, to the Universe or whatever. I was offering up my heroic services to an event in my summer's future, an announcement to the world that I was qualified for the job. Even though I had no idea what the job entailed.

I closed the journal with a sense of satisfaction. After I hid it under the mattress, it struck me that I hadn't really done anything; I was pleased with myself for writing a few random goals down on a piece of paper. The more I thought about how absurd the list was and, by extension, how stupid and pathetic I was for even considering myself hero material, the more miserable I became. When Ken approached me and Demian late in the day about coming with them to a big house party in Sausalito, I was feeling numb.

"Do we hafta go?" I said, speaking for Demian without even asking what he wanted.

"Suit yourself," Ken said. Mom strolled in to the living room. "We can just leave them here tonight, right, babe?"

My mother looked at us with something unreadable on her face, but which I took as disinterest. She nodded at Ken. "Fine."

Demian looked bored, and I thought about what our night home alone would look like: TV, junk food, and more boredom. I spoke up, again for both of us. "No, we'll go."

The truth was, even though I was bumming out pretty hard, I really didn't want to be alone with just Demian. To be his babysitter, to be responsible for entertaining him and caring for his needs. I didn't want to be his mommy, while his real mommy, *our* mom, was out enjoying her night and not caring for Demian's or my needs.

Mom nodded her head again in that noncommittal way, like she didn't care what we did with our Saturday night. Was it too much for me to expect her to take charge, to force us out of the house and into a party with other people? Too much for her to say, "Hey, Steve, come on! You've been moping here all week. Let's get out and have some fun at a party. It'll be good for you."

But it *was* too much. It would always be too much for her to try to figure out what it was that I needed from her—or even just *ask* me—and for her to give it to me.

THOUGH WE WALKED INTO THE PARTY together as a family, after we had filed through the door and our jackets were thrown into a back bedroom, our unit quickly separated. Mom sent us off to play with the other kids while she and Ken headed into the kitchen for a drink and probably some smoke. Demian and I shuffled toward the room where the host's son, Gary Reese, and his friends huddled around a TV set.

"No way." Demian saw what was on the screen and he clenched his fists in excitement. "They've got *Pong*."

He moved swiftly inside the room, stood behind a small group of three or four kids—the oldest about fourteen, the youngest a little older than Demian—and watched Gary and a barely teen girl I'd never seen before play a video version of Ping-Pong. The straight lines that wavered on each side of the TV screen paddled the small white circle back and forth, the speed of the ball increasing as the volleys continued. My brother stood mesmerized, but I was hungry. I figured Demian could handle himself there in front of the TV while I searched for food.

The music soared all around the big house, Elton John belting out a song about rock being young, and Suzie and him having so much fun. Moving through the halls that were filled with adults who ignored my presence and forced me to press my way past them toward the kitchen, the unnamed feeling I'd had earlier spiked. Was it depression? What was that supposed to feel like, exactly? Instead of a dull numbness like before, I experienced the song as nostalgia, a loss of some fleetingly remembered childhood joy. I wondered how I could feel nostalgia from a song I'd only heard a handful of times and how it could cause me to long for a period in my life that I wasn't sure ever existed.

I was a mess, with butterflies pounding my gut and a powerful urge to cry building up inside. I entered the kitchen and grabbed the first foodstuff I saw: tortilla chips and a block of cheddar cheese.

I looked across the kitchen at a guy in his twenties, sporting a severe buzz cut, an earring in his left ear, a tie-dyed poncho down to his knees, and huaraches on his hairy feet. "My degree's in chemical engineering, but who wants to wear a fucking lab coat the rest of their life until they become that tight ass from *The Graduate* spouting shit about 'plastics.'" He spoke to a woman his age in a flowery dress that barely covered her butt and a pair of high-heel leather boots. "But the money's pretty fucking good."

The woman twirled a strand of blonde hair that looked almost white. "The serious money's in real estate. My sister got her license last year, and she's hemorrhaging the shit. She's been pressuring me to get my own license, but I like what I do just fine."

"What's that?"

I ate my cheese, sharp, and chewy like gum, while I listened to the next Elton John song and watched the two adults do small talk. It felt good to focus my attention on something other than my own melancholy.

"I'm a masseuse." She held out her arms. He set his plastic cup of wine down and held her hands. "They're small but powerful. Don't let my size fool you—I can get you to nirvana with these beauties."

The man brought her hands close to his face. "They *are* beauties," I think he said, before he led her out of the kitchen.

The cheese and chips finished, I rummaged over the card table full of food and boxed red wine as a fresh wave of adults entered the kitchen. Half of them seemed drunk or stoned, talking too loudly and moving erratically. I looked up at the clock over the refrigerator and felt instantly sad again. Barely nine o'clock, but it felt so late already.

I turned my head back to the table as a guy with grease stains on his fingers shoved a lit joint under my nose, almost burning it. "You want a hit?"

"No, no, I'm, uh, cool," I muttered. He shoved it even closer, grinning like Frank Zappa on the cover of an album Ken had played so much the record finally started to skip. I backed up, watched his eyes glaze over and lose sight of me. He laughed to himself, then put the joint to his lips and sucked in until his cheeks disappeared into his mouth.

Once he'd wandered out of the kitchen, I sneaked back to the table. A fondue pot rested on a bed of pot holders in the middle of it, steam rising in still-burning swirls. I peeked in to see a black hole, spit bubbles outlining the circle of cooked chocolate. I readied myself to spear a marshmallow and dip it in the pot when Demian and two boys from the playroom entered.

"Grab some wine," one of the boys, older than Demian, fished a plastic cup out of the sink. "She said she'd drink it."

Demian hadn't seen me yet, too involved with his new friends. "Why does she talk like that?"

"Duh. She's deaf." The other boy, short and wiry, swiped a cup of his own and filled it from the wine box next to a rack of dishes. Demian eyed the red wine as it flooded into the cup, his face flushed and excited. He had tried alcohol before—Ken had let him sip from his beer bottle a couple of times when he thought Mom wasn't paying attention—but he never seemed to enjoy it. I thought Demian did it to impress Ken, and now he seemed to be trying to impress his new friends. Friends he'd never see again after tonight.

"Hey." I left my marshmallow undipped and joined Demian's little group, desperate for external distraction. "What are you guys doing?"

"My brother." Demian rolled his eyes at the two boys, who laughed into my face. A chill ran from the top of my head down my arms and tightened into a noose at my fingertips. It felt white, electric, and unpleasant.

"My brother," I said in a whiny, mocking voice and then laughed like a maniac at the three of them. I turned quickly, in search of the bathroom, before I could see or hear them react.

I ROAMED THE HOUSE FOR NEARLY an hour, listening in on conversations that made little or no sense to me until I was thoroughly bored. My appetite was gone; the smell of pot and body odor in the living room had made me slightly nauseous, and all the smoke in the air caused my head to spin. Mom and Ken stood together in the dining room, engaged in a discussion about God and the collective unconscious. It sounded "deep," Ken's code word for something that I rarely understood, so I spent a few minutes listening in and trying to decipher it, translate it into a meaning that made sense to me.

I finally gave up and ventured outside, into a back yard that was spacious and unkempt. A two-car garage, behind dead grass and overgrown weeds, stood detached from any sign of a driveway. One of the wooden doors was halfway open, light from inside trickling out to me. The air was cold and damp; my jacket was inside the house, commingled in warmth with all the other coats. A cluster of clouds above me hid the moon, but my eyes adjusted quickly to the dark. What sounded like a radio and small, tinny voices giggling drifted toward me from the garage. I slipped in unnoticed and counted at least a dozen kids.

Demian huddled with his two playmates from the kitchen. A couple of girls my age talked to Gary, the son of the couple throwing the party. A small group of eight- or nine-year-olds played spin-the-bottle with an empty green wine jug. No kissing, only spinning and giggling.

Empty of cars, the garage was filled with boxes, bikes, camping equipment, and recyclables spilling out of cardboard boxes. The radio I'd heard was a small transistor, resting on a wooden shelf filled with loose tools and scattered nails.

A commercial ended, followed by a voice identifying the channel as KFRC. "Aw, Jesus!" erupted from a darkened part of the garage. A body emerged from the shadows of an overhanging shelf lined with dead house plants. It was a big kid, probably fourteen or fifteen, with facial hair, red like the thick mop on his head, grown into a beard. Joining the beard were a constellation of freckles and round, inflamed pimples.

"The music sucks and it's freezing in here, fuck," he yelled to nobody in particular. He wore a white tee with a cigarette pack rolled into one arm, a pair of cut-off jeans, and he was in his bare feet. *What an asshole*, I thought. *No wonder you're cold, you jerkoff.*

I watched the redhead pick up the radio and manhandle the dial to another station. He passed by country music, a religious sermon, and a classical channel before settling on a KISS song.

"Now this here, this rocks!" he strummed an invisible guitar and flashed his tongue as if he were Gene Simmons. He looked like a retarded lizard.

Gary stopped flirting with the two girls long enough to say, "Aaron, my folks have some sleeping bags over there, if you're cold."

Aaron, the redheaded lizard asshole, flashed Gary a Spock *V* sign with his splayed fingers before reaching up into the garage rafters to pull down an Army surplus sleeping bag. He unzipped it, fit his entire body inside while standing up, then hopped back toward the shadows.

Before he could disappear into the dark, a girl staggered out. It was the girl I'd seen playing *Pong* earlier. She looked about thirteen, with her shoulder-length brown hair in pigtails and a half-empty cup of red wine in her hand. Everyone in the garage stopped whatever they were doing. Aaron and the girl had taken center stage.

Like a femme fatale from the old movies I watched on UHF late at night, she drained the bottom of her cup and tossed it over her shoulder. Then she got in the sleeping bag with him. She kissed him—not the other way around—and they almost slammed into the floor, she went at him so hard. On the ground, he zipped the bag up to their heads.

When she threw her shirt and panties out, they landed near the spin-the-bottle group, and every one of us moved in for closer looks.

The bag wriggled around like a snake racing through a meadow, Aaron now on top of her and emitting loud, unpleasant grunting noises. Strange, guttural noises also escaped from her, and I suddenly realized she was the deaf girl Demian's friends had talked about in the kitchen.

"Oh, man, I think they're doing it," a boy squealed.

Nervous, excited laughter filled the garage. The redheaded guy continued to grunt and writhe inside the bag. It flopped around until it rested directly under the one source of light in the garage: a bare, single light bulb shining from the center of the ceiling.

A nasally voice from the back porch of the house penetrated Paul Stanley's vocals and the redhead's own squeals. "Aaron, Aaron, where are you? We're leaving."

The squeals abruptly stopped.

"Aaron!" came the voice from outside the garage, this time with more urgency.

"Ah, shit." He fumbled around inside the bag, tugging at the zipper until it opened. He scurried out of it, half-dressed and staring through his captive audience in a foggy daze. He squeezed into his cut-offs and circled back to the girl, still inside the sleeping bag. "I gotta go," he said, and for a moment I thought he might break down and cry.

When he was gone, the garage went silent. Expectant. The deaf girl, her naked body fully visible with the bag open and the harsh spotlight hanging above her, ran a finger along her belly and stared at the small pool of sweat on her stomach. She cupped her small breasts and giggled an overly loud, scratchy laugh.

The KISS song had ended, and "Born to Be Wild" zipped through its catchy chorus. An older boy startled all of us, suddenly accompanying the radio with his full-throated voice, acting like the alcohol had just kicked in. I watched him bellow into an empty beer bottle as if it were a microphone and he was on stage at the Fillmore, where Mom had taken me to see my first concert when I was three. I think it was Cream. Or maybe the Yardbirds. The singing boy was twelve or thirteen and tall for his age. Long arms and legs, a really skinny kid with shaggy black hair that came down over the tops of his eyes in bangs. Similar to my hair, but a funhouse mirror reflection of me. Or me of him.

I heard footsteps behind me, new kids stumbling onto the scene: a five-year-old girl in a pretty pink dress with a wide bow and a boy, maybe eight, smiling through his harelip. I saw Demian and his friends, in the same spot they had staked out when I first came in, transfixed. Demian lifted a cup of red wine to his lips, grimaced, swallowed, and then laughed. I started toward him just as the deaf girl stripped the sleeping bag from her body like a husk.

I watched her move to the singing boy's voice, dancing to sounds she couldn't hear. I stopped and watched her reach out to him with the same hands that had touched her own breasts. He whipped the beer bottle over his shoulder with such force that it struck the wall of the garage and shattered. She opened her mouth into a grin, revealed a gap in her teeth and a tongue bloody from wine. He jumped on top of her and they both wrestled themselves onto the sleeping bag.

My heart pounded, my eyes fixed on her body under the bright yellow light. I was excited, turned on, but I was scared for her. I was scared for Demian, and for some reason I was scared for me too.

The boy took off his shirt, and she helped with his pants. He crawled on top and thrust himself at her small body, on display for all of us to see. I broke my gaze long enough to find Demian again. I edged through the gawking kids, most mesmerized but others holding their hands to their mouths, giggling. I reached Demian and yanked the cup from his hand.

"Hey!" He gave me a dirty look, his two buddies fixated on the show under the light bulb.

I ignored him and whispered, "Let's go."

"I don't want to go!" he said loud enough that the two boys looked over.

One of them said, "You're not going, are you?"

"You should do her next," the other one said to me, laughing. "She's all for it."

I stood there stupidly, holding the cup full of Demian's wine, not sure if I should drink it or chuck it. "No, I don't think so."

"How about you, Demian? You're into it, ain't you?"

Demian's eyes shifted up and down, and he looked as if he was about to wet himself. "Yeah yeah," he said, rubbing his hand over his crotch. "Fuck fuck fuck. Hahaha."

I had never heard him cuss like that before. I worried about how much he'd had to drink and how drunk he might be.

I was feeling sick again, nauseous. The radio seemed louder, and the deaf girl was making those creepy, screechy noises again. The two boys laughed.

"I saw it in a movie," Demian told his buddies, emboldened by the wine and the morsel of sexual knowledge he thought he possessed. "That movie we saw. With Mom and Ken. I want to do that to her. With my ... penis."

He laughed, the boys laughed, and I'd had enough. I tossed the cup into an empty corner of the garage, grabbed Demian by the arm, and dragged him toward the door. As we moved behind the excited throng of kids, I noticed the five-year-old girl. Scared, confused, she lay on the floor, sobbing into the hem of her little pink dress, the bow wet with her tears.

Demian protested loudly behind me as I passed her. I wished that her parents had never brought her to this party and wondered where the hell they were and if they even cared about her.

As we reached the door, I stopped. An adult, a man at least thirty if not older, stood half inside and half outside the garage, smoking a cigarette and calmly staring at the two kids having sex on the sleeping bag. I thought he should say something to them, do something for that little girl on the floor, but he looked right past us, the flame from his cigarette casting a reflection of fire in his eyes.

I ran around him, my hand gripping Demian's wrist. Outside the garage, the moon had broken free of the clouds and shined down on me as brightly as the bulb had shined down on the deaf girl. More kids wandered toward the garage, while inside the house the parents and other adults remained oblivious. All but the one by the door, smoking his cigarette while he watched little kids fucking in front of other little kids.

Not saying or doing a goddamned thing.

Chapter 10

MOST OF THE FOLLOWING WEEK I spent close to home, still under the influence of that same unrest and sadness that had crept up on me after the bike ride and then blazed with intensity the night of that party in Sausalito. I couldn't concentrate enough to read more than a *MAD Magazine* or the funnies section of the *Chronicle*. My mind was now as flabby as my body and I secretly wished that school would just hurry up and get here—that summer would shove off and become fall—so that I would be forced into some kind of structure, some regimen where I was responsible for producing homework, showing up for class, and hopefully emerging from my rut.

Sunday came and for the first time in what seemed like a long time I was excited about something. Mom hadn't taken us to Grampa and Gramma's for Sunday dinner in months, and I missed them and the ritual that less than a year ago had been twice-a-month. Demian and I had spoken to Gramma on the phone since our last visit to their house, but it wasn't the same. I loved them so very much, understood they truly cared about what my brother and I thought and did and wanted to do. Around them I understood safety, and structure, and rules even. It was a wonderful feeling, more so lately.

We arrived at their house in Fremont just before five. Gramma always served dinner promptly at five, so there would be little time for extended hellos before we jumped into food. Mom likely planned it that way, so she could avoid getting into any kind of heavy discussion with her mom until later in the visit.

We rang the bell and were greeted by the barking of two papillon dogs, Milsie and Chew-Chew, who had been alive as long as I had. They recognized us right away. Grampa got generous with hugs as we walked through the door and said Gramma was finishing dinner. He took us into the family room, where big band music played, the old-timey stuff with all the instruments but no singing. Demian and I played with the dogs while Ken disappeared into the bathroom and Mom made small talk with Grampa.

"They treating you well down there at good ole Ma Bell, Rose?"

She snickered. "I don't really care how they treat me, as long as they pay me at the end of the week."

"Sure, sure. You're not working for free, heavens no." Grampa laughed kindly, but Mom didn't even crack a smile. "Well, now ..." he said, his voice softening. "Okay, then." He saw Demian and me with the dogs and left Mom to join us. I gave him another big hug. "Boys," he said, "I've got a present for you. Wait here, I'll get it."

At that moment, Gramma entered the room, wiping her wet hands on a pristinely white and pressed towel. "No you won't, Howard. Dinner's ready, and I don't want all my hard labor getting cold or going unappreciated."

Demian and I abandoned the dogs to greet her, showering her with our kisses. Ken came back from the bathroom, and she embraced him, leaving Mom for last. "Rosemary, you're looking lovely. I would kill for your hair, so long and lustrous." She reached out to touch her daughter's hair, but Mom jerked, almost violently, backward.

An awkward silence. Even the dogs had gone quiet.

"Well," Gramma smoothed her apron, forcing out a smile, "let's eat, shall we?"

The main dish was home-cooked and delicious, a hearty and yet healthy-tasting stew, all chunky with meat and vegetables. I had seen my grandmother cook before, and it seemed nothing like the chore it was for my mother—it was an invigorating, creative task for her, full of joy and satisfaction once all the preparation and ingredients and cooking time had been weaved together to produce a meal for her family.

When all of us were at the table, hot plates and covered bowls of food spread out over the flesh-colored, crocheted tablecloth, Gramma stretched her arms out and said, "Grace, please." Mom's face got a pinched look to it, like it always did when this part of dinner came, but she took my hand on one side of her and Ken's on the other. Gramma said a few things about God and his glory, and the feast that surrounded us, as well as something nice about Mom and Ken and us boys all here under their roof once again. Then our hands were free to dig into dinner.

"Please don't feed the dogs, Demian," Gramma said gently, when she caught my brother dropping small pieces of buttered bread onto the floor where Milsie and Chew-Chew had encircled his feet.

Demian showed Gramma that his hands were now empty. "Sorry. It's just ... I'm just ... I'm happy they're okay. This dog, that lives near us, he—"

"Demian, eat your dinner, sweetie." Mom leaned across me, straightened the napkin over his lap.

"I just, I—"

"That's enough, Demian."

"Rosemary, what's he talking about?" Gramma had stopped eating.

Mom's tight-lipped smile met Gramma's pursed lips, and she said, "It's nothing. It's not a big deal, Ma. Some random creep put some poison into ground beef and fed it to a neighbor's dog."

"Oh my God," Gramma said, dropping a fork onto her plate with a tinny clang.

"It happened a few weeks back, and nothing else has happened since. It's really not a big deal."

"That's horrible. Did they catch the person?"

Mom ran a hand down her braid. "No, Ma, but it seems like an isolated thing. We don't have any pets, so we're fine."

"What about the boys?" Gramma's voice had what sounded like panic in it.

Mom stared at Gramma, her anger simmering. "What about them?"

"Well, the neighborhood, I mean, is it safe?"

"Yes, Mother." Mom's voice had gone tight. Cold. "We live in a safe neighborhood."

"But if—" Gramma started to stand up, but Grampa took her hand and placed it in his lap. She looked startled, her mouth caught half-open. I watched Grampa stroke the back of her wrist, and after a few moments she said, "So, how is everything with dinner?"

After dinner, as we all sat down to watch Lawrence Welk, Grampa brought out a present for us—a backgammon set, a game he, Demian, and I had played on occasion. I lost the first game to Grandpa, and then Demian tried his luck. Mom lured Gramma into the living room, and Ken got up and changed the channel to *60 Minutes*. I watched Grampa and Demian for a while, then wandered to the fridge for a little after-dinner grazing. Gramma raised her eyes at me from the family room.

"Dessert is coming," she said, "so try not to ruin your appetite for it." She turned back to Mom, and I found a couple of carrot sticks in the crisper. At the kitchen table, I could hear the TV, as well as Grampa and Demian playing their game. But I heard Mom and Gramma's conversation from the other room the best.

"It's just for a few days, okay?" Mom's voice, strained and pouty. "You've done it before, I don't understand why you're acting all put out."

"I'm not 'put out,' Rose, I just would have appreciated at least a week's notice beforehand. And that's not my only concern. How can you afford it?" Gramma asked.

"We're fine," Mom said.

"You are? Time away from work and Ken out looking for a job? That doesn't sound as if you have a lot of extra money to go throwing it away in Santa Cruz for three or four days."

"Will you take them or not?"

"Of course I will. Any time they need to come over here, they are beyond welcome. But I want to know what this trip will do to you financially. We can't continue to loan you money that you obviously have no intention of paying back."

"That's not true. We do," Mom said.

"Has Ken found anything yet? And how are you making the rent every month?" Gramma sounded concerned.

"We're managing. Will you stop hassling me all the time about money?"

"You need to take more responsibility, for those two boys and for yourself. It's not my place to lecture Ken myself, but if he's the reason you keep coming to your father and me for money, then that may change."

"So you'll take them?" Mom's voice seemed tired, sounded heavy.

"Yes, Rose, I would love to have them stay here next week."

"That's all you had to say. You didn't need to make me work so hard."

"I love you, Rose, and I want you to make good choices with your life. When I see—"

I heard heavy footfalls, then a door down the hall slammed. A moment later, Gramma came back into the kitchen. She seemed lost in thought, and kind of sad, but when she saw me still sitting at the table, she gave me a smile, unaware that I'd heard their conversation.

I had no idea Mom and Ken planned a trip for themselves, but over the past year or so a pattern had slowly emerged that confirmed my belief that I was rarely the first one they consulted before making decisions that affected all of us.

"Are you ready for dessert?" Gramma asked, and led me back to the refrigerator.

TUESDAY NIGHT, DEMIAN AND I WERE back at our grandparents' house, our suitcases full of clothes and toys. Mom said they'd be back sometime Saturday. She thanked Gramma and even gave her a hug before leaving us behind with a cheerful, "Be good. Love you."

It was already past dinner time, but Gramma still had food prepared for us. Never one to turn down a meal, I allowed myself a hearty portion of meatloaf and garlic-flavored mashed potatoes, which tasted like something you'd eat in a fancy restaurant. Demian picked at some vegetables, apparently still full from the half a P-B-&-J he'd had for dinner at our house. When we had finished clearing our own plates and given some love to Milsie and Chew-Chew, Grampa picked up our bags from the living room and showed us to our room.

"I'll be the bellhop," he said, wearing a plaid sweater-vest over a white, button-down shirt and holding the battered but functional suitcases Ken had picked up from Goodwill that day especially for our trip, "and you boys are staying at this here four-star hotel. Follow me to the Presidential Suite, if you please."

Demian's cheeks puffed out, trying to suppress a giggle, as Grampa led us down the small, carpeted hall to Mom's old room. It was at the end of the house, just past the main bathroom, and when we reached the closed wooden door, Grampa stopped. He placed the bags on either side of the door, then made a big show of fumbling in his baggy wool slacks for keys. He withdrew his hand with an invisible ring of keys, his fingers nimbly searching for the one that would fit our hotel room lock.

"There it is," he said finally. "You know, boys, this is a pretty big hotel, where all the celebrities and big-wigs like to stay, so it takes a while to find the right key." He fiddled with the lock, building suspense for what lay behind the door. "I've seen 'em all, everyone from Bob Hope to Bob Barker. They've all come through here. But only United States presidents have stayed in this particular suite."

He turned to us, his hand frozen in mid-air, like he had a key inserted in the door handle, ready to unlock it. "What presidents do you think have slept here?"

Demian looked up at me, his hands fluttering at me to answer quickly. "How about President Nixon?" I asked.

"Lousy tipper, breath kind of bad, but very presidential." He stared at Demian. "Who else?"

"Umm … President …. Umm … President Washington?"

Grampa smiled. "I cannot tell a lie. He did *not* stay here. But I have a feeling he chopped down that apple tree we used to have out front." Demian stared at the closed door, his feet shuffling through the green shag carpet that he liked to pretend was the softest, furriest grass in the world. Grampa raised his eyebrows at me and then turned the invisible key. Inside the room, I recognized the two twin beds: the one Mom had slept in as a girl, and the other an addition when Demian was born, in anticipation of his staying here. Demian and I had stayed in this room before, the last few times right after Mom had met Ken when my brother was just out of diapers. There was a vanity against one wall, the mirror round as an oversize Frisbee, and a chest of drawers that stopped at my throat. Directly across from the open door was a large window, covered by off-white drapes, which framed a view of our grandparents' back yard.

Grampa stepped away from the door and did a bow. I pushed Demian inside and he immediately jumped on his bed, the springs squeaking. Grampa deposited the suitcases in front of the closet door and then turned to me with his palm up. I just stood there, not understanding what it meant. He cleared his throat and shoved his hand closer to my nose.

"For the service ..." His eyebrows scrunched down, coming together like a huge caterpillar that had been chopped in half.

I finally got it. "I'm supposed to give you a tip?"

He nodded. "Anything will do, sir. A twenty-dollar bill, loose change ... the lint from inside your pocket."

"What did Nixon give you?" I plunged my hands into every pocket of my jeans.

Grampa's nose curled up like he smelled something unpleasant. Like a fart. "The fine Republican president from our own Golden State left me the lint from inside his navel."

I reached into my front pockets and dug deep, as if my hands were searching for something real. I pulled out an invisible bill, clutched between my fingers, and placed it in his open hand. "A thousand dollar bill. It's not counterfeit or anything. You could totally spend it if you wanted to."

He closed his hand over my tip, said, "Thank you, sir," and then turned and walked out of the room without another word.

I shoved at the heels of my shoes until they flopped off my feet and onto the carpet, and then I joined Demian on his bed. We jumped up and down, flying from bed to bed, until Gramma came in and told us to brush our teeth.

THE DINING ROOM TABLE WAS SET for breakfast when Demian and I straggled in before 7:00 a.m. I could have easily slept a few more hours, but Gramma wanted all of us to eat our bowls of shredded wheat, milk, and fruit together before Grampa left for his job at the GM plant, where he was, in his words, "a white-collar, collared-white, manager-type." So after making our beds and opening the drapes to let the day in, we joined our grandparents in reciting a brief morning prayer before digging into our food.

"You said that *amen* with a fair amount of gusto," Gramma said to Demian while she poured milk over his homemade cereal. "It's a fun word to say, isn't it?"

He dug his spoon into the bowl, nodding, and took a big bite of Gramma's food. When she handed the milk to me, Demian's lips pursed inward and he gave me a funny look. He swallowed before asking if she had any sugar.

"She's a great cook," Grampa whispered to Demian after Gramma had gotten up from the table, "but she has a tendency to forget that you boys like the sweet with your breakfast meal."

Gramma came up behind them, sprinkled a teaspoon of sugar into Demian's bowl. "I don't forget. It's that I prefer they don't rot their teeth under my roof. *No* roof, actually, but I can only control what happens when they're here with me."

"Amen!" Demian shouted, and I laughed because I heard it as a response to what Gramma had said about control and her lack of it, instead of what it actually was: him giving her a loud cheer for adding sugar to his cereal.

Gramma laughed, too, but when I yelled, "Hallelujah," to join in with the fun, she met my eyes and shook her head. I decided then not to ask for any sugar, and just added more strawberry and honeydew to my shredded wheat.

THE SMELL OF SPICY APPLES FLOATED from the kitchen to the living room, and although I knew the constant snacking worked against my goal to lose weight, it was hard to resist. A Mantovani record spun on the hi-fi set in the corner of the room, the towering speakers on either side of the maple cabinet spilling out more of that music without words that my grandparents loved. Both Demian and I were on the floor, pencils buried in the open workbooks that Gramma had given us after breakfast. Mine was filled with math problems specifically for sixth graders, and Demian had letter and word worksheets in front of him. At first I'd complained, citing summer as a homework-free zone, but Gramma argued a lot better than I could—all about keeping our skills up, not allowing our brains to go to mush, and just the plain fact that she "said so"—and it was easier to figure out a few fractions than do battle with an old lady so intent on victory.

Gramma's feet were next to my head before I noticed she had entered the room. "Snack time." She kneeled down, the tarts smelling fresh and delicious. "How are you finding that workbook? I went to a teacher supply store, so I assumed this would be challenging for you."

I reached up to take a pastry off the tray, but my fingers wavered. I pulled my hand back down to my side. "Pretty good. Not too easy but not too hard, either."

"Just right!" Demian snorted, propped up on an elbow beside me. "What's that, Gramma?"

He got to his feet, put his nose into the tray. "They're apple-and-raspberry tarts," she said. "Healthy, homemade, and not bad in the taste department. Try one, Demian. In fact, try two or three." Gramma placed a stack of them into his open hand. He stared at the food, unsure about it.

"I'm not so hungry." He stuck his hand back toward Gramma.

"Demian," Gramma said, lifting a compact treat from the top of the pile, "I know that you are about as fond of food as you are of bee stings, but in my house you need to eat." She pushed it toward his lips, and he opened just enough for her to slip it onto his tongue. "Chew, please." He chewed for about a minute, until she said, "Swallow ..."

He looked over at me, and I gestured with my chin for him to eat.

"Not horrible, right?" Gramma placed her hand on his cheek, still kneeling down so they were face-to-face. Demian shook his head. "Good. Now, if you'll have another."

She stayed there, holding the tray and gently urging him to eat until his hand was empty. "Thank you, Demian."

"Why isn't Steve eating too?" Demian wiped a crumb from the edge of his mouth and poked it inside with his thumb.

I leaned up on one knee, patted my belly. "There's no more room in there. Here," I said, reaching out for his hand, "touch it and see."

His little dimples appeared, and he stepped away from my reach.

"If you boys have had enough studying for one afternoon, you can go outside now. Your grandfather will be home in about an hour, come in then." I closed the workbook, and Demian followed Gramma back into the kitchen.

"Can I have one more, Gramma?" Demian said.

"Nothing would make me happier." She handed him one of the tarts, but he opened his mouth instead. She fed it to him, like a momma bird taking care of her babies.

OUR GRANDPARENTS LIVED ON A CUL-DE-SAC, and from their porch I could see the door of every one of their neighbors. There were only nine houses on the block, which let out onto a straightaway that led to a bigger street farther up. Most of the cars that came onto their street belonged to the people who lived here, their friends, or folks who mistook the block for a thoroughfare.

Clouds were scattered above us high in the sky. A welcome breeze prevented the sun from making me sweat. Demian and I wore T-shirts and shorts, standing on the front lawn and looking for something to do. Gramma had told us we weren't to leave the block, so we played a game of invisible hand ball against the driveway until the sound of music captured my attention. From a few houses down, the Four Tops or The Temptations or The Miracles (that whole "Motown Sound" was a favorite of mine, but I sometimes found it difficult to tell the groups apart) drifted (The Drifters?) up the street, the harmonies tinny and muffled.

A long pair of legs, in oil-stained jeans, jutted from beneath what some of my friends from school called a muscle car. The hood was open, and beneath the music I heard a constant *ping-ping*, like a hammer beating on a hollow tree. I wanted to walk over, lean down, and see who was under there and what he was doing. I thought about daring Demi an to venture into their driveway but knew that wouldn't be very responsible. What if the guy was really mean or had an attack dog hiding in the shadows of the garage?

"You wanna walk?" I asked Demian, handing him the invisible ball. He took it. Nodded. We headed in the opposite direction of the muscle car house, my face planted forward but my eyes darting over to where the doo-wop sounds played and the hammering continued.

Demian hopped past me. "Look, I'm a rabbit," he said. He turned around, his front teeth dangling over his lower lip while his nose twitched. Then he hopped more frantically, circling back behind me and then past me again. "Now I'm a hare."

"Same thing," I said, feeling like I wanted to hop myself but afraid whoever was underneath that car might see me and start laughing.

"Now I'm a turtle," Demian said, on all fours and moving slowly over the warm sidewalk. He rolled over on his back in a neighbor's front lawn. "Now I'm a snake." He hissed and moved toward a display of ceramic ducks. He slithered past the momma duck and pretended to swallow one of the chicks, making loud smacking noises.

"Sick," I laughed, unable to help myself. It was funny, and it felt good for those muscles in my face to move.

Demian kept me entertained all the way to the end of the block, transforming himself with every shouted, "Now I'm a . . ." Once we had crossed the street, headed toward the neighbor's garage, I had a newfound courage to peek my head inside it. By the time we got there, the music had stopped, the hood was down, and the legs underneath the car had disappeared.

GRAMPA PULLED ME ASIDE AFTER DINNER, just the two of us moving toward the garage like we shared something conspiratorial. "I got you a little something on my lunch break," he said, once we were at the top of the short staircase. He flipped the light on, and between my grandmother's car and a small oil stain covered with kitty litter stood a big cardboard box. "Go ahead and open her up."

The box was wider than my body, and when I tried to lift it off the ground, I couldn't. A picture of an old guy in a blue jumpsuit stared up at me as I looked for a way to open the box. Grampa handed me a box cutter. "Be careful, it's sharp. That there is what the salesman at the sporting goods shop called the Jack LaLanne special."

I looked up at him, not any wiser about what was inside.

"It's a weight set," he said, cupping his hand around my bicep and giving it a playful squeeze. "This is your summer to get yourself fit, isn't that what you said?"

I nodded, so excited about the idea of having my own workout equipment that I nearly cut my finger slicing open the top flap of the heavy box. "But it's not my birthday yet," I said.

Grampa leaned down and pulled the first weight plate from the box. "No, it's not. And this is not your birthday present. This is something else."

Within ten minutes, all the equipment was laid out in the garage: an unassembled bench, plates ranging from two-and-a-half pounds all the way up to fifty, a set of dumbbells, and a barbell we lifted out of the back of Grampa's backseat together.

"You like it?" he asked, as we followed the instructions on how to put the bench together.

"Yes. Yes, yes!" I hugged him, and he rubbed my back with his strong hands. "It's so … so great."

"It's not only a gift for you, Stephen, but one for me as well. I was actually kind of selfish when I walked into the store today. I was hoping if I bought this for you, Gramma and I might get a chance to see you more often. At least as long as summer lasts." He screwed a leg onto the black vinyl bench seat until it wouldn't turn anymore. "I know you boys are going back at the end of the week, and your mom doesn't really like to … Well, never mind that. But maybe you can come down on your own. Are you old enough to ride the BART by yourself?"

"Sure," I said, handing him another leg, "Mom has let me do that all kind of times."

"Then you ride over here—bring Demian too if you like, that'd be nice—and spend a little time with your grandmother, then with the weights. I can always try to knock off work a little early—Damn," Grampa said, as the screw went in at a weird angle and he lost his balance. I picked up the screwdriver and handed it to him. "Nah, you go ahead. My steady hands are not as steady as they used to be, I guess."

He guided me with his own hands, helping me fit the flat tip of the screwdriver into the small screw. I twisted it as he held the bench and the leg together. "That's it, you got it. Just keep at it till it's as tight as it goes."

When we were finished, one set of the legs wasn't as flush against the garage floor as the other set, but Grampa said it hardly mattered—I had done a terrific job on it.

"Here, lie down on the bench. I'm going to teach you a few of these exercises."

I rested my back against the padded vinyl as he placed the barbell in my outstretched hands. "Thank you, Grampa. I love it."

"And I love you. When you win Mr. America, you can tell them who got you your first set of weights."

"I will," I said, and felt stronger then than I had ever felt before.

Demian and I spent the day reading, doing more homework, and running errands with Gramma, so by three o'clock we were ready to go out on our own. We played in the back yard with the dogs until I heard the faint sound of Stevie Wonder's harmonica.

"Let's go," I said, heading out the side gate toward the street. "And don't let them out."

This time I had more courage than the day before, determined to see what was under that hood. The closer we got to the garage and that muscle car, the more nervous I became. The pair of oil-stained jeans leaned against the front bumper now, and I could see that they belonged to a blond-haired boy in his teens. His feet tapped the garage floor in beat with the music as he peered at the car's engine.

Just as I was about to lead Demian up the driveway and introduce ourselves, I chickened out and kept walking.

Before we had passed his house, he yelled to us. "Hey!"

"Hey!" Demian waved and then ran until he was beside him. He stood on his tiptoes, trying to get a peek at the car's guts. I quickly followed him. "Whatcha doing? Is that your car? What's all the stuff in there?"

"Sorry," I said, standing next to Demian, "he gets, um, excited."

"That's cool," the boy said, then wiped his hands on a green towel before offering his hand to Demian. "I'm Phillip Mosely. What are your guys' names?"

"Demian O'Neill. That's my gramma and grampa's house over there."

"I know them," Phillip said. "They're real nice people."

"I got a loose tooth," Demian said. "You wanna see it?" He stuck his hand inside his mouth and wiggled it around.

Phillip chuckled, and I nudged Demian aside. He danced around while he yanked at his teeth. I introduced myself and told him I liked the music he was listening to. We talked about music for a few minutes until Demian interrupted us. He wanted to know about the car, whose it was, what all the junk inside was, if Phillip had any dogs; he wanted Phillip to know that we lived in Berkeley and went to school and where did he go to school, here in Fremont?

Phillip told us to stand by the grille of the car, which was split down the middle. I stood in front of the side that had lettering embedded in it, while Demian stayed close to Phillip. "This is a '66 Pontiac GTO, one of the bossest cars ever made. My dad bought it from a junk dealer last year. Thing was in horrific shape, just awful. But we spent a bunch of weekends working on it together, getting the body back to factory mode, the interior reupholstered, and now it's up to me to get it road ready."

He explained the different parts of the engine to us, using words like *intake manifold* and *throttle valve* that I hadn't heard before. To me, it looked like a giant puzzle that was never going to fit together into a thing that I recognized. What I did understand was that he had a dad, one who had spent all that time with him, teaching him something that seemed useful. And important.

My father never cared much for television, called it the idiot box, and was in favor of Demian and me using our own imagination, rather than letting what was on TV do our imagining for us. Because I could barely read, and Demian hadn't even learned his alphabet yet, our father borrowed jigsaw puzzles from the library. The ones he brought home for us to play with after dinner were simple but full of color and oddly shaped pieces. They kept us busy for hours.

For my sixth birthday, one of the presents was from my father: a thousand-piece reproduction of the Eiffel Tower. He had never been to Paris, but on occasion he had read aloud from *The Hunchback of Notre Dame*, *A Moveable Feast*, and, somewhat inexplicably, *Tropic of Cancer*. My mother had read *Madeline* to us, so I knew exactly what the structure was when I saw it.

We all began working on it about a week later, making a space on the hardwood floor right in front of the little-used TV set. My father had taught us to work from the outside in, gathering up all the edge pieces and corners first, to build the square outline before moving slowly inside of it. Two nights into it, the base of the tower began to take shape. There were still at least six hundred or so pieces left. My mother had gotten frustrated with it that first night, since it became her job to keep Demian from stomping on it and kicking the puzzle around the living room.

But Dad had stuck with it.

When my enthusiasm flagged at the end of that second night, he kept me focused and engaged on the task at hand. "Always finish what you start," he'd told me, both of us on our bellies, noses almost touching. "If you abandon something too soon, you'll never know what could have been."

"I know. But the picture on the box, that's what it's gonna be. Right? So why do I gotta do it all?" I could feel his breath on my face as I spoke, a not-unpleasant mix of tobacco and hummus swirling around me.

"Because you gotta," he said simply. "Because Father knows best." He laughed then, a small sound, pushing its way up through his chest.

I had every intention of finishing that puzzle. I waited for him to get home from work the next night, but he had made plans with friends. The night after that, he told my mother that he had quit his job. Over the next week, the puzzle sat there on our floor, unfinished, as my parents argued through the nights and into the early mornings.

And then, one night, he was gone. Forever.

I think we sold the puzzle at one of the yard sales my brother and I set up. Or I threw it in the garbage. By then, I was sure my father was never coming back, so there was no use keeping it. Who gave a shit about some stupid tower in some stupid country that I was never going to visit anyway? I was happy to be rid of it.

Phillip let us tinker around with some of his tools, showed us where he had replaced panels and buffed out scratches. We then piled inside and pretended to drive the streets of Fremont, the convertible top down and our long hair whipping behind us in the high-octane speed of the wind. When we came back down to Earth, out of the car and back in the driveway, I saw that Grampa's car was parked in front of our grandparents' house.

"We gotta go!" I yelled to Demian, and we both looked at our watches. It was almost five thirty. Two hours had zipped by in Phillip's garage, and we were late for dinner.

"Your dinner is cold," Gramma said to us as we ran through the back door, Milsie and Chew-Chew yapping at our return.

"Sorry, Gramma, really." I looked at the table, the plates set but empty of food. "We didn't go more than a couple houses down. I just must've lost track of time or something."

"Or something." She was pissed. "You both have watches—that Grampa bought you—so there should be no plausible excuse why you were late."

Grampa sat at the kitchen table, reading a newspaper and staying out of the discussion.

"I said we were sorry. Jesus!"

Gramma's face turned a few shades redder. "That kind of talk is unacceptable in this house. Stephen!" She raised her voice up to get my full attention. "Do you understand?"

I nodded slowly. Anger still roiled around in my belly.

"No TV tonight for either one of you. And, Stephen, you'll do the dishes." She went to the stove, where a pot simmered over a low flame. "Wash your hands and we'll try to have a pleasant meal together, now that we're all finally here."

Dinner was tense at first, all of us eating reheated casserole and overcooked corn on the cob. I didn't know if Gramma expected me to apologize to her again, but I had no intention of saying anything more about it. I sat silent, thinking, Who the hell eats dinner at five o'clock every night? It was ridiculous, especially when it didn't get dark until almost eight. It was rare if we ate dinner before six thirty at our house, and that suited me fine most of the time.

As a mini-protest, I ate as slowly as I possibly could, nibbling at the edges of my chicken casserole and barely touching the corn. I was hungry, but I hoped that when Gramma saw how little I had eaten she would understand it was too early for me to have gained any kind of healthy appetite.

Demian ate his normal small portion, with Gramma gently urging him to eat more.

When I finished doing all the dishes by myself, I peeked my head into the living room. They were watching the news. "I'm done. Gonna go to bed now, I think."

Grampa looked up. "It's not even seven o'clock. I thought maybe we'd do a few sets of curls or work on your shoulders, if you weren't too tired."

"I'm too tired," I lied. I wanted to be alone.

In bed, the sun still bright enough outside the window to fill the room with light, it was too early for me to fall asleep. My head spun, strangely relieved that I had been punished for not following Gramma's demands but also angry that it was a rule I never would have had to follow under my mother's roof. I knew that Gramma would forgive me, but it felt like crap to know that I had upset her, and it was stupid of me not to eat the good food she had fixed for us.

I reached into the bottom of my suitcase and opened my journal. Avoiding the summer goals list, not in the mood for the disappointment that would accompany all of those uncompleted goals, I started a new list of all the foods I ate at home. I wrote down *Breakfast*, underlined it, and on the line below spelled out *Cocoa-Puffs*, *milk*, *donuts*, *leftover pizza*, *chocolate milk*, *candy*, *Pop-Tarts*, and *toast*. I devoted another page to *Lunch*, and a third to *Dinner*, jotting down everything from peanut butter and jelly sandwiches to Flint's barbeque with extra sauce. I recalled as much as I could of the foods I generally ate, adding salad and cooked vegetables, even though they rarely made it to my plate. Then I wrote down all the foods Gramma had given us in the three days we'd been their guests. When my wrist got sore and the sunset began draining light from the room, I stopped writing.

I compared the lists, happy to find certain foods that appeared on both menus, but surprised at how little they matched. All the bread from Gramma was whole wheat or rye, while Wonder Bread was the staple at home. I hadn't downed a single glass or can of soda in the past few days, had eaten more fruit and fresh vegetables than I'd ingested in the past three or four months, and even the sweets Demian and I had been given were sugar-free or naturally sweetened. Even with me consciously choosing the healthier choice at home since I'd started trying to lose weight at the start of summer, the food and the portions that my grandparents served had actually made me feel better than I had since I don't know when. I wasn't feeling bloated or stuffed, and my energy seemed higher, my head a little clearer.

Maybe it was the change of scenery and the break from my usual routine, added to the fact that I was monitored more closely than I had been in who knows how long, that attributed to my physical change. All I knew was that Demian and I weren't looking forward to going back home so soon, not when we were being cared for so well right here.

I COULDN'T FALL ASLEEP. IT WAS only ten o'clock, far earlier than I normally went to bed, and lying in the dark with only the sounds of Demian's tiny snores made me restless.

Out of bed, I moved as quietly as I could down the unlit, narrow hall that led to the living room and kitchen. A light above the stove was on, the only illumination in the entire house. I went straight to the refrigerator, not from hunger but from habit. I stared into the brightness, with the milk and yogurt and vegetables and leftovers in Tupperware all lit up and on display.

A voice from behind me asked, "Didn't get enough dinner, Stephen?"

I slammed the fridge door shut, harder than I intended, and turned to face Gramma. It was dark again, but I could see she was in a big terry cloth robe. I stood in front of her in just a T-shirt and my underpants.

"I'll go to bed," I said, and started to walk back to my room.

"I didn't ... I wasn't trying to embarrass you, Stephen. If you're still hungry, sweetie, then you're still hungry. I realize you didn't eat much tonight."

She had tried to make me feel bad; I could hear it in her voice. It was her first reaction when she was in the presence of something or someone she disapproved of, but she was usually quick to make an attempt to hide it. I chose to see the good in her, despite her short temper and knee-jerk criticism. My mother never did acknowledge all the good things Gramma had done for us, and I didn't think she ever would.

"I know. Thanks." I turned around again, and she placed her hand on my shoulder.

"Sit a minute," she said, and I pulled my shirt down over my underpants. She flipped a switch on the hanging light over the kitchen table. We sat across from each other. "You're a night owl, aren't you? Just like your mother."

"I guess," I said. I looked at the fridge. "I wasn't going to eat anything, I just … I'm really trying to lose some weight this summer."

"Grampa told me how much you like the gift he bought you." She smiled at me, and I wondered if they were her real teeth or dentures. I knew Grampa wore dentures, but I wasn't sure about her. "Any excuse to have you over more often is fine with me."

"I wish Mom still brought us over for dinner on Sundays." I wanted to say more, ask her what had happened, but I knew it was between them.

"I do, too. It would be nice if—"

I couldn't help myself. I blurted, "What happened with you and Mom? Why doesn't she like you?"

Gramma seemed surprised at my outburst. I hadn't meant to say that about her, it had just come out.

"No," she said, recovering from her initial surprise, "your mother does not think too much of me, does she?" She sat with that thought for a while. "It's my fault, although I wish she could forgive me just the teeniest bit."

"What did you do?" I asked, not meeting her eyes.

"I pushed her too hard. That's what I think it was. It was so long ago for me, but for her … She acts as if it happened just the other day." Gramma paused, and I stayed quiet so that she could say more. Because I knew there was more.

"I don't really blame her. I know I've always been strict with her. I think you got a little taste of that tonight." She glanced at me and I looked up at her for just a second. I nodded. "When she got to be a teenager, she wanted to roam, but I wanted her to be safe. I wanted her to stay my little girl. I held on tight, and I lost her.

"She was my only child. Your grandfather and I wanted to give her a brother or sister, but God had his own design on our family. So I cherished the one child God did allow us, and then I smothered her with rules and my own insecurities. It wasn't fair, I know that now, but she made it so … hard, sometimes. So defiant. Which only pulled for my own …." She reached her hands out for mine. I fumbled them in my lap and planted them on the table in front of her. She took them and said, "You asked why she hates me, and it's all those things … adult things … I said and more. But I think your mother never forgives me for the time I struck her."

My mouth went slack. It opened, and I quickly closed it. "You … hit her?" I whispered.

"I did. It's something I will regret for the rest of my life, but … at that moment, I believed that she deserved it." A long time went by before she said another word, and when I looked up, I thought she might be crying. I wasn't sure until she cleared her throat and said, "I was wrong."

We sat there under the bright glare of the lamp and it was just too much for me to stay quiet. "Why did you hit her? What did she do?"

Gramma squeezed my hands, then pulled her arms back to her sides. "She was supposed to have been at the library, studying with her friend Suzy. When she was late, I got worried. I chose to trust that she would be fine, that she simply lost track of time, like you and Demian did today. It got later, and I peeked out the front door every minute or so, expecting her to come walking down the street with an apology in hand. What I saw was a car parked a few houses down from ours. She got out, and I saw a boy, what looked like an older boy, behind the steering wheel. She was only sixteen, and I remember he had facial hair and looked college-age, maybe even older. A *man*. I stood on the porch and waited for her. The car backed up, and when the headlights turned on, she saw me. I remember it so clearly … She stopped and looked behind her, at the man and his car that was now driving away. Then she straightened her body and headed toward me.

"She got to the porch and past me, went right into the house without saying a word. I followed her, of course, into her bedroom. She closed the door on me, but I … confronted her. I told her I was sick that she lied to me, that she was with some man instead of studying with Suzy. She muttered, well … '*Blank* Suzy!' … And it was the first, but not the last, time I was shocked by her language. I asked if she had been necking with him in the car, and she said she had. And that's when I slapped her. Hard. I left a mark that she had to cover with makeup the next day.

"I had never ... I had never done that before. Not to her. Not to anyone. She just made me so angry—her defiance, her independence, it turned me into a violent person for that one brief moment. If I had just apologized, tried to make it better ... Instead, I grounded her for the rest of the school year. She missed her junior prom. Not that I would have let her go anyway. After that, she was never really mine anymore. The day she turned eighteen, she moved out of my house and in with a girlfriend of hers. At least, that's what she told me. Who knows?"

She was silent again, and I think she forgot that I was there for a minute. Then Gramma looked at me. "Does that story ... does that make you hate me too?"

"No," I said.

"I didn't deserve her forgiveness, not for what I did. But I wanted it, even expected it at a certain point. But she's never really forgiven me. Not to this very day. She loves me, I know that. But, yes, Stephen, I believe she hates me too. Both things can be true at the same time."

"Yeah," I said, understanding her exactly, "both things *can* be true."

We sat there for a few more minutes, then she said good night.

Grampa was up early, so Demian and I were too. He sent me into the attic for a small wooden box. When I brought it down, he opened it to reveal a crisply folded American flag, the stars so white my eyes got blurry.

"We may not be the most patriotic folks on the block—that distinction goes to Harv Peterson—but we know when it's respectful to show our loyalty to country." Grampa was going all corny again, like with the bellhop stuff, but when he unfurled the flag, his eyes got far away. Sad.

"Grampa, what's wrong?" Demian asked, tugging at his sleeve.

A nervous laugh escaped Grampa, and he rubbed his hand gently through Demian's hair. "Just remembering, that's all. I don't know how much you boys know about history, and our part in certain wars. I never served in the armed forces, much as it would have pleased me to wear a uniform and do my sworn duty. I was too young for WW two, and by Vietnam I was too darn old. Korea was my one chance, I guess, but your momma was still a little bitty girl then, and leaving her and your grandmother seemed like something I couldn't have lived with. I still get a twinge, though, every time I think about it. So that's what the flag is for, for me doing my small part every Independence Day."

He went to the closet near the front door, moved a rack of coats aside and pulled out a metal pole. "What's Independence Day?" Demian asked.

"Fourth of July," I said. "You know." I turned to Grampa, "He knows." I was embarrassed by Demian, his ignorance about the holiday. It reflected badly on me, somehow, but more than that, it seemed to reflect poorly on Mom. I was still angry that she had left us here without any real warning, but she was my mother and it was my job to protect her from other people thinking negatively about her. I could think rotten things about her, could call her names in my head when she made me feel stupid or sad, but nobody else was allowed to have those thoughts about her. Nobody.

"Why is it called that?" Demian pressed.

Grampa set the pole against the front door, the flag draped over the dining room table. "They don't teach this stuff in school? That *is* disappointing."

He sat us down and gave us a history lesson, and it wasn't so much the words that made me pay special attention—I'd heard most of them before and read about it all in my school books—but the way he said them. There was reverence in his voice, and pride seemed to surge through his entire body when he told us about the battles for freedom, and the founding fathers, and the liberties that we enjoyed that so many other countries in our world were deprived of. He went on for too long, and when Demian's legs couldn't stay still anymore, Grampa finished by saying, "And fireworks!"

The speech had inspired Grampa, and after we held the ladder as he placed the flag above the front door, he drove us to a fireworks stand on the side of a busy road. He bought sparklers and snakes, bottle rockets and smokers, and that night we had our own pre-Independence Day celebration. In the driveway, the sun setting behind us, Gramma sat in a plastic lawn chair while Grampa supervised us. He watched me as I positioned a bottle rocket away from the house and toward the empty street, lighting a match to the wick and stepping back to see how high that sucker could fly. I watched Demian as he carefully struck a match to a sparkler, which he waved around with enthusiasm and something that could only be labeled glee.

When all the fireworks had been lit, Gramma handed us a garbage bag and the garden hose. After cleaning the driveway to her satisfaction, we brushed our teeth, got into our pjs and under the covers.

"Mom and Ken are coming tomorrow," Demian said from his bed next to mine. "I can't wait, I can't wait," he chanted. "Yay!"

I stared at the ceiling, a small knot suddenly balling up in my stomach.

"Yay," I said back.

Chapter 11

The Fourth of July had finally arrived, the bicentennial big deal that been hyped for months now, all over TV and in the newspaper, at the gas stations and even in the stores along Telegraph Avenue. Demian and I had personally bought into the celebratory hype firecracker, bottle rocket and sparkler, even though based on everything I'd been told by Ken, I wasn't sure I was supposed to have pride about being an American, if it meant kids my age in oppressed foreign countries led by CIA-placed dictators had to work in factories at slave wages in order to keep their families from starving to death.

It was Sunday, the day after we'd been picked up from Gramma and Grampa's house. Both Mom and Ken were sleeping in. Demian wasn't in his bed, but I could hear the strains of *The Three Stooges* theme song wah-wahing from the living room. I followed the sound out there, then got myself cereal from the kitchen.

Two hours later, Godzilla rampaged through Tokyo, and our bodies were molded into the sofa. Mom and Ken were dead to the world in their room. The plan for the day had been for us to hang out—something we as a family excelled at—and then around three head across the bridge to Golden Gate Park, where a large fair was going on, with rides and attractions and Fourth of July fun. It was about an hour's drive, but that still left time for us to enjoy a day in The City until it got dark around eight, when the fireworks spectacle would be in explosive bloom.

That was the old plan.

"We're just a little short right now," Mom said around eleven. Mothra was dragging Godzilla around by his huge tail. "Our trip to Santa Cruz cost a bit more than we expected, and that's not your fault, it just means we won't be going to San Fran today. We'll catch some fireworks around here, though. I'll find out where we can see them, and we'll do that tonight, okay? For now, you two can watch as much TV as you want. How's that sound?"

"It's okay, Mom," I said. "We understand." And we did. There was no other choice.

Demian smiled and gave her a thumbs-up. When she had left and we could hear the shower running, Demian curled up into the sofa like a wounded animal. "She promised," his eyes glistened, and all I could do was nod. I focused on the TV, and let the big lizard do my screaming for me.

THE STARRY PLOUGH WAS DECORATED FOR the holiday with red, white, and blue coasters on the tables and plastic, mini American flags hanging from the ceiling. It was five o'clock. The new plan was this: dinner at the pub, a few drinks for Mom and Ken, then off to the Berkeley Marina, where a massive fireworks display awaited us.

Demian and I ate our early dinner in silence, ours the lone family in the place. Only two of the bar stools were filled—a man and woman spoke loudly to each other in a language I didn't recognize. I ate a salad with tuna fish, part of my plan since being at Gramma and Grampa's to eat healthier. Ken had laughed when I ordered it and then tried to pretend he hadn't. I ignored him and even asked for the Italian dressing on the side, something Gramma had said I could do in restaurants.

When the sky darkened outside the big window facing Shattuck, the pub filled up, but the festive atmosphere was completely lost on me. Demian tap-tapped my knee with his fist. He was antsy, like me, to get a seat up close to the fireworks display in the Marina.

I glanced over at Ken and Mom, reminded of that night before the last day of school. They grooved on their bench to the music, both with beers in front of them. Ken's eyes stayed shut as he whispered the words of the song.

"Mom, are you guys almost finished? We need to get to the park. It's almost dark."

Ken opened one eye, looked down at me, muttered, "On the side ..." and then laughed to himself.

Mom took a sip of her beer, which was almost at the bottom of her glass. "One more round, okay?" she asked me, but

I refused to look at her. I saw her hands reach across the table to Demian. She held his limp hands in hers. "Okay, honey?"

I saw him nod from the corner of my eye. She gave his hands a tiny squeeze before releasing them. When I looked up, Ken was already on his feet. "More sodas for the boys too," she told him.

I had a glass of water in front of me, and Demian was drinking apple juice. He started to say something, but I put a gentle hand on his leg. I shook my head slowly when he met my eye.

A half hour later, they were on their second last round, and Ken was in the middle of a story I couldn't really follow. I knew Mom had no intention of going anywhere, for fireworks or anything else, that night. My brother and I silently stewed.

Until the song came on.

It was a song I had heard on the radio a lot that summer. It was a Chicago tune, and when they started singing about the park and Saturday and the Fourth of July, I lost it.

"This sucks!" I didn't know I was yelling until the words had shot out of my mouth.

"Whoa," Ken said, "what's the disaster here?"

"Like you don't know," I said, staring into reddened eyes that had trouble focusing on me. I turned to Mom, "Let's go, Mom. We're gonna miss the fireworks!"

"You challenging me, Daedalus?" Ken was drunk.

"That's not my name, *Kenneth*, and you know it." My fists were balled up under the table. I could hear my voice shaking, my throat so tight it hurt.

He put his beer down hard, wobbling as he sat up straight. "You need to respect me, little boy."

"The fuck I do," I said under my breath. But they both heard it.

"Hey!" my mother said.

Ken snarled, "What'd you say?" A second later he was on his feet, his face flushed with a combination of alcohol and anger. I had seen hints of his temper but never quite like this. Mom noticed it, too, because she stood up right away. "Ken, sit down." He didn't move. She put a steady hand on his shoulder. "Sit down. I'll talk to him."

Ken tried to stare me down, and I blinked first. He shook his head like a dog after a bath, then headed to the bar, almost tripping over the long bench.

Mom leaned over the table, her face inches from mine. Her voice was as steady as her hand had been. "What do you think you're doing?"

"What do you mean?" I held her gaze. Demian trembled beside me.

She gave me that sideways glance, the one that said, *You think I'm stupid?* The one she used when I thought I was pulling one over on her, and she didn't have the patience to tolerate it. "What am I supposed to do with you when you pull this nonsense?"

Take my side, I wanted to say. I kept silent until she sat back down and finished off the puddle of beer in her mug.

"Demian and I want to see the fireworks," I concentrated on not raising my voice. Mom turned her body toward the bar, where Ken fished out his wallet and slapped a bill down.

As Ken waltzed back to us, Demian fidgeted beside me. "I really want to go," he said, and I thought there would be no way she could refuse him.

"Then go," she said.

I looked at my brother, both of us not sure what she meant. We turned to her, waiting for more. The Chicago song ended, and Martha and the Vandellas sang that we'd be dancing in the street.

Ken slid a fresh mug in front of Mom, and she laced her fingers around it. "You want to see the fireworks, then go. You're both old enough to make that kind of decision for yourselves."

We are? I thought. I stared at her so hard my sight began to blur. She had promised us one thing, taken it away, and then promised something else. And now she was taking that back, too.

My body moved before I knew what it was doing, and I was up, peering down at Demian's blond head. "Come on," I said, and he got to his feet right away. There was no hesitation, and I was surprised to find him standing next to me, ready to leave the bar without them.

"We'll see you at home," Mom said. "Have fun."

I wanted to cry. I wanted my mommy. But she was nowhere to be found.

Demian waved at them as I led him out of the pub.

The Marina was too far for us to go without a car, but I knew we could see the fireworks from Indian Rock Park, which was a lot closer. We ran home, grabbed my bike, and got to the park just before the sun went down. My brother and I watched the fireworks among a throng of Berkeley families, the crowd politely cheering when the grand finale of explosions ended. I was celebrating the birth of my country, while simultaneously mourning the death of my childhood, ambivalent about all this new freedom I'd been given. I had too many big ideas in my head that I couldn't get a firm grasp on, lost in wondering about what responsibilities now belonged solely to me, and if I had the right to ask any questions or if I was supposed to just know it all by now. I imagined myself as an old man, with a long beard and my head almost reaching the ceiling of our house. At a round table in the kitchen, Mom and Ken sat with Demian. They were as small as he was, maybe even smaller. I served them all dinner, bellowing down at them, "Make sure to eat all your vegetables, and do all your homework before bed." Ken cried, and suddenly he was a baby, demanding that I change his diaper. Then Mom and Demian also became babies, and they began crying with Ken. My head brushed the top of the ceiling before bursting all the way through it. Once the top half of my body was completely through the roof, I stomped on the three babies below me. Crushed to death, they all stopped crying. I shoved myself through the rest of the house and ran down the street, growing taller and higher until I couldn't see anything in front of me but stars.

As we walked down the dirt path to the street, skidding in the dark, I asked Demian what he thought about the light show.

"The fireworks at Gramma and Grampa's were more fun," he said. And I knew exactly what he meant.

STILL ANGRY FROM THE NIGHT BEFORE, I got dressed early on Monday. When I heard Mom leave for work, I dragged our velvet-covered footstool from the living room onto the front porch. A block of shadow reached from the middle of the street to beyond my porch, but I could feel heat settling down on me from above. The bright glare of the sun climbed the back of Mrs. Hunter's house, peeking over the roof at me. I turned away from the glare and counted pot-holes in the street until the red, blinking spots faded from my eyes.

From the house at the end of the block, Mr. Takadakos, our landlord, limped down his steps and headed toward me. Only a little taller than me, he wore brown pants that sagged at the waist and cuffs. He pulled them up as he walked, his lips moving like he was talking to himself. He wasn't particularly big or scary, just really old, and old people (with the exception of my own grandparents) made me uneasy. His wife had passed about half a year earlier, and while he had always been a grouch—he even had the same bushy eyebrows as Oscar from *Sesame Street*—he seemed to get more cantankerous as the months of his loneliness rolled along.

"I don't like this," he muttered to himself as he approached our walkway. He stared at the lawn, yellowed and bare to hard dirt in places. Finally, he adjusted his gaze slightly upward and stared at me as if I were some crab grass sullying his property. I picked up Demian's discarded Slinky from the ground and moved it back and forth between my palms, hoping somehow it would make him go away.

"You live here, you need to take care of the lawn. *You* are responsible for the upkeep. Look at it. Dead!" He seemed to get angrier with every syllable, and I knew I couldn't handle him alone.

I yelled inside the open door, "Ken!" I wasn't sure if he was awake or asleep, but I hoped he was within earshot. When he didn't appear at the door within a minute, both the landlord and I staring at the door as if we were waiting for a magic trick to reveal itself, I excused myself.

Ken was asleep, alone in their bedroom. The room smelled like cigarettes and burnt candles, and he lay in the middle of the bed, his mouth open. Snoring. "Ken," I shoved his back. It was one of the few times I had ever touched him. He felt even more solid than he looked.

He craned his neck around, as if he had no idea where he was. "Landlord." I jutted my thumb toward the front door, then got out of there.

Ken came outside a few minutes later in his dingy blue cutoffs, shoving his head like a turtle through the neck of a stained white tee. I stood off to the side, wondering how he'd handle the old guy.

"Mr. Takadakos," he started, all his teeth showing, "nice to see you. How was your Fourth?"

"You owe rent." The old guy walked closer, and waved his hand at the lawn. "And you need to take care of this lawn. Look at it."

"Yeah, I tell the kids to water it—even pay them to do it—but you know kids." Ken chucked a thumb behind him at me on the porch."

"It's the fifth of the month, and I have no check for the rent. I am tired of always asking for it, for it always being late."

"You're right. One hundred percent, and I'm sorry you even had to come over here for it. Truly, an apology is in order." He spread his arms out, and for a second I thought he was going to bow. When Mr. Takadakos roughly crossed his dark, hairy arms over his chest, Ken said, "Rose is gonna write you a check, soon as she gets home. She's at work, working hard. She works, works, works to pay the bills, and rent, of course."

"You bring it over. Tonight." He stood there a moment, squinting as if he was trying to read Ken's mind. He uncrossed his arms and slowly limped away, back to his house. "And take care of the lawn!"

Ken waved to him, "You have a good day now, Mr. Takadakos." Ken trudged up the walk toward me. "If you feel so inclined during your *busy* summer days, take a hose to this fire hazard and help me keep that old fuck off our backs."

He passed me, and I didn't bother giving him an answer. I heard Demian's voice—"Good morning"—and a "Hey, small fry" from Ken. Then Demian was on the porch, looking bored and full of energy at the same time. From my spot on the porch, I could see Ken plop himself down at the living room coffee table and crack open a book.

I left Demian standing there, eyeing me like he was waiting for direction, and went back into the house and our room.

Five dollars and two handfuls' worth of change sat next to my underwear in the dresser. I scooped it up, passed Ken without a word, and lightly punched Demian on the arm as I continued toward the street. "Come on, let's go somewhere."

WE WALKED UNTIL WE GOT TIRED, in front of a bus stop on Shattuck and Carleton Street. I sat down next to a crumpled, pored-over *Chronicle* and reached for the Datebook section. A skinny piece of paper fluttered out of the folded pile of news.

"Oh, wow," Demian said as he reached down to pick it up. "A transfer."

"Cool. That's worth, like, twenty-five cents," I said.

"Remember when I found that five dollars?" He wriggled around on the bench. "'Member, Steve? This is just like that. Huh?"

"You're a lucky kid."

"Yeah. Lucky. That's me."

"Wanna see a movie?" I hovered over the movie ads, for *The Omen* and *Silent Movie*, before settling on the theater listings. "What about *Midway*? The TV commercials look kinda good. Lots of explosions and stuff."

"I guess," Demian said, still enraptured with his rare find. "This is good till twelve o'clock noon."

"It's playing at the Rialto," I said, more to myself than to him as I scanned the paper. "But that place sucks. You can always hear the movie playing right next door to yours. Hey, it's at the Oaks. We catch the 18, it'll take us over to Solano."

"And I can use the transfer!" Demian yelled.

Thirty minutes later, the bus entered the Northbrae Tunnel, and I imagined that we had been swallowed up into the stomach of some great beast. When we reached the other side, I experienced pretend relief as we were spat out, like Jonah or Pinocchio. Above the city of Albany now, the bus stopped in front of the movie theater, the street slanty and steep. I stared at the movie posters behind glass, wondering how one of them would look on my bare bedroom wall, how exactly I could get hold of one, and if I should use thumbtacks or tape to hold it up.

Demian wandered over to the box office, a squat booth much like the one outside the UC Theatre, where a few weeks earlier Ken had gotten into it with the ticket guy, and we had watched two people having sex on each other in a Paris apartment. I got a little memory chill, like mental goose bumps, but shrugged it off when I noticed our movie was about to start. A woman in her fifties, at least, sat reading a magazine inside the booth. I joined my brother at the glass window and pulled out my five-dollar bill.

"Two for *Midway*, please," I said, "for the twelve o'clock show."

I held out the money, but her hands didn't move from the magazine. "Are your parents with you?"

Why would our parents be with us? It was the middle of a Monday, a work day. Demian and I were the only ones standing in front of her. I shook my head at her, tried to give her the bill again.

"It's rated PG, son, parental guidance. You can't get in without an adult." She gave me a pathetic little 'sorry' shrug.

I suddenly got really angry.

"Parental guidance *suggested*," I corrected her. "*Suggested*!" I said again, my voice raised for effect.

"Sorry, it's just too violent. Come back with your parents, okay?"

My throat closed up, and heat flooded through my face. It was hard to speak. "That's … that's not okay. We see PG movies all the time."

She closed the magazine and clasped her hands together, which exposed her age spots, and gave me a look that seemed genuinely sorry now. But it was too late. I wanted to see *Midway*, and I intended to see it right then and there. "We've already seen *Patton*. And *Taxi Driver* too!"

The old hands moved to her chin. She looked like Gramma then, genuine concern and care in her expression. "Well, that makes me sad. Those movies are completely inappropriate for boys your age."

I stared at that face, full of compassion, and knew that she was right.

"Fuck you, you fucking bitch!" I grabbed Demian's hand, my whole body trembling now, and led him away from the box office and down Solano Avenue. I shoved the money back in my pocket and felt dizzy. I stopped in front of the pizza place two doors down from the theater and let go of my brother's hand.

"You okay?" Demian asked, and the anger built and built until my eyes were crammed with tears. I fought to keep them from escaping. When I slapped my palm against the brick wall a few times, flecks of red scratched it raw. Scowling at my hand, I wondered if this was what the inside of me looked like, scraped up and slightly bloody. I kicked the wall, mad at it as if it had hit me, and my mouth burst open with sounds like hiccups. My body seemed to fall out from under me, and I crumpled to the sidewalk, crying until my jaw hurt and my face was wet. I forgot where I was, with no awareness that Demian was next to me, and gave myself completely to the feelings that had been building up, rising against a dam until the pressure was too great. Something inside me exploded, and along with all the sadness, there was also a sensation of relief. It was like I was a balloon, blown up so big there was no more room for any more air, until someone went and stuck a pump in the small opening and forced in some more. Then it, *I*, popped, with all the air transformed into tears.

The crying stopped once I'd run out of energy, which left me exhausted and without any breath. I opened my eyes to Demian kneeling over me, his hand stroking my shoulder like I was a cat. He whispered, "It's okay, it's okay. Don't cry, it's okay." I rubbed the wetness from my face and saw that Demian was scared; he blinked rapidly, and his heels batted against each other like Dorothy and her ruby slippers.

I used the wall to push myself up. "It's over, Demian." I forced out a smile, to give him the impression that maybe I had been joking around, that it was all a silly little show I had put on. My smile faded, then I gently lifted his bangs away from his face and said, "I'm sorry."

He wiped some moisture from his own eyes and stopped knocking his feet together. I looked for something to say. Something to do. To make us both normal again. To make him feel safe.

Past his ear, a smudge of sand flecks clinging to that hollow space, I saw a metal rack stacked with paperback books. "You want to go to the book store? Then some ice cream at Ortman's?"

He nodded, so I led him down the street, both of us staring at the ground. There was old, blackened gum that looked like tar imbedded in the concrete sidewalk, and as we approached a huge window filled with hardcovers and textbooks, I stepped on cigarette butts scattered like birdseed. Before we reached the blue doors—one wide open, the other closed—I glanced at Demian. He was walking toe to heel along a crack that had started at the curb and weaved itself up to the bookstore threshold.

Inside, Demian and I gave friendly hi's to the bearded old guy at the counter and then to the younger guy—this mass of hair and tie-dye—shelving books near the front door. A few customers roamed the aisles, walking on a linoleum floor of ugly cream-colored squares that were occasionally interrupted by faux-marble gray-and-black squares. A pregnant woman with a baby carriage next to her and a golden retriever at her feet leafed through a book of black-and-white photographs. Demian wanted to go to the kids' section, for Charlie Brown books. Near the back of the store were the fiction paperbacks. We split up, and he scavenged through the comic-strip books while I searched for more Jack London.

They didn't have any used copies of my favorite author's adventure tales, just new ones. Two of them had cover prices over eight dollars. I pulled out my wrinkled, pathetic bill. Abe Lincoln stared through me, bored or maybe indifferent to my financial plight. I had a little over a dollar in change, but that still wouldn't buy me what I wanted.

Demian bounded up to me, a coffee table Peanuts book in hand, his cheeks flushed. "Steve, look." He flipped through the pages—Linus, Snoopy, and the rest of the gang flashed by so quickly that my eyes were unable to focus on even a single panel. "This has got, like, *all* of them."

"How much?" I asked, my voice flat, but my anger rising again.

The dog with the pregnant lady barked suddenly, and we both looked in her direction. "Umm …" Demian thumbed his way back to the first, blank, page, where a pencil mark covered the upper corner. "Fourteen dollars?"

"Too much. We don't have it."

"That's a lot," he said, softly, letting the book collapse to his side, head down as he shuffled back to the children's books. "I was hoping it would be just a little." I stared at his small, fragile back, feeling his disappointment.

I spent a few more minutes in my own section of the store, and when I saw Demian wander toward a table of new books, I knew what I had to do.

Less than three minutes later, I stood next to my brother as he pawed through a huge cookbook with as much interest as the face on my five-dollar bill had given me. "Let's go, this is lame," I said, making a beeline for the exit.

I had made sure the old guy at the front of the store wasn't near the open glass door before I casually sauntered out, my eyes on the faded peach linoleum floor.

"Hey, kid!" I heard the old man behind me, but I picked up my step and fast-walked to the door.

"Stop that one," he shouted, but I was already outside, escaping down the sidewalk toward the corner. The sun was hot and brighter than I ever remember it being, and I squinted as I turned my head to say something to Demian. But he wasn't there. He wasn't there, running behind me.

I stopped, shielded my eyes, and looked up the street. The old guy, standing next to the mass of hair in a tie-dyed Cal T-shirt, held on to the back of Demian's shirt. My brother's tiny face scrunched up, staring at me. His mouth opened wide, but no words came out. Instead, sobs tore out of him. The old guy glanced at my brother, then pointed at me. Crooked his finger for me to come, like a dog.

Inside the store, behind the counter, all four of us sat. Demian had fortunately stopped crying, and the old guy, the owner of the store, held three paperbacks, all with Charlie Brown on their bright-colored covers, in his hands.

"You honestly believed you could steal from me, you little shit? You see those mirrors?" he pointed at the back of the store, but I didn't turn to look. I knew they were there, but never once did it cross my mind that he could actually see me stashing the books down my pants. "They're for making sure I don't get robbed blind."

For some reason, I wasn't scared or intimidated by the way he talked to me. I was calm, knew I'd probably go to jail. But I didn't care. When his assistant, the hair guy, clucked, "That was a real low-class move, you two," I stared through him.

"I should call the cops on you little thieves, so they can throw you in a cage downtown. But I'm gonna call your parents, let them sort this out." He picked up a phone on the counter and I saw his knuckles go from red to pinched white. "What's your number?"

When he finished dialing, I said, "Good luck getting a hold of anyone." Mom was still at work, and Ken was probably listening to his music with the headphones on or out doing whatever he did when he wasn't at home.

"Hello?" the old guy said into the phone. "Yeah, I've got your two boys down here at Mahar Books." He paused, listening. "Yeah, we sell a lot of copies of that here. Look, um ..." He looked at us. "What are your names?"

I didn't want to tell him our real names, then realized I had given him our real phone number, instead of a fake one.

"Steve and Demian, they stole some books. Can you come down here and settle it? I really don't want to bring the cops into this." The old guy listened, his face suddenly disfigured as if the person on the other end of the phone was saying something crazy. Then he said, "Okay, thirty minutes then."

He turned to us. "Your dad is coming. You can just stay back here until he arrives and think about what you've done."

He reminded me of a substitute teacher I'd had in third grade for a week when Mrs. Lee had been sick. I remember one day he made the entire class sit at our desks and think about all the mistakes we'd made in our lives, what we'd done to disappoint those around us. We were eight!

"He's not our dad," I said, not sure why I was correcting him. "Boyfriend."

"Yeah," he said. "That makes sense." He made a strange face again, then turned back to the counter where he grabbed a stubby pencil and began writing prices into the first page of a small pile of books.

"FIRST I GOTTA DEAL WITH MR. TAKADAKOS, then drive all the way out to Albany for this crap. You ever think about me being inconvenienced in all this? You ever think about that, Steve?"

Demian and I sat in the backseat of Ken's Rambler, the car radio playing the Grateful Dead. "I dunno," I said, looking out the window as we entered the tunnel and headed back to the house.

"You dunno? You haven't come off my shit list yet, after what you did last night at the pub. That was seriously uncool, man, disrespecting me in there like that. That's still a conversation we need to have. But not with Demian here."

"Why not?" Demian said, sitting up straight in his seat, tugging self-consciously at the lap belt I had forced him to wear.

Ken caught his glance through the rear-view mirror. "'Cause you didn't do nothing wrong. Your brother's the one seriously out of line."

"What'd you do wrong?" he asked me, but I shushed him.

Ken tried to catch my eye in the mirror, but I focused all my attention on the world passing outside my window. Every little bounce, each bit of force that was generated by Ken's car meeting the road, shuddered through my body. He constantly raged about having to get his shocks replaced, as if some malevolent force had placed a hex on his shitty car, but he never did. I'm sure he reasoned that if it wasn't his fault for the car not working properly, then it wasn't really up to him to solve the problem. Living with him, day after day, I learned how effectively rationalizations can serve you when your sole intention is to avoid responsibility and blame.

We passed Live Oak Park, and I wished we had just gone there for the day instead. But I was ready for some punishment, primed to be grounded or at least chewed out some. I knew what I'd done was stupid, made me look like a crook. Worse, it made me look like a poor jerk who couldn't afford a few kids' books.

As if reading my mind, Ken barked, "And if you're gonna steal a little of the merchandise, pinch something that's worth getting caught over. Make sure it's rare, or expensive at least. Can't you just read that stuff in the funnies, you gotta read a book of that junk?"

"It's not junk," I said, not sure if he could hear me over the lame music. "It was for Demian."

"Anyway, your mom'll deal with this when she gets home."

Demian sat up straighter. "Don't tell her! Please."

"It's okay, you didn't do anything," I shook my head at him. "It's all me."

"Hey, being a fuck-up is nothing to be proud of," Ken said, lighting a cigarette while he steered with his legs.

I wanted to punch him in the back of the head, make him run the car onto the sidewalk or into a tree. Instead, I whipped ninja throwing stars at him from my eyes and said, "I'm not a fuck-up, Ken."

"Well," he said, as he chucked a lit match out the car window, "that's news to me."

AT HOME, KEN WENT BACK TO his book without bothering to say anything more. Mom wouldn't walk through the front door for at least four more hours. I knew that Ken had no intention of keeping me inside the house all that time—he planned to leave any punishment to her—but still I didn't venture outside.

"Is it okay if I go over to Rafe's?" Demian asked me when we were both in the bedroom.

"Yeah, go." He didn't move. "You're not gonna get in trouble, Dem. It was my fault. I shouldn't have done it."

He wrestled with a booger inside of his nose, digging around with his finger as he said, "Why are you mad all the time now?"

"Am I?"

He pulled out something small and hard, then wiped it on his jeans. His head bobbed up and down.

"Well … I'm not mad at you," I said.

"If you want, I'll be mad too." He contorted his face into something that resembled anger. He had trouble pulling it off.

"No, don't be mad. Be happy. Like Richie Cunningham. Or J.J." They were from two of his favorite shows, *Happy Days* and *Good Times*, and I could tell it cheered him up to think about them.

"And you can be cool, like the Fonz. And like …" he paused, thinking on it.

"Like J. J.'s mom," I said, and he laughed with all his teeth showing. I pulled a *MAD Magazine* from a pile of stuff on my bed and waved at him with it. "Go to Rafe's. I'm just gonna read."

"I think this is gonna finally gonna come out," Demian poked his front tooth with his finger. I could see it move back and forth in his gums like a swinging door. "Tonight, I think! Or maybe tomorrow. Or the day after that. Hopefully not the day after that day, though. No."

"Smell you later," I said, kicking off my shoes in his direction.

I hopped up onto my bedcovers, and he closed the door behind him. After reading a few pages, I dropped the book to the floor, got under my covers fully dressed, and fell asleep.

I CONSIDERED MAKING A SALAD OR fixing dinner for everyone from whatever I could scrounge up in the fridge or from inside the cupboards, hoping to somehow lessen whatever punishment I was in store for when Mom got home. I had never stolen before, or at least never gotten caught at it, so anything was possible as far as TV restrictions, my allowance, or access to my bike. She didn't as a rule hand out much in the way of punishments, but I had missed out on favorite shows for particularly mediocre report cards and neglecting certain chores she'd assigned.

It was difficult for me to remember the last time she had really laid down the law for bad behavior, from either Demian or me. In fact, there had been little more than a glance of mild curiosity at my report cards for over a year, ever since my brother started kindergarten, and the chores usually went undone without a word of warning or otherwise.

Realizing that whatever disciplinary action Mom could muster would probably be manageable, I forgot about food prep and instead watched TV in the living room with Demian until she came home from work around six. She gave us a tired hello and went straight to her bedroom. Ken was in there, the only reason we were camped out in front of the TV, and I figured he'd tell her what had happened.

Fifteen minutes later she joined us, her work clothes replaced by a summer dress that looked almost like a nightie. Ken followed behind in a pair of cut-offs, his chest and feet bare. "Hey, you boys wanna turn the boob tube off? Your mom needs to talk with you."

She didn't look pissed, just exhausted. I turned the TV off, and back on the couch Demian sat close to me.

"Ken told me what happened today, but I want to hear it from you two." She sat in the chair facing us, and just as I began to tell her the story, I noticed the bottle of lotion in her lap. It was from the Body Shop on Telegraph, and I could see the label, then I could smell it: cocoa-butter cream. Ken wandered into the kitchen, and Mom squirted yellow cream into her hands before rubbing it into her ankle, then up along her leg to the thigh.

I was distracted, trying not to look at her hands caressing her shaven legs, so white they looked like warm milk. Reminded of the night after the movie, a vivid picture forming that I wasn't sure belonged inside my head, I found a spot of wall behind her head and spoke to that. "So we tried to go see a movie at the Oaks Theater, but they wouldn't let us in because of the rating, so—"

"What movie?" she asked, head down, hands focused on all that rubbing.

I told her. Even though my eyes stayed planted above her, I could still see what she was doing. Her hands just rubbing and rubbing.

"It was rated what?" She had moved on to the other leg.

"PG. Parental guidance *suggested*," I said.

Ken came back into the room with two bottles of beer in his hand. Mom took the one offered, and he sat cross-legged beside her chair. He reached his arm out and touched her shiny leg. His fingers gently tapped her calf, as if he was playing chords on a guitar.

"How was the movie?" Ken asked.

I stared at his stubble-ridden face, glad to take my eyes off the wall, and said, "We didn't see it."

"You didn't listen," Demian said to him, and I wished he hadn't.

"I was in the other room," he said to Demian, then held out the neck of the beer bottle for me to see, foreign writing all over the damp label. "Getting something from the fridge that *I* actually paid for."

"Stephen. Tell me what happened in the bookstore," she said.

I could look at her now, the lotion put away, her legs crossed at the ankles, and her face very Mom-like at the moment. I dictated the events in the store as plainly as I could, without defending my actions, sure to exclude Demian from anything I'd done. When I finished, she sat back and took a sip of her beer. Her eyes traveled over me and then Demian. I wanted that moment to last, not because I was afraid of her punishment, but because the attention was nice. I felt connected to her then, like I had been once before.

"Well, I think you've learned your lesson today. I'm thankful he called Ken instead of the cops. None of us needs that kind of headache. Just try not to do it again, okay, Stephen?"

And then she was finished.

The talk turned to dinner. She was too bushed to throw anything together, and Ken had a sudden craving for flautas. As they got dressed to go out for Mexican food, I sat on the couch, stunned. Even Demian looked at me, surprised. I didn't expect much, but I was prepared for some kind—any kind—of penance.

When he spread his lips wide at me and tapped excitedly on my knee, muttering, "Cool," I turned and stormed off into our bedroom. I was convinced that whatever I did from now on—good or bad—would be ignored by everyone. I was afraid that if I was never punished for my behavior, I would never be rewarded for it, either. So why did any of it even matter?

LATER, AFTER THEY HAD GORGED THEMSELVES on burritos, flautas, chips, and sweet-spicy salsa—I ate a small salad, still on my diet but mostly because I was too out of it to rouse an appetite—we watched Johnny Carson. Demian had already fallen asleep on the couch, and I struggled to understand why the monologue was so funny to that invisible audience who laughed every three seconds. I was ready for bed. After I helped Demian out of his jeans and under the covers, I went to brush my teeth.

The TV in the living room was off, and Ken and Mom had moved to the bathroom. I suddenly had to pee, so I waited outside the door, trying to hold it while the faucet ran and they talked.

"—just show the old guy some tit," I heard Ken say. "He'll back off the rent, and then we'll scrape it together."

"If you'd get a job, he wouldn't be bothering us again." Her voice was tired but firm.

"I'm gonna be flush soon, it's just a rough market out there right now. You know that, babe." I heard what sounded like Ken brushing his teeth, then a loud spit. The water stopped running. "I'll find something, and then we'll have enough to get a place even better than this one."

"I don't want to move. I just want you to—"

"With his wife gone, he's probably horny. And lonely. Just give him some ... just a little ... I know he'll kick some more rent off." The toilet flushed, and then the faucet started up again. When the water stopped, I thought they were finally finished in there. My bladder was full, and I was ready to barge in when Ken spoke again. "It worked out all right last month." Ken's voice was calm. Gentle. "Right?"

My mother's voice suddenly sounded exhausted. "You've got to stop buying so much grass. And find a job, Ken, I'm serious."

"Consider it done."

"I'm going to bed," she said. She walked out into the hall and looked surprised to see me there.

"Gotta pee," I said, holding my crotch with both hands to help give the impression that I wasn't eavesdropping on them. "Bad."

She said good night, and once Ken traipsed out of the bathroom, without a look or a word for me, I ran inside and did my business. As I brushed my teeth, fragments of their conversation swirled around in my brain, and I tried to make some kind of sense out of it.

In my room, the lights out and Demian already asleep, I lay in bed as my eyes adjusted to the darkness. I hadn't understood exactly what Ken and Mom had been talking about, but the feeling I had was that it was dirty and rotten. I couldn't sleep. When I did finally close my eyes, I saw Mr. Takadakos driving his car down a deserted road. My mother snuggled up against him in the front seat, naked from the waist up. The car pulled over, and our landlord began massaging her chest, calling her "Ava," the name of his dead wife. While he unbuckled his old man trousers and got on top of her, Ken sat up in the back seat, chanting, "Do it, do it, do it. Pay that rent. Pay that rent."

For the first time since I was Demian's age, I woke up crying.

Chapter 12

SENECA WAS BACK. FINALLY. I WAS convinced she would never come back from Seattle, or if she did, that she wouldn't bother to call me again. I figured she eventually came to her senses and understood that showing me any kind of encouragement beyond simple friendship had been a stupid idea. Especially after seeing me with my face full of banana split. But no, she called. And I was home to answer the phone.

The phone call was short but to the point. We'd spend some time together, the next day. I offered to pick her up, either walk to her house to get her or bike her around with me. She thought it was better to meet somewhere, something about her dad being home and not thrilled about her doing anything like "dating" yet. Yes, this was a date! She mentioned Edy's, a diner on Shattuck, and I agreed without hesitation.

It was only after I'd hung up that I tried to figure out how I was going to afford lunch for both of us, with a chocolate shake or something for dessert. After the conversation

I'd overheard a few nights back, about how broke my Mom and Ken were that she might have to have sex with old Mr. Takadakos, I'd given up my allowance the next day when she brought it to me and Demian. He looked at me like I'd lost my very mind, and there was no way I could tell him why I was doing it. He took his dollar from Mom without argument, and I wondered if he still had it.

I spent most of the morning figuring out ways to pay for the date. There were books in my closet I thought I could sell to Moe's for a few bucks; comics that wouldn't hurt too badly if I got rid of them; a search under the couch cushions and around the house for loose change and abandoned paper money could be fruitful; offering myself up to do a few chores for Mrs. Dillon, who lived across the street, might get me the money I needed; or hitting Demian up for the piddly few bucks I knew he had in his piggy bank could be a solution.

I piled up a stack of books and comics, rifled through the furniture in the living room without success, knocked on Mrs. Dillon's door to find she wasn't home, then finally decided I'd ask my brother for the cash. He gave it to me that night, with very little resistance, probably because I told him that as soon as his tooth came out the Tooth Fairy was going to relinquish some cash of her own. I promised to pay back the twelve bucks and change as soon as I could. It was more money than I expected to spend on my date with Seneca, and I wasn't sure how borrowing Demian's stash helped Mom with the rent money, but when I took it, a confidence surge ripped through me. If I could pay for a date, then maybe I could deserve to have her as my girlfriend. I knew from movies and TV that girls loved for guys to buy them things and take them places. They liked pretty things and fancy places, and Edy's was a good start. I would worry about buying her jewelry some other time.

I walked along Shattuck Avenue the next day, self-conscious about the clothes I wore, afraid that the late morning sun would turn me into a sweaty mess before I reached the diner. The thirty-minute trip gave me time to relax and then worry, to run scenarios in my head about Seneca becoming my girlfriend, followed by alternate versions where she broke up with me before our first kiss. Then I worried about kissing her, the first kiss with a girl I really liked. I had kissed a few girls before, but they had been on dares at parties, and I always felt small and stupid after it was over, like it had meant so much more to me than it had to them.

Outside the restaurant, I checked my watch and saw that I had time to cross the street to the library and use the bathroom. I never considered using the one inside the restaurant, not willing to chance Seneca seeing me exiting the men's room and suffering the shame of her knowing that I had just peed in there. Or worse. So I ran into the main branch of one of my favorite haunts and checked myself out in the mirror. My hair was too long and unkempt, my cheeks too plump, and my neck flesh too gross, but it was as good as I was going to get.

Inside Edy's, I approached the hostess podium and waited. A woman older than my mother, with her blonde hair wrapped in a bun and wearing a black-and-white checkered uniform, winked at me from a few tables over. When she finished taking an order, she bustled over to the podium and gave me her full attention.

"Hey, sweetie, what can I do you for?" It was a little before 11:30, and the place was already more than half full. But she didn't rush me or make me feel unimportant. I liked her right away.

I stumbled but finally got it out that I wanted a table for two. She scooped up two laminated menus and asked, "This something special, or maybe just lunch with your mom?"

"Something special," I muttered, and she looked behind me.

"Well, how about I seat you now, find you a nice little table, and I'll keep an eye out for—what's her name?" She led me to one of the red leather booths by the window and not too close to the kitchen.

"Seneca."

"Beautiful name. And I'm sure she's a beautiful girl." She made a ceremonial little bow, ushered me into the booth, and then placed the two menus at its edge. "This is our best table in the house, reserved for young men who arrive early to meet their girl."

She left me alone there, and I let the phrase *my girl* roll around in my head for a little while. Seneca entered the restaurant a few minutes later. I watched the blonde waitress excuse herself from a table and intercept Seneca. She wore a flower-pattern dress, with bows in her hair, and she looked nervous, which I was happy about; I tried to calm my own twitching, roiling stomach.

The first few minutes were awkward but amazing, and by the time we were halfway through our lunch, it was like we were back in the classroom. That easygoing, casual way we had with each other was back, as if it had been a day, instead of so many long weeks, since we were together. She told me about her trip to Seattle, where her mom was, which she said was wonderful and sad. When we got on the subject of books, I told her all about Jack London, and she went on about Louisa May Alcott and Laura Ingalls Wilder.

We had hardly touched our sandwiches, but when our waitress asked us about dessert, I consciously avoided the ice cream, especially the banana split. I asked what her favorite pie was, and she told me. It was, simply, the best piece of apple pie I had ever eaten. When the bill came, we had our first official fight.

"Ix-nay, Eneca-say," I said when she pulled out her money purse.

"Stephen, I brought money so I could—"

"Nope. Not happening." I put my hand over the bill, and she tried to pull my fingers off it.

She was laughing when she said, "Let me just pay for half."

I covered her hand with my free one, and stared at her wide, liquid-blue eyes. "Nuh … uh!"

I released her hand and went to the counter, waving the bill at her in victory as she sat in the booth with a fake pouty look on her face. After tipping big—I did the math in my head for 20 percent of the check, which my grandfather had told me once was "a generous token of appreciation for fine service"—we went outside and into the summer heat of the afternoon. She suggested we go across the street to the library, and I caught myself before I accidentally blurted, "Hey, I went to their bathroom right before lunch!" We moved through the fiction stacks, where I let my fingers tap the spines of novels by Doctorow, Oates, Roth, and Updike: all authors whose books took up space on Mom and Ken's shelves at home that I hoped to someday feel old enough to read. In the A/V room, we looked at the comedy albums her dad played for her—Bill Cosby, Bob Newhart and George Carlin—and made fun of the opera records and Pat Boone collection.

Seneca showed me an album cover with a picture of Anita Bryant wearing a big floppy hat. "Isn't that the orange juice lady?"

"Yeah, I think so. My mom hates her," I said, and then poked Anita in the eye with my thumb.

"Why?"

"I don't know. Maybe she doesn't like that orange juice," I said.

We left the library with books in hand: I had a copy of the Jack London stories that my Pepsi fiasco had ruined, as well as *Little House on the Prairie*, which Seneca told me was her most favorite book in the whole world. She left with a book on Brussels and Steinbeck's *The Red Pony* that I suggested, a book I couldn't believe she had never read.

It felt like the natural conclusion of our date when we left the library and crossed the street back to the diner, where we had begun. But I didn't want it to be over just yet. I offered to walk her home, over on Ellsworth a few blocks from our school, and she said sure. Afraid her dad or one of the neighbors he had asked to keep an eye on her might see us together, she told me I could only walk her as far as the corner of Blake Street.

At her block, she stopped, and her eyes shined at me. "Thanks very much, Steve. For lunch, the pie …" She searched my face for more to say, "… The walk."

"Uh-huh," I said stupidly, not blinking as we stood there face to face.

"So …" she said, crossing one leg over the other and tapping her big toe on the hot sidewalk.

"So …" I said back, then leaned in for a kiss. I didn't make any sudden moves, just kept my feet planted on the ground and stretched my head toward hers. She closed her eyes before our lips met. I shut my eyes and kissed her.

It was nice.

Mouths closed and dry, the kiss started as small pecks, like I'd give to a sister if I had one. Or to my mom. But then there was moisture between us, and her lips opened slightly. I felt her short breaths in my mouth, and I started to get hard. My pants were loose, but my body wasn't pressed up against hers, so I wasn't worried about her feeling how excited I was.

But I was excited. And the more she breathed her sweet-tasting breath into my mouth, the more I wanted more from her. I wanted my mouth to be swallowed up by hers, to be inside there with all her teeth and tongue and gums and all of it. I remembered what I'd seen in a foreign movie Mom and Ken had taken us to see, where the actors on the screen had kissed like snakes, using their tongues on one another.

With the introduction of my tongue into Seneca's open mouth, she stopped moving her lips. I was suddenly kissing her without her kissing me back. My erection now pressed against my pants, but I was so lost in exploring her mouth with my tongue that I didn't notice anything.

Suddenly she pulled her head back from me, lightly placed her hands on my chest. "Stephen," she said softly.

I snapped to right away, eyes open and hyper aware. It was difficult to figure out what she was thinking at that moment. "I'm sorry, I …." I didn't know exactly what I had done, but I felt shamed by it, like I'd pushed something special past where it wasn't special anymore. I hated myself at that moment, and I turned quickly away from her.

"I … I better go," she said to my back.

I nodded, looking into the gutter a few feet away.

Then she was in front of me, and I was looking at her blouse. "Hey …" she said.

"I didn't mean to …"

"I had fun, Stephen. I kinda froze when you … did that thing with … you know. Maybe we can … try it again next time." She put her arms around me and gave me a warm, full hug.

I finally found the courage to look at her face. "Next time?"

She kissed me quickly on the lips, before I could react, and then ran up the street toward her house. She turned once and waved, her eyes playful. Beautiful.

Chapter 13

I RAN HOME FROM OUR DATE, determined to shed as many pounds from my oversize frame as I could before the next time we saw each other. I called Gramma to see if I could come by on the weekend to visit them and work out on the gym Grampa had bought especially for me. It depended on my mother, she said, but she was enthusiastic about seeing me, and maybe my brother, too, soon. I planned to talk to Mom that night, and even if she didn't want to see her own mother, I'd travel out there on my own or with Demian in tow.

With my thoughts on him, he and Rafe came in through the back door, ending their pilgrimage at our kitchen in front of the fridge. The carbonation fizz from a bottle of Pepsi, sounding like a hundred balloons deflating simultaneously into the air, filled the house. Then Rafe burped. Both of them laughed.

"Hey, save some for me," I yelled from my place on the couch. I lay lengthwise over the two big cushions, hands behind my head, nestled into a pillow Mom herself had crocheted when I was a baby.

"We're going back out," Demian said from the kitchen.

"Where you headed?"

"Just out," Rafe said, but I could tell from his voice that he was hiding something.

The springs wheezed as my body left the couch. I wiped my damp hands over the front of my jeans and walked barefoot into the other room. They stood against the sink, both drinking plastic cups filled with soda. Sweaty, they looked out of breath.

"Where you coming from?" I asked.

Demian pointed to the camera on the kitchen table. "Willard. Seeing if we could find the Wee-wee Guy."

"Wee-wee Guy," Rafe laughed. He seemed punch-drunk. Nervous.

"Did you find him?" I grabbed my own cup and poured a big splash of Pepsi into it, then fished the ice cube tray from the freezer and pulled the metal lever until cubes broke free. A few of them hopped the tray and skidded along the table.

Rafe caught a piece of ice before it slid off, and held it out to me. "Nah, nothing yet. But we did see—" Demian's stare stopped him mid-sentence.

I sipped my drink and eyed them over the top of my glass. Waited.

Demian felt my gaze. A big, dismissive grunt came out of him. He said, "Eric was there. With some friends."

"That turd has friends?" I blurted, before I'd meant to. I then asked the question I should have asked first. "You okay?"

"Yeah. He didn't see us. But we ran anyway, just in case." Demian finished his soda and rummaged in the cabinet. "You hungry, Rafe?" Rafe shook his head, and Demian pulled out some Ritz crackers. "We've got peanut butter."

"You got bananas?" Rafe asked.

I remembered that we didn't have any kind of fruit in the house. No bananas, no apples, no oranges, not even a lone grape rolling around the bottom of the crisper drawer in the refrigerator because as a family we were boycotting them. Curious, I looked to see if we had any vegetables beyond a head of lettuce in there. I came up empty.

"Ken's doing the shopping now," I said, and Rafe nodded. He knew exactly what I meant.

"I got some bananas at my house, if you want to come over." Rafe didn't say it to be mean, but Demian suddenly looked embarrassed. He scratched at some imaginary itch just below his knee.

"You guys stay here. I'll run to the Co-op and grab some stuff." I knew I had enough money left over from the date to at least buy a bunch of bananas and maybe a few Red Delicious from the grocery store up the street. "Just hang out, I'll be back."

I didn't wait for them to answer, just went back into the living room, dressed my feet, and then jogged out the front door. I realized I had a lot of energy, which I wanted to burn off.

When I got home, with a bagful of fruit, Demian and Rafe were gone. I put the groceries away, washed an apple, and let my thoughts drift back to Seneca.

THAT NIGHT, I HAD MOVED FROM thinking sweet thoughts about my first date with a girl to obsessing over pushing the kiss too far at the end of it. I wasn't sure if she liked me, or hated me, or, worst of all, felt completely indifferent about me. I threw myself into watching TV so that I could replace my anxious thoughts with mindless ones. Demian gnawed on a Red Delicious behind me, the distracting crunch and smacking of lips affecting my concentration on a rerun of *Baretta* I had missed the first time around. Mom and Ken sat beside each other on the couch, dinner served and finished by nine o'clock, and everyone winding down for the night. I scooted across the rug from my place by Mom's feet and turned the volume up. Before I could do a reverse scoot, Mom told me to turn it back down.

"But I can't hear what anyone is saying over Demian and that stupid apple." I wished I had never bought them. I turned to glare at him once I'd lowered the volume. "What are you eating for anyway? We just had dinner."

Ken piped up, "You're bulking down, so your brother's bulking up. He's doing his part to keep the universe in perfect harmony." He chuckled, then went back to his book.

I stared at Demian until he finished chewing. He swallowed and then said, "I gotta get my tooth out. Nillie, she's in first grade and pretty smart, she told me. Use a apple, that'll do it."

"Well …" I said, talk of Nillie and school awakening thoughts of Seneca. I needed to hush Demian up so that I could immerse myself back into the show. "Just … be quiet about it, okay?" I said weakly.

"'Kay," he agreed.

Less than a minute later, Demian yelled out in surprise. "My tooth! My tooth!"

By the time I could focus on the show again, it had switched to a commercial.

I WAS TIRED, READY TO FALL asleep, but Demian still bounced around with what seemed like infinite energy. I tossed off my jeans, decided I wasn't in the mood to brush my teeth, and beat my pillow into a misshapen lump. Demian removed his front tooth from the pocket of his shorts and rolled it around on his palm.

"If you keep screwing with it, you're gonna lose it," I said, desperate to turn off the bedroom light and go to sleep. It was one sure way to put my Seneca-brain on hold for a few hours. "Just put it under your pillow so the Tooth Fairy can take it."

"How much she gonna give me, you think? Fifty dollars, maybe?" Demian held his hand straight out, the tooth resting in the center of it, and let it lead him to his pillow as if it had a mind of its own.

"You're high. How about a buck, maybe. I only got a quarter for my first tooth. But with inflation and all, you'll probably get a dollar."

"Neat," he said, placing the tooth down gingerly onto his sheet. With great ceremony, he laid the pillow on top of it.

"Now, go to sleep or you won't get anything."

Demian bounded over to the door and yelled, "Lights out" as he flicked the switch. I couldn't see him, but I heard him pad back onto his bed. He whispered to himself, "Come on, Tooth Fairy, I'm ready for my one dollar now. Thank you."

THERE WAS NOTHING THAT NEXT MORNING for Demian to be thankful for. His tooth still lay in the exact spot under his pillow where he had placed it the night before. No paper currency or small pieces of silver lined his bedsheet. Mom had forgotten.

I made up something elaborate about how the Tooth Fairy had probably been overworked and couldn't make it to our house but that she would definitely be by after he went to sleep that night. It was the best I could do, and it felt shitty to look at the way his face had collapsed into a frown. His very first lost tooth had been neglected by a deity he had, up until then, maintained complete faith in. That was how I felt about our mother too, but it was my job as big brother to shield him from the truth. He deserved to hold on to a happy fantasy as long as he possibly could.

I shifted attention to a happy thought of my own: Seneca and her soft lips pressing against mine. Demian found distraction in a piece of Silly Putty and the comics section of the *Chronicle*, and our day had begun.

BACK IN BED AGAIN, THE NIGHT'S darkness shrouded over our little house, I listened to Demian's breath as it drew in to his little body, then pushed back out. The tooth was under his pillow, awaiting a second chance at fairy removal. I had once more assured him, just before he fell asleep, that she would definitely be making a stop on Emerson Street before the sun came up.

Earlier, Mom had been stirring something in a pot, which smelled vaguely of dinner, when I snuck away from Demian and Ken on the couch and joined her in the kitchen.

It took her a while to notice me, her mind off on one of its trips to somewhere else, somewhere *better* than where she was at the present moment. "Hey, how long you been standing there?" she asked.

"Not very," I said, but I could tell she was put out that I was here at all. Her eyes were tired, and she seemed more interested in the glop beneath her wooden spoon than in anything I could say or do.

"Dinner'll be ready in a bit. You can tell me about what you did today at the table, okay?" she said. This was my cue to leave her alone and go back into the living room.

But I had come in here with something to say.

I checked behind me, the TV noise loud enough that I knew Demian wouldn't be able to hear anything from the kitchen. "You forgot about his tooth."

"I did what?" she said, surprised I was still there.

"Demian's first tooth. You were supposed to take it and put money under his pillow. You didn't."

She didn't respond. I waited.

The spoon traveled around in the pot, clockwise, then counter-clockwise. The sounds of the abrupt tick … tick … tick of the clock above my head and the laugh track in the living room sailed around my ears.

"Mom?"

"I heard you. What do you want me to do about it now?" She was defensive, as if I had screwed up, instead of her.

"Well," I started, dragging the word out with what I understood came across as sarcasm, "you could not forget anymore."

She glanced back at me and stopped stirring. She dug into the back pocket of her jeans, came up with nothing, and then searched her other pockets. A couple of bills popped out of her front pocket like rabbits out of a hat. She peeled off a one-dollar bill and held it out at me. "Here, you do it for me. You're the elephant who never forgets."

I heard it as *you're the elephant who never thin gets*. I knew that wasn't right, but a rush of embarrassment shuddered through my body anyway.

"I'm not his mother," I said, shoving my hands deep into my own, empty, pockets. "It's your job, not mine."

She looked stung, her mouth tight and grim. Her hand closed around the dollar and crumpled it into a small ball. "Your little mouth these days, Stephen. I swear. It's becoming very," her voice got louder, "very tiresome."

I stared down at my shoes, the holes in them big enough to show the gray-white of my socks.

"It's not okay for you to speak to me like that," she said.

I told her, "I'm sorry." I didn't mean it.

Mom looked toward the living room, where the faint sounds of canned laughter continued. I looked at the side of her face, not meeting her eyes when she focused on me. "Just … make sure he puts it under his pillow close enough to the edge so I can reach it without waking him up. Can you do that for me, Stephen?"

I nodded, then left the room. By the time we were all together at the table, I had completely lost my appetite.

Sitting in my bed in the dark a few hours later, wide awake and listening to my brother sleep, I wondered if Mom would remember this time. I didn't have to wait long, because a few minutes later, she sneaked into our bedroom, walking softly in what sounded like her bare feet. She hovered over Demian's bed for a few seconds, then put her ear to his face. I closed my mouth, inhaled and exhaled through my nose, and witnessed the Tooth Fairy close up.

From my sideways view, I squinted to see her reach under his pillow once, then again. She squatted down and ran her hand along his head. The sound of his peaceful, uninterrupted sleep continued. As she stood quietly beside his bed, she appeared to stare down on him. Her hand caressed his head, which sparked memories of when she used to do that to him all the time when he was awake. I remembered how she used to do the same thing to me too. It had been a long, long time since she had done it, but I still remembered how she did it and how it felt.

Her gaze shifted toward me, and then she did something strange. With her free hand, she waved at me. A friendly, silly kind of thing. I waved back.

Mom gave him a final caress before she kissed his head. I watched her stand erect and waited for her to leave just as she had come.

"I left him two dollars," she whispered, suddenly in front of my face. She squatted down, a spicy but not unpleasant scent to her breath. She reached her hand out and stroked my hair, gently. It was exactly how I remembered it.

I closed my eyes as her fingers softly scraped along my head. My breathing stopped in the hope that I could save this moment, capture it like a bird, until I was ready to set it free. I released my breath through my nose, quietly, before her hand left my head.

I woke up the next morning, unable to remember how long she had stayed there beside me until I fell asleep. All I knew for sure was that she'd been there. I touched my hair and pictured her fingernails traveling lovingly, deliberately, across my scalp.

THAT WEEKEND, DEMIAN AND I WENT to stay with our grandparents. Mom and Ken were invited over for Sunday dinner, but they bowed out, with an excuse that it was "a tiring week for the both of us." Mom *had* seemed out of it for most of the week, and while she blamed it on her job, I knew that it was because of our landlord. I couldn't get Mom and Ken's conversation about the rent out of my head, so when she left her checkbook on the kitchen table, I snuck a peek: a check dated July 7 to Mr. Takadakos was made out for one hundred dollars less than the June check. The difference between the June and May checks was only thirty dollars, and everything before May was consistently the same amount. Math was never one of my strongest subjects in school, but I knew that one hundred dollars was a hell of a lot more than thirty, so whatever Mom had done with our landlord in July was a hell of a lot more than she'd done with, or to, him in June.

Ken still hadn't found a job, but he did seem to be spending less time at the house smoking dope and more time out doing whatever he was doing. I had no idea if he was going on interviews, drinking coffee at the Med on Telegraph with his college buddies, or reaching for enlightenment under a Bodhi tree, but I knew he didn't land on the couch until right before Mom got home from work, and that arrangement worked for me.

Despite that, I was lately more open to a vacation—however brief—away from that house and those people, so Demian and I took Gramma up on her offer to spend the weekend in a different house, in a different town, with different people. I biked the two of us down to Ashby BART station, where we caught the train to Fremont.

I loved Berkeley's huge, unruly houses, the wild murals, telephone poles plastered with guitar lesson flyers and anarchic slogans, and I never tired of the lunacy and commotion of Telegraph Avenue. But pedaling my bike through

Fremont, with Demian's small hands holding my shoulders for balance and support, I discovered that there was comfort for me in this place that lacked any pretense of being unusual or unique. My heartbeat was steadier here, my body more relaxed, and my mind filled with a quiet that I was acutely aware of. I coasted down the small decline to my grandparents' house with an inexplicable sense of being where I belonged.

BOTH OF US HAD A GOOD time, with Grampa teaching me new exercises on the weight machine in the garage, while in the kitchen Gramma taught Demian how to make dishes out of a recipe box she had gotten from *her* grandmother. It was mostly uneventful, which is what made it so memorable.

When we got back home late Monday morning, the first thing I did was call Seneca. The phrase *next time* had run through my head ever since the end of our first date, and I was overly eager for our second date. She was home when I called, and our conversation was brief but fruitful. I offered to pick her up at the corner where we shared that kiss, but she wanted to come to me, to see where I lived and then make a plan from there. We talked about biking together—she would ride her Schwinn over to my house, and then we would bike up Ashby toward the Claremont Hotel, or maybe into Rockridge. She insisted on taking me out to lunch this time, so we made plans for the next day at noon.

Tuesday didn't come quickly enough. After two showers and three changes of clothes, I was ready for our date to start. I had cleaned my room and sprayed enough Lysol into the upper reaches of the house to kill all the nasty odors that permeated the air. The smells of Ken's feet, burnt weed, fried food, and farts had been replaced with bacteria-fighting, lemon-scented chemicals. It wasn't exactly fresh air, but it was clean.

Mom left for work and Ken wandered off to parts unknown before I took to cleaning and detoxifying the house. Demian got up late, his stomach upset. He had a constant, annoying sniffle that got on my nerves. I let him laze on the couch in front of the TV until eleven forty-five, and then I told him to beat it because Seneca was on her way over.

"I don't wanna," he whined. Then he sniffled for probably the thousandth time that morning.

"Jesus Christ, Demian, just do it."

"I don't feel good," he said, then coughed to prove it. He looked weird with his missing tooth, which made me angrier at him for some reason.

I finished a last minute dusting of cobwebs from the corners of the living room, then pointed to the back door. "Just go outside, then. In the back yard. Take some toys and just … stay out of our way." I went into my room and came out with a few of my comic books. "You can read these if you want. I'll come get you when we leave, okay?"

He lifted himself from the couch with exaggerated effort but took the comics and disappeared into the back yard. I locked the door behind him, to make sure we wouldn't be bothered.

AT TWELVE FIFTEEN, I THOUGHT SHE was just a little bit late. By twelve thirty, I began to think I'd given her the wrong address. After staring out the front window every ten seconds until it was almost one o'clock, I called her house but got no answer. I went outside and checked the doorbell. It rang loudly through the house, sounding around the rooms in a flat, echoey gong.

By one fifteen I sat sulking on the couch. I called her once more and again got nothing but an endless series of rings heard by no one. Then I got paranoid that she actually was home, refusing to answer the phone because she knew it was me on the other end. She had realized that I was a monster, a creepy fat-ass who couldn't control himself or his disgusting tongue. She had made a mistake about seeing me again, so she had decided not to come to my house and was letting her phone ring until I got tired and gave up.

So I gave up, stopped calling, went into my room, and slumped against the windowsill. I looked toward the back yard, where I'd left Demian, but didn't see him. Lying on the bed, I glanced at the two books from the library: the London book and *Little House on the Prairie*. I had read almost half of the Wilder book in preparation for our next date, poring over it so that I could discuss with her all the details of the Kansas farm and the Ingalls family while we had lunch after our bike ride. Angry at Seneca, but mostly at myself, I swatted the crappy girly book off my nightstand and into the wall.

When I finally got up and dragged myself into the kitchen, I heard Demian's sniffling by the back door. I unlocked it, saw him sitting on the pair of concrete steps with his eyes closed and his body rocking back and forth. "You can come in now," I said, before I moped toward the fridge and swigged a big gulp of Pepsi right from the glass bottle.

In the living room, my eyes rested on our dishwater-gray Ma Bell phone, and I used all my willpower not to pick it up and call Seneca again. It was now past two o'clock, and the day, my *life*, was ruined. I wanted to curl up in bed, wrap all the covers around me, and descend into a sleep that would last forever. I wanted to stop feeling sad, and angry, and defeated, and start feeling numb. Or even comatose with sleep.

Instead, I rushed out the front door, without saying anything to Demian, and walked to Trevor Kreumann's house. I had seen him only once since school had ended, hanging out with that asshole Ryan on College Avenue, so I figured our own friendship was kind of over. But he lived only three blocks away from Seneca's house, and I needed to be *near* her, if I couldn't be *with* her. Avoiding her block completely, for fear of actually seeing her or of her seeing me, I landed at Trevor's front door with adrenaline coursing through my body. I hoped Ryan wasn't there, but if he was, I would stand up to him, not hold back about what I thought of him. I was nervous, jumpy, and when Trevor answered my knocking, I grabbed him in a hug and lifted him off the ground.

"What the fuck?" He swatted me in the head and I dropped him.

"Sorry," I mumbled.

"You wanna come in?" he asked, like nothing had happened.

"Ryan here?" I peeked my head in his door, and he flung it wide open.

"No! Why would he?" I followed him inside, and he sat on the floor in front of *Gilligan's Island* on his color TV. We had a black-and-white TV at home, and it was a thrill to see how red Ginger's hair was, and how the Skipper's shirt looked so blue.

Trevor shoved a bag of corn nuts at me after taking a handful first. I said thanks, and the sound of two mouths crunching competed with the Professor's latest invention.

We sat and watched without saying anything, just passing the bag back and forth until the show ended. "You wanna watch *The Monkees*? Or you wanna do something else?" Trevor poured the last few kernels from the bag into his mouth, crumpled the foil wrapper, and chucked it under the couch behind him.

"What do you wanna do?" I asked him, still too unsettled to make any decisions on my own.

"You bring your bike?" Trevor did a weird maneuver where he leaned back, hands splayed out behind his head on the carpet, his legs bent underneath him. He looked like a four-legged, upside-down spider. From this pose—which looked painful, a shape I could never manipulate my own body into—Trevor pushed off his wrists and catapulted himself up into a standing position. I was impressed.

"No bike," I said as he rubbed at a little rug burn on his palm.

"We could walk up to the avenue," he said, putting on shoes. "You got any money?"

I had about six dollars in my pocket, originally reserved for my second date with Seneca. It now burned a hole in the front of my jeans, desperate to be spent recklessly and immediately. I nodded and said, "I could go for a couple of Top Dogs."

He laughed, looked at me. "Thought you were off those things. For Seneca, right? She ever come back from … where was it?"

"Seattle," I said. "No, never heard from her."

He walked out the front door, and I followed. He left the front door unlocked, which seemed like an oddball thing to do. It unsettled me. No one at my house ever forgot to lock a door, front or back, when we left. I wondered if his parents would get mad if they found out, and what kinds of broken rules it took for other people's parents to punish their kids.

"Top Dog, then." Trevor leapt off his small porch and onto the sidewalk. His ankle twisted and he fell into a heap. "Aw, shit."

Trevor's older brother, Art, a sophomore at Berkeley High, appeared from their driveway at that same moment. "Smooth move, ex-lax."

"You okay?" I leaned down to help him up.

"The little retard is fine. Hey, Stevie, what's up?" He chucked his chin at me. Art wore his hair short, had the beginnings of some upper-lip hair, and was decked out in black jeans and a white tee with a black A in the middle of a circle.

It was a cool design, and I figured he got it specially made, like a monogram or something. His parents both worked, and Trevor never seemed to be without a few dollars on him. Their house had enough room for four kids instead of two, but Art lived in the garage, which had been converted into an apartment just for him. He even had his own fridge and TV inside. I'd only been back there once, but I thought it was even cooler than Greg Brady's attic pad on TV.

Trevor limped around for about a minute before quickly recovering. "Dad give you any money yesterday?" He put his hand out to Art, waiting.

Art tried to slap him a hard five, but Trevor yanked his hand back, then caressed his curly hair with it. "Too slow."

Art threw a karate kick that just missed his brother's solar plexus. "Get bent, little fuckwad. I ain't got no money fo' yo ass."

"No?"

"No, you simpleton pud. What do you want money for, anyway? You'd just spend it on stupid shit." Art threw a few air punches at Trevor, then a roundhouse kick. "Where you going?"

"Telegraph." Trevor turned to me, said, "Come on, let's go," then ducked away from a wild side-armed lunge by his brother.

"I'll go with. Gotta make a stop at Rasputin, see if they got any more U.K. bootlegs."

I knew Rasputin was a record store, but I didn't think they sold shoes too. Instead of asking, I kept my mouth shut, because Trevor seemed to understand him. "Those things are a total rip-off. They sound like garbage."

"And you eat garbage. From a garbage mound."

"Yeah. Made out of bootlegs."

Art flicked Trevor in the ear with his finger. He turned to me. "What kind of music you like, Stevie?"

"I don't know. Elton John's cool, I guess. I like Elvis. And The Beatles, too."

Art nodded, walking up the slight incline backwards, facing me and Trevor. "Elvis, the king, nice. Elton's a gaylord, but he can sing the shit out of those songs. But the Rolling Stones are way hotter than the Fub Four."

"Art's in a rock band, so he thinks he knows everything about everything," Trevor said to me, then stuck his tongue out at his brother.

"Try again, you pimple. It's a *punk* band. Better than rock."

"Louder. That's for sure." Trevor side-stepped around an ivy bush jutting out from a front yard, and he lost his footing. Art saw it, dropped back a few steps, and leaned into his brother's ear. I slowed down, pretended to see something fascinating in the direction opposite them, but heard Art when he asked, "It still hurts?"

Trevor lowered his voice, said, "A little."

"We can go back, no problem," he stopped, gently squeezed Trevor's shoulder. At that moment I yearned for a big brother, someone who cared about me. Someone who was looking out for me.

"Nah, it's fine." Trevor resumed walking, and Art bounded ahead to take the lead again.

When we got to Telegraph, they were arguing about music again, and it felt good to be out with them instead of moping at home over Seneca. Thoughts of her popped into my brain when I wasn't expecting them, coming as single lines from songs, usually with *she* in the lyric. Gone, it was going to take giving money to the devil to get her back. The lyrics came and went, along with images of her, but I tried to concentrate on our walk down the avenue. My stomach was rumbling, and I knew Top Dog was near.

We passed Shakespeare, and I craned my neck toward the latest books displayed in their window. There were so many I wanted to read, with the hope to someday have enough money to buy a bookstore of my own. Halfway down the street, the guitar strums of a stringy-haired guy in his early twenties wafted toward us like cigar smoke: heavy and unpleasant. When we were in front of him, Art stopped. On the ground, near the guy's bare feet, sat a straw hat with a red bandana wrapped around it. At the bottom of it were a few nickels and dimes and what looked like Canadian currency. A few pesos, too.

"'Blowin' in the Wind,'" Art said directly to the singer, who was trying his best to channel Dylan. "Relevant. Hey, lemme ask you a question. Is this the *only* fucking song you know?" The guy looked up, lost the flow of the song, and stopped singing.

"Hey, man, I don't need your bad vibes raining down on me here. I'm trying to lift everybody up, raise some consciousness here, not bum the world out."

"Then how about getting a job, or at least playing a different tune, you loser ass." Art leaned down and laughed into his face. I didn't think it was funny, and I couldn't understand why he was being so mean to this guy. But I wanted to believe he had a good reason.

A knot formed in my stomach, and I stared at the guy as Trevor and Art walked toward the corner. The guy with the guitar met my eye and said, "You think I'm a joke, little man of our future? It's you and your poisonous friends who are the true joke."

He picked up the chorus of the song again, his voice scratchy and off-key.

"You're a condescending piece of shit," I said, the phrase something I'd heard at one of the parties Mom and Ken had dragged me to. It felt right coming out of my mouth, even though it didn't belong to me. There was something about this guy that reminded me of my dad, and for a moment I was speaking directly to him. "You selfish asshole, with your stupid dreams and your bullshit talk. You and your music, they all suck!"

I stood there, still seeing my dad's face superimposed over guitar guy's. I thought maybe he would stand up, tell me to screw off, or maybe even hit me for calling him so many names. Instead, his own face reappeared, his mouth slightly open and his eyes staring at me with what looked to me like kindness. Compassion, even.

"You got some demons in you, little man," he said, and held out a wilted daisy from behind his ear, "but they don't own you. You got you some powers no one can take away." I opened my hand and took the flower. "No one."

Staring at the yellow petals brushing up against my pinkish fingers, my breathing stopped. A slight, intense ringing filled my ears for a moment, pushing out all the other street sounds. I looked up the block, where Trevor and his brother waited for me. "You're wrong." I crushed the pathetic little daisy into my fist before throwing it back at him.

He shook his head, picked up the flower and put it back behind his ear. As I ran to the end of the street, he slapped the guitar before fingering the strings again and sang, "Yes, how many times must a man look up / Before he can see the sky?"

Still running, I puffed up my cheeks, and as the air rushed through and around me, I pursed my lips and with all my might blew straight into it, feeling defiant and resolute.

IF I WASN'T CALLING, OR THINKING about calling, Seneca, I was hanging out with Trevor, and sometimes Art, acting out all my aggressions around the city. I verbally harassed the street people of Telegraph, homeless men who begged for spare change and had animated conversations with themselves, as if there were actually someone speaking to them. With the encouragement of my friends, I wrote *College sucks dick* and drew penises on some of the buildings around campus, and even stole a couple of Whatchamacallit bars from the corner store on Euclid, over in Northside.

When I was at home by myself, I felt stupid for doing what I was doing, but I didn't want to stop. Demian acted as if he was sick, and not like himself, but I was annoyed by all his ailments and left him alone most of the time. The nights

Mom and Ken cobbled a dinner together for us, Demian was sullen and I managed to eat entire meals without saying a single word. Mom and Ken weren't speaking to each other much, so all of us in one room was like a doctor's waiting area where four people who didn't know each other lost themselves in their own thoughts and ignored those around them.

I had wandered around Seneca's neighborhood, trying to find her house, confused and nervous. If she saw me hanging around her neighborhood or by her front door, she might act like I wasn't there. Or worse, she could run away from me, screaming loud enough to make everyone come out of their houses and call the cops on me. I had done or said something awful, which had led to her decision to stand me up, but I wished I knew what it had been.

On Friday, three days after Seneca had stood me up, I called her again. I needed to know exactly what I had done wrong. This time, she answered.

She said hello, her voice small and beautiful.

"Seneca? It's me, Steve."

"Steve?" There was a long, painful pause. "I can't talk to you anymore." She sounded almost robotic.

"What do you mean?" The air around me seemed to change, as if my ears had popped, and it was like I could hear the ocean. "Did I do something?"

"I just … Please don't call here anymore. Please." Her breath whooshed into my ear, and it sounded like she was about to cry. And then she hung up.

I stood in the living room, with the dead phone in my hand and my pinky twitching on its own. I called her back. The line rang and rang, until I slammed the phone down. What the hell had happened? What had I done that was so bad to make this girl I cared about so much actually cry? I tried to think of something I had done, or said, to make her not talk to me. Was it the kiss, the one with the tongue—was that it? But we had talked after that, made plans for another date; it didn't make sense.

Then I thought maybe it had nothing to do with me. I was relieved while I imagined that maybe someone in her family had died. A grandparent or a cousin, maybe. I pictured her dad losing his job, or maybe even her mother dying. Suddenly, there was a reason for it all. Seneca was headed back to Seattle and couldn't face telling me because she was so in love with me.

I stuck with the last thought, built it into something that felt true and real, and moved forward with my summer, a summer without Seneca. It still felt sad, horribly unresolved, but the invented scenario made me feel better about myself, that I wasn't responsible for whatever tragedy had separated the two of us and our future together.

I was feeling more generous overall, so when I saw that Demian was still sulking around the house even though his sniffles were long gone, I offered him one of the chocolate bars I had filched the day before. He lay in bed, looking at his wall full of erratically spaced poster art, and I nudged him with the candy.

"Demian, eat this," I instructed, and he rolled over to face me. He hadn't bathed in a couple of days, and his hair stuck out like a clown's, his mouth sticky with a thin gloss of white goo.

"Not hungry," he mumbled, pulling the covers close.

I wanted to eat it myself, but I controlled my appetite and placed the bar on our shared dresser. "You still sick or what?"

"I don't know."

"Wanna watch some TV, or go walking somewhere? I got money." I knew I should have given any cash I had to Mom in order to help make the rent, but I also wanted to bring Demian out of his funk.

Demian didn't move, so I said, "You need to go to the doctor? You okay?"

He got up then, jumped out of bed to show me he wasn't sick. "I'm okay. Okay?"

I looked closely at him, and he just didn't look like his normal self. Something was definitely wrong, but I had no idea what it was. "Are you sad about something? I mean, I get sad about stuff. You wanna tell me?"

He stared at the floor for a long time, then swiveled his head up at me. His mouth opened, but nothing came out. He started to cry that little-boy cry, an odd mixture of full-throated fierceness and gut-wrenching weakness. I put my arms around him in a tight hug, and he let me. He cried non-stop for almost ten minutes. I patted him, I rocked him, I whispered in his tiny ears that everything was going to be okay, everything was going to be okay.

The tears stopped, his heartbeat slowed, and he broke our embrace. Wiping the tears away on the sleeve of his ironed-on

Sigmund and the Sea Monsters tee, he walked out of our room. I followed him into the living room, where Ken sat on the couch smoking a cigarette and reading *Mother Jones* magazine.

Ken looked up as we entered, staring at Demian's wet face before giving me a hard glance. "Were you two fighting?"

"No," I said, elongating the *o* in a denial that was also like, *How dare you even ask that of me.*

"Why's he crying then? Why are you crying?" He got up, as if to go comfort him—I suspected that Ken had noticed, despite his continuous streak of self-absorption, Demian not acting himself lately—but he didn't move quickly enough. My brother whipped himself around and fast-walked back into our room and shut the door.

"Steve, what's that all about? Are you sure you didn't do something to him?" Ken seemed genuinely concerned, which was weird.

"It's just his time of the month," I said, not knowing what that meant, exactly, only that I'd heard it before and it seemed to fit Demian's behavior.

Ken stubbed out his cigarette and sat down on the couch again. He seemed relieved that I was making a joke out of it, like the pressure was off him to actually do something that might be misconstrued as an act of fatherly concern.

"Don't worry, he's okay," I said, to put his mind completely at rest.

"*Bueno*." He reached toward a stack of record albums and fondled a Linda Ronstadt cover. He was over it, his interest in my brother dried up and deserted like an old dog turd.

Chapter 14

The summer felt like a marathon I hadn't properly trained for. Only mid-July, my desperation to be back at school and forced into a routine had me agitated and aimless. It had been days since I'd spoken to Seneca, and Demian had gotten over his cold but still seemed sluggish and distant. My discovery about Mom and the special favors she'd been doling out to our landlord, Mr. Takadakos, in exchange for a break on the rent, had put a pressure on me to bring some money into the house. Somehow.

Demian and I sat in front of the TV on a Monday morning, a rerun of *The Andy Griffith Show* that we'd both seen at least five times boring the hell out of us. I decided it was time to get our own jobs. I couldn't actually do much outside of read books, ride my bike, and struggle with math problems; Demian's skills were fewer than that. I searched for inspiration from the shows we watched, where kids like Wally and the Beaver went door-to-door in their neighborhood, seeking jobs doing yard work or handyman tasks. Our yard looked like shit, and I didn't even know if we had any tools in our back garage, but we had to try something.

I bullied Demian into looking for work alongside me, figuring that if we worked as a team, our combined knowledge of labor—however minuscule it was on both our parts—would amount to just enough so we could get through an hour or two of posing as hired hands. We crossed the street to Mrs. Dillon's house, a good place to start. She was a widow, a nice lady in her late fifties who was a fixture in the neighborhood. Her Army colonel husband had been killed in Vietnam, and she never remarried or had any kids. She seemed to like kids, though, which was why she was our first stop for possible work and cash.

"Why, hi there, boys," she said in her slightly southern drawl, greeting us on her front porch. "How's summer treating you?"

"Swell," I said, still thinking about Wally and the Beav. Demian said the same when her eyes fell on him.

"Wonderful. You need something? Your momma send you over to borrow some flour or sugar or something? Or you just come by to keep me company while I watch my soaps on the TV?" The door opened wide, but we just stood there, unsure what to do next.

Demian turned and looked up at me, his feet slowly marching in place. I said, "We were wondering ... I mean, do you have any, um, work? We could do?"

She smiled, but her forehead got all wrinkly at the same time. "Well ..." She drew out the word, like the high note in an Aretha Franklin song. "You mean along the lines of weeding the lawn or . . ." Mrs. Dillon stole a glance across the street at our front lawn. I followed her eyes, and suddenly my entire body felt like it was being attacked by pinpricks of heat.

"Never mind, Mrs. Dillon. Forget it." I turned to Demian, took his hand. "Let's go, Demian. Thanks," I said to her as we started for the three steps down to the walkway and toward the houses where our job hunt would begin anew.

"Wait, Stephen. I might, well, I might have a task for you."

Inside her house, she offered us lemonade from her refrigerator, the lemons hand-picked from a tree in her back yard, the sugar genuine C&H brand. "Not the thrifty stuff," she said, "but the good stuff." We drank it standing up in her kitchen, my head swiveling around the room while Demian kept half his face buried in the jam jar he'd been given as a glass.

After we'd eaten a small plate of vanilla wafers and animal crackers, I asked her what the job was. I knew she would pay us whatever it was worth, and maybe a little extra just because.

Her cat, Mildred, which she had told us more than once was named for an old black-and-white movie character that Joan Crawford had "played to perfection," meowed loudly from the other room. "Oh, darn, the door's shut," she said to herself, then turned to us. "Before we get to that, I want to show you something."

She led us to the bathroom door, where Mildred pranced in front of it, the sounds of warbling loud and full. The cat was gray, with patches of white all around. I didn't know what kind of cat she was, but I thought she had sad eyes.

Mrs. Dillon pushed open the door, and Mildred the cat padded onto the tiled floor and leapt onto the toilet seat. "It only took me six months to train her. Watch this."

We all crowded into the small room, my hip pressed up against the sink's exposed pipes. Demian leaned forward from his spot between me and Mrs. Dillon. When the cat began to pee into the toilet, he burst into giggles.

"You think that's funny—which it *is*—you just wait."

We waited, and then the cat squatted its haunches even lower into the toilet. Her tail reached higher and higher toward the ceiling, as if it had a mind of its own. Then a long, brown blob inched out of Mildred's butt.

"Eww, gross," Demian said, and cackled so loudly that the cat looked up and almost lost its footing on the plastic seat. "The cat's pooping, Steve." He pointed at the scene as if I had been somewhere else.

I watched the cat push out another piece of poop, the sound of it when it hit the water echoing slightly in the bathroom. A little water splashed back up onto Mildred's quaking leg, but she didn't seem to mind. I had always thought cats hated water.

"Ta-da!" Mrs. Dillon spread her arms out proudly. The cat extended its little claws and scratched on the seat as if in a litter box. Then Mildred jumped down to the tile and padded out of the room.

Demian continued laughing, feeling bold enough to look inside the toilet bowl. I thought it was weird, and I didn't know exactly how I felt about having watched a cat take a crap like a person did. It made Demian laugh, and given how he hadn't been doing a lot of that lately, the oddness of it all was okay with me. I joined him at the toilet and took a peek.

An hour later, Demian and I finished our peanut butter and jelly sandwiches on Wonder Bread with the crusts cut off. Sitting in Mrs. Dillon's living room, the walls covered with pictures of her dead husband and medals he had been awarded, I turned another page of a red leather-like photo album while she narrated.

"And here's Henry in Trafalgar Square in the middle of London, England. You can barely see him ... Look, there's his sweet little self ... That was V-Day, the end of the war. I was home back in North Carolina, worrying my little head over him. We weren't married yet, but I did my part for the war. I was no Rosie the Riveter, mind you, but I did my share of stitching parachute harnesses and bringing my momma's pies out to the boys waiting for their marching orders over at Camp Lejeune."

Her finger hovered over the small figure in the photograph she had identified as her husband, her shiny red nail like a sea of blood in all that black, white, and gray. It was as if she looked *through* the picture, to some place beneath it, or beyond it, and as she spoke, her voice seemed to drift to another place as well.

Another hour later and the albums lay spread all along the carpeted floor. Mildred licked herself between two of them, her furry backside pressed against the spine of the red leather book. Mrs. Dillon fished into her purse and reeled in paper money. She handed two crisp dollar bills to me and two to Demian, then opened her front door. We followed her, where she thanked us for our hard work, and told us we were welcome to come back any time. There was plenty more work for us to do, she said.

As we crossed the street back to our house, Demian held the money up to my face. "Why did she give it to us? We didn't do nothing."

I looked both ways before darting across, then squeezed between two parked cars before landing on the sidewalk, with my brother close behind me. "She's a nice lady," I said. "That's all."

Demian nodded, agreeing, and I looked back at her house for a moment. She still stood at her front door, looking toward us. I waved at her, but she didn't wave back. The way she stared past me, I knew she was seeing something—experiencing a memory—that was another world away from me, Demian, and this entire neighborhood.

BECAUSE A LOUSY TWO DOLLARS WAS never going to be enough to help Mom with her situation, Demian and I went back to Mrs. Dillon's house the next day. She had told us to come back again, although I'm sure she hadn't meant right away. I was feeling restless and powerless, though, with a need to do something before August was here and the rent came due again.

She found chores for us in the back yard, pulling weeds and sweeping up. It didn't take long, and between the two of us we earned only six bucks. Maybe Mrs. Dillon could tell by my face that I was disappointed. She reached into her purse and pulled out a twenty-dollar bill. Then she hesitated, probably realizing how much money it was. It *was* a lot of money, and I was wondering if she planned to give it all to Demian and me, and for what, exactly.

"You boys know Mrs. Hunter, from up the street?" she asked. When we both nodded, she said, "Terrible thing about her dog. I don't believe she has gotten over it yet. Although how could she, with Humphrey being the only thing she had left once her husband ..." She trailed off.

I grew impatient, seeing that twenty in her hands and thinking what Mom would say when I handed it to her tonight. At that moment, I didn't care what I had to do to get it, I just wanted it. I wanted the bad dreams to end and thought giving her this money might help that happen. "What about her?" I asked, trying to keep the desperation out of my voice.

"Well," she said, coming back to us from wherever she'd drifted off to, "Mrs. Hunter, I'm sure, could use the help of two strong young men. Some yard work, shopping for her perhaps, and probably some tasks around the house. If I give you this money, will you go offer yourselves to help her ... for free?"

Demian craned his neck up at her. "How is it free if you give us money for it?"

"Demian, shush," I said, a little more strongly than I had wanted. "I'll explain it to you later." I held out my hand as politely as I knew how and said, "We can do that. For sure."

She hesitated again, looking at the twenty-dollar bill in her hand, and finally placed it in my open palm. I shoved it in my front pocket and steered Demian toward the door before she could change her mind.

Just as we reached the porch and were heading down the stairs, she spoke. I froze, my hand unconsciously grasping at the front of my pants. I didn't want to give that money back. I *wouldn't* give it back. It was mine now.

"Stephen, don't forget to take some tools over there with you. You know, a hammer and a screwdriver. A toolbox with all of that inside would be ideal, if you have it at home." She waited for a response, which I gave in the form of a nod.

I honestly had no idea if we had any tools, not remembering a moment in my life when anyone but the landlord had ever fixed anything inside, or outside, our house. I certainly had never used a hammer before. It should have felt strange to realize that, but it didn't faze me. It just *was*, like so many of the things in my life I'd never done before. Another normal abnormality, in a childhood filled with them.

DEMIAN WENT IN THE HOUSE FOR a drink while I journeyed to our dusty, cluttered garage. It was at the end of our cracked and weed-strewn driveway, a detached building like the one at the house in Sausalito, only a whole lot smaller. It was big enough to fit Mom's or Ken's car, but so filled with boxes of miscellaneous stuff that there was no room. I assumed it was all just clothes and junk Mom had collected but didn't have room for in the house. Some of it was Ken's crap too. I hardly ever ventured back here, except on the few occasions when it rained and I had to put my bike inside. Mostly I forgot, which is why the paint was so rusted and the chain needed constant oil, even in the summer.

I flicked the light switch, but the bulb was burned out. I opened the door wide, letting the sun in, so I could look for tools. I pushed aside an old lamp, Bekins Storage boxes, and a thing that looked like a desk but that I knew was a sewing machine. I couldn't remember Mom ever using it.

On the back wall, a dusty shelf stood above my eye level. On it were things that looked like they had been useful once but were now forgotten: a cardboard box of Ivory Snow, a pile of copper wire, cracked and broken bricks, oil-soaked rags, empty bottles. And a toolbox.

I reached for it but couldn't quite get my hand up high enough to grab the handle. I looked around for a ladder, which apparently we didn't have. My old red wagon, with *Radio Flyer* written in white on the side of it, lay overturned in the far corner of the garage. I dragged it over by its shovel-like handle, and was reminded of pulling Demian around the neighborhood in it, back when he was two or three. He could barely speak full sentences then, but he knew how to scream "Faster faster," even if it came out of his mouth sounding like "Fatter fatter." The wagon rides ended when I pulled him past a group of older kids who laughed at me, not him. The taunts from them of "Fatter, fatter, boy" and their trumpeting elephant sounds made my palms sweat and my brain empty of all thought. I ran us all the way home and stashed the wagon in the back of the garage. Demian asked for more rides after that, but I acted like I didn't know where the wagon was, until he pushed so hard that I told him some asshole had stolen it, so he was shit out of luck. He never asked about it again.

I yanked the metal body until it was under the shelf, then tested my weight on it. The hard rubber wheels didn't burst, so I got in and reached for the toolbox. I lifted it down into the wagon, then scouted the dusty, splinter-hazard of a shelf for anything else of interest. Some loose change stuck to the wood, caked on by something sticky and gross. I needed the money, so I peeled it up and shoved it in my pocket.

Searching for other treasure, I scooted the wagon down a few feet, to the far end of the shelf. Cans were grouped there. I lifted them up, reading one as paint thinner, another as Raid, the other ones too faded to make out. In the middle of the cans, crouched out of sight, was a box of rat poison. It looked fairly new, the yellow of the box still bright. I held it up, catching the words on it from the sunlight straining in through the open door, and it seemed about half-empty. I hadn't seen any mice or rats anywhere in the house, so I didn't know what the box was doing here.

Then it came back to me, what I had been looking for in the Johnsons' garbage the night after Mrs. Hunter had confronted Kirby about her dog, Humphrey. He had been poisoned: small pellets of what looked like rat poison found stuffed inside a small piece of raw hamburger meat. I opened the lid of the box, though I was afraid to touch the stuff inside, and took a peek. I put on my imaginary detective cap, earned from reading all of those Hardy Boys and Sherlock Holmes books, and tried to deduce something.

If this was the poison that had been used on Humphrey, whose was it? My first thought was that Kirby had stashed the unused box in our garage, cagey enough to know it wouldn't be smart to put it in the trash can outside his own door. I chewed on that a while, until my arms broke out in goose bumps as a mini-flood of memories flashed through my mind.

I carefully pushed the lid down, placed the box back onto the shelf, and rearranged the cans back to their original spots around it. By the time I had put the wagon back and carried the toolbox out of the garage, it was clear to me exactly who had killed Mrs. Hunter's dog. It was a scary realization, and I had no idea what to do with that information. None at all.

I TRIED NOT TO THINK ABOUT Ken, or his reasons for wanting to poison a harmless dog, while I took a big swig of Pepsi from the bottle in our fridge. Something Humphrey had done must have pissed him off enough to make him commit murder—barking too loud when Ken was trying to read or trying to sleep, pooping in the grass near his car, or some other heinous injustice the dog had committed against him—which got me wondering how much Demian or I would have to piss him off to make him poison one of us.

"What's in there?" Demian, now at my elbow, asked.

I looked down at the tool box and belched. "Snakes. I wouldn't touch it if I were you."

He laughed, then stopped, his brow furrowing. A look up to me, then to the box. "Why are they in there? Where did you get them?"

"Why, indeed?" I asked, then grabbed the handle and headed for the front door. "Come on, we got twenty bucks to earn."

By the time we got to Mrs. Hunter's house, Demian had figured out that I was kidding about the snakes. The conversation somehow made its way to ants in our pants, then to the farts of various insects, and when Mrs. Hunter opened her door to us, we were in tears and couldn't stop laughing.

"Well, you boys sure are in good spirits today, that's clear. You come over here to infect me with the giggles?"

I made an effort to compose myself while allowing Demian's laughter to run its course. I stared at Mrs. Hunter in her ubiquitous housedress and thought of the right words to say. "Mrs. Dillon told us you might need some help," I started. "You know, handiwork stuff, so we wanted to do whatever you needed done. She already paid us, on your, um, behalf, so it will not cost you a dime. Or even a penny." I gave her a genuine smile at the end.

"That's mighty neighborly of that fine woman, and I'll have to fix up something as a ways of thanking her. Come on in. Let's see what needs doing around here."

Her house had a musty, unpleasant smell to it, with multiple odors combining in a way that made it difficult for me to breathe. There were dog odors, even though Humphrey had been gone for over a month now, and sharp, acrid cooking smells: a deep-fried, burnt scent that filled the entire house. Demian put his hand over his nose, but I swatted it away before Mrs. Hunter could see him.

She led us through the front room, which was filled with tower-high piles of newspapers and magazines, some tied in neat bundles and others teetering above my head. A purplish sofa, with dog hair all over the ripped and faded cushions, stood in the center of the room, a color TV planted in front of it.

"Don't mind any of the mess, just come on through," she commanded, and we moved into the kitchen. The smell of smoke and grease was the worst in here, and I almost gagged. I swallowed it back, with my mouth closed as I tried desperately to hold my breath. Demian tugged on my shirt, and I swatted his hand away. We had been paid the twenty dollars, and nothing was going to keep us from earning it the way Mrs. Dillon intended.

"You hungry? No trouble to fix you up something quick," she said, poking through cupboards that were disorganized and filled with Co-op brand cans and packages.

"No, thank you. We want to help *you*," I said between short gasps of air. The more I tried not to inhale any of the smelly fumes, the more my forehead and the backs of my eyes hurt. "Do you have anything outside for us to do?" I practically pleaded.

Mercifully, she opened the kitchen door and led us down a small wooden staircase, painted the same faded green as the house. Surrounded by a fence that ran up one side of Essex and made a sharp turn onto Wheeler Street was her back yard: half concrete and half dying brown grass. The big toolbox was still in my right hand, and I did a few quick curls with it to keep my arm from falling asleep.

She gave us instructions to clean the back yard of the dog droppings, reminders of the life that Ken had for some reason ended, all of which were either brown and shriveled or as white and chalky as the concrete. Then we were supposed to mow the lawn with a mower that looked older than Gramma and water it down "real good."

Mrs. Hunter watched us work from the top step of the staircase, her regular breathing raspy and loud. Sometimes she spoke directly to us, while other times she seemed to be speaking to herself. "We may be poor, but God gave us all this lushness, all this green," she said, and I looked up to see her attention focused on the view over her fence. "The flowers and trees and birds singing is free, true enough."

When we finished with the back yard, Demian followed me back up to the kitchen, where the old woman was going through her pantry. I told her the work was done, and she gave a startled shake.

Facing us, she said, "Well, I had planned to bake Mrs. Dillon a nice pie to show my gratitude, but I'm plum outta the ingredients I require. Can't even make a pie crust with what I have here, and my fruits are all eaten up." She moved slowly into the other room. Demian looked at me, like he wasn't sure if we should follow her. I shrugged but kept my feet planted on the filmy, stained floor.

She struggled back into the kitchen, purse in hand. She collapsed into a skinny metal chair next to the faded yellow Formica table and began to pull everything out of the overstuffed black purse. She separated a capless pen, a scrap of paper, and a handful of colorful bills, which I recognized as food stamps, from the rest of the heap. Demian could not keep from fidgeting as Mrs. Hunter scribbled down a word or two, then closed her eyes, jotted another word, closed her eyes again, repeating the sequence over and over until she held the paper out.

"If you boys are still on the clock, could you go on up to the supermarket and get me the things off this list?" she said, and I nodded. I took the paper from her, and she counted out fifteen dollars' worth of federal money and placed it in my hand. "There should be enough there for all that, plus a piece of candy for the both of you."

At the Co-op, we found everything she wanted, loaded all of it up in a grocery cart, and still had some change left over for Mrs. Hunter after we had checked out.

"What about the candy, Steve? She said we could get some," Demian looked longingly at the four small shelves of candy and gum—next to the *People* magazines, *National Enquirers*, and fashion magazines—near the checkout line.

"We don't need it, Demian," I told him, eyeing the change in my hand that I knew meant more to Mrs. Hunter than it ever could to us. Yes, we were poor, but she was old and poor, and alone in that house that smelled like jail or death.

I tried to make it up to him by wheeling the cart out of the parking lot and telling him to get inside. He did a funny little dance, then squealed, before climbing up into the belly of the cart. I steered it down Ashby, back toward Mrs. Hunter's house. It was all downhill, so once I built up some speed, I jumped onto the back of it and we sailed the sidewalk, past all the houses and trees, past the weeds, and alongside the cars driving by us in the opposite direction.

At Wheeler, I maneuvered us past a huge patch of ivy and stopped at the sour grass growing wild near the street. I plucked a few stalks, snapped the yellow flowers from the tips, gave one to Demian, and gnawed on my own. Inside my mouth, the green casing popped and released the wet, bitter juice, which swirled around my teeth and down my throat. I chewed and chewed until it was all gone. Then I went back for more.

I didn't even hear him until he was almost in front of us. "Hey," Kirby said, jogging toward me from across the street, "could I get that cart?"

I looked at Demian in the shopping cart, his body so small and vulnerable in there with the big bag of groceries. I tried to meet my neighbor's eyes, but he towered above me. I focused on his chin and mustered up a weak, "I need to take it back to the Co-op."

"They won't miss it." He lifted Demian out and planted him next to me. He grabbed the grocery bag and pushed it into my arms. I cowered there, feeling like I'd been bullied. It reminded me of that night in the pub with Mom and Ken, when Ken had made me feel so small and powerless.

Demian stood with his head down, his body shaking slightly. Feeling protective, I gathered the courage to look up, where Kirby had hold of the cart's handlebars. His crazed pile of blond curls danced back and forth as he reached the corner and then disappeared onto Ashby.

"Fuckhead," I said, my throat suddenly dry and my thumbs trembling at the edges of the grocery bag. I was aware of the car sounds, a *whish-whish* as they traveled east and west on the busy street where Kirby had our hijacked cart. Birdsong mixed with the traffic noise, my ears full of all the sounds in the world. I stared into the sun that roared its brightness above me until my eyes teared up. I closed them, seeing spots, and I was afraid I might throw up.

I steadied myself, gave Demian a little nudge with my elbow, and walked to where one old lady was waiting to make a pie for another old lady.

DEMIAN HAD WORN HIMSELF OUT, JUMPING on our beds and fighting imaginary pirates until sleep swept over him like a huge wave and he crashed onto the shore of his pillow and was still. Wide awake from all the soda I'd been drinking, I fingered the twenty-dollar bill in my pocket and knew what I had to do. The entire point of working was to help Mom out, so she didn't have to do anything bad with Mr. Takadakos anymore. Twenty dollars was a lot of money. I just wasn't sure it was enough. But I had to try.

Before I ventured out of my room, my thoughts leapt to the poison I'd found in the garage. Maybe we had a rat problem, and Ken had taken care of it without bothering any of us. I had no proof, really, that he had had anything to do with Humphrey's death. The decision to try to forget I'd ever seen the poison came at that moment, and I forced myself to give Ken the benefit of the doubt that he could never do something so cruel and heartless and sick.

Out in the living room, Mom and Ken's friends listened to our stereo and sat on our furniture. I looked around, as always, for any kids my age, but found only adults engaged in smoking, drinking, and talking.

I tried to blend in, out of place in my own house, but quickly realized that no one even seemed aware of my presence. Alone in the kitchen, I thought about eating a piece of cheese that had fallen onto the floor. Then I heard Ken make his bleat of a laugh. *Don't eat that cheese!* a voice inside my head screamed. *He probably poisoned it. Just for you!* My mind had already betrayed the pact I'd made with it. I kept my eyes off the floor and did my best to avoid running into Ken.

I followed the sound of Mom's voice to her place on her favorite chair. She sat cross-legged on the thin cushion, fingers fondling one of her handmade baskets. Across from her, one of the few other women there sat on our ratty ottoman that was covered by a paisley sheet. They looked deep in conversation, so I waited patiently in the hall for an opportunity to proudly hand Mom the twenty.

"—getting a degree that's this side of useless," Mom's friend said, her teeth too large for a mouth that seemed to never close completely. "You've got a good, solid job, even without it."

Mom wrapped her small hands around the top of the basket, lifting it up and then down, in a kind of hypnotic motion. "So I didn't miss out? I chose the right path? Good for me."

"Rose," the woman said, placing her hand lightly on my Mom's foot. Her leg jerked back from the touch.

"Pa*tricia*," Mom said, her voice high and strange, like she was making fun of her. Patricia's mouth closed suddenly. I could see her big teeth pushing against her chapped lips. "Do you look at my life and see something you want for yourself?"

I backed into a shadowed part of the hall, suddenly hoping she wouldn't see me.

"Hey, Rose, I never once tried anything with Ken," Patricia raised her hands up, like you see people do on TV when the cops have their guns pointed at them.

"Don't be stupid. That's not what I meant." Mom straightened her legs and gave a small kick at the ottoman. "And you know it."

Patricia's lips spread wide, and all I could see were those teeth. "I know, I know." Ken laughed again, this time from the kitchen, and both of them turned their heads toward the noise. "Is he what *you* want?"

"He takes good care of me." Mom seemed to react to some look of Patricia's that I couldn't see when she said, "Not financially, of course. But he makes me happy. He makes me laugh when I'm sad."

"That's nice." She touched Mom's foot again, which rested on the ottoman between Patricia's legs, and this time it didn't move. "I get sad too. About some of the choices I've made, the men I've allowed myself to fall in love with. What do you get sad about?"

Mom stared at her hands, lost in them for what felt like a long time. She finally looked up at Patricia and said, "The little girl I'll never have. The boys I *did* have. Their constant presence, and the way they sap so much of my energy with their neediness … The man who said goodbye when

I wanted him to stay with me forever." A long pause, as the music seemed to get louder. Janis Joplin wailing, drowning out the next thing Mom said.

"What would you be doing, what kind of life would you be living, if not this?" Patricia asked. Mom leaned toward her, until their heads almost touched. When she spoke, I couldn't make out the words. She looked like she was sharing a secret, a secret life that I would never know.

They hugged, and then Mom was out of the chair and heading toward the hall and me standing there. "Is Demian asleep?" she asked when she saw me.

"I think so," I said.

"Okay," she said, and I wanted her to kiss my head or touch my shoulder. A small gesture. A tiny show of affection. I wanted to get it without having to ask for it.

I watched her disappear down the hall and into the bathroom. By the time she shut the door, I had already spent every penny of that twenty dollars in my head. The desire to save her from our landlord had completely vanished.

DEMIAN AND I DIDN'T REALLY TALK much over the next two days, mostly because I decided to ditch the odd-job nonsense after what I'd heard Mom say to her friend, and I began to leave early each morning to spend time with Trevor. I knew that if I kept my mind and body busy, it would be more difficult for my thoughts to drift back to Seneca and what my summer *could* have been. So Trevor and I trekked all around Berkeley, even up to the Rose Garden and into the heights of North Berkeley, where his slightly older cousin, Nathan, had just moved into a mansion-like house with his lawyer dad, from D.C. We ate what Nate called "gourmet food" for lunch—which didn't taste that different from a regular bologna and cheese sandwich, except the bread was really crunchy and had a bunch of herbs in it—played with his massive train set down in the basement, prank-called a bunch of strangers, and pretty much goofed off until it got dark.

When Trevor's big brother, Art, was around, he'd wander up to Telegraph with the two of us in tow, pocketing the occasional book from Moe's or clay pipe from one of the head shops. I thought we were pushing our luck every time we took our five-finger discount, and I was terrified of getting caught. At the same time, I wanted to see the look on Mom's face when she had to come down to the police station and get me out on a shoplifting charge. I felt guilty about stealing, especially from the bookstore where the guys behind the counter had bought some of my crappy used books in the past, but Demian wasn't ever with me like he was that day at the bookstore in Albany, so I knew the only one who'd get hurt if I got caught was me. I could live with that possibility, if not the unavoidable eventuality.

It was a Thursday night, around five o'clock, when I got home from another day of running wild in the streets. The house was empty. Thankfully, there was no sign of Ken, and Mom wasn't due for another hour, but I was surprised not to find Demian in front of the TV or in our room. The bedroom seemed different, especially his side of it, but I didn't notice anything wrong right away. I was bored, so I ventured down a few doors to Rafe's house to check on Demian.

"Hi, Stephen," Rafe's mom opened the door with that tone in her voice which meant she still didn't like me.

"Is Demian here?" I leaned my head around her body to stare into a house that was cleaner and roomier than mine.

She looked behind her, squinted as if trying to see what I saw. I heard the squeal of Eva, Rafe's little sister, from one of the bedrooms. "No," she said, "he's not."

"Oh, okay." I stood there in front of her, feeling dumb. "Is Rafe here?"

"We're about to sit down for dinner. Can it wait?" she asked, her hand on the door as if ready to slam it in my face.

Rafe appeared from behind her, Eva in his arms. "Mom, I think she pooped." She took the handoff from Rafe, and as she shut the door on me, he rushed over and kept it open. "Steve, hey, did you get him?"

His mom wandered off to change a diaper, and Rafe came outside and stood next to me on the small porch.

"Get who?"

"Demian got clobbered by Eric today. He didn't tell you? Oh, man, it, well, scary, it sucked, we were so freaked out. I figured you ..." Rafe wobbled back and forth, his cheeks blown up and spittle leaking from his lips. *Weebles wobble, but they don't fall down*, I thought, channeling my brother.

"He ain't home," I said. "You know where he is?" I knew something was really wrong then. Demian should have been home.

"Yeah, no," Rafe said, and I headed off.

"Send him home if you see him, okay?" I yelled. I was almost two houses up the street now.

"You gonna kick Eric's ass?" Rafe yelled and I stopped.

"Where does he live?"

He shrugged and looked up into the sky, where the sun had already started its slow rotation westward, toward sunset. "Don't know. But I can find out."

"Find out, Rafe. 'Cause I am going to kick his ass. I'm gonna put a serious hurt on that piece of shit."

"Hell yeah!" Rafe said, pumping his arm up in the air like he was at a rock concert or something.

Back in my house, I checked all the rooms, and when I couldn't find Demian, I checked the back yard. In our bedroom, one of the drawers was half-open. Clothes, *his* clothes, were missing. I looked inside the closet. Things had been moved around, piled up like he'd sifted through them. I saw my bookbag but not his. My hands grabbed at whatever was under his bed—a gum wrapper, half-broken action figures, a ripped comic book—but his backpack wasn't there.

"Fuck, Demian," I said aloud. I was freaked out and pissed off at him for not being home. What the hell was he doing? Where the hell had he gone?

Ken strolled in around six, and I ignored him. I taxed my brain trying to imagine all the places my little brother might go at this hour. When Mom came home a little later, I rushed at her.

"Honey, I just walked in," she said when I told her Demian was gone. "Can I get a minute to change my clothes, unwind before you bombard me?"

I moved aside, so she could go into her room. I stood there, Ken on the couch picking his toes with a matchbox and humming to himself. I didn't believe Demian had actually run away from home—he was only six, how far could he travel before he got hungry or homesick?—but he didn't know Berkeley as well as I did, and I was afraid of it getting dark, him getting lost, and something bad happening to him. He had been acting so strange, it made sense that he might do something that wasn't characteristic of him, like packing a bag and taking off.

Five minutes later, Mom still hadn't re-emerged from her bedroom, and now I had to listen to an album Ken had put on with a woman screaming at the top of her lungs at somebody called Gloria. I had no idea how long Demian had been gone, but I wanted—I needed—to find him before the sun went completely down. Storming out through the back door, I yelled to whoever might be listening, "I'll be back." I hopped on my bike and pedaled toward the places I knew he knew well.

I biked up to Le Conte, rode through the playground where two kids his age were leaping off the jungle gym. They hadn't seen him, so I rode up one street and down another, up and down like that until I reached the campus. By now it was well after seven but still light outside. I headed back with the hope that he had already gotten his adventure out of his system and was sitting at the dinner table with Mom and Ken.

An hour later, it was dark, and Demian still hadn't come home. No phone call, no sign of him. I alternately stared at the clock, the door, the phone, then back to the clock as the minutes piled up without any word.

"Mom, can you do something? I'm really worried."

"Demian's fine, Stephen, just relax. What about his friends, do you have any of their numbers?" Mom asked me from the couch, a glass of red wine in her hand. She and Ken had eaten dinner while I kept watch in the living room.

Vigorously, I shook my head. Both of them weren't the least bit alarmed or concerned, positive that he would walk in the door at any minute. "He's never this late. Ma, come on!"

"What do you want me to do exactly, Stephen? Drive around the neighborhood looking for him? He's responsible, he'll come back soon." She took a sip and ran her tongue along the top of her lip.

"What about the backpack? And Eric Zydenski beating him up today? He's gone, Mom. He's gone!" I held back tears, scared and angry.

"Melodramatic much?" Ken said, then smiled at me like we were best buds. I ignored him and turned to Mom, still hoping she could see reason.

She placed her wine down, then focused what little attention she had on me. "Okay, let's do an inventory. What'd he take with him? His backpack, right?"

I nodded, gave Ken a quick dirty look, and then rattled off a list of things I'd deduced were gone from our room.

"His clothes, shirts definitely, underpants, socks. Oh, his little windbreaker." I moved into the kitchen, shouted out from in front of the fridge. "The bologna package is gone. Half the bread. Looks like the pickles are gone."

"The pickles? Which ones?" Ken's voice drifted to me from the other room.

"The sweet ones."

"Aww, man. I love those," he said. "I'm actually jonesing for one of those right now."

I slammed the refrigerator door, hoping it was loud enough for Ken to get how pissed off I was at him. The silverware drawer looked full, but the junk drawer had been rifled through. Trying to think of what all we kept in there, I shouted, "I think he took the flashlight."

I ran to Mom, the wine glass at her lips, her front teeth visible as she sipped. "Why would he take the flashlight if he's planning on coming home before dark?"

She froze for a moment, and looked suddenly worried. Scared. She put the glass down on the coffee table, hopped up, and headed for her room. "Let me get my shoes on and we'll go right now."

Ken yelled at her from his place on the floor. "Hey, we got people dropping by in a few." A half-smoked cigarette smoldered between his fingers, a section of the *Chronicle* on the rug at his dirty feet.

Mom had her sneakers on and grabbed her leather fringe jacket by the door. "That's fine. Just don't let them eat all the brie in there. I want some when I get back."

I followed her out. She pushed past me and stuck her head back in the living room. "And don't smoke our entire stash, okay?"

I could see him from outside on the porch, through the window that looked onto the street. He stared at her, dumbly.

"Okay?"

"Okay, okay," he said, then went back to reading the paper.

I got into the passenger seat of Mom's Dodge just as the last colors of sunset faded behind the horizon.

BY TEN O'CLOCK, WE HAD BEEN to four of Demian's friends' houses, driven up and down Ashby Avenue, and traveled past the school again. I had run out of ideas for places he might have gone, and as we neared Willard Park, my hopes for finding him had vanished. I tried to stay positive, then clung to the idea that maybe he had gotten tired or scared and headed home finally. If he wasn't there, the next place we'd have to go would be the police station.

"Call home, then," Mom said, "if you think he might be there." She pulled into a well-lit gas station that had a pay phone. She placed a dime in my hand, and I raced off and into the phone booth. Out of habit, I checked the coin return for change. It was empty.

I dialed our house. It rang. And rang.

A man's voice I didn't recognize answered, "Yeah?!" Loud strains of guitar and drums filled the earpiece from the other end.

"Ken? I want to talk to Ken!" I said, yelling to be heard over the noise.

"What? Who is this?" he said. Then I heard a mumbled, "I don't know who the fuck this is, man."

"Hang it up," another voice said.

Then the phone went dead. I searched my pockets for some change. Nothing. I tried not to panic and ran back to the car. I silently prayed for Demian to be home and safe.

"Is Demian here?" I yelled as I ran in the front door. Mom was still outside, coming in from the car. The house was filled with half a dozen of Ken's friends. Sprawled all over the living room, they ate our food, drank our booze, and listened to our turntable. "Is Demian here?" I interrupted Ken and a girl in beaded clothes and moccasins who looked like Pocahontas.

"This is Stephen," Ken introduced me to the girl. I didn't care about her, I just wanted to know if my brother had come home yet.

The girl held out her dark-skinned hand, black hairs covering her bare arm. "Hi, Stephen. I'm Arielle."

"Ken Ken Ken," I said, staccato-like, freaking out. "Where is he?"

Mom walked in then, her eyes tired. I ran to check the bedroom. He wasn't there. When I came back, she stood at the door, waiting for me.

"I'm going to the police station. Do you want to come?" she said.

"I should stay here. You know, if he … when he calls." I didn't want any of their friends touching the phone or hanging it up again.

"I'll be back soon." She held out her arms, and I fell inside them. "It's going to be fine, Stevie. Okay?"

A short burst of tears escaped me, but I kept the hug short. I had been taught not to trust the pigs, that they were all corrupt, but I hoped there were at least a few Berkeley cops who cared enough about missing kids to try to search for my brother. I knew they weren't like Kojak or Baretta on TV, super cops who always caught the criminal or saved the kidnapped victim, but maybe they weren't as bad as Ken always accused them of being.

Once Mom left, I became aware of how loud everything in the living room was: people talking, music blaring, feet treading on the hardwood floor, people laughing, bottles clinking against tables and chairs. A song ended, followed by the cyclone-like sound of the turntable needle as it reached the record's end. A moment later, the tonearm was lifted by someone, and a new album replaced the old one.

It was Elton John, with a voice that could be scratchy and defiant one moment, mellow and vulnerable the next. Sitting Indian style on the cool hardwood of the short entrance hall that connected the front door to the living room, determined to be the first face Demian saw the minute he got home, I closed my eyes and listened to the music. I tried to filter out Ken's voice and those of his loud friends. I wanted to exist in that special space that a song occupied, that bubble of life where the lyrics created images and the images expanded to create a place I could slip right into. It was safe in there, wrapped around the funny-looking notes of the music, this world of escape.

"Let me get a hit of that," I heard a male voice say a few feet from me. I wondered if the smoke in the air was affecting these thoughts of separate universes created from songs. I wondered if Demian running away had made me crazy. I wondered if it was all my fault that he was gone.

"Levon" started up, one of my favorite songs from Elton, and I began singing the lyrics to myself. When the *New York Times* declared that God was dead, one of Ken's friends by the record player hooted and raised his arm, then pumped his fist a few times.

"God is dead, hallelujah!" he shouted. All six or seven people in the room looked his way.

An older guy, one of Ken's professors when he was still a student at Cal, chuckled as he rubbed an unruly white beard. "If He ever existed, that is," he said.

Ken seemed to propel himself off the couch to turn down the music, like a dog leaping to please its master. He stared at the professor as if he were a rock star on a stage or something.

Ken's friend, wearing a beer-stained poncho, his teeth crooked and yellow, shook his fist again. "That's the debate, isn't it? Is God a construction by those few who hold the power striving to control the masses, or a true force in the cosmic universe? Where do you fall, Professor?"

The professor stroked his beard again, then wiped his fingers on his tan corduroy pants before addressing the living room as though he were teaching one of his classes. "Is He an abstraction or is He a truth? I'm not a scientist, merely a lowly philosopher—" Here he stopped himself in dramatic fashion to laugh at his own joke, or whatever it was supposed to be, before continuing, "But I'll enlighten you if you wish, on what this deity is all about."

For the next fifteen minutes, phrases like *godlessness as Marxist revolt*, *strict commitment to faith and the gospel*, and *the orgasm is proof enough for me that God exists* bounced around the room but didn't seem to stick anywhere solid. I strained to hear the music under their discussion, wanting to escape back to that special musical space while trying not to imagine Demian dead somewhere. Or worse.

I must have dozed for a while after that, because next thing Elton John was gone and my mother walked in the house. Her face was angry, pulled tight. It softened when she saw me sitting on the floor, blocking her passage inside.

"Why don't you go to bed, Stevie?" She helped me to my feet, and I felt groggy, weak.

I asked her what time it was, unable to focus on my watch. She said it was after midnight. She told me she had given the police a school photo of Demian and that they would do their best to find him. Her voice wasn't as convincing as I needed it to be.

"They think he probably went for a sleepover with a friend and just forgot to tell us. I'm inclined to maybe agree with them." She led me into my bedroom, pulled back the covers, and gently pushed me down. I kicked off my shoes and let her tuck me in, all my clothes still on.

"He'll be back in the morning, Stevie," she said. I didn't believe her, but I was too tired to argue, too defeated to fight any longer for my little brother. "Get some sleep." She shut off the light and closed the door behind her.

I lay in bed and stared at the ceiling, lit from the moonlight outside the window. Whenever a car drove down our street, I followed the sweeping shadows above. The voices from the living room were loud but indistinct.

A pair of feet padded across the far side of the living room to a spot not far from my bedroom door. "What's up with the little guy?" Ken's voice.

Mom hissed, "One of them hit on me. I'm there for my son, and the creep is leering at me and asking about my hair. Bastard." She started crying then, a soft, restrained thing.

"Aw, babe," Ken said, and the floorboard outside my door creaked with his movement. "It'll be all right."

Hearing my mother cry scared me, because it happened so rarely. I couldn't help wondering, though, if she was crying because Demian was missing and she was worried about him or if it was because some cop had come on to her.

I HAD BARELY CLOSED MY EYES all night, but somehow I slept. I dreamed of Demian walking in the snow with his ratty bookbag, a pack of wolves surrounding him. Their red eyes were like infernos against the whiteness of their fur and the falling snow. He seemed scared but determined to continue moving toward wherever he was headed. The sound of the party breaking up pulled me out of the nightmare. With the images slowly receding, although not slowly enough, I made a wish that Demian was back asleep in his bed. When I looked on his side of the room, there was no sign of him. Just an unmade bed and a rumpled pillow.

When the sun brought light into my room, I tumbled out of bed. Still in my clothes from the day before, it seemed easy for me to start the day where I'd ended it: worrying about where the hell Demian could be. Out in the living room, pillows were scattered along the floor, next to ashtrays full of cigarettes and roaches, surrounded by wine glasses, beer bottles, and stepped-on particles of food. The smell of smoke and incense hung in the house. I went to open a window when I saw Mom curled up on our big chair. She jerked, startled when I moved past her.

"Demian?" she asked.

I turned to face her, her eyes bloodshot and raw. "No, Ma, just me." I paused, then asked the question, already knowing the answer. "Did he call?"

She rubbed her nose with the palm of her hand, then plucked something small from the edge of her eye. She mouthed no and then got up and hugged me. I had wanted to cry all night, but for some reason I resisted it now. When she released me and said, "I need to get ready for work," I knew why.

I gave her a hurt, questioning look. She immediately got defensive. "I have to work, Stephen. I'm the only one around here making—Ken will stay here with you today. Hopefully, the police will call. Demian will call. Or come home. I want someone to be here when that happens. Okay?"

I let her go, then picked up the phone to make sure it was working, not off the hook or dead from Mom or Ken not paying the bill. The dial tone was strong. My fingers hooked into the holes on the front of the phone, letting six of the numbers click-clack down. I stopped before I dialed the last of Seneca's number. I hung it up and listened to my stomach grumble. Hunger or nerves, I wasn't sure which. So I went into the kitchen and rooted around in the cupboards for something to eat.

That was when I noticed all the soup was gone. And the can opener.

MOM LEFT A HALF HOUR LATER, and Ken got up a little after that. He wandered into the living room, where I sat watching something or other. Not having my brother there beside me, or anywhere in the house at 8:00 a.m. on a summer morning, felt more than bizarre. It felt wrong. Ugly.

Ken's big toe knocked over a half-full bottle of Heineken; a flood of liquid and foam spilled onto the wooden floors. "Ah, shit!" he said, and scurried into the kitchen. He sopped up the mess with paper towels, and I stared at the tiny pools of beer he missed.

"You doing okay?" he asked, after he'd tossed the towels in the garbage and lit up his first cigarette of the day. "Yeah," I said, hearing the deadness in my voice.

"Hey, I'm gonna hang out here today, okay? Your ma wants me to be here with you when Demian comes home. And he's gonna come home, feeling stupid that he spent the night at one of his little buddy's houses without telling us." He took a long pull on his cigarette, and I felt the urge to bite him.

"Don't call him stupid," I said. I got up, walked the entire length around the coffee table to the TV, rather than sidle past his hairy legs, and turned off the TV.

"Steve, hey, I wasn't calling him—you know, I'm just trying to ..." Ken ran out of steam. No fucking way was I sitting in this house all day with him.

"Later," I said, and walked out the back door and to my bike along the side of the house.

"Where you going?" he asked to the wide open door, but he didn't get off the couch and didn't raise his voice.

As I rode past the side of the house, I heard the sound of the TV in the living room come to life and tried to imagine my father doing something different from Ken if he was here. I hadn't seen him in so long, didn't even know if he was alive or dead, still in New York City or somewhere in the jungles of Peru or even back in California. Wherever he was, I was suddenly desperate to know if he ever thought of Demian and me.

I HAD NO IDEA WHERE TO go, or how to find Demian, but I rode anyway, down Ashby and into neighborhoods I'd never seen before. I pedaled back up to the Claremont Hotel and weaved around windy streets that led up to houses and lives that I had coveted and dreamed about inhabiting. I felt sorry for myself, wished that my life was something that it wasn't. I took a turn off a curb strange and my chain made a crunching sound just before it went slack. I fixed it in front of a three-story house with a brilliant view across the San Francisco Bay, my fingers wet with oil.

I rode back down to Telegraph, headed toward campus, traveling up and down all the streets intersecting the avenue. Cruising down Ellsworth and approaching Stuart Street, I saw a Hare Krishna wandering around like he was lost. I had never seen one—faded pink robe, bald head but for the long ponytail, worn sandals, and an indecipherable look of either bliss or stupidity—alone. This one had glasses, wire-rimmed, and he looked like Woody Allen. He also had a handful of what looked like flyers. I stopped my bike near a patch of ivy to watch him.

He looked nervous, walking up the short walkway of a one-story house. After he had knocked a few times, he left one of the flyers on a welcome mat in front of the door. When he approached the house next door, I scooted my bicycle and myself over to the welcome mat. I expected to see a picture of Krishna on the flyer, with the words of a chant and some cult-like propaganda. Instead, I saw a picture of a frightened-looking Demian, with what looked like a bruise on the cheek under his left eye. Below the color photo was a simple question: *Is this your child?* and two phone numbers, one belonging to the temple, the other to the BPD.

"Hey," I yelled, riding up behind Woody-Krishna. He turned, giving me that simple, unreadable look. I stopped and pointed at Demian's face. He stared at me, then his face seemed to brighten, a facsimile of a smile forming. My finger started shaking and my voice caught in my throat. I managed to get the words *my brother* out.

"Yes," he said, pointing at Demian with me. "Come." He turned and started to run up the street, toward the temple. I tried to pedal, but my legs shook too hard. Off the bike, I held the handlebars and pushed it up the hill.

Inside the temple, I waited in a room filled with pamphlets, wild flowers, incense, and images of Krishna. An ancient-looking man with a white dot on his dark-skinned face and wearing saffron robes festooned with swirling scarves, entered the room and gave me a small bow. "You are the boy's brother?" he asked, with such kindness in his voice that I started to cry. He embraced me in a way that allowed all the tension to drop out of me, like water rushing over a falls and into a calm stream.

He chanted something into my ear, a prayer that repeated itself every few words, but all I could hear was an internal voice chanting, *My brother is safe, my brother is safe.*

Chapter 15

AFTER WIPING AWAY A FEW TIRED tears at the Krishna temple, I thanked everyone around me and rushed home to call Mom. The police had already called the house and, fortunately, Ken had been there to answer it. Mom was on her way to the police station to pick him up. I thought about biking over to meet her but figured it would be best to just hang tight and serve as a welcoming face when Demian got home. I was relieved but also pissed. Why hadn't he just told me what had happened with Eric? Why hadn't he been able to confide in me that he wanted to run away?

The leader at the temple had told me that Demian had sneaked into their gardens the day before and hid. One of the young kids had found him, and they had played for a while before more kids came along. Demian wanted them to shave his head like theirs, but while one of the kids was heading back to the garden with a razor, an adult had stopped him and then discovered my brother. He had refused to tell them his name, where he lived, his phone number, or anything that could get him back home. He simply said he had run away and wanted to join their family. Demian had used the word *family*. He ended up staying there for the night while the older people talked about it. First thing in the morning, they took a Polaroid of him, printed up flyers, and sent the majority of their members around the neighborhood looking for his parents, while a few others drove him down to the police station with the hope that they could get him back home.

When Demian and Mom finally walked in the front door, I was a mixture of hurt, anger, and happiness. He looked at me, but didn't say anything. I called him a doo-doo head, then playfully punched his small arm. Ken gave him a hug that was too hard and a "Welcome home" that was too loud and boisterous. I watched Demian go limp inside Ken's embrace. Mom put his backpack in our room, then took his hand and led him to the kitchen, where she made him a glass of Nestle's Quik.

"So he's … okay?" I asked her after he'd eaten something and Mom had put him in his bed to rest. She was back off to work, to finish the day out.

"He's fine. Or he will be." She looked at our closed bedroom door, then leaned down to me. "Don't tell your grandmother about this, okay? Another headache I don't need."

Ken left at the same time Mom did, so it was just the two of us in the house. I wanted desperately to talk to him, to figure out what he had been thinking. I wanted to wake him up; I wanted to punch the wall; I wanted to pack my own bag and head for my own idea of escape. Instead, I got down on the floor and did a bunch of push-ups. Then I did a bunch of sit-ups. After that, I cleaned the mess from the night before until I was sweating and my energy for flight or destruction had left me.

I crept into our bedroom, not wanting to bother Demian. I lay on my bed, picked up my copy of *Rumble Fish*, and started reading it again from the beginning. Hoping to learn something about what I was feeling, and how to deal with it.

Demian stared over at me from his bed. His body covered but with his head peeking out of the blankets, he said, "Hey."

"Hey," I said. He turned his face toward the wall, and I continued reading my book.

A DAY LATER, IT WAS MY eleventh birthday. July 24, 1976. I had waited all summer for this day to come, but now that it was here, I didn't care. The timing was off for feeling celebratory, with Demian back but not quite himself, Mom more distant than normal, and Seneca in hiding from me. The only upside: I was in the best shape of my short life. My clothes were already too big for me, and I was only eating three meals a day. I had even convinced Ken to buy vegetables and fruit, despite his protests. He was the most non-organic hippie I'd ever seen.

Mom went out of her way to make the day special for me. I was honestly surprised that she even remembered it. But she actually had a plan, created just for her and us; Ken was apparently free to spend his Saturday any way he wanted, as long as it didn't involve us. That was fine with me. I *did* think it was weird that he wasn't invited to a "family" celebration, but I didn't advocate for him, given what I believed about him and a box of rat poison, and she seemed set on being alone with her boys on my birthday. I think she also wanted to go out of her way for Demian, to bolster his own mood and give him a reason to be happy that he had failed in his plan to join the Hare Krishnas.

The morning started with breakfast at a restaurant on Grove Street, about a twenty-minute drive from our house. I sat in the front seat next to Mom, my window down slightly to allow the breeze to swirl around my face. I rolled it down farther and stuck my head out, thinking about dogs doing just this, with a full understanding of why they enjoyed it so much. I let my tongue roll out of my mouth for a few seconds, then felt self-conscious and closed my mouth. Above us, trees still in full bloom leaned into the street—their branches and leaves dipping so far down it was like they were going to fall on top of the car. Or maybe even try to reach out and touch us, they felt that close.

When we came out of the tree tunnel, Demian perked up behind me. "There he is!"

On the corner, just ahead of us, was someone my brother and I knew as "the waving man," because he stood out on his front steps and waved at the traffic, a smile always lighting his face. He was black, a little older than my grandparents, and from what I'd heard, he was retired and did his waving bit pretty much every morning, then returned inside to spend the rest of the day with his wife. There was a lot of traffic that passed by his house, going in both directions, so I'm sure his arms got tired.

"Honk, Mom, honk!" Demian screamed from the back-seat as we got closer to his house. She seemed distracted, and I was afraid she hadn't heard him, that she would once again fail by denying him a great deal of joy in exchange for her doing so little. But she tapped her horn twice, which got the man's attention. He looked down at us through a pair of glasses and gave Demian an extra-special wave with his big orange work gloves, calling out, "Have a *good* day."

We all waved as we drove past him, Demian huffing and puffing he was waving so furiously. When he was done, he dropped back into his seat and said to himself, "Cool."

The restaurant was called Fat Albert's, and both Demian and I got excited about that, since we had watched the Bill Cosby cartoon a bunch of times, but Mom said it wasn't named after *that* Fat Albert. Then the word *fat* kind of stuck in my craw, and I wondered why, when I was so conscious of my weight, she would pick a place on my birthday with that word in its name. When we walked in, though, I knew exactly why Mom had picked it, and I forgave her instantly.

The entire place was covered in Jack London memorabilia.

There were black-and-white photographs of him at his typewriter, with his wife in a hammock, as well as a bundle of his books lining the upper walls. But the best thing was our table itself, which had a laminated top over a collage of his writings, pictures, and one-line witticisms. I soaked it all up, my obsession with London renewed, my thoughts of travel to Alaska and the Yukon freshly ignited. It was a great start to the day.

Even Demian appeared to enjoy himself, and he made short work of his whole-wheat pancakes, dousing them with butter and maple syrup. I happily ate my granola and wheat toast, while my mother picked at an omelette. The conversation meandered around safe topics, away from Demian's disappearance, and I realized that if Ken were here with us, he wouldn't be able to avoid bringing it up, most likely ruining the good mood we all shared.

Mr. Mopps', a toy store I'd heard about but had never actually been inside before, was the second surprise. Located across the street from the restaurant, it took up almost a third of a block. Inside, the place was covered from floor to ceiling with books, toys, puzzles, kites, bikes, nearly everything a kid with money in his pocket or a grandmother on his arm could want. I got myself a couple of books of Mad-Libs, something I figured Demian and I could both have fun with, two Tintin books, and a Steve Austin action figure that was as tall as one of my brother's legs. Mom let Demian pick out a Lego set, even though it wasn't his birthday. I didn't mind.

When we got it all to the cash register, Mom pulled out her checkbook.

"I'm sorry, we don't accept checks," the gray-haired woman at the counter said. "We take cash and MasterCard, however."

My mother dug through her purse. "I didn't bring much cash," she muttered, pulling out the few dollar bills stashed inside. She fumbled with the purse until a man and a little girl stood behind us. The girl held a handmade doll in her hand, her face bright and shiny. I gave a pleading look at my mother until she noticed them and put her purse down.

"I can … I can go to the bank, withdraw some money," she said.

The woman at the counter smiled kindly at us before saying, "I'll just hold these for you, until your return."

As Mom led us out of the store, my birthday presents unceremoniously shoved to the floor behind the counter, my hands curled into tight fists. I looked at the man withdrawing a hard plastic credit card from his wallet and then glared at his beautiful daughter. What had she done to deserve a father who had enough money to buy her whatever she wanted?

BY THE TIME WE GOT TO the bank it was closed, and wouldn't open again until Monday, when Mom would be back at work. She offered to go back to the toy store and buy me a few of the presents with the cash she *did* have, but I told her it was okay, I could wait. I knew that was the answer she wanted to hear.

"I'm sorry, Stevie," she said in the car on our way home, and I did my best not to sulk. Demian sat quietly in the backseat, staring out the window with his bottom lip pooched out and his hands glued to his cheeks.

When she stopped the car in front of our house, I swear I heard Mom say, "Stupid birthdays" to herself as she got out. Demian looked up at her suddenly, so I got the feeling I'd heard it right. Neither one of us moved, the heat of the midafternoon creating small puddles of sweat on my arms and at the back of my neck where my collar made me itch. By the time I got out of the car, I was convinced that this was what eleven would feel like for the next year. I was resigned to the idea of constant disappointment.

SUNDAY MORNING CAME, AND I DID something I had never done on my own before: I went to church. Mom and Ken were asleep as usual when I asked Demian if he wanted to go somewhere with me. He was sullen but restless for something to do, so we walked to the only place of worship I'd been to in Berkeley, a Protestant church on Parker Street. It had a good-size parking lot and a ton of stairs that climbed up to the three big wooden doors, but inside it wasn't so big. I didn't feel intimidated walking in there with Demian next to me, even though compared to the other people around us we were terribly underdressed. Most of them, even the kids, wore ties and sport coats, or nice dresses and polished shoes. Demian wore a ratty T-shirt, jeans, and his scuffed Keds, while I had on my usual sleeveless workout tee, shorts, and tennis shoes. But even though we were dressed like we were, the only looks we got were kind and accepting.

It felt good to be in God's house.

Fifteen minutes into the service, I was bored, and Demian fidgeted so much I was tempted to kick him. We sat in our pew between an old couple and a family with three girls, the two of us reading from the same Bible, then warbling along with the congregation from the same hymn book. The singing seemed to invigorate us both, and eventually Demian settled down and I found myself feeling calmer than I had in a while.

I thought about the few times Gramma and Grampa had taken us to their church, in Fremont, where they knew everyone there and dressed us up in clip-on ties, blue jackets, slacks, and tight brown loafers that we used Grampa's shoehorn to squeeze our feet inside.

"My handsome boys," Gramma said to us the last time we had gone, many months before. "These are my grandsons," she told everyone we met inside the church. She held us close and gave us sugarless mints throughout the service to keep us happy. Demian sang with his squeaky, off-key voice alongside Grampa, while I tried to match Gramma's strong, soulful voice as it carried itself high above all the voices surrounding us. After the whole thing was over, I felt lighter than my fat body usually made me feel. My ears rang from the chorus of hymnal singers, and my fingers tingled in a way that comforted me somehow.

In the Berkeley church, that Sunday after my birthday, I had some of the same feelings rise up in me. Demian and I were part of a community, in a place where structure and ritual were not frowned upon. We belonged to something greater than ourselves, a small world where we mattered and were cared for. The parts of the sermon I didn't understand seemed the most important, as if hidden within or just below the surface of his convoluted speech were the exact ideas and lessons that I needed to clearly grasp. I followed the pastor when he preached about higher duty and a connection with God as the place where faith lived, but the problem was that that faith hadn't even been born for me yet. I wanted to believe, was eager to mold myself in His image. I opened my heart to the power of the gospel, allowed myself to feel love for every being, recognizing that they felt love equally for me.

Not long after Demian and I left the church, removed from that place of devotion and severed from the overpowering sensation of unity, my heart closed again.

RAFE WAS WAITING FOR US WHEN we got back home from church. Instead of going inside to check in with Mom and Ken, we all walked toward the Ashby BART station and the weekend flea market. None of us had any money, it was just something to do. By the time we passed Shattuck, Rafe had told me everything that happened that day with Eric. Demian had clammed up every time I brought it up with him, until I finally gave up, frustrated that he was keeping more secrets from me. When Rafe gave me the blow-by-blow, starting with the taunting and ending with the beating, I was furious. I wanted to tear that little bastard Eric a new one.

"I don't want you to beat him up," Demian said to me, right after Rafe told me what street he lived on. "I don't."

"Well, I do. I'm gonna fucking smear that little queer," I said, imagining my foot pummeling his head.

Rafe looked at me strangely, then said, "You're gonna play games with him?" Smear the Queer was a game some of us had played during recess when I was in elementary school. It was basically a little-kid version of rugby; we tagged whoever had the ball, no tackling involved. During one recess, a teacher stopped us and said the name of the game was demeaning, and unless we changed it, we couldn't play it. Shortly after that, we abandoned it and played games with no names.

"Was that what he was playing with Demian? Fucking games?" I wasn't mad at Rafe, but he was pissing me off, so I got all up in his face. He cowered, and I was satisfied. "Didn't think so."

We passed stalls selling antique furniture, handmade clothes and trinkets, garage sale style junk, including toys that had been played with past the point of their usefulness. I thought of stealing a couple of comic books from a stall that was run by a kid my age and a dad more interested in listening to the A's game on his transistor radio than watching his merchandise. I remembered Demian was with me and decided against it.

By the time we'd gone through every aisle, the hot sun making me both thirsty and hungry, we were all ready for some refreshment.

"Come on to my house. Mom went to my auntie's with Eva. Dad says you can come over if you wanted." Rafe lumbered out of the station and back toward Emerson Street, so we followed.

At his house, I decided I still had energy to burn, so I drank water from his hose out front and took off for a run toward Telegraph. I also thought I'd pass by Eric's house to see if my brother's bully was available for a proper shit-kicking.

I DIDN'T FIND ERIC, BUT I came home both refreshed and exhausted from jogging around town in the late-July weather. Demian was on the couch watching *Wild Kingdom* with Mom and Ken, who looked as if they'd just woken up. It was after six o'clock.

I showered, then stared into the foggy mirror, searching for any signs that I'd gotten a year older. No hint of a mustache, not even a trace of peach fuzz on my upper lip. My shoulder and bicep muscles stood out more clearly than they ever had before, and being wet made them look even bigger and cooler. I admired myself in the mirror until Mom walked into the bathroom.

"Oh, shit, sorry, Stevie." She backed out and closed the door. Embarrassed, I stood where I was until I knew she had wandered back out to the living room or into her bedroom. I waited two full minutes, then slunk out of the bathroom.

In the hall, before I got to Mom and Ken's bedroom door, I heard her voice. She was pissed.

"Because I want to get it over with. It's almost the first," she said.

Ken's voice was calm, relaxed. "So you're gonna shower for him. Why?"

There was silence, but I could still hear her breathing. I didn't dare pass by their room at that moment. I thought I should go back in the bathroom, but I felt stuck in the hall, dripping small beads of water onto the wooden floor.

Finally, Mom's voice exploded, "Get a fucking job already!"

"Hey, don't speak to me like that," Ken said, not raising his voice.

"We're broke, and I can't do all of it by myself. I can't even afford to buy birthday presents for my son, and now I'm keeping us from getting evicted by doing *this*? And you're allowing it? You need to start pulling your weight, Ken. Pronto!"

I heard Marlin Perkins's voice from the other room, the words *tiger* and *prey* reaching my ears.

Ken let out a big breath and said, "You're right. This is on me. The bullshit ends tonight. This is the last time you need to even deal with him." A long pause, then, "So, we cool, babe?"

"I need to get in the shower," she said, and then Mom was in the hall. I kept my head down, with my hand wrapped around the towel like I'd just come out of the bathroom. I didn't look up for any reaction from her, just moved past her and went straight to my room.

I heard the water of the shower run through the pipes under my bedroom floor. The sun was almost down outside my window. I turned on the light before the dark had a chance to engulf the room.

MONDAY MORNING I HEADED OUT BEFORE the sun rose, to get a run in before stirring up trouble with Trevor and maybe Art, too. Still worried about Demian, I thought about inviting him along, then figured he was better off being far away from us, especially if we planned to lift more stuff from the Telegraph Avenue stores. I also wanted to track down

Eric again, and I definitely didn't want my brother around when I found his attacker.

I had heard Mom come in late the night before, after Demian and I were already in bed. We both heard her crying in her room, and while I felt sad for her, I also had figured out a label to affix on her that I'd learned from church: *immoral.* I didn't necessarily believe that she would burn in hell or any of that weirdness, but I did judge her for her behavior, for her choice to lay down with our landlord in exchange for less rent money. I thought she should have been a stronger person, should've gotten a job that paid more, or figured out another way to deal with us being broke so often. Poor.

As she cried and I secretly blamed, Demian stared at me through the dim light that the moon's pursed lips had blown into our room. I turned my body away from him, closed my eyes, and tried to think of other things.

On my run, I passed Manny's house and saw him sitting on the stoop playing jacks with his sister. We hadn't hung out in a couple of weeks, so I asked if he wanted to come with me to Trevor's. They had met each other a few times, and had gotten along, so I figured it was cool to bring him along. He said yes right away, the small rubber ball from their jacks game flying wild and into the street.

As we walked off, Juanita said, "Manny, get my ball for me."

"Get it yourself," he said, not looking back at her.

I heard her start to cry. "I'll tell Papa that you were mean to me. I'll tell him."

Manny whipped around and ran back to the stoop. He grabbed her arm and yanked so hard her feet left the ground for a second. "You don't tell him nothing! You hear?"

And then he punched her in the stomach. Hard.

A gush of tears and urgent cries poured out of her now, but all he said was "Let's go," to me.

I had gotten mad at Demian plenty of times, even batted him around a little, but I could never have imagined hitting him like Manny hit his sister. I wanted to go to Juanita, see if she was all right, but Manny stared at me from two houses up the block. I abandoned her and ran to catch up with my friend.

ART WAS OFF WITH HIS BANDMATES, so Trevor, Manny, and I watched TV in his living room and looked through Trevor's mom's *Our Bodies, Ourselves* book. I had seen it before, but Manny hadn't and got really into it. As he turned pages, he kept asking questions: "*That's* what it looks like?" and "Why's she got all that hair down there?" and "Man, those titties are big, huh?" Trevor and I laughed the more excited he got, until the TV went off, the book went back into the bookcase, and Trevor got us outside.

"I know where we can see *real* naked girls. You guys wanna see?" He took our blank stares for yes and led us a few blocks over to Dwight Way, and into what looked like an apartment complex.

"This is where a whole mess of Cal students live," Trevor told us, "and nobody cares if we trip around in here. Me and Art've been here like a hundred times."

We wandered in from the parking lot, and Trevor led us through their cafeteria, where we helped ourselves to soft-serve vanilla ice cream from a machine. We carried the cones through a common room, where a college guy with hair down to his butt and big mutton chops did yoga poses while another guy had his head buried in a bunch of textbooks. "Hiya," Trevor said loudly as we passed through, but neither of them looked up.

By the time we got to the roof, we'd seen guys and girls hanging out in their rooms studying, smoking pot, and sleeping. There was no sign of the naked girls Trevor had promised us. I was actually kind of relieved, not sure what I was supposed to say or do if we ran into a girl with all her body parts out for us to look at. When we didn't find anyone on the roof, Trevor said, "Bust," and we went back out the same way we came in. He and Manny grabbed more ice cream, but I passed. Amazingly, my appetite had been shrinking and shrinking. I ate, sure, but I wasn't hungry all the time, the way I had been.

Heading back to Trevor's house, I could tell they were both a little deflated by our trip, but I had an idea. A minute later, we were all running toward Eric Zydenski's street, hair flying back from our faces and feet pumping. A few blocks later, they were both out of breath, but I was just hitting my stride. We slowed down to a leisurely walk, swiping sour grass and farting around in the ivy.

Halfway down Oregon Street, I saw him. He was alone, walking right toward us. "Look!" Manny blurted. "That him?"

Eric saw me, and his mouth dropped open. I ran at him. He turned and darted away like a little jackrabbit. Suddenly hungry for his blood, I was a wolf chasing after prey. I heard Manny and Trevor close behind me. Manny even took up a war cry, like a banshee or an Apache Indian or something. We were closing in on the scared bunny.

I was almost on top of him when he vanished off to my right. Still running, I looked behind me to see Eric almost at the front door of a house that looked like it hadn't been painted or cared for in a hundred years. I turned around and now Manny and Trevor were in front of me, trying to beat him inside. By the time all three of us landed on the porch, Eric had already made it inside the house, and the door was locked.

"I'll try the back door," Trevor said, and I believed he was ready to actually go into the house to get this kid if he could find a way inside.

Seconds later, loud barking made my head involuntarily jerk upward. Then I heard Trevor, laughing and running back toward us from the back yard. "Holy shit, that dog's big."

Manny looked panicked. He started to run toward the sidewalk when Trevor said, "He's chained. And there's a fence." He jerked his head at the barking sounds, and when I looked to see the four-foot-high wooden fence, I also saw Eric staring at us from a small window.

I ran to the window, raised my fist at him like I planned to bash it in. He flinched but didn't move away. I screamed at him, told him I was going to kill him for what he did to my brother. Manny and Trevor joined in with the threats, Trevor going so far as to bang on the house itself. We yelled obscenities and gave him angry looks until he moved away from the window and went somewhere in the house.

"You think he's calling the cops?" Manny asked.

We looked at each other, considering it.

"I know where you live now, fucker!" I yelled, loud enough for the whole neighborhood to hear.

Trevor cupped his hands over his mouth. "Sleep well, you little shitbag!" he screamed, his voice cracking on the syllable *bag*.

I led us back to the street, where we patted each other, congratulating ourselves for scaring the little bastard who had hurt my brother. We made plans to come back every day until we found him and beat the snot out of him.

I WOKE UP FROM A MIDDAY nap, alone in my room, disoriented. My hair was damp with sweat, a few longish hairs stuck to my pillow. As I shifted uncomfortably in the bed, intent on falling back asleep, I heard voices in the living room. No music, just talking. I rolled my body off the bed, onto the floor, and managed to tweak my ankle. I rubbed it and put my eye to the keyhole. I could see blurry movement, but that was it.

I wanted to go out there and into the kitchen for some cereal, but something about the hushed tones, the lack of music, made me hesitate. Ken was talking to someone. Maybe Kirby. I wondered if they could possibly be talking about the death of a certain dog. I had to know.

I turned the doorknob and pulled the door open just enough so that I had a view into the living room. A long-haired guy I had never seen emptied a pouch of tobacco into a Zig-Zag paper. His yellowed fingers were visible even from all the way in my room, and Ken's bare foot pressed against the side of our coffee table.

"Where am I gonna go?" Ken asked. His friend just rolled his cigarette. "She's my everything, man."

"So why all the issues?" A tongue jutted into my eyeline. I watched it drag across the length of the paper's edge.

"Back in April, I asked her to marry me," Ken said.

His friend sucked on the ends of the cigarette. "Even with those kids?"

"Yep. You know what she said?"

They weren't talking about rat poison or Humphrey, so I willed myself backward. But I couldn't move. I wanted to know what my mom had said, even though I thought I already knew.

The friend didn't answer, so Ken said, "'Not divorced yet,'" in a voice that kind of sounded like Mom's. But not really.

"How long's it been? When's she gonna do the unhitching?"

"Maybe never."

Smoke floated toward the door, and I worried for a minute that it would make me cough, and then Ken would get all pissed off that I had been eavesdropping on him.

I wanted to hear the rest of this.

"You get a ring and down on one knee and all that shit?"

Ken said, "Yeah. All that shit. And for that, I got her telling me that she has no plans of ever getting married again."

"So, she's just gonna keep being married to this guy who beat a path elsewhere? Just, because?"

"Because she still loves him, obviously. More than she loves me. More than she'll ever love me."

"Kenny, that is cold."

"She hurt me, man. She just … kinda shut the door on any sort of future for us, didn't she?" Ken's toes bent forward, then back, flexing faster and faster.

"Well, any kind of *traditional* future." A burst of smoke exhaled from his friend's mouth.

"So, am I a chump for sticking around, then? Not hauling ass and finding some woman more emotionally open to hitch my wagon to?"

"I ain't about to judge love, brother. Sometimes it just is what it is. Married, unmarried, married to someone else … it don't make sense, even when you think it does. It's the abstraction that has vexed many a man greater than you or I. It's been the cause of wars, the death of civilizations, and a whole lot of nasty shit. But it ain't going away anytime soon. 'Specially not from you."

The smoke drifted closer to my door. I shut it as quietly as I could and remembered the letters and the poems my father had written to my mother. Demian had followed me into the garage that same day I found the rat poison, after we had finished our work for Mrs. Hunter and I was putting the toolbox back. I was pretty sure that he'd never find the poison way up there on the shelf, but if he saw the wagon I'd hidden from him, he wouldn't understand why he had been lied to, so I tried to intercept him. But he hadn't even noticed the wagon; he was curious to know what was in all the boxes. Why he picked that moment of that day, I don't know—boredom, the memory of me in there earlier with tools and imaginary snakes, maybe—but he didn't seem like he'd be redirected out of the garage until I delivered something worthy of his interest.

I helped him open some of the boxes near the front of the garage, but Mom's old clothes and knick-knacks from our old place with Dad didn't put a spark into Demian. We ventured farther and found a box with a bunch of picture frames wrapped in newspaper. The date on the *Chronicle* pages went back to 1973, just before we'd moved here to Emerson with Ken. I unwrapped one, black ink smearing onto my fingertips. I wiped them on my jeans and pulled out a small gilt frame with a picture of Mom as a little girl inside it. It looked like a school picture, from maybe when she was in second or third grade, a little older than Demian. Gramma had probably given it to Mom, and here it was, buried in a Bekins box inside our garage.

"Who's that?" Demian asked, and I waited for him to try to figure it out for himself. "Is that Mommy?" he finally said, and I nodded. He took it from me and stared at the girl with bushy eyebrows and her hair in pigtails. "She doesn't look like Mommy, not really."

I dug deeper and unfurled more newspaper to reveal a picture of Mom and Dad, standing in a park and holding hands. He had a moustache, and his hair was the longest I had seen it. He wore a paisley shirt, loose-fitting pants, and sandals. Mom had on a short dress, with small birds embroidered onto the hem. They both looked happier, and younger, than I ever remember them being. It was their wedding day.

After we unearthed more time capsule photos, I carefully rewrapped them. I thought Demian would have gotten bored at this point, but it seemed to have only piqued his curiosity. While my hands got blacker and blacker from the newspapers, he dived into a small box. Inside were envelopes and letters and lots of small books. I wiped my hands to touch them, but the ink refused to come off.

I told Demian that I didn't want to touch them, for him to hold one up so I could see what it was. With great ceremony, he took his time picking just the right one, like picking a number from a hat that would mean a grand prize for one lucky winner, and when he'd chosen it, he held the envelope up.

"Open it," I said, and his tiny fingers unfurled the back flap until a letter was revealed. He pulled it flat and held it in front of my face. It began, *Dearest Love*, and ended with what looked like Dad's name, Thomas. It was a love letter to Mom, full of big words and the biggest of words, *love*, repeated throughout. Demian giggled as I read it, excited about the treasure he had found. A glimpse into a past where neither one of us existed, but right here in these pieces of paper was where the foundation of our futures was being built.

I read a few of them, Demian dutifully holding up each page in front of my face so that I didn't sully them with my smudged hands. He giggled less and less the more I read. His eyes got a little dark, it seemed. Distant.

"What's wrong?"

He rubbed at the underside of his nose and said, "Nothing."

"Why nothing?" I asked.

"'Cause. I don't know."

"You don't remember him. Do you?" He was quiet. His eyes fixed on something at the rear of the garage. He didn't blink. "Does that make you sad?" He didn't answer. "It's okay if it does. I know it's not fair you didn't get to see him as much as I did."

He sat still.

"What do you want to know?" I asked. "About him?"

"He loved Mommy. Right?"

I nodded.

"He loved us?"

"I guess." I paused, wondering that myself. "Sure."

"Is he dead?" Demian asked.

I rubbed my chin, then remembered I had ink all over my hand. I considered wiping the smudges off, but it didn't matter. Not really.

"I don't think so. He could be."

Demian nodded over that one.

"But probably not," I said.

My own feelings about him were at that moment strangely absent. I saw him in my mind's eye, a series of afterimages from the photographs, as well as moving pictures from my own memories of him, when he was close enough to touch. The musky smell of him came back too, if only for a few seconds. I saw these fragments of my father, sensed him, but any emotion I was supposed to feel—sadness, anger, pity, love—wasn't there. I just had a hollow little space where that part of me was supposed to be. A vacancy inside my head, or something.

"Did he write this, too?" Demian held up a handwritten poem of about twenty lines. It didn't have his signature on it, like the letters, but it looked as if it could have been written by the same hand.

I told him he did, then read it aloud. All these years later, I can't recall a single line from it. I do remember that it didn't rhyme, unlike most of the poems I was used to from school. I thought it sounded sophisticated, like he had spent a lot of time figuring out which words to use. I'm not sure if I liked it or not, but I know that I didn't really understand it. Which means that I probably thought it was pretty good.

At least, knowing that part of the reason he left us was to pursue his poetry, I wished for it to be pretty good. Because if it wasn't good, if it was really awful, then how could it possibly be more important than we were? And if we weren't more important to him than shitty poetry, then how could Demian and me be anything more than shit? How could we ever matter? To anyone?

I MISSED MY MOTHER. SHE WAS right there, living in the same house with me, but I felt so far away from her. Abandoned.

As the night dragged and the TV droned on, I watched my bored mother caress her long strands of hair. I fixated on the gentleness and care she afforded herself, and I wanted some of that for my own.

"Mom, will you cut my hair?"

She looked up at me, drawn away from her own, impenetrable thoughts. "It looks fine, sweetie. Let it be."

I ran my hand through it; it was full of tangles, long and thick—my ears were so hidden they were just an idea—while the back of my hair draped down past my shoulders and the bangs nearly covered my eyes. It was time for a trim, if nothing else.

"I just … It's too long. Can you please cut it shorter?" Demian and I had never been to a barber shop, had never gotten a professional cut. Mom was the only one who cut our hair. Period.

She let out a sigh, a full breath's worth, and I knew she was annoyed. She dug into her knitting basket and pulled out a pair of silver scissors with long, sharp blades. I didn't actually care about the length of my hair, not really—I just wanted an excuse for her to touch me. Like she did to Demian when she played the Tooth Fairy a few weeks back. Like she did with me, when she ran her smooth fingers over my scalp and made me feel safe. And loved.

"Come over here," she barked, patting her hand on the ottoman in front of her.

I left the spot on the couch next to Demian, and Ken gave me a side-long glance as I stepped over his splayed legs.

Mom straightened me by the shoulders, then ran a hand quickly over the top of my head, down to the tips of my hair that lay over the back of my T-shirt. The *snip-snip* of the scissors was followed by a short pause, before she slid the scissors into my mass of hair.

Less than five minutes later, there was a smattering of hair surrounding me on the ottoman and littering the floor, and she was done.

"Go take a look," she said, and as I headed into the bathroom, she replaced the scissors in the macramé bag and relaxed back into her chair. The TV droned on.

The reflection in the mirror looked exactly how it had looked earlier in the day when I had stared into my pudgy face. Except now I was missing a few strands of hair. The bangs still fell over my eyelashes and curtains of hair remained in their old position over my ears. I touched the back of my head and could barely tell any difference.

"It doesn't feel short enough," I said when I came back into the living room.

Mom looked up at me, her half-empty wine glass between her fingers now. "It looks really nice," she said. "Sweep up the hair for me, okay?"

I went into the kitchen, got the broom and dust pan, and did what I was told.

"So, you gonna run away again?" I asked Demian later that night. He sat on his bed, sulking. "Or *try* to, at least." I was feeling nasty. Mean.

He ignored the question, just looked down at his sheets and said nothing. I tried to remember when this *other* Demian, this terrified and quiet little boy that I hardly recognized, had shown up. It was definitely before Eric had beaten him up, and right around the time he got sick. I knew *something* must have happened to make him like this, but he wasn't telling me anything. I decided to keep pushing.

"What happened with that guy from the park?" I asked.

He wrenched his head up and gave me a look I couldn't read, although there did seem to be a little panic in it. "Kirby?" He made eye contact with me for the first time since we had left the living room.

"No, not Kirby, the flasher guy. Did you and Rafe ever find him?"

Demian's head went back down to his hands in his lap, but he didn't answer me. He started to rock his body in a strange circular motion. It wasn't something I had seen him do before.

"Did you?" I asked again, worried now. I thought about what I'd heard in the schoolyard and seen on the cop shows on TV, about "perverts" and what they did to little kids. A blast of heat rushed through my chest, and my tongue felt numb.

"Did he … did he do something to you, Demian?" I didn't want to know the answer. What was I supposed to say if he said yes?

He shook his head no, looked at me with his mouth turned down like he was about to cry.

"Then what *is* it? What's going on with you?"

"I can't ... I can't tell you." And then he was crying.

"Tell me, Demian. Right now," I said.

He wiped his nose on his sleeve and wouldn't look at me. I leaned my knee onto his bed and grabbed his arm. "Tell me!" I squeezed his thin arm, feeling bone. "Goddammit!"

When he cried out in pain, I let him go.

"Fine. Screw you then! Crybaby shithead!" I hated him, wanted him to curl up and die. This wasn't my brother; this was somebody else. Somebody I didn't want to be responsible for. Not anymore.

THE NEXT DAY WHEN I WOKE up, Demian was on his bed, staring at me. "You okay?" I asked, and he shrugged. I sat up and said, "I'm sorry. Yesterday. Sorry."

We watched cartoons until Mom left, and Ken joined us on the couch, dressed in the nicest clothes he owned.

"I got a few interviews today. For a job. You boys want to wish me luck?" He tucked in his shirt and smiled at us, proud of himself.

"Luck," I said, my eyes still on the TV. "Wishing you."

"You're such a pain in the ass," he said, but he seemed relaxed, confident, and in a good mood. "You boys have a good day. Summer's gonna be gone before you know it. Take advantage of it."

Then he was gone. August was almost here, and Demian and I sat watching TV when we could have been taking advantage of our summer vacation like he said.

"Wanna go to Telegraph?"

"Nah," he said.

"Fill it to the rim … with Brim!" a commercial blared, and I realized I didn't want to zone out all day on the couch.

I got up, switched the TV off. "Come on. I'll show you the big pipe I found on campus. It leads all the way to Cardonices Park."

"Okay." Demian plodded into his bedroom, to get his shoes.

"Hustle, boy, time's a-wastin'," I repeated something I'd heard in a movie or somewhere.

I heard him giggle, and it sounded like the Demian I knew.

We were in Strawberry Creek, the small stream that ran through Cal, our feet wet and the entrance to the pipe only a few feet away, when a campus cop found us. "You two, outta there," he said from above. I thought about making a run for it, knowing he probably wouldn't come all the way down the side of the dirt incline to grab us. But there were rocks, big and small, scattered in our path, and I was afraid either Demian or I would slip and break our heads open before we could make our escape. So we climbed out of the water and up to where the fake policeman stood, hands on his hips in a pose that looked like he'd rehearsed it a bunch of times in front of a full-length mirror.

He pulled out a notebook and took down our names, "for future reference," and then told us to "find other amusement." We left campus, and I remembered the housing co-op on Dwight Way that Trevor had shown Manny and me. I didn't have money for anything, and the thought of having free ice cream cheered me up. I knew it would cheer Demian up too.

"We're not gonna *steal* it, it's there for free. They don't mind," I told him when we entered the building's cafeteria. There were a few people eating at the two long tables inside, and I chickened out. I walked past the soft-serve machine and moved toward the staircase. "We'll get some later. Let's check out the roof."

We didn't see anyone on our trip up the stairs, but the roof was packed with people. The gravel floor crunched under my shoes, and a guy playing a guitar raised his hand, warding off the sun to see who we were. I recognized him as the yoga guy, with his mutton chops and long hair. This time he was completely naked, though, the guitar covering his lower half.

"*Namaste*," he said, and I nodded at him like I was responding to my name. Demian stood on the landing behind me, his hand wedging the door open. I waved him onto the roof, and he left the darkness of the staircase for the bright sun above. The edge of the roof was covered in hardened black tar, appearing wet with the heat. I touched it and peered over, into the parking lot below.

"Check this out," I said, and Demian kneeled down on the gravel next to me.

"That's a long way down." He pointed at the ground.

I grabbed a handful of tiny silver-and-black rocks and sprinkled them over the side of the roof. We watched them land and then scatter over the concrete. I sprinkled some gravel in Demian's hand. He dropped the pieces one at a time, watching their descent with awe.

"If you or me fell, we'd drop a lot faster than those tiny rocks," I said, thinking about one of my school lessons that dealt with velocity and weight, rate of speed in comparison to something or other. I suddenly got a little schoolsick.

"Don't fall then," Demian said, and put both his hands on me, pretending to push me. He even had a discernible smile on his face.

"Too late," I said, then put one of my legs over the side.

"No, don't!" he yelled, suddenly scared.

I brought my leg back onto the gravel and told him I was just kidding around. We walked the length of the roof's edge, looking over the side as we went. We could see the campus from one side, then Telegraph Avenue from another. I wondered if the last side of the square roof would allow us to see our own house. When we reached that final side, I heard whispers.

A man, as naked as the yoga guy with the guitar, lay on top of a woman who was also naked. She was much younger than him, skinny and pasty white, a rainbow-colored towel spread out below her. He had a long beard, flecks of gray in it, and he pressed down on her body with his hairy legs and fat belly. She was whispering what sounded like "No no" in a steady cadence, while he whispered, "Yes yes," in response. She had her hands on his hairy butt, and she squeezed it every time she said no, like they were playing a silly game. He grunted, both of them unaware that we stood less than five feet away from them.

I thought the guy was kind of gross, and the whole thing seemed funny to me. Demian grabbed my shirt, and I could feel his body shaking. He pulled me toward the roof's door, oddly determined to get us both out of there in a hurry. When we were in the stairwell and the door was shut behind us, I asked him what was wrong. He let go of me and rushed down the stairs as fast as he could.

The cafeteria was empty, so I walked to the soft-serve machine. Demian was already halfway to the exit door. I ran after him, and once outside, he started to cry.

I figured he had been spooked by what he'd seen on the roof, the couple having sex on the blanket. "Did you see his butt?" I joked. "Hair-ree!"

Demian didn't laugh, just kept crying. "Is she okay?" he sputtered, looking up at the roof. "She … she … she's okay?"

"Yeah, she's fine," I said. I rubbed his back and made shushing sounds to calm him. A few residents of the complex had to edge past us to get through the front entrance, so I led Demian over to a shady spot in the parking lot. We sat next to each other, and I watched his breathing slow.

"You feeling better?" I asked.

He nodded a weak yes. Then he shook it hard: No!

There was silence for a while. I wanted to comfort him, but I had no idea what his deal was, and I was reminded of the other night in our bedroom, grabbing his arm when he wouldn't talk to me. I didn't want to hurt him again, so I said, "I can't read your mind, Demian. You gotta clue me in." I put my hand on his back again. "I want to know, okay?"

"Kirby," he said, so low I almost didn't hear it.

"From next door, *that* Kirby? What about him?"

Demian said, "He did … something."

A woman's cackle erupted from one of the open windows above, and both of us jerked our heads toward the sound. Another short burst of laughter, and then there was silence again, except for the intermittent traffic noise in the street behind us.

"Kirby did something? To you?" My heart was pounding, and I was scared, so scared that Demian was damaged, that he was fucked up beyond anything I could possibly do. Like with his bully, Eric Zydenski, this was information I was getting too late, way past the point when I could have had some impact on future events, when I could have maybe done something to stop it.

Images, memories, whatever they were, came into my head: Demian walking into the gutter as we passed Kirby's house; Demian crossing the street before we walked up Emerson toward Wheeler; Demian taking the long way around on his own, bypassing the house entirely. I couldn't remember when exactly he had started doing this, or how many times I had seen it without really taking notice of it, but the pattern finally revealed itself to me.

I was too afraid to ask him more, and I waited for him to answer me. His avoidance of Kirby's house brought me back to when I was about eight, home alone with a cold, or maybe it was a fever. Ken and Mom were at work, and Demian was in daycare. I felt crappy enough to stay away from school, but after sitting around the house in my pajamas for a few hours, I was bored. In the kitchen above the sink sat a big box of matches: long wooden sticks with round red nubs at the end. Mom had let me use them to light the burners on top of the stove once or twice, so I knew how they worked.

I plucked out a match and swiped the red against the sandpaper-like side of the box. Fire came alive on the thin stick. I felt its heat and marveled at the colors of the flame. After lighting two or three of these—holding them from the very bottom until the fire had transformed them into blackened fragments—it was time to try a new trick. I tore a sheet of paper towel from a roll and leaned against the sink. I struck a match, lit the towel by its edge and watched fire spread. Then, as I grasped the towel between my thumb and forefinger, I turned on the faucet and doused it in cold water.

The next sheet lit went up slowly, like the other one, but the towel was consumed much quicker than I expected. The sleeve of my pajama top was ablaze before the flame caught my attention. It crept up my arm toward my shoulder, and I panicked. I dropped the wisp of the burnt towel into the sink and flapped my arm in the air like an idiot who thought he could fly. The flame whipped up and down with my arm, and somehow I realized how ineffective my method was, so I frantically shoved it under the faucet. I turned on the water and the blaze made a single, loud fizzle before going out.

A small cloud of smoke lifted from my sleeve, and I doused my arm in a stream of water for at least two minutes straight before turning off the faucet. I was faced with a crispy, scorched pajama top, with a hole that allowed me to see my pale arm underneath. I ran to the bathroom, ripped the top off, and examined myself as if I was a doctor. No burns, no marks on my arm at all, which gave me a moment of relief. But that didn't quiet my panic. It didn't stop the humming in my ears and the flurry of erratic noise in my head.

Shirtless, I ran to all the windows and looked out: into the back yard, the side yards, the front yard, searching for witnesses to my pyromania. There was no one outside I could see, so I set about hiding all the evidence of my crime. I got dressed in street clothes, balled up the pajamas, top and bottom both, with the spent matches and burnt paper towels in the center, and headed out. I shoved the package under my shirt and tried to appear normal, scared as hell that I would run into someone, anyone, and they would stop me, call both the cops and my mother, and my life would be over.

I passed no one, saw only a car or two as I made my way up to Wheeler and all the way to the corner at Prince Street. There I found an overgrown bush, a deep one with dense foliage and space to stash incriminating evidence. I shoved the non-flame-retardant pajamas down into the middle of it, where it was swallowed up by green and hidden from sight. I walked down Prince, strolled back and past the bush, staring at it from every angle I could manage. I doubled back, then ran all the way home and tried to think of anything else but what I had done. It was impossible.

For an entire year after that morning, I avoided that side of Wheeler and that bush with the thought that if I even got near it, Mom would somehow be psychically alerted to my crime and it would be revealed that I had burnt my pjs and nearly set myself, and the entire house, on fire. She never found out, but when I finally worked up the courage to walk past that bush, it was with the still-vivid recollection of what had gone down there. Even though the pajamas were long gone by then, the day itself was planted deep in my mind and would never completely vanish.

So whatever had happened to Demian, whatever he had seen or done or had done to him at Kirby's house, I was sure that it was an event or—God forbid—multiple events he would never forget. I knew his memory of the *something* would be specific and full of detailed truth, if only I could get it out of him. He had gotten so good at keeping secrets lately, but I knew this was a secret he could no longer keep to himself. He had to let it out. He had to share it with me. After that, I didn't know, but I knew he was going to tell me right there in that parking lot.

And he did.

"You can tell me what happened. I won't tell Mom or Ken. I promise." I wasn't sure that pledge could be kept, but I needed him to trust me.

"You remember that day," he said, and then went silent.

"What day?" I prompted, trying to be patient.

"That girl. Your girlfriend."

I tried to will his eyes to meet mine. He kept them locked onto the ground at his feet.

"You mean Seneca. She's not my girlfriend." Goose bumps, a sense of embarrassment, tingled on my arms. "She never ... We never ..." I trailed off, in my own head.

The thought of something happening to her brought me back. "Do you mean ... when she was going to come over? *That* day?"

He nodded, then closed his eyes. I knew everything would need to be pried out of him. Impatience, followed by anger, welled up. I balled up my fists and gave it time to pass. When it had, I whispered, "Did she come over? Did you see her?"

He nodded again.

I had no idea what any of this meant. I was so confused, but I kept pressing him, as gently as I could manage.

"Where did you see her?"

"At ... at *his* house."

"Kirby's?" I shouted, beginning to understand something I couldn't possibly ever really understand. I lowered my voice and asked, "Why was she at Kirby's house?"

"She thought ... she thought you were in there. He told her." Demian kept his eyes down. His voice was small, but I caught every word.

"So she went inside?"

He nodded. "He took her bike."

"You were in the back yard when you saw this?"

"Uh-huh."

"And ... did you see anything else?"

"Uh-huh." A long tear crawled down his cheek. It dropped onto his shoe, and then more tears followed.

I wanted to scream, to pound my fist into something. Instead, I steadied myself and placed my hand over his.

"You saw them? Inside the house?" I pictured Demian's view of Kirby's house from our back yard: the front door, the side of the green house. I could see the one big window and two smaller windows on that side, all of which were visible over the wooden fence that separated the houses.

"The big window?" The sweat in the middle of my palm spread outward. His hand was so hot beneath my hand.

"What were they doing?" I said, and Demian looked up at me for the first time. His face was soaked with tears, and his eyes were comically wide. His mouth quivered, lips pressed tightly over his mouth. "What was *he* doing?"

I squeezed his small hand, not enough to hurt him but enough to get him to open his mouth. "Was he hurting her?"

"Uh-huh."

I waited.

"He got on top of her."

"In the bedroom."

"Her hair. I saw it. It was shaking up and down."

"Did you hear anything? Did you hear her?"

He shook his head. "I couldn't. He said stuff, though."

Fractured images of Kirby hunched over Seneca, with her mouth screaming and his laughing, skittered across my mind. I heard her cry out.

"What ..." I couldn't catch my breath. "And she ... and then?"

My eyes blurred, covered in rising water. I felt like I was drowning.

"Did he see you?"

"I don't, I don't know. I ran to the door. Our door. It was locked. You locked it. I sat there. And sat there." He shook now, like he was in Alaska. Shivering cold, even though it was a warm summer day.

"I'm sorry," I said to him. But I was thinking about Seneca. Picturing Kirby doing things to her that Demian and I had seen in *Last Tango*, that we had seen in that garage in Sausalito, that we had just seen up on the roof of the student housing complex. Things we never should have seen.

I wanted to rip my brain out and throw it on the ground. Stamp on it until all those thoughts were crushed and destroyed and out of my head. I closed my eyes to push them away, but it made them worse, more intense and more real.

I opened my eyes, pulled Demian to his feet, and led him out of the parking lot and toward the street. I wanted to run away from the guilt I had for ever inviting Seneca over. For locking Demian outside and allowing him to see what he saw. For being responsible for not knowing what a monster Kirby was and not chopping his fucking head off his fucking body before all this could happen. It had been my job to protect them from him, and I had failed.

We walked back home, and I fixated on how it wasn't too late to kill the monster. I knew it was stupid to think that

I could literally do that to another person; I knew it was a sin and, more importantly, I knew he was a grown man and I was only a kid. But I didn't care. I knew it had to be done, and I knew that I was the one who had to do it.

Chapter 16

In the aftermath of Demian telling me about what Kirby had done to Seneca, my mind seemed to empty itself of everything. I had no clear thoughts, the struggle to fully comprehend what had happened to her and how I needed to feel about it making me weak and indecisive. There was a strange numbness in my brain, a vacancy similar to the depressive thoughts I had after the bike ride to Oakland. There should have been anger, disgust, sadness, but it was all too much for my eleven-year-old brain to process, so it simply shut all emotions out and went cold.

There was a moment, me on my bed, the thin sheets old and unwashed but comfortable draped over me, when my foot brushed against a Jack London book that was almost a week overdue. It was one of the two books I'd checked out from the library with Seneca. The other book, a *Little House on the Prairie* novel that she had implored me to read, I returned shortly after Seneca stopped taking my calls. I had stewed for days, angry at her and myself. The thought that I'd pushed our first kiss too far, that I had rushed something that deep down I didn't even want to hurry along, had made a scrambled mess of my brain for weeks. When Demian confessed the real reason for her behavior, my anger shifted elsewhere, with a fury and blind rage that I never knew existed within me.

I wanted to recapture that wrath, with the intention of focusing and then unleashing it on the one person who deserved it: Kirby. My depression was too great that day for me to clear all of the mud and fog out of my brain. I considered other options, things that would help Seneca and also make sure Kirby was punished. I wondered if I should call the cops, call Seneca's dad, tell Mom and Ken? Maybe I could convince someone older and bigger than me to find Kirby in the park and hurt him really bad. All my options seemed like good ideas until they seemed like terrible ones. I was too paralyzed by my own addled mind to make any decision, good or bad. So I made none.

The next morning, Rafe was at our door before seven o'clock. I heard banging, and my first thought was that Kirby had figured out Demian and I knew what he had done to Seneca and he was trying to break in and shut us up permanently. When I saw the little guy from down the street through the colored glass in the front door, I relaxed. I let him in, told him to stop huffing and puffing or he was going to blow the whole goddamned house down. He laughed in that snickery way he had, then showed me the newspaper in his hand. It was the *Berkeley Gazette*, which Ken called a crappy rag and the reason why he subscribed to the *San Francisco Chronicle*, despite still not having a job to pay for it.

I didn't know what Rafe wanted me to see until he pointed at a grainy black-and-white photo. It was a close-up of Kirby, sharing the frame with part of a police officer's hat and half a face, staring directly at the camera. The hair, those creepy eyes, his jagged scar, all came through even with the poor quality of the reproduction. It was him, all right. Below the photo was a story about a sweep of the Berkeley parks for drug dealers and "illegal activity" that had been conducted the day before. Some councilman had deemed August "Lawfulness Awareness Month" or something like that, and this was apparently the first stage of that awareness, conveniently timed with the councilman's bid for re-election. "That's your neighbor, right? The one we saw at the park that day?" Rafe was excited, as if he was the one responsible for busting Kirby. Before I could answer, he looked around the house. "Hey, is Demian up?"

I said no, then asked if I could hold on to his paper for a minute. I wanted to read the article again, to make sure it had really happened.

"Wake him up," Rafe said, shaking the arm that held the newspaper. "Show him, show him."

I went into our room, where Demian was groggy but already awake. I had a few moments of hesitation, worried that my brother would tell his little buddy everything he had told me about Seneca and Kirby. But I knew that was now our secret, just his and mine, so I let Rafe inside. He sat on Demian's bed and showed him the paper, while I threw on some shoes and grabbed a couple of quarters from the dresser. Once Rafe and Demian had abandoned the newspaper for a pile of Wacky Pack stickers stashed on the floor of the closet, I ran out and down the street. At the liquor store, I bought the Saturday *Oakland Tribune* and my own copy of the *Gazette*. Manny lived right up the block, and I wanted so badly to tell him, to tell anyone, what Kirby's arrest meant to me. But I didn't. I just sat outside, against the chipped green wall of the liquor store and pored through both papers. There was a small article in the Oakland paper about the park sting, mostly listing the parks—Live Oak, Willard, People's Park, and a few others—but not including photos or any mention of Kirby Johnson.

I unfurled the *Gazette*, found the page with the article Rafe had shown me, and read it again and again until I couldn't stop smiling. There was still a part of me that wished I had found the courage to carry out some kind of revenge on him in Seneca's name, but ultimately I was just a scared little boy and this was the greatest outcome I could have hoped for. If I had been the kind of kid to embrace the hippie-speak of Ken and his friends, I'm sure I would have considered the timing of his arrest a significant "synchronicity" and seen the bust as a form of "cosmic justice." Instead, I just let my anger go and celebrated Kirby's bad fortune.

Back home, Demian and Rafe sat at the kitchen table, eating Life cereal while Ken talked to them in between puffs on his cigarette. "The pigs can't hold him for long, not for simple possession. No matter how much grass he had on him, they'll try to book him for intent to sell, but it won't stick."

"Why not?" Rafe asked, as if Ken's one class in criminal law at Cal made him Melvin Belli.

"Marijuana isn't really a drug, and everybody knows it. Not like other drugs. Shit, they should've legalized it years ago." Ken stubbed out his cigarette butt onto a half-eaten English muffin on his plate. "Hey, Rafe, you wanna see a fat bud?"

I wanted to say something to Ken, without creating a whole scene. Rafe was a good kid, but he had a big mouth, and I didn't want him telling his parents that we were doing a pot show-and-tell at our house. His mom already hated me for some reason, and I didn't want to give her a reason to not like Demian too.

"Hey," I moved my body in between Rafe and Ken, kneeling down and locking eyes on my brother, "you guys going to that fair at LeConte today? They got the bookmobile and a bunch of free stuff they're giving away." I felt Ken's breath on my neck.

"Free?" Rafe said, and I knew I had their attention.

Ken lit up a cigarette, the hot smoke he exhaled brushing against my neck and settling in my hair. Demian stared at Ken behind me, his gaze communicating to me that Ken was pissed. Then I heard the chair behind me squeak, and he was out, into the other room. A minute later, the stereo was turned on and The Band started singing about being lonely in Times Square and the certain fruit you weren't supposed to taste.

I wondered if they had any food at the school fair, and before the song was over, I had both boys out the door and headed up there to find out.

THAT WEEKEND WAS THE LAST SHRED of normalcy Demian and I enjoyed for the rest of the summer. On Monday, the *Berkeley Gazette* again ran a picture of Kirby, but this time it was his mug shot, and the story was about him molesting a little girl in the same park where he'd been arrested for selling pot. The girl, her name withheld, had seen his picture in the paper on Saturday and come forward. Kirby's bail hearing on the drug charge was supposed to be that Monday, but with the new accusation, he was being held without bail until further charges could be filed. As a community service, the paper was running his picture on behalf of the Berkeley Police Department, suggesting the possibility that he had molested more kids.

By midday, I had seen the same kind of article in both the *Chronicle* and the *Tribune*, and it seemed like a part of the neighborhood had seen at least one of the papers that morning. Mrs. Dillon stopped me when I passed her house to ask me if Demian and I were okay. She hinted around the idea that one or both of us had possibly been "touched" by Kirby, her hands fluttery and her eyes constantly peering over my head and toward the house next to ours. I told her he hadn't done anything to us, we hardly even saw him around, and her hands settled down and came to rest against her flower-print dress. She told me what a tragedy it all was, and hoped to God that he hadn't hurt any other children.

I knew there was at least one more girl he *had* hurt, and I suspected that there were definitely more girls out there. I couldn't do anything about the girls I didn't know, but I felt it was my duty to do something for Seneca.

Her phone rang and rang, without answer, the first couple of times I called her. When I tried her around four o'clock, she picked up.

"Seneca, it's Steve." Silence on her end. "Did you … see the paper today?" I waited for her to say something, but the breathing on the other end was my only clue that she hadn't hung up on me. "I know what he did. Demian … my brother … he saw you. He saw *it*."

The breathing turned to what sounded like crying, but it was faint and the butterflies in my stomach made it hard for me to hear her clearly. "I want to. I want to help you, Seneca. Can I? Please?"

"Nothing happened. Nothing!" she screamed in my ear. I waited. "He said …" She sobbed into my ear now, trying to form words. "He said he would kill you. And your brother. If I ever … if I ever said … anything."

"I'm … I'm sorry," I said, my stomach seizing with a cramp. Then I was crying. I tried to hold the phone away so that she wouldn't hear, my nose running junk into my mouth. I stood like that for what seemed like minutes, trying to contain my tears and listening to her own over the phone. Finally, I pulled it together enough to ask, "Does your dad know?"

She cried again. "I can't. I can't tell him. I can't tell … anyone."

"Why not?" I asked, feeling stupid and powerless.

"Because I can't! That's why!" she screamed at me, then started to cough over the tears.

I waited for her to say something else, not sure what else I could say. I wanted to tell her I'd be right over to her house, that we'd tell her dad together, and that we'd all go to the police station together.

She hung up. I called her back right away, but she didn't answer again.

Heading to my room, the phone rang. I nearly tripped over myself trying to pick it up, expecting it to be Seneca.

"Stephen? It's Grandma," the voice said. I said hi and she asked, "Everything okay? You sound funny. Have you been crying, sweetie?"

"No!" I shouted, louder than I intended. "I'm not a cry-baby." I sounded more like Demian than myself.

"I know, Stephen, I know. How are you?" she asked.

"Fine," I said. I wanted her to keep talking, to stay on the line and say Gramma-like nice things to me, but I was stuck coming up with words to say to her.

"Did your mom tell you I called? I've been trying to reach you, ever since your birthday." She sounded concerned, a hint of exasperation under her breath.

"My birthday?" I asked, like an idiot. "You mean last week?"

"I want to take you out to lunch for your big eleventh birthday. And of course buy you a present. Or two. Or three." I laughed when she started to say, "Or four."

"When?" I asked, looking at the time and realizing it was way past lunch. "Tomorrow?"

"Tomorrow … yes, tomorrow would be lovely. What time would you like me to pick you up, Mr. O'Neill?" She was doing the English butler voice she did sometimes, when she was prepared to spoil me.

"Can Demian come, too?" I asked, not wanting to hog Gramma all for me. He asked about her at least a couple of times a week, and every Sunday we weren't at their house for dinner, he wondered aloud why.

"Of course. Your grandfather's working, but the three of us should make for fine dining companions, don't you think?"

"I think," I said, and then we made plans for noon the next day.

When I told Demian that night, he jumped up and down like a pogo stick, unable to contain his excitement. I still hadn't figured out what to do about Seneca.

Mom and Ken didn't come home until almost ten thirty that night, and by then Demian and I were under our covers with the lights out and consciousness drifting away. Mom had called a little before six to tell me that Ken had gotten a job, so they were going out to celebrate. She didn't say where, or why we weren't invited, only that there were TV dinners in the freezer. She told me to take care of my brother, they'd be home later, and then she hung up. I'd like to think that she had said, "I love you," before letting the phone go dead, but I'm pretty sure she didn't.

They would have read about or heard the news concerning Kirby by then, and I was dying to hear what they had to say about it. Ken had invited the monster into our house and probably bought grass from him, so I was sure he'd have a reaction to the arrest and the molestation charges. But I didn't get the chance to ask about it that night, and by the next morning, he was out the door with Mom for his first day of work.

Gramma got to our house just before noon, dressed in her flowy colored top and long skirt, and when I saw her come up the walk to the door, I yelled to Demian, "Crap, she's dressed all fancy. Change!"

The doorbell rang while my brother and I tossed off our T-shirts and quickly buttoned up shirts that she had given us for Christmas. Demian's was now too small for him, his white belly showing just above his belt, and mine was way too big, hanging off my new, smaller frame. He and I shuffled to the door, greeted by a peal of laughter as we opened it to Gramma.

Five minutes later, back in our original tees, we left the house for lunch. She had made a reservation at a French bistro in North Berkeley. When she saw the disappointment and confusion on our faces, she turned to me in the passenger seat of her car and asked, "Where do *you* want to go? It's your birthday."

"That sounds fine," I said. "The French place."

She made a U-turn at the next block, and soon we were on Shattuck, pulling into a parking spot. "I'm thinking

Italian might be nice." Sitting in Giovanni's, at a booth with the red high-backed, leather-like seats, we ordered pizza and spaghetti, while Gramma indulged us with refills of Coke. She had remembered this as one of my favorite places, somewhere she'd only been once before, years ago, and to thank her, I stuffed myself and let my appetite go crazy.

Back in the car, she said softly, "That was nice," before getting back into traffic. "So, where should we go for your present? Ssssss? Presents. Is there a toy store you like?"

Inside Mr. Mopps', Gramma let us roam around while she admired a handmade doll display. "It's his birthday," she had whispered to Demian when we first walked in, "but you go ahead and pick something out too. Whatever you want, okay?"

Gramma had given me free rein in the place, not limiting what I could or couldn't have. I knew she and Grampa weren't rich, but they could afford to splurge on their only grandchildren once or twice a year. When my arms were full of big-ticket items—a motorized airplane, a Hot Wheels track, and a set of roadster cars—I looked behind the counter. The same woman who had been there on my birthday was there now.

"Do you remember me?" I asked, after dumping the expensive toys in one of the aisles and approaching the front of the store. "I was here about a week ago."

She peered at me, pinched her glasses, and pulled them down her nose. "Yes. I think so."

"Do you still have the … things, toys, that you held on to for us?" I pointed at the floor behind her.

She rummaged in the back, found a white bag with a piece of paper safety-pinned to it. She lifted it up for me to see that *O'Neill* was written in black ink on the small scrap. "Is this it?"

I nodded. "Be right back." I went to Demian, who was cradling a huge box of handmade building blocks. "Put it back," I told him. He looked at me like I had just kicked him in the nuts.

"Why?" he whined. "Gramma said I could have it."

"I know. But put it back. We're getting something else."

Gramma met us at the counter, where the woman had already removed our toys from the bag and began ringing them up. "What did you boys get?" she asked, looking at our toy loot. The Steve Austin doll was there, along with the Tintin books, the Mad-Libs, and the Lego set I'd picked out for Demian. All the things that my mother didn't have the cash to buy. All the things I doubted she would ever come back and get for us.

"Didn't you want that airplane, Stephen? Where is that?" Gramma looked along the counter for it.

I pointed at the few toys next to the cash register. "Nope. That's all."

"I told them before, we don't accept checks," the woman said when she gave Gramma the total.

Gramma pulled a credit card from her purse and said, "That's fine. I have cash. I have MasterCard. Whichever you prefer."

The woman took the card, placed it in a metal rectangle thing that looked like a funky mouse trap, put a white slip of paper over it, and then pushed a lever back and forth like she was playing air hockey.

Gramma stared at our toys, then at me, her brow furrowed. "Did your mother—"

"Here you are," the woman handed her back the card and a receipt. I took the bag and fished out the Lego set for Demian.

"Thanks, Gramma," I said, and nudged Demian to say the same.

I wanted to tell her everything, rat my mother out on this thing with the toys, Demian running away, and even her immoral acts with our landlord. I wanted Gramma to know, I wanted Mom to be punished somehow, but I kept everything to myself.

THAT TUESDAY NIGHT, MOM AND KEN did come home right after work. When she called us from our room for dinner, I made a big point of bringing my *Six Million Dollar Man* action figure with me. I placed it next to my plate, looked through the eye, and was generally pretty obnoxious with it.

"New toy?" Ken asked dumbly, once Mom had served us quiche she'd bought on her lunch break. It was cold, but I wasn't very hungry anyway.

"Gramma got it for me today," I said, looking through the astronaut's bionic eye at Mom. "For my birthday." I took a bite, enjoying the strained silence at the table. "And Demian got a Lego set." Another bite, holding the tension. "From Mr. Mopps'."

Mom finished her food and put the plate in the sink. She brushed by me on her way to the cupboard. She had to prepare; company was coming.

THE CELEBRATION OVER KEN'S NEW JOB hadn't ended, because by nine o'clock there were already over a dozen people in our house. The music played, and the alcohol flowed, but the pot supply was short.

"Hey, sorry, my dealer got busted last week. Can you believe that? For selling to an undercover pig," Ken handed a Heineken to the Arielle woman, who wore another Indian-style outfit. Demian was in bed, but I had made a point of staying in the living room, close to Ken in the hopes of hearing him talk about Kirby. Did he know what our neighbor had been up to with those girls before he went to jail? Would he have done anything to stop him if he knew? Did he even care?

Arielle took the bottle, flicked the foam from the top of it with her tongue, and gave Ken a pouty look. "Not down with that. I wanted to get high."

Ken stared at her mouth, then down at her chest. I looked around for Mom, to see if she was seeing this, but she wasn't in the room.

"Oh, we can still get high," he told her.

"I'd like that," she said, then whispered something in his ear I couldn't hear.

He looked around, her mouth hidden in his hair, and caught me staring at him. Ken pulled himself away from Arielle and came toward me. "Where's your mom?"

I shrugged, still looking at him with a hard stare.

"What the fuck's your problem?" he said with his teeth clenched, and I knew he was drunk.

"Nothing," I turned away from him and headed into the kitchen.

"That's right," he slurred. I heard bare feet slapping on the floor behind me. My head snapped forward, and it took me a second to realize I'd been hit. Stunned, I craned my neck around. Ken looked ready to hit me again. "I got a job today!" he yelled at me.

I wanted to say, *Hooray for you, asshole*, but my mouth wouldn't work. I couldn't believe that he had actually punched me. In the head. It was something I knew he had wanted to do for a long time—in the pub on the Fourth of July, the fury in his eyes revealed how much he would have liked to have pummelled me—but I never imagined he'd actually do it. Especially not with my mother in the house, or with all these other people around. At that moment, he and I were the only ones who knew what he'd done. The kitchen was empty, everyone out in the living room or on the front porch.

"It's high time you started giving me the respect I deserve. I'm tired of your shit!"

Mom walked in midway through his rant to me, her eyes bloodshot, both hands wrapping her hair into a bun. She looked at us, trying to understand what was happening.

"Ken?" she said, steadying herself against the fridge and trying to focus on both of us at the same time.

"This fucking kid." He swatted the air like there was a fly, before going back to his friends in the other room.

"What did you do?" she said, like she was disgusted with me.

"Nothing," I said. "I wanted a snack."

"You wanted a snack? Right!" She opened the refrigerator door and said, "So go ahead. Eat."

I stood where I was, looking at the floor. There were bread crumbs and dirt ground into it. How long since any of us had cleaned in here?

"Every time you go out with your grandmother, you come back acting all full of yourself. You think she treated me so good?"

I didn't look up at her.

"Don't need this. Going to bed." And then she was gone.

I HAD GIVEN UP ON LISTENING to Ken and his college compadres talk philosophy and politics in their intoxicated and altered states. When Arielle led him out into the back yard alone, I knew I'd been at the party too long.

Demian lay on his bed, looking at one of my Mad-Libs books, when I came in. I took off my watch. It was almost eleven. "What's an adjective?" he asked, sounding out each syllable.

"It's a description of something, like ... *pushy*. Or *loud*." Even with the door shut, I could still hear every word sung by Paul Simon, his plaintive voice forcing its way from the living room.

"What's a verb?" he asked, and I walked him through one of the games. Demian came up with some funny words, and we read the story a couple of times before I was ready for sleep. I changed into shorts, then hit the light. We lay there in our beds, the sound of conversation outside our door almost as loud as the music. After about thirty minutes and two album changes, I turned to Demian in the dark.

"You still awake?" I whispered to him.

He responded right away. I said I'd be right back.

I was tired, and grumpy, and still pissed off that Ken had actually hit me. Most of all, I was hurt that Mom hadn't come to my defense. Again.

In the living room, I said, "Can you guys turn the music down a little?"

Ken was back in the house, on the couch next to his old professor, with Arielle close by. "We can't sleep."

Ken's eyes struggled to focus on me, standing there amid the group of about ten people, all gathered on the floor near the couch. "The adults are talking here. Go back to bed."

"We can't," I said, trying to make my voice heard above an elongated drum solo, "because it's too loud."

Ken stood up, and I thought he was going to come at me, with a punch in the face this time. Instead, he moved a few feet to the record player and turned the volume up even louder. Back on the couch, he took a defiant slug from his beer bottle.

When the song finally ended, I hadn't moved from my spot. The professor leaned in close to Ken, said something, and then went over and twisted the volume dial on the stereo down so low I could actually hear the conversations around me.

Ken splayed his hands at me, arms midway to his chest, as if to say, *There! You happy now?* I wasn't happy, but I figured now Demian might be able to fall asleep. I was wide awake.

In the kitchen, I found an overripe banana and decided to take my chances with it. I stood in the doorway, stared at Ken's group as the conversation seemed to veer into a direction I'd been waiting all night long for it to find.

"Diddling little girls, huh? That sounds pretty serious." From the floor, a guy wearing a tie-dyed turtleneck and cargo pants sipped red wine from a tall beer glass.

"Hey," Ken said, seated in the lotus position on the couch, playing with his toes, "innocent until proven guilty by a jury of your peers. Don't assume anything without the facts."

"Man, the cops don't need facts. Lawyers can make up whatever shit they need to sell their case." Turtleneck made a disgusted *psssh* sound.

Sergio, one of Ken's friends I'd seen working at La Peña the few times Demian and I had been dragged there for live music, stood up. "And when did any man, working outside the corporate structure, earning a living from what the earth provides, free from the stranglehold of taxation, when did he ever get a fair shake from our judicial system? If they can't make their bullshit charges stick, then they turn around and trump up something bigger and badder so you get put away. Create lies designed to discredit you, demonize you, and ultimately destroy you just because you don't fit into society's norm. They're all terrified of what they don't understand, so they choose to crush it out of existence."

The professor stood up, and I was ready for the lecture portion of the night. "You make a good point, yet it's only history repeating itself, *ad nauseam*. This is nothing new, a man accused of a crime unjustly, stripped of his rights as a human being based merely on conjecture. Or less. But the more fascinating approach to the quandry presented here is whether this crime he's been accused of *is* truly criminal. Is the act of love between what society considers 'an adult' and what it labels 'a child' legally or morally unjust?"

He had the attention of everyone. They hung slavishly on his every word. The banana in my hand was forgotten as I struggled to understand what was being said.

"Foucault argued, quite forcefully, that there should be no moral implications for a man who has 'come of age' to bed a boy or a girl who has not yet reached that stage of life." My mother wandered into the room while the professor spoke, looking half-asleep. She didn't see me standing in the kitchen. "Why then, in the second half of the twentieth century, in an atmosphere of love and acceptance here in the heart of the evolution of revolution, is it unacceptable for people of any age to choose who they want to love, regardless of age or, for that matter, sex?"

He rubbed his hands, like he was awaiting a challenge from the room.

Arielle spoke up. "Love is phenomenal, right, but it has to be a consensual act. Mutual love."

"Is love really so narrow?" The professor took a sip of his drink, then spoke directly to Ken. "Should it have constraints on it? Isn't it the only thing that's still truly free anymore?"

One of the guys on the floor raised his hand, like he was in class. He waited until the professor acknowledged him before asking, "What about air?"

"Freedom isn't even free anymore, if it ever was." The professor seemed to ignore the question, riding the wave of his own ideas. "Even those of us who purport to be 'liberal-minded' are rarely '*open*-minded,' especially in the case of behavior that does not conform to our expectations. How can we justify something we don't fully comprehend? Our own ignorance is at fault in these cases, not the individual's right to live a life in accordance with their own belief system."

"Like *Lolita*, right?" somebody else said.

"Yeah, Humbert Humbert," the turtleneck guy said. "Nabokov's descriptions of that girl made me horny, I'm a little ashamed to admit."

My mother had sidled herself into the space between Arielle and Ken, just as he fumbled through their bookcase. He pulled out a book, the one they were talking about, and held it up for the room to see, as if it was his turn during show-and-tell.

"Why ashamed?" the professor challenged. "This is a perfect example of the constraints we place on ourselves, as we were *programmed* to do since birth. Self-censorship, yet on a sub- or even un-conscious level, is what we are all guilty of. Why not feel what we feel, express what we have desire for, without fear of punishment or the overwhelming terror of being shunned by *society*?"

"But what about the girl?" Arielle asked. "The victim of these desires?"

"There is no victim." The professor shook his head vigorously.

I heard myself mumble, "Bullshit," too low to be heard. I moved slowly into the living room, catching my mother's eye.

The professor said, "The girl herself becomes irrelevant in this discussion. I'm speaking toward the notion of our free wills becoming oppressed by moral codes that limit expression, that make thoughts and actions obscene when they are not."

"But the girl—" Arielle was cut off midpoint.

"Is *irrelevant*. She doesn't factor into it. Simply, she does not matter."

"Yes, she does," I said, standing behind all of Ken's friends sitting on the floor. No one knew I was there until I spoke. Suddenly, they were all staring at me.

The professor looked like I had said something funny. Mom stood up and told me to go to bed. Ken clenched his fist like he wanted to break something. Or break me.

"A future debater, welcome." The professor opened his arms wide, as if inviting me into the conversation. "Or are you only a contrarian? I say yes, you say no no no, is that it?"

"I apologize for this, Professor. Please, ignore him," Ken chucked his thumb toward my bedroom, gritted his teeth.

"It's difficult to ignore the voice of youth. They are unfiltered, freer with their words and actions than we can ever hope to be again." He walked toward me, the sea of his former students' legs parting for him as if he were Moses. "Speak your mind, young man, as only you can."

I stood there, feeling the heat in my cheeks rise all the way up my face and through my scalp. The professor seemed to be laughing at me with his small, squinting eyes. He waited for me to say something, the room quiet. My mother stepped near us but didn't say anything.

"No more?" he asked me. "I *am* disappointed. Perhaps it *is* time for you to go to bed, yes?"

"No," I said, and he laughed. A few people behind him laughed. Mom and Ken, they didn't laugh.

"The natural-born contrarian, how delightful." He suddenly seemed bored with me, returning to his spot near Ken and the couch. "Do I now need to revise my earlier statement?" he asked his adorers. "Do children factor into our interpretation of constrictive societal mores after all?"

Mom placed her hand on my arm. "Steve, you're embarrassing Ken. Will you go to bed now?"

"I'm embarrassing *him*?" I looked at her, feeling rage building and building and building. "Fuck him!"

I felt eyes pull away from the professor and land on me. "And fuck you!" I screamed at them. "This fucking thing sucks!"

She grabbed my arm, shushed me while trying to physically push me toward my bedroom.

"You're all sons of bitches. You don't know shit!" I pushed Mom off me and kicked a half-full beer bottle across the room.

"Stephen!" Mom yelled, grabbing me from behind.

"Go to bed!" Ken screamed at me, losing his cool completely.

I looked at all the adults staring at me, who probably thought I was stupid. Or crazy. The professor stared at me in a way that made me feel like an animal escaped from its cage. Maybe I was dangerous, maybe I wasn't, but he was keeping his eye on me.

"You don't even know her. It wasn't her fault—it was his!"

"What are you talking about?" Mom's grip on me loosened; her voice sounded softer, concerned.

Arielle said, "Was that girl his friend?" to no one in particular.

"I think he brings up a good point about blame." The professor chuckled, trying to pull the focus off me and train it squarely back on him. "Who *is* to blame in a case like this? The man in question *is* educated, yet the manner of his dress, what he chooses as his commerce, leaves him open to scrutiny and suspicion within a society built on antiquated ideals ..." and then he *was* the focus, and I stood there listening to my own fevered heartbeat.

Mom said, "Honey, it's late. You're obviously tired ..." She tried to steer me toward my bedroom, but I didn't budge.

Behind me, one of the guys said, "Who knows, there's always the possibility that this is like a case of buyer's remorse. You know, she actually wanted it, and liked it, but now—"

I squirmed out of my mother's hand and turned to face them. "She didn't want it! She didn't! Not from that ..."

My mouth went dry. The tips of my fingers tingled like I had electrical current in them, and I screamed, "That motherfucking asshole rapist cocksucker! She didn't want *him*, she didn't ask for *that*, you fucking piece of shit loser hippie fucks!"

The words rushed out of me, like a tsunami.

Ken came toward me in the next moment, unable to control his own temper anymore. My mother stepped in front of me, said, "Don't!" and I had time to escape back into my room.

I heard Demian breathing, but I didn't say anything to him. I hoped he was asleep, hoped that he hadn't heard what I'd said in there. As I climbed into bed with all my clothes still on, I heard the professor's distinctive voice say, "That was certainly a bit unnerving."

The house emptied out over the next fifteen minutes, and the music was turned off, but I didn't fall asleep at all that night. Demian shuddered once, as if in the throes of a nightmare. I went to him, wrapped his blankets tightly around his body, just the way he liked them, and whispered in his ear that I loved him.

I realized how alone we were, how little anyone outside this room cared about either one of us. Then I saw Gramma's face in my head. And Grampa's. I knew there was a better life out there for both of us.

Chapter 17

THE MORNING AFTER THE PARTY, THINGS seemed to come into focus for me, clearer than at any other time in my life. I decided that for the rest of the summer, if not the rest of our lives, Demian would not be left alone. Even though I now had plans that were too adult for him to be a part of, he *was* a part of it all, so I intended to bring him with me everywhere I went. In the calm of pre-dawn, wide awake, I made two new entries in my Things to Do This Summer list. *Look out for my brother* was a goal I had already committed myself to, probably from all the way back to the night he disappeared. Definitely once he told me about seeing Seneca and Kirby. So I knew that was one goal I would do everything possible to accomplish. The second one was more complicated but was directly related to the first. I wrote, *Get us the FUCK out of HERE!!* and envisioned Demian and me living in Gramma and Grampa's house. This goal, it was bigger than the Heroic Act. A whole lot bigger, and not completely within my control. But it was the thing I wanted most of all, and I was ready to fight, as hard as I possibly could, to make it come true.

I didn't even want to look at Ken or Mom, so I woke Demian up before seven. We both dressed and headed out on my bike. I had enough money for the BART train, and change to make a phone call when we got there.

At the Ashby station, we boarded a train for Fremont. I called Gramma from the station, trying to sound like everything was normal and that we just happened to be in the neighborhood. When we got to their house, she was standing in the driveway, waiting for us.

She fed us breakfast and touched both of us a lot, stroking our hair and shoulders like she hadn't seen us in a long time, instead of just a day. I told her we liked our presents a lot and about Demian and me doing Mad-Libs. He told her what he remembered about one of them, and the mood in the dining room lifted for a minute.

Gramma seemed to sense that I had a lot on my mind, so she sent Demian into the back yard to pick blackberries off the vine. She promised she'd teach him how to bake them up into a pie if he brought back enough berries. Then she pulled up a chair close to mine.

"Okay, spill it. What's in that sharp little head of yours, Stephen?"

I took a few deep breaths, feeling like I needed more air in my lungs. I peeked around the corner, to be sure Demian was out of earshot. Then I told her everything that had happened that summer, starting with us walking home alone the night before our last day of school, and ending with Ken hitting me. I'm not sure if I said the exact words, "I don't feel safe," but it was how I felt. How Demian had felt when he ran away from home and tried to become a part of the Hare Krishnas.

She let me talk, only stopping me to ask a specific question here and there, to keep the sequence of events clear in her head, as she put it. It was exhausting telling her everything I wanted to share with her, with someone who actually cared enough to listen. But it was also a relief, like I had unburdened myself of something my brain and body couldn't wholly contain. I even told her about the shoplifting. And about Seneca and what Demian had seen. When I told her that, that's when she started to cry.

After I finished it all, she stood me up and wrapped her arms around me. She hugged me hard, all of her old-lady strength channeled into that embrace. She held me until Demian came back with the berries. Then we all made a blackberry pie.

SHE CALLED MOM TO ASK PERMISSION for us to stay through dinnertime. Gramma didn't drop any hints about what I'd told her, only said that we had come over to get a birthday present that she'd neglected to give me the day before. I saw her forehead crinkle during that pause in the conversation, knowing that Mom had probably said something mean to her. But Gramma kept her tone cheery, promised to have us back home before it got dark, and then lightly hung up the phone.

"I don't want to go home," I told her when she hung up. Demian was in the other room watching TV. "Never."

"Baby, I know. I know. But that's your home." Gramma cupped her warm hands around my face.

"I want to stay here. Demian too." I said a little prayer in my head, something I'd prayed for the night before. "For always."

"I wish that too," she said, "I truly do. But …" She let the thought hang unfinished. I sensed that her mind was suddenly working on something. A solution.

Grampa came home, surprised to see us there. We did a couple of sets in the garage with the weights, and I showed off the new definition I had in my upper body. He showed me *his* muscles and said, "I'll arm wrestle you any time, buster."

After dinner, the bike was loaded into the rear of their station wagon and Grampa took the wheel. Gramma sat beside him, while in the back seat, next to Demian, I fiddled with my seat belt. We took the freeway, listened to a big band 8-track on the car radio, and then the ride was over and we were home. I didn't unbuckle my belt right away, our house looking gold and alive as the sun set in front of it. This was not where I wanted to be, not anymore. Demian stared at me, awaiting my cue.

"Boys, you're home," Grampa said, and Gramma met my eyes. "Your ma's waiting for you, I bet."

He unloaded the bike and walked us to the door, Gramma staying in the car. When I went to hug her through the window, she whispered, "We'll talk, okay?"

Ken met us at the door, exchanged some civil, nonsense words with Grampa and then we were inside.

"The prodigal sons return," Ken said, then laughed, even though he didn't seem to think it was funny. He went into his bedroom, and a few minutes later Mom came out to the living room. Demian and I stood, unmoving, as stiff as my bike, which was propped up on its kickstand next to us. We gazed at each other, like we'd done something wrong and were about to be punished. But we hadn't done anything, and we never *got* punished, so it was a confusing moment, heightened by uncertainty and the shame I felt about betraying Mom.

"Are you going to leave that in the house?" she asked, and I opened the front door behind me. Demian followed me, and together we pushed the bike to the side of the house and through the gate. Mom met us at the back door, stood with her hand on the top of it, holding it open for us.

"Are we in trouble?" Demian asked her.

"For what?" She shut the door behind us. On the kitchen table were two plates, the remains of their dinner.

"I don't know." My brother's legs leaned in on one another, and he rubbed his palm over his crotch. "I gotta go."

He ran to the bathroom, and I stood in the kitchen with Mom. She stared at me, like a coiled snake ready to attack. "So, we're going to talk about last night."

"We are?" I looked at her chin, not meeting her eyes. Her face was framed by her long, black hair, and I imagined if I looked up, I would turn to stone.

"I didn't teach you all those horrible words. No one in this house speaks like that. We *respect* people in this house."

"You do?" I met her eyes, ready to do battle.

"Sit down," she said, and we both sat in the kitchen. Demian came back, zipping up his pants. "Honey, can you go watch TV or something? Okay?"

When he left, she leaned in close to me. "Is this my punishment for not buying you those toys? Is that what this is?"

"No," I said. "Try again."

She shook her head, then bit her upper lip. "I don't want to play games, Stephen. I'm too tired for all that. Just tell me what's going on."

I didn't want to tell her anything. I didn't trust her to care. Not about Seneca, or Demian, not about Ken, or the way she treated me like I was a drain on her energy. A waste of her time.

"Fine. Suit yourself," she said, getting up and going in the other room, as if to make my point for me.

"Did you talk to him?" I heard Ken say from the other room.

"It's more trouble than it's worth," she told him.

KEN HAD HIT ME ONCE, AND I knew he probably had it in him to do it again. The first time had been a surprise, something I wasn't expecting. I don't think he expected to do it, either. He had never been a violent man, not as far as I had experienced him, but I think my mother's refusal to marry him had changed him. After that happened, back in April, he lost his steady job, more than likely poisoned Mrs. Hunter's dog, pushed Mom into the whole Mr. Takadakos affair, and hauled off and punched me in the back of the head. He had lost control of his world, and how he wanted it to go, which made him act in unpredictable ways.

I wanted him to find that anger again, that unpredictability, in time for me to use it as ammo against him and Mom. To unlock the escape route that would lead from our house into our grandparents' house, I needed something extreme to occur.

I was in the garage again today, I wrote in my journal, *and I saw that rat poison just sitting there on the shelf. I don't want to believe Ken could do that, kill poor Humphrey. But if not him, who? Mom? I don't think so. It was Ken. In my mind, he's just as bad as Kirby, next door. Worse, maybe. Who knows, maybe Ken even knew about what Kirby did to Seneca. And those other girls.* I paused, shocked to see this vague suspicion of mine written down like that. More real now that it was right in front of me, but another accusation that I honestly hoped wasn't true. A sharp pain tugged at the upper part of my side. Like a cramp. *They were friends, right?* I wrote. And the last thought came, the one I knew I shouldn't write, the one thing I believed truly was a lie. But I wrote it anyway: *Maybe he even did some of that stuff too.*

I read it over and wondered if that would be enough. Enough to make him act, to hit me again, maybe this time right in front of Mom. I ripped out the page with the summer goals I had set for myself and shoved it inside one of my Tintin books before I carried the open journal into the living room and placed it face-down on top of the coffee table. I moved aside an ashtray and a small stack of record albums so that it would be in clear sight of Ken.

I CAME HOME THAT NIGHT A little after six, most of the day spent walking and listening to the barrage of thoughts that flooded my head. Summer was ending, and what was my life going to be like when I got back to school? I wondered about Seneca, and Kirby in jail, and about how much I wanted to be far away from everything. And everybody.

Both Mom's and Ken's cars were parked out front, but they weren't in the living room. I instinctively glanced at the table where I had left my journal. It was gone. I heard a conversation from Mom and Ken's room, and to avoid them, I went into my bedroom. Demian was splayed in the middle of the room, hands on his face as his wide eyes stared into the multi-colored panels of one of my Hulk comics. He kicked his feet in the air behind him and looked up at me for the briefest of seconds before staring back into the book.

I stepped over him to get to my bed, where the age-yellowed sheets lay half off the mattress and my blanket snaked from the foot of the bed onto the floor. I started to straighten the mess up when there was a knock at our door.

"Stephen, hey, you're home. Good. Ken and I are going to Ashkenaz for a few hours. Have some dinner and do a little dancing."

"Are we going now?"

She stared at me, like I was stupid. Or deaf. The look felt mean. "You and Demian are staying here. There's some canned soup, and I brought home a half a sandwich leftover from work. You can make a meal out of that, right?"

"Okay," I said, my eyes not meeting hers.

Demian suddenly came to life. "What are we doing, Mommy?"

She looked farther into the room to see him but didn't make any moves to come inside. "You keep doing what you're doing, baby. We'll see you after bedtime."

I couldn't look at him. I didn't want to see what he felt, all of it etched on his little, trusting face. I watched her shoes change directions and move into the hall and out of my field of vision. I pushed the door so that it closed with the tiniest click.

When I shuffled back to my bed to finish making it, I noticed something visible underneath the pillow. It was my journal. Closed and placed below the spot where I would put my head tonight. Where I was sure to find it, clear in the knowledge that it had definitely been read.

I shoved it out of sight and waited for the next humongous shoe to drop.

18

GRAMMA PROMISED THAT WE'D TALK, AND we did. We spoke the next day, and every day up until the weekend. She had done the hard sell to get us all out to Fremont for Sunday dinner, and my mother had reluctantly agreed. This was the first phase of our plan. I was disappointed that there had been no signs from Ken that he had read my journal—no dirty looks or aggressive tones—and I wondered if he had even looked at it. Without a definitive act of violence from him that I could use against him and Mom, I needed to become a spy in my own house. I observed neglectful parenting decisions, jotted down notes in that same journal, hidden away again, about the things said and the injustices done, all in an effort to gather enough evidence in order to serve up a solid, Perry Mason-tight case for moving out. I loved my mother, even had feelings for Ken despite myself, but this wasn't our home anymore. My brother and I deserved something else. Something better.

Gramma said Sunday was about "testing the waters" with Mom, seeing how open she might be to my idea. There would be no mention of all the intel I had gathered, nothing about Mom being unsuitable to raise us any longer. Gramma could be a crafty old woman when she set her mind to it, and I was counting on her craftiness that Sunday night.

"So," Gramma said, after dinner was finished and the dishes cleared, "we miss these grandsons of ours. We'd love to see more of them before the summer's over."

Demian and I were off in the living room watching TV while the adults spoke at the kitchen table. I positioned myself as close to the kitchen door as I could, hanging on every word of their conversation.

Grampa said, "And I'd love to help Stephen reach his weight goal before he goes back to school. He's really gotten himself fit, yes he has."

"You want to take them for a few days?" Mom asked.

"I was thinking more like a week. How does that sound?" Gramma's voice was full of innocence, not tipping her hand.

"Sounds great," Ken said, more enthusiastically then he'd probably intended. "They love spending time with you two," he said.

By eight o'clock, plans had been made for Gramma to gather us up the next day for a week spent in Fremont. From the backseat, as Ken drove us home, I thought about something I'd read in a book, about someone cooking a frog in a pot of boiling water. It was apparently a French delicacy, frog's legs, but they were tastiest if boiled alive, rather than dead. This young French guy, the hero of the book, had set out to impress his girlfriend with his cooking. He had gotten himself a couple of frogs and thrown them in a pot of water that had been boiling on a high flame for over thirty minutes. The minute he dropped them in, they hopped out. He tried to cover the pot with a lid, but they kept getting out. He finally called a chef friend of his, who told him the best way to cook a living frog was to put it in a pot of cold water. *Then*, he was told, place it on the stove, with the burner turned so low the critter couldn't feel the heat. Slowly increase the heat, the chef said, until the moment when the frog finally succumbs to the boiling water, unaware that it had been cooked alive.

I imagined this was what Gramma was doing to Mom. Me, I would've just jumped to the chase, told her that Demian and I were getting the hell out of that house and moving in with our grandparents. But my grandmother was like the chef, and she knew that kind of approach would only pull for a negative reaction from my mother, and no way would we ever be allowed to move anywhere. So, she placed Mom in a pot of cold water for a week, and then slowly began to turn up the heat.

Our time at Gramma and Grampa's went by quickly, the day beginning at a certain hour and ending at another specific hour. Our days were structured in a way they never had been before. There was time assigned for play, for reading, for shopping and errands, and even time for some TV.

We were encouraged to make friends with the neighborhood kids, but we had a curfew, and neither one of us dared go over it. At night, we all had a home-cooked meal together, talked about our day, and then played board games and boned up on a little math and reading until bedtime.

The week ended, with Mom and Ken expected to come over for Sunday dinner and then return home with us. Gramma planned to ask them if she could keep us for another week. This would help Mom get comfortable with the idea of us being gone, which would ultimately make her more amenable to my emancipation from her. A monkey wrench hurtled into our plan when Mom said she didn't want to come over for dinner and told Gramma to bring us back after we'd eaten.

"They're having such a good time, Rose. Why don't you leave them here for another week?" Gramma let me sit near her while she talked on the phone to Mom. Demian was out in the back yard with Grampa. I was nervous, but Gramma probably knew Mom better than anyone, and now she seemed as determined as me to have us with her. For always.

"No, I understand. You miss him—them. Yes." Gramma had slipped, tried to cover. I knew Mom's favorite was Demian, who gave her no trouble, no reason to change the way she treated us. "Well, why don't you come to dinner during the week? That way—"

A long pause. I was dying to know what Mom was saying.

Gramma finally had a moment to speak. "I'm not entirely sure why you're getting so worked up." Another pause. "No,

I *know* that they are your sons. This isn't about … Brainwashing? Oh, really, Rose, you've got to be joking."

By the time the conversation had ended and Gramma hung up the phone, she was fuming. "Honestly, your mother is losing control of herself." She looked at me. "Sorry."

I shrugged, feeling no loyalty to that woman over on Emerson Street. "What'd she say?"

"We can bring you back tomorrow afternoon," she said.

"So, are you? Is that it?" I started to shake a little, not wanting to set foot in that house again.

She noticed me shivering, ran her hand along my arm. "Is this really what you want, Stephen? Is this what Demian wants?"

"Demian …" I hadn't told him my plan, hadn't given him any reason to think that our visit here was part of a larger maneuver to separate ourselves from Mom and Ken.

"I think you need to tell him. *Ask* him what he thinks. What he wants," she said.

"He's six," I blurted. "He doesn't know what he wants. Does he?"

"And you're only eleven. Eleven years old, Stephen, making choices that someone your age shouldn't need to make. Are *you* sure? Is this the wisest thing to do?"

"It is. For me. I don't know about Demian," I said.

"Ask him. Then we'll all talk. All right?" She took my hands in hers, rubbed them.

Now I felt like the frog in the warming water, knowing if I jumped out of the pot I may survive, but sure that if I stayed with the way things were, I would boil alive.

DEMIAN WAS OUTSIDE, PLAYING WITH A neighbor's cat who had wandered over to Gramma and Grampa's back yard. I joined him, letting its long tail furl around my leg and listening to it purr.

"He's like Mrs. Dillon's cat," Demian said. He lay on his back and let it crawl over his belly. Milsie and Chew-Chew barked from behind a closed glass door that looked out onto the lawn, but the object of their attention seemed oblivious to the dogs' insistent threats.

I asked my brother if he missed being home, missed the neighborhood and his friends. If he missed hanging out with Rafe. He shook his head no, and the cat settled on his chest. He hugged it to him.

"Does being there make you want to run away again?" I asked. He didn't say anything. "Does being *here* make you want to run away?" He shook his head no again. "Do you want to stay here? With Gramma and Grampa? With me?"

Demian stared at me, and I wasn't sure how much he understood about what I was asking him. I didn't want to put words into his mouth, I wanted to let him be the one to choose. Allow him to make a decision that he wouldn't later regret. I didn't know if that was possible.

"What if we didn't live at home anymore? What if we lived here?" I rubbed the scruff of the cat's neck as it purred on top of Demian. A small breeze rustled the blades of grass around us. My hair flew into, then out of, my eyes.

Demian said, "We could … do that?"

"Maybe. Would you want to?" I asked.

"Without Mommy?" He sat up, and the cat jumped down, onto the grass.

I shook my head. "No Mommy. No Ken."

"Are they going to die?" His upper teeth gnawed methodically on his lower lip.

"No." I held his arm. "No. They'd still be there. But we'd be here. We could visit them, talk to them on the phone. I'm sure they'd visit us. But … we wouldn't live with them anymore."

He sat there with an expression of someone thinking very hard. I wondered how his mind operated, what his thoughts looked and sounded like.

"And you'll be here?" he finally said.

"I'll be here, Demian." I stared at him, wanting him to believe me, to trust me. "Forever."

"Then okay," he said, and got to his feet. "I've gotta pee."

And that was it. Now came the hardest part.

I HAD A LOT TO THINK about, now that the decision had been made. Early the next day, Monday, I let Gramma drive me to the BART station in Fremont. She gave me a big hug while Demian sat in the backseat, reading a comic book.

"You be brave," she said. "We love you."

When I reached the Ashby BART station, I still didn't know exactly what I planned to say to Mom, how I would argue my case against living with her and for Demian and me moving in with our grandparents. I needed courage. When I reached Shattuck Avenue, a potential source of that strength presented itself to me.

I hesitated on the sidewalk in front of the building, feeling a slight breeze rush by me whenever a large truck or bus passed. I stood there at the corner, assaulted by the street sounds while I alternated my gaze between the spinning candy-cane stripes behind the cylindrical glass and the two concrete steps up to the front door of the barber shop. A man, fifty or so, with a newspaper in his hand and a neatly trimmed mustache on his lip, emerged from behind the glass door and stopped.

"You lost?" he asked, his hand positioned flat against the edge of the door.

"No," I said, before I rushed up the steps and past him. He chuckled, and the street sounds were muted as the door shut behind me.

It was warmer inside than out, a small circular fan that hung from the ceiling rotating slowly. I stood at the counter, which was as high as my nose, and started to lose my nerve. There was one man getting his hair cut by another man in a white smock. Two other men sat in the plastic chairs with their backs against the big window. There was a second barber, older than the first, who swept up hair around an empty chair. All the men were black. None of them noticed I was there.

The sharp tang of unfamiliar hair supplies tickled my nose, and I stared at the pictures on the wall of male hair models as a way to ground myself. I was afraid of being in a place that I didn't know, unsure if what I intended to do here would help or hurt my impending conversation with Mom, so I planted my feet on the black-and-white checkered linoleum floor and just waited.

"—don't know where she got the idea church was the place to shame me for not calling and asking her out for a second date … but there she was, in the middle of the pew shaking a finger at me while the preacher was doing his best to save all of our poor pitiful souls."

I didn't look up to see who had spoken, but his voice was deep and sounded a little sad.

"Hallelujah, indeed, brother," another man said, laughing a deep belly laugh.

I smiled, that laugh infectious. It reminded me of Demian.

"Hey, Youngblood!" A different voice than the first two spoke loudly, in my direction. "Whatcha selling? Magazine subscription?"

I didn't understand the question. Then I remembered I had my backpack on. And here I was, a kid in a place for adults. I swallowed hard and asked him, "Do you … cut white hair?"

The belly-laugh guy, wearing the white smock, erupted into a laughing fit. The man in the chair getting his hair cut also laughed.

The second barber leaned his broom against the wall and walked toward me. He had the name Gerard stenciled on his light blue smock, just over his heart. "Hair is hair, son," he said. "You got it, I'll cut it. Is that cool with you?"

I took off my backpack, loaded with library books, my journal, and a water bottle. "That's, um, cool with me. I have my own money."

The barber named Gerard grabbed a green cape and whipped it outward with a snap. "Come on up—get in this chair here."

I wasn't sure exactly how to maneuver myself into the chair, almost slipping as my foot touched the low metal step, but there wasn't any more laughter aimed at me, so I figured I handled myself okay.

"How do you want it cut?" he asked, as the conversation about the woman and the church resumed next to me.

"Shorter," I said, feeling the weight of my hair on every inch of my head.

Behind me, I heard the small metal crash of scissor blades meeting each other. "A trim?"

I saw Mom's face. "Short," I said, louder than I had intended.

One of the men in the chairs by the window, as old as Grampa, said, "Boy knows what he wants," and gave me a wink.

I tried to relax in the big chair, listening to the *snip-snip* and imagining bunches of hair dropping like bombs to the floor. The two men who sat near the window didn't seem to be waiting to get their hair cut. One of them, who looked like he could be in high school, chewed on his fingernails and looked unhappy. The older man read a magazine that was the same shape as the *TV Guide*, but it was called *Jet*. It had a woman in a leopard-print bathing suit on the cover. I didn't recognize her.

I tried to fit in, ask about something we might have in common. "Do you know Mrs. Hunter? She lives on Wheeler."

"She a black lady?"

"Uh-huh."

The high school finger chewer threw up his hands, a tinge of anger in his voice. "Man, ain't all us don't know each other."

"Yeah, that's just a myth," the barber next to me said, then laughed that laugh.

"Perpetrated on us by the white majority," Gerard said. He emphasized all of the syllables, in a singsong, jokey way. I wasn't sure if it was okay to laugh myself, so I stayed quiet.

"Ain't no joke," the older kid by the window said. "That kind of ignorance is pervasive, and it don't help nothing."

The barber beside me switched off the electric clippers in his hand. He stared at his son. "College boy showing off now. Don't make me sorry I'm spending all that money on your education."

"It's junior college. You ain't even paying for it. Government's footing that bill."

"Out of my taxes. Don't forget I'm paying for your books. And the roof over that too-big head of yours. I'm doing all that."

"And he 'preciates it," Gerard said. "Don't you, Carl?"

"You just love keeping the peace." The gray-haired man with the Jet magazine spoke up. "Look at you."

"Look at you, old man ..."

The conversation, a kind of friendly banter among these men, veered from subject to subject. I kept silent, nervous about all the hair that was being cut from my head, while excited to be a part of this adult world that was unlike the adult world of my parents and their friends.

Somebody brought up politics and the corruption that always seemed to go hand-in-hand with that profession. Now it *was* sounding like my parents and their friends.

"—and the politicians just like the cops just like the rich businessmen screwing all of us and keeping us from living decent lives." The college kid, Carl, said.

"Now, don't go generalizing. I know that school teaches you better than that." Gerard spoke up behind me. "There are good folks doing those jobs too. Well-meaning people out there doing more than just trying to make a buck."

Carl chuckled. "You so naïve. Seriously, you can't see the constant, evil bullshit they shoveling down our damn throats?"

I felt Gerard pull the scissors away from my head. But it was the other barber, Carl's father, who spoke. "Quiet now. We got us a kid in here. A customer. Be respectful."

"I ain't saying nothing wrong. I'm just ..." Carl trailed off.

His father said, "You just ... behave yourself."

Gerard's scissors were replaced with an instrument that whirred. When the metal touched my head, the vibrations made me jump. He laughed softly and put a hand on my shoulder. "Don't worry, I'm not gonna hurt you. But something tells me, when they get a look at this hair, your momma or your pops just might do you some harm."

She just might, I thought. And I felt I was ready for whatever was about to happen.

It was six o'clock when Mom walked through the front door of her house. I no longer thought of the Berkeley house as *ours*. I no longer thought of us as a real family anymore.

"Ken home?" she asked me, as I sat on the couch reading a new book I'd checked out from the Fremont library. I had used the new library card that had my name on it. Gramma had signed Demian up for one too.

"Didn't see him." I put my book down, gave her my attention.

"Oh my God! What did you do to your hair?" Mom asked. She reached her hand out to touch it, then retracted it.

"I had it cut." I paused, for effect. "About time."

"Well, it looks … really awful. You look like you're in the military or some goddamned thing. Did Grandma do this?" Her anger sparked at the thought. "Did she do this to Demian, too?"

I ran my hand along the prickly ends of my new-shorn hair. It tickled. And it gave me strength. Courage. "It was my idea. With my own money. Demian didn't get his cut."

"Well. That's a relief, I guess. Are you and Demian hungry?" She walked into the kitchen. I followed her. "Or did Grandma do her early-bird dinner routine with you already?"

"Demian's not here. He doesn't want to come home. Never." I used my dramatic voice, trying to fill my words with as much importance and finality as I could.

Mom dropped her purse and jacket on the kitchen table, washed her hands at the sink. "So now you and your grandmother are colluding against me? Poisoning the well for Demian?"

I wasn't sure what she meant, so I said, "I don't want to live here either. Not with you."

She laughed. "If not with me, then who? You want me to move out?" She sat down at the table. "If this is your pissy little way of 'getting back at me' for whatever horrible thing I did wrong … then go ahead and get it out of your system. You want to stay with your grandparents for another week, fine. But that's all. Do you understand? No more."

"They say we can live with them."

"Who? Who says? *They* don't have the right to say. You're my son. Not theirs!" She got up, opened the refrigerator, and then slammed it shut. "Not theirs!"

"Why do you care? I thought I was more trouble than I was worth. Right?" I was trying to be strong. To be adult. She wasn't making it easy for me.

"I didn't … I didn't mean that." She came to me, put her arms around me. My arms stayed at my sides. "I've been … a little crazed, lately, if you haven't noticed. Ken lost that job he just got. So, maybe I haven't been completely … all there, you know?"

I made a mental note of that, logged Ken's lost job into my spy book to tell Gramma about later.

"I love you, Stephen, you know that," she said into my ear.

Staring at her feet, which were snug inside leather sandals, I whispered, "No, I don't."

She acted as if she hadn't heard me, then released her grip on me and sat back down. "What if we go to a movie, huh? Did you ever get into that movie you wanted to see? What was it, that war movie? We could go see that, just you and me. Tonight."

"I don't wanna," I said. "I want to go back to Gramma's."

"Fine," she said, her mood turning dark. "Go back there if it's so great. It wasn't so great when I was living there."

"It's not so great living here, either," I told her.

Her head swung up, and her hair swept over her face. She looked at me between long strands of black.

"Then go. Go, you ungrateful little shit. Go live with those prison guards. Go live by their rules, instead of mine."

You have no rules, I thought to myself, but didn't say.

She pointed at my bedroom, "Go and pack all your clothes, all your fucking little toys that she bought for you, and move to shitsville Fremont. Just you and your grandparents, living happily ever after and all that bullshit."

"And Demian," I said.

"What?" she demanded, pulling the hair away from her face.

I didn't answer her, feeling the urge to cry. But I wouldn't. I would not cry.

"*You* can go, Stephen. I give *you* permission to get the hell out of here if that's what you want. But Demian's not going with you." She got to her feet, pointed her finger at me.

All kinds of thoughts scurried around in my head. I grabbed one and spit it out. "You want him to run away again? Because he will."

"No, he won't," she said weakly.

"He hates you. He told me," I lied.

Her mouth contorted, and she gasped air in. Then she was crying. I wanted to take back what I said. But it was too late. I had pushed and plotted this far.

"I love him. I love you. He's too young to be without his mother," she said, in between sobs.

I had stabbed the bull in the ring with more than a few swords, and I wasn't going to stop thrusting the steel in now. No matter how much blood was shed. "He's been without his mother for *this* long ..." I let the words hang.

The front door opened and suddenly Ken was in the kitchen with us. My mother's head was down, arms at her sides, with her long hair covering her lap. I stood near the sink, my arms folded.

"Hey," Ken said, "somebody die?"

Mom continued to sob. He walked over to her, started to massage her neck. She whipped her body up, threw her arm at him. "Get away from me!"

"Hey, what the fuck?" he said, taken by surprise.

"Get out of here. Get out! Just leave us alone! Now!" she screamed.

He glared at me. "What did you do, man?"

"Get out!" She stood up, her arms flailing, face wet with tears and snot. "Leave us alone!"

"Jesus, all right." He backed away, put his shoes back on, and went out the front door. It slammed so hard the diamond of colored glass inside it shuddered. I waited for the crashing sound of broken, shattered glass. But a moment later, all was silent. Except for my mother's crying.

"You want to be tarnished by her?" Mom asked me, wiping her tears away. "You want to be imprisoned, subject to her whims, her shackles? She'll squeeze the pulp out of you, leave you barren and shell-shocked. Is that what you want for yourself? For your brother?"

"She cares about me. They care about us," I said, my legs weak and wobbly. It took all my strength just to keep myself standing up straight.

"Really? Is she the one who made you write those vile lies in your journal? That's what a loving grandmother does?"

"When did you … read my journal?"

"You left it right out in the open for me to find it. Or was 'the plan' for Ken to find it? And do what, exactly?"

I didn't want to reveal anything, but I also didn't want her to believe that Gramma had put me up to it. "Hit me. Again."

"He hit you?" Her eyes focused in on me, and I thought for a second there was compassion there. But it vanished too quickly for me to be sure it had ever been there. "I'm not really surprised. The way you've been acting, you probably deserve worse."

I swallowed. I couldn't speak.

She folded her arms and sat back against the wall. "He didn't even see your journal. Your *big* plan failed, little one. *I* saw it, and read it for the prank it was—a way to rile us up—and I should have thrown it in the trash. But I didn't."

She had put it under my pillow. Not him.

"What about Humphrey?" I asked, a bit of strength welling up inside me. "He poisoned him, didn't he?"

Mom leaned forward, her arms still linked across her chest. "No." She held my gaze for a long, long moment. I believed that that's what she believed. Then she sat back again. "And even if he did … that's none of your concern. Is it? Are you trying to be a cop now, Steve? Bust all the wrongdoers of the world like they do on all those mindless TV shows you watch? Huh? One neighborhood at a time? Who's next? Mrs. Dillon? Mr. and Mrs. Fisher? Me?"

I met her gaze. She was bullying me now. I didn't like being bullied.

"This is the end of this." She shook her hair, like she was clearing her head. "You are absolutely, positively *not* going to live there. That is unacceptable. It's ridiculous and stupid, and something that is *not* going to happen."

I stared at her, not sure what to say next. Because I knew it was going to happen. There was no way this would continue to be my home.

"I'm your mother! Not her. Not him." She thumped her chest and yelled, "Me!"

I waited for her to say more. She calmed down a little, and then I said, "I'm going to call Gramma."

"Go," she said, violently wiping the wetness from her face with the back of her hand. "Go call that bitch. Tell her I'm coming to pick up my son." She grabbed her purse and slammed the front door behind her.

And just like that, it was over. And I had lost.

Chapter 19

THAT NIGHT, MOM BROUGHT DEMIAN HOME. For good.

Two days later, Kirby Johnson was released on bail while he awaited trial.

The next day, I wandered the streets of Berkeley and found myself outside Trevor's house. He wasn't home, but Art was there at his garage apartment. He invited me in, loud and abrasive music jangling my nerves. It sounded like nothing else I'd ever heard.

"You like it? The 101ers, bootleg stuff out of England. They're fucking *mental*." He shook his body chaotically with the music.

I stood just inside the door, with its thick carpeting, waterbed in the corner, books and records and weights scattered all over the floor. Art looked to me for a response to the music, and I bobbed my head as if I liked it. "Cool."

"Trevor's out, but you can hang here if you want." He pointed at a La-Z-Boy chair and I fell into it. He grabbed an album cover and read the back of it with intensity.

"You haven't been over in a while. All that plucking freebies on the avenue spook ya?"

"Nah," I said, "just stuff happening. You know."

"Yeah, sure. I heard your brother ran away." Art tossed the cover across the room like a Frisbee and gave me his attention. "He came back, though, right?"

I sat up in the chair, but the design of it forced my neck and body backward. It was a really comfy chair. "He's … yeah. He's home now."

"Where'd he go?"

"Hare Krishnas," I said, embarrassed as the words left my mouth.

"No shit!" He laughed. "Sorry. But they're, like … I don't know."

"They were nice," I said softly, barely heard over the thumping of the drums.

"Well, as long as he's okay, that's all that matters, right?" He smiled, then tapped his fingers on his knees.

"He's fine." I hadn't told anyone about what Demian had seen, about the horrible thing that had happened to Seneca. I don't know why I told Art, but I did. I didn't say her name, or Kirby's, and I didn't even share enough with him so he could have figured it out. But I told him what I felt, in fragments, as best I could. "My friend … Someone mean hurt them … really, really hurt … I wanna get this guy back … bad … only a kid … Don't know what I can do … stop him from hurting them again … or anybody else."

To Art's credit, he let me stumble through it, not clear on any of the details. But it seemed to me that while we sat in that small, airless room he called his pad, my friend's older brother shared in what I felt. I wished he was my brother, my protector, as he said, "Well, that fucking sucks. For you and your poor friend. Sucks!"

As we listened to the loud, urgent punk rock coursing from his waist-high speakers, Art's emotions heightened, and he expressed the anger I felt in a way I could not. "Fuck that prick, fuck! If someone I cared about, somebody close to me, got hurt by some dickwad, I would do serious damage to them. You know? I'd take a knife to their belly, or slit his goddamned neck. That'd do the trick." He swung his wrist around, demonstrating the movements, as if he had a knife in his hand. "Fix that fuck but fast. Keep him from doing anything to anybody again."

Then he fell into the beat of the music, thrashing his arms and body around the small garage. He was full of energy and rage that I could only admire; I knew I could never duplicate it.

When I left Art's pad, after thanking him for letting me hang out, I wondered if it had all been a show, an act he had put on that was spurred by the frantic music and not by a genuine desire to do violence to another person. He was angry *for* me—that was how it felt—and I was in a place where I needed that shared emotion, or at least a human form of mirroring the things I had inside me but couldn't get out. It was a reminder that I had my own power, strength that I had never tapped into but that I knew existed. Immense will that could manifest itself into something great and wonderful and dangerous.

It was time to put the failures of the summer far behind me, with a singular goal in front of me. Even though it was the craziest thing I could ever imagine doing, it was the only thing worth doing. And I was, finally, ready to do it.

It was a Thursday, the small Batman-shaped alarm clock-radio on my dresser nearing the 11:00 a.m. mark, and the house was empty except for me and my book. Mom was off at work, Ken had already lost his new job and was supposedly out job hunting again, while Demian had been invited to spend another afternoon at Fairyland with his friend Twahn and his mother. The windows were closed; the air outside crept through the walls and heated up my room. I finished the last few paragraphs of a Jack London story, where an Eskimo slaughters a powerful bear, and closed the book with a satisfying clap.

Fully dressed, my hands still sweaty from gripping the library book during those incredible last pages, I leapt off my bed and went to the window. The entire side of his house was visible from where I stood, the peeling paint and curtained windows caught in the glare of the hot sun above. I had done my research, knew that Kirby was on house arrest, that his parents had mortgaged their home for his bail, and that he was due back in court in a few weeks.

I had spent the past week keeping track of everyone who moved in and out at the Johnsons' place. I learned that his father left every morning at seven thirty and came back around five thirty. His mother got picked up by a friend in a Chevy Rambler at eleven on the dot, and based on my eavesdropping I learned that they drove to a church in Oakland where she prayed for her son's soul. I hoped God was turning a blind eye to her pleas for mercy, and that once I had killed him, he would be sent straight down to Hell.

The Rambler pulled up in front of the house next door. I waited, unmoving, until Kirby's mother got into the car and was driven away. He was inside, alone now, but I had only a vague idea which room in the house belonged to him. My nerve had been activated, his mother would be gone for at least two hours, and it was time to move.

The window near the back of Kirby's house, which faced the side of our detached garage, remained slightly ajar. I had performed my own stealthy reconnaissance on it the day before and peering through the open space afforded me a view of both a shower and a toilet in the tiled room. It would be a tight squeeze, with no guarantee that I could wedge it up any farther, but the window was my only way into the house.

Standing in my room, thinking about what I planned to do, my heart pounded like it did when I ran or worked out. But I felt strong. Invincible. In the past week, when I looked at my shirtless body in the closet mirror, I convinced myself that I had a bunch of big, new muscles. More important than the outward appearance, I felt stronger, faster, less like a total fat-ass and more like someone who could plunge a knife into a guy more than a foot taller than me and almost fifteen years older.

From the back of the closet I dug out my school backpack, with my old binder and a handful of lined paper still inside. As I scribbled down my own last will and testament, just in case things went a lot more wrong than right, I thought about what Demian would do without me around. Legally signing over my every worldly possession—including my treasured comic books that had once meant so much to me—a big dose of guilt attacked me. How could I leave him alone, with only Mom and Ken to look after him, if I got arrested or killed? Would Demian feel like he was responsible, since he was the one who had seen it all, and then dared to tell someone—me—about it?

I finished writing the note. After I placed it and a box of comics on his bed, I went into the kitchen to remove the biggest, sharpest knife we had, and walked out the back door. I stopped thinking about Demian and thought only of Kirby.

He had lived in the house next door pretty much his entire life, from the time he was a young kid and all through his years at Cal, up until now. After graduating with a degree in political science, he had worked mostly menial jobs and then, at a certain point, seemed to have just given up on working altogether. He was a loner, who rarely had friends over to his house, and he came and went at all hours of the day and night with no significant objection from the parents who still supported him. The scar on his forehead had come from a really bad car accident when he was a teenager. I learned all this, and that he was twenty-five-years old, from

Mrs. Dillon across the street. Her love for gossip was almost as strong as her love for daytime soaps. During my week of surveillance and fact finding, I knew she would be a source of information on Kirby and the Johnsons. I lied and told her our TV was on the fritz and that I was desperate to watch something. Anything. Between bites of oatmeal raisin cookies and during the commercial breaks on *All My Children*, I had pried open all the knowledge and educated guesswork about the neighborhood that Mrs. Dillon possessed—everything she, ultimately, couldn't keep to herself. By the time her soaps were over and the local news started up, I knew my enemy as well as I figured I ever would.

In the back yard, holding the kitchen knife's long blade flat against my leg, I stared at the crack in the Johnsons' bathroom window. I could hear and sense things so intensely my body seemed to hum like a tuning fork. Everything was magnified, all my senses wide open and intensely focused. My body must have been coursing with adrenaline, the fear tamed for the moment as I peeked into the window and listened for any sign of Kirby.

An intermittent drip of water at the sink sounded like a crash of waves against a sea wall in my present, heightened state. I gingerly placed the sharp knife onto the window's far edge, then pried up the wooden bottom with my palms. Once I wiggled my body inside and retrieved the knife, I edged toward the door and listened for any noises in the hall.

I sneaked out from the tiled floor onto plush, wintergreen carpet that looked like an overgrown lawn. My hand, damp with sweat, gripped the knife firmly as I trod down the unlit hall. With no idea which room belonged to Kirby, I depended on Demian's recollection, and the room he had pointed out to me, where he had seen everything happen. I slid my fingertips along the hallway wall, a beige-colored strip of wallpaper leading me to the bedroom door.

Anger swept over me as unwelcome images flooded my head. I saw Seneca the way Demian had seen her, pinned down under Kirby, his flop of curls covering her face. His body pressed into hers, rapidly and with great force. Red spots suddenly appeared in my vision, and I whipped the closed door forward, propelled by a burst of courage. Knife raised, my heartbeat spiking, I entered the room prepared for violence.

It was empty.

A pair of heavy curtains were parted slightly at the middle of the window, the one that Demian had seen into that day, allowing the sun to mark the fully made queen-size bed with a thick line of dull yellow. I surveyed the room where a rapist lived, where he spent his time making plans to hurt girls like Seneca. It slowly became clear, however, that this was not his room.

Religious artifacts lay scattered around the room, a rosary tangled around a black faux-leather Bible on the nightstand. A crucified Jesus slumped forward, nailed to the wall above an antique dresser. Next to the mirrored closet—the doors closed, but with a line of space between them like a glass table cleaved right down the middle—stood a pair of black dress shoes. Beside the shoes, a tan stool and a silver shoe-horn that brought to mind a deformed ice cream scoop.

This was his parents' bedroom. My courage left me. I stood dumb, not sure what to do next. I was suddenly cold, my body shivering and my arms breaking out into goose bumps. The knife in my hand glistened from the small rays of sunlight piercing into the room, reminding me of its purpose here.

I made myself move back into the hall, to continue my hunt for this man, this grown adult, who had hurt the girl I cared for and upended my entire world. I had a purpose, the clearest one I had ever had in my life: revenge. Justice. Now on the forest of carpet, I shuffled past a half-open door filled with boxes and stacks of magazines. It looked like a guest room, used as storage. I thought I could hear music, muffled, playing from the floor below me.

At the end of the hall, I saw the staircase. Leading down. The steps were covered in the same shag rug as the hallway, muffling my feet as I glided over them. I placed one foot down, then joined it with the other foot on the carpet below. I repeated the movement until I'd descended into the basement. The sounds, the music I had maybe imagined, had stopped. The silence was so complete, I heard that steady hum the absence of sound makes. I waited.

A few feet from the bottom of the steps was a room, with the door slightly open. The faint amount of light coming from the room seemed to be generated by a night light or maybe a lava lamp. It took everything I had, every shred of courage that I had saved up for this very moment, to use the sharpened point of the kitchen knife and push open the door.

A wail, a scream, met me at the door, and I jumped backward. Strains of guitar and drums followed, and then Bob Marley's voice filled my ears, imploring me to lively up myself. My heart slammed against my ribcage, and I thought I would piss my pants right there. I couldn't see anyone, the light low, the sound of the music so loud it was like a physical wall, a barrier I couldn't see past.

My eyes adjusted, and I saw him, the back of him, move away from the door and toward the center of the room. He turned, then fell backward into something. I squinted, trying to understand exactly what I was looking at, while hoping he couldn't see me standing just inside the room across from him. A minute or minutes passed, and I watched his arms and legs splay, the core of his body sunk deep into what I now recognized as an enormous green bean bag. His eyes looked closed, but I couldn't be sure. He lifted a joint to his mouth. Smoke escaped from his moist lips, a gesture both obscene and fascinating to watch. I was terrified, afraid to step any farther into the room and equally unable to turn around and run away.

I let the smell of the potent smoke reach me, the knife handle sweaty in my tight fist. The darkness of the room finally gave way to more light, and I stared at all the posters on his wall: glossy reproductions of Bob Marley, Ralph Nader, and Steve McQueen above a small Buddhist shrine where incense burned. On the other visible wall, pages and pages ripped from magazines were tacked up in a seemingly random, haphazard way. There was the smiling face of the Jackson 5's little sister Janet, Kristy McNichol, Jodie Foster from her Coppertone ads with the dog tugging on her bikini bottom and dressed as a prostitute in *Taxi Driver*. All young girls, from TV, movies, and fashion magazines like the ones I'd seen at Trevor's house. I recognized the girl from *Paper Moon*, her lips pouty and suggestive of something perversely sexual.

"You live next door. I don't recall placing an order for a neighbor boy." His voice drifted toward me from his spot near the floor. It sounded raspy, slow. Less than six feet away from me, he took another hit and exhaled in my direction. "I don't go in for little boys. Now, if you were a girl ..."

His laughter made my forehead ache, made it burn like someone had lit matches behind my temple. Marley squealed more, and I suddenly saw myself from outside myself. I watched the scene, as if I were watching a movie in a dark theater. My hand raised the knife above my head. My foot inched forward a step. Kirby, his curly blond locks draped below his eyebrows, leaned up on his elbows, which made him sink deeper into the bean bag chair.

"That's a big knife for a little boy." He laughed, then coughed out a small trail of smoke. "Although, you're not such a little boy, now are you? A big boy, a fatty boy." He sat up, stared at my movie self. "Daedalus," he said, dragging out the *s* so that it sounded like air escaping from a tire. Or like a snake.

Kirby stubbed out the lit end of his joint, then swallowed the roach. I was back in my body when I felt a small trickle of pee go down my leg. "Whatcha gonna do?" he whispered, seducing me.

"Kill you," I said, unaware that I had started swinging the knife back and forth in front of my body. "I'm gonna fucking kill you." The words rang in my ears, and I was ready to do murder. I was ready to die.

"Daedalus," he said, his voice calm. "Is this a Joycean tragedy we have here? Or something lowbrow and slightly distasteful, like Dirty Harry or Charles Bronson? A revenge flick come to life."

The song ended, followed by loud clapping, and the faint hiss of the record spinning on his turntable. He smiled at me, his teeth big and white. My vision blurred from the sweat dripping over my eyelids.

Another Marley song replaced the last, filling the silence.

"So," he asked, "are you going to stand there doing nothing? Why don't you use that thing to go make me a sandwich." He flicked a finger at the knife, which I had stopped swinging but still pointed in his direction. "We're not going to fuck, you know, so you might as well feed me. Or you could bring your little brother by here. *He's* sweet. Like a little girl. You don't turn me on one lick, but that angel child … I could make that work … *nice*."

"You … stay away … from him," I said. My voice sounded unconvincing and weak. I swung the knife again, afraid the sweat on my palms would make the hilt fly into the air.

He stood up, waved his arms, and yelled, "Courage!" His body moved slowly toward me.

I held steady to the knife. But I had lost my nerve. I turned around, ready to bolt back up the stairs and out the front door when he grabbed the back of my collar. His fingertips pressed into my neck.

"Where are you *going*?" he hissed into my ear.

I felt my entire body whipped around, and as I was swung to face him, I slashed his bare arm with the long blade of the knife.

Kirby grasped his arm, blood trickling from the cut and down toward his wrist, but he didn't call out, didn't say a word. He stared at me, with a look that conveyed surprise and maybe even some admiration.

He laughed, a deep, brassy laugh that I had heard from other people when they were really stoned. Blood landed on my shirt and in my face as he flung his sliced-open arm at me. As I blinked, he reached for the knife. I backed away, the blade still pointed at him, but he continued flicking the blood at me and moving forward.

I tightened my grip on the knife and jabbed it at him, praying it would make him stop. But he didn't stop. My back was pressed up against his bedroom wall, nowhere for me to go. I kicked out at him but lost my balance. My head snapped back and slammed against the wall. My body dropped from under me, and I landed butt first on the floor. Kirby barked another strange laugh and dropped to his knees. He pulled on my outstretched legs and dragged me a few inches across the carpet and closer to him. The blood dripped from his arm onto my jeans leg as he moved his hands up my body, on his haunches towering over me.

I still held the knife in my hands, squeezing so tight it felt like I might break the handle. He pushed down on my legs, using them to raise himself upward and to his feet. The force on my knee made me cry out, and as he pushed harder on it, one of his hands slipped from my leg and he lurched forward.

His face was suddenly on my chest, his matted curls across my face. My knee throbbed now, but it was the moisture, the wetness around my knuckles and fingers that made me scream. I felt Kirby's big, smooth hands cover mine and his head wrenched backward. The entire blade of the knife—I could only see the hilt of it and my hands covered by his, and all that blood—was lodged deep into his throat.

I tried to yank the knife out, wrenching it away from where a steady stream of blood poured out, but as I pulled, so did he. His hands slipped off mine and his fingers closed over the mass of blood that was now his throat. I clung to the wooden hilt and pulled, but his tugging at his own throat prevented the knife from sliding out.

His eyes focused on a spot above my head before his eyes rolled upward and then closed. His hands fell away from his neck, and as he fell backward, the blade of the knife came free. Marley screamed on the record, and I screamed inside my head. My hands shook, little spatters of blood flecking my jeans. I stood there for another ten minutes without moving, my entire body shaking and my mind howling. I must have been in shock, immobilized by what I had just done with my very own hands. Words, in a voice I didn't recognize, bled from my ears. *You killed him.*

The screaming in my head eventually stopped. I let go of the knife, my fingers sticky and forced together like they had crazy glue on them. I waited for the tears to come. Instead, the theme to *Baretta* whistled through my brain. The police. They would come, and I would be put in jail and that would be that. I was willing to die to kill Kirby, but the idea of spending the rest of my life in juvenile hall and then a real prison was something I wasn't willing to do.

I thought about killing myself, to avoid all the trouble I was now in, but I had no desire to die. No reason to die. I had tried to run, did my best right before it happened not to hurt or stab or kill Kirby. I had changed my mind, lost my nerve. Even after what he said about my brother. But it still happened. I still killed him. But I hadn't meant to. Truly, I hadn't meant to do it.

But I had, and my choices were to wait and try to tell the cops everything I *hadn't* meant to do, even though I had broken into his house deliberately, with an eight-inch blade in my hands. And the evidence of my intent, even if I had "changed my mind" midway through, was the lifeless body of Kirby Johnson lying face-up in an unholy amount of devil-red blood.

I began to hiccup, loud bursts of violence in my throat. It made it difficult to think, the interruption of sound and fury every few seconds. I tried to focus on the lessons learned from all the cop shows I had watched over the years, but every time I got close to a criminal plan that would get me out of a murder charge I was clearly facing, a hiccup would jerk my head upward and jostle my thoughts.

There was so much blood on the carpet under and around Kirby's body, I couldn't conceive of a way to clean it all up. What would I do with the body? Hide it? The strength I had wasn't enough to haul a grown man anywhere. My heartbeat quickened, and then another hiccup swept through me. I held my breath, but still they came. I did my best to ignore them. When I was finally able to concentrate, as I scanned the room for some kind of solution, the ashtray came into focus.

One of the things a few of the smarter crooks on *Baretta* and *Adam-12* and old *Perry Mason* shows did in order to throw suspicion off them was to cover the first crime with a more serious crime. Something that created fewer questions for the police about guilt or innocence. Matches, roaches in the ashtray, the smell of pot in the air: fire.

It had been so easy to set my pajama top on fire, when I had no intention of doing it. With intention, I picked up the matches and surveyed the room. What should go up first? What would burn most, spreading the fire quickly through the basement so that Kirby's charred body would hide the knife wound through his neck? The hiccups still made my body move involuntarily, but I managed to block them out enough to embrace the criminal—an evil, unrepentant human being—that I needed to be in order to free myself.

My fingers begged to shake as I struck the first match, but I willed them to stay steady. The London story "To Light a Fire" popped into my brain, and the fear that this was an impossible task paralyzed me. It passed, after a moment of dread, and I waved the lit stick under a poster on the wall. One of the actresses was set ablaze. The wall buckled and turned black, but it was the section of poster that floated to the carpeted floor that set the fire in motion. Record albums fed the small inferno and spread to the hi-fi set, then consumed more of the carpet. As the room heated up, and sharp, undulating daggers of red-yellow flames reached Kirby's curls and singed them, my throat ached with phantom pain.

I forced myself to pick up the knife—the murder weapon in Cop-TV-speak—and rub it into the carpet, in order to get the blood off the blade. My nose was filled with an acrid smokiness mixed with the sharpness of fresh blood. Cramping in my stomach joined the pain from my throat and I threw up. I retched loudly, sweat beads forming at my temples.

The fire in the room was building, but I wasn't sure my stomach was done with me yet. I waited a few moments before backpedaling out. I stopped at the foot of the carpeted stairs. Once the flames had enveloped Kirby's hair and face, I ran up the stairs and into the main hall. My clothes were soaked in Kirby's blood, and I struggled to avoid dripping any of it on the floor as I moved. That was important to me, more visuals from TV shows warning me against leaving a trail as I reached the bathroom window and squeezed out. I leapt over the short fence, careful not to stab myself with the knife or stain the wood slats with blood. I kept my head down, afraid of anyone or anything, even a bird flying overhead, seeing me as I rushed away from Kirby's house.

I walk-ran to the back of my house, keeping close to it as I sidled around the garage and toward the back door. The tiny gravel on the driveway scattered and crunched under my shoes; the sound was deafening. My senses were heightened to a dizzying degree, the intensity of the sun on my head unbearable, the smells of the smoke from the basement overpowering. I had left my back door unlocked, but a fear that it wouldn't open seized me, and I looked up at that moment.

Mrs. Dillon stood on her front lawn, watering it with a brilliant, too-bright green hose. Sunlight reflected off the tiny ring of metal where the water poured out and onto the grass. Her head shifted as I reached the door. I fumbled to open it. It was too late. She stared at me, in my bloody clothes and with the knife in my hand, and put a hand to her mouth. I pleaded with her, in my eyes, in my brain: *please please please shh shh no no quiet please please.*

The door open, I stepped into the coolness of the laundry room and gently shut the door behind me. In the living room, I peeked out the window where across the street Mrs. Dillon stood with the hose in her hand. It looked like she was really thinking hard about something. She glanced at the house, but even though I could clearly see her, I knew she couldn't see me through the curtains. Her feet stayed planted on the lawn, but her head swiveled around, reminding me of a chicken.

After I had watched her for more than a minute, her indecisiveness about whether to cross the street and knock on my door or stay and water her lawn drove me mad. I had to get out of the bloody clothes, ball them into a pile with the knife and the journal and my will, shower all of the stickiness off of my body, my face, my hair, and then find a place to hide the damning evidence before the house next door caught fire and the fire engines came and the police came and the neighbors moved into the street and the commotion started and I would need to go outside and pretend I had been sleeping inside, even though my hair would be wet and hopefully no one would notice because now it was so short like I was in the military and the smoke would be so heavy and the flames would be licking every inch of the house and the firemen would be using their big hoses to put it out and keeping it from spreading to my house and Mrs. Dillon would please please please keep her mouth shut about what she saw which was me standing by the door with a knife in my hand and blood all over me right before the fire started and she knows that I did it that I set that fire that I killed the man inside who they will eventually find and they will wonder what happened and oh my god will they see the hole in his neck and wonder if he got that before the fire or after and what the hell would put a hole that size in a man who burned to death how would that happen who is responsible it's the boy next door he did it the fatty boy next door with the new haircut and the guilty look on his face in his walk he did it and he will burn just like Kirby except it will be in prison and he will never be safe his brother will never be safe and their lives will be over.

Except … what I had done was the Heroic Thing. The goal I had tried to achieve all summer. The selfless act. And that would make it all right. That would save me. And no one would say a word against me or suspect that an eleven-year-old boy could do something that horrific or inhuman to another human being.

But I would know, and I would find it difficult, sometimes impossible, to live with what I did. And the fact that I was never punished for it would haunt me, would fill me with the gravest dread for years and years. Because what I did was evil.

I was the boogeyman now. I was the thing I feared most of all.

Chapter 20

ONCE THE FIRE I HAD SET in Kirby Johnson's house was extinguished, there was another one still alive that needed tending. It had simmered all this time, but Gramma finally turned the heat all the way up on the pot, with Mom inside and unaware that she was about to explode. Forced out of our house on account of the smoke that clung to our walls and threatened to cling to our lungs, Mom and Ken packed everyone up for a temporary stay in Fremont. With all of us under her roof, dependent on her hospitality and kindness in a time of uncertainty, Gramma wielded her determination and ferocity. She advocated for Demian and me, for our safety, for a life rich with consistency, love, and maybe most important, clearly defined boundaries.

In addition to the smoldering house next door and all the potential dangers and disruption inherent within that arrangement, Gramma had thrown everything else against her: the abandonment in the middle of the night, the sexually inappropriate movies, the late-night parties and exposure to drugs and alcohol, sexual predators selling her those drugs, and finally the physical abuse. While she and Grampa had it out with Mom in the living room—Demian and Ken out back, me in the kitchen catching every word—thirty-plus years of my mother's animosity toward her mother and father came out in a flood. It was my grandfather who buckled, but my grandmother propped him up and together they pushed until she snapped. Then she broke.

Ultimately, it came down to an argument of finances. With Ken out of work again, and Mom barely making the rent, even with the sexual favors to Mr. Takadakos, she just couldn't afford to take care of two boys. That was how my grandmother framed it, sold it to her in a way Mom couldn't deny. Even if the house was eventually habitable, they wouldn't be able to afford it any longer. With Demian and me in Fremont, she and Ken could move into a smaller place, something they could realistically pay for.

Over the next week, all the arrangements were made. Our bedroom was transported to their house, we were enrolled into our new Fremont schools, and a deal was struck. We would live with them for a year, with full visitation rights given to Mom. Because of the violence Ken had shown me, and because Gramma wasn't convinced that he could control his anger, he was no longer welcome in their home. Also, at least one of my grandparents had to be present whenever he was around us, at the old house, a new dwelling, or elsewhere. I figured Ken honestly couldn't give a shit if he ever saw either one of us again, so this small stipulation became a complete non-issue as far as I was concerned.

The summer ended, Demian and I settled into our new rooms, our new house, our new lives. Mom called Demian almost every night, and occasionally she spoke to me too. The conversations were always cursory, her voice filled with an undercurrent of anger and disgust. I longed to call her, to ask how she was, to tell her that I loved her and even missed her, despite everything. I didn't call, but I couldn't stop imagining how things might have been different, what may have happened between us if the girl I so desperately wanted to make my girlfriend had never biked onto our street that day. Would Demian and I have moved to my grandparents' house, and away from our mother, if Kirby Johnson hadn't raped Seneca Reed, with my brother a witness to everything from the other side of the fence? Would Ken have hit me, would I have said things to my mother that could never be unsaid, if that day had never happened? I know that Kirby would probably still be alive. And I wouldn't be the murderer that I undoubtedly am. I wouldn't have done something I could never, ever take back, no matter how much I wished and dreamed and prayed for a different outcome on that day.

I had to live with the knowledge that I was truly capable of evil. I convinced myself that I was the Devil's son, from that movie *The Omen*. That crazy nurse was screaming *my* name, not my brother's name. I was Damien, the unholy child who needed to be destroyed. The desire to tell someone, to turn myself in to the police, was unbearable at times.

I came close, many, many times, to confessing my sin—the greatest sin one could ever commit—to Gramma. But I never did. The guilt, the shame, the self-loathing I felt was my punishment, my own cross to bear. It was selfish, and unjust, and ultimately self-serving, but I didn't dare make an admission to anyone. Ever.

I also felt fear, acutely aware of the one person out there who knew what I had done. I waited in agony for that other shoe to drop, to come crashing down on me and rip apart the world I had finally secured for myself and Demian.

When the police questioned me after the fire, I expected them to have a warrant for my arrest, based on Mrs. Dillon's eyewitness account of me—blood-soaked and with a knife in my hand—leaving the crime. Instead, they asked me only if I had seen or heard anything prior to the blaze, and warned my mother of the possible risks of smoke damage, given our proximity to the smoldering carcass of a house just outside our door. There was no reason to suspect an eleven-year-old boy, not when the source of the fire was from deep in the bowels of the Johnson house, where a suspected drug dealer and pedophile most likely started it himself, whether accidentally or as a deliberate, guilt-induced suicidal act.

It was a few weeks after the fire that Mrs. Dillon visited me at Gramma and Grampa's house. She had gotten the address from Mom and wanted to see how Demian and I were doing. She brought a pie, one that Mrs. Hunter had baked special for us, a few toys for Demian, and a bouquet of flowers for Gramma. I thought she hadn't brought a gift just for me until the visit had come to its end. She said her goodbyes, then asked me to walk her out to the curb, where something waited for me in her car. For a brief moment, I was afraid her adored Mildred was in there, the toilet-trained cat my inexplicable gift for creating death and chaos in a neighborhood that craved only quiet and order.

Mrs. Dillon pulled an envelope out of the glove compartment, but she neglected to hand it to me for quite some time. She stared at me, *into* me, and tears welled up in her eyes. I shifted back and forth, the afternoon sun baking my close-shaven head like I was under a giant magnifying glass. I wanted to turn and run back into the house, lock it and pretend that the piece of paper in that envelope was not somehow related to the murder I had committed. A copy of her testimony to the police, or a warrant for my arrest and eventual conviction.

"My husband said something to me once that I never did forget, and I wanted to share it with you." She placed the crisp, egg-white envelope into my slightly trembling hands.

I stared at it like it was something alien and possibly dangerous. "Do you … want me to …" My thoughts drifted off. I didn't know what to do.

"Open it, Stephen," she said, as she helped me remove the paper from inside. It had handwritten words scrawled on it, words that looked as if they were written in another language. My brain finally arranged the cursive into words and sentences that I could understand, and I read them, speaking them aloud in my mind.

In war, the note began, *you are faced with choices that no man should ever have to face. The character of the man is determined by his making the choice that not only protects himself, but others. And the choice ... the choice is never easy.*

I didn't understand what it meant when I had finished reading it, not really, but I knew that it was Mrs. Dillon's promise to me that the secret we shared would never be shared with another person.

"Thank you," I said, not able to look her in the eyes.

She hugged me, a gesture that she had never offered before but one that felt in that moment both familiar and welcome. She held me until I wrapped my arms around her and returned the embrace. "You be safe," she said, and it sounded like a truth, a statement of fact rather than a wish.

That night, before our first day in our new schools, Demian and I ate a home-cooked meal and for dessert had the apple crisp pie from Mrs. Hunter. After that, we watched a movie on a UHF station, something Demian and I had seen before. Gramma and Grampa had also seen it before, when they were much younger. Gramma even remembered seeing it with Mom, so long ago. It was a Marx Brothers movie, *Horse Feathers*, and it seemed like the funniest thing in the world.

"I still like that Harpo guy the best," my brother said, the two of us awake in our beds, the lights out.

"Yeah," I said, "me too."

Acknowledgments

Over the many years of my discovering what this novel was, what it meant, and how its story wanted to be told, I have had a bounty of readers, cheerleaders, and mentors. Thanks to Frank X. Gaspar and his writing class at LBCC, who were the first people to see the early chapters. The core of the novel was written in the USC MPW Program, and I gained invaluable guidance and motivation from Gina Nahai and my fellow students in her workshop. Rita Williams was the first to see a mostly-completed draft, and Judith Freeman read my first full draft; as my advisors at MPW, they both brought their expertise, patience, specificity and encouragement to every meeting we shared.

To those who read full drafts and never pulled your critical punches, I am so very grateful: Lynn, Kathy McCullough, Donna DeLacy (you read it *twice*!), Kerrin Piche Serna, Wendy Scheir, Juan Alvarado Valdivia, Mary & Victoria, and Michael F.X. Daley. I also want to thank all the gifted readers from my classes at MPW, as well as all the wonderful writers at Skidmore and Squaw Valley, who gave me such helpful feedback on my workshop chapters.

To Janet Fitch, my first real mentor, I want you to know how much I appreciate the kindness you've always shown me, and the confidence you've given me as a writer; you are glorious. To Gina Nahai (again), thank you for being so open and gracious and positive, from the first time you read my early chapter in class, up to your offer of reading the entire manuscript and helping me navigate my way toward publication; you have no idea what your generosity has meant to me through all of this.

Also, thanks to Aaron Iverson, who saved me from myself at just the right moment; Kristin Thiel, for the copy edits; to Bela and his wonderful staff at Viento y Agua who, over the years, poured me hot coffee (with *that much* non-fat milk), toasted the everything bagels, and allowed me to spend many, many hours working on this novel in the most inviting space imaginable; and to my boys, who demonstrate, every day, how important it is to be present and exist within each moment, and who have taught me how to step away from all the work and stress and just *play*.

The final words of thanks are for Lynn, who is everything. Without you, this book would have never materialized, and I never would have learned how much love I have to give or allowed myself to be so fully loved.

About the Author

JUSTIN MCFARR grew up in the Bay Area during the 70's and 80's as a latchkey kid. He is a proud graduate of both UCLA and the MPW program at USC, and has attended the New York State Summer Writers Institute at Skidmore College and the Community of Writers at Squaw Valley. His short stories have been published in numerous magazines and online journals, and will be collected in the forthcoming *Controlled Chaos: Stories* from Wheeler Street Press. He currently lives in Los Angeles with his family. This is his first novel.

www.justinmcfarr.com